# THE TOPAZ MAN

PRESENTS

# A Dream Come True

*Five Powerful Love Stories by*

# Jennifer Blake
# Georgina Gentry
# Shirl Henke
# Anita Mills
# Becky Lee Weyrich

**JENNIFER BLAKE** is the author of 37 successful historical romances, including *Fierce Eden*, *Sweet Piracy*, and *Love and Smoke*. *Love's Wild Desire* was her first novel to make the *New York Times* bestseller list and went on to sell one million copies. In the years following, three more Blake historicals have made the *Times* list, and her books have appeared on *Publishers Weekly*, bestseller list and national chain bestseller lists.

**GEORGINA GENTRY** is the author of 11 historical romances, including *Half-Breed's Bride*, *Apache Caress*, and *Nevada Dawn*. Her books have made the *Reader's Market* bestseller list, and national chain bestseller lists. She has won two Lifetime Achievement awards from *Romantic Times* for Western Romance and Indian Romance.

**SHIRL HENKE** is the author of 12 romances. Some of her recent books are *Terms of Surrender* and *Terms of Love*. She has won six *Romantic Times* awards, six *Affaire de Coeur* awards, was a two-time finalist for RWA's Golden Medallion award, and received Bookrack's Bestselling Romance of the Year award for *Night Wind's Woman*.

**ANITA MILLS** is the author of eight historical romances, the most recent being *Falling Stars*. In four years, she has received 15 nominations and eight writing awards. *Autumn Rain* and *Falling Stars* made romance and mass market bestseller lists, and they received huge praise from fellow authors and reviewers.

**BECKY LEE WEYRICH** has published 18 romances. She has made national bestseller lists and *Heartland Critiques* listed her book *Sweet Forever* as one of the Best Reads of the Year. She has won two Reviewer's Choice awards from *Romantic Times* and received their Lifetime Achievement award for New Age fiction.

# BUY TWO TOPAZ BOOKS AND GET ONE FREE ROMANCE NOVEL!

With just two purchases of Topaz books, you'll be able to receive one romance novel free from the list below. Just send us two proofs of purchase* along with the coupon below, and the romance of your choice will be on its way to you! (subject to availability/**offer good only in the United States, its territories and Canada**)

Check title you wish to receive:

☐ *WILD WINDS CALLING*
**June Lund Shiplett**
0-451-12953-9/$4.99($5.99 in Can.)

☐ *A HEART POSSESSED*
**Katherine Sutcliffe**
0-451-15310-3/$4.50($5.99 in Can.)

☐ *THE DIABOLICAL BARON*
**Mary Jo Putney**
0-451-15042-2/$3.99($4.99 in Can.)

☐ *THE WOULD-BE WIDOW*
**Mary Jo Putney**
0-451-15581-5/$3.99($4.99 in Can.)

☐ *TO LOVE A ROGUE*
**Valerie Sherwood**
0-451-40177-8/$4.95($5.95 in Can.)

☐ *THE TURQUOISE TRAIL*
**Susannah Leigh**
0-451-40252-9/$4.99($5.99 in Can.)

☐ *SO BRIGHT A FLAME*
**Robin Leanne Wiete**
0-451-40281-2/$4.99($5.99 in Can.)

☐ *REBEL DREAMS*
**Patricia Rice**
0-451-40272-3/$4.99($5.99 in Can.)

☐ *THE RECKLESS WAGER*
**April Kihlstrom**
0-451-17090-3/$3.99($4.99 in Can.)

☐ *LADY OF FIRE*
**Anita Mills**
0-451-40044-5/$4.99($5.99 in Can.)

☐ *THE CONTENTIOUS COUNTESS*
**Irene Saunders**
0-451-17276-0/$3.99($4.99 in Can.)

*Send in coupons, proof of purchase (register receipt & photocopy of UPC code from books) plus $1.50 postage and handling to:

**TOPAZ 🔽 GIVEAWAY**
Penguin USA, 375 Hudson Street, New York, NY 10014

NAME_____

ADDRESS_____ APT. #_____

CITY_____STATE_____ ZIP_____

# THE TOPAZ MAN PRESENTS
# *A Dream Come True*

## *Jennifer Blake*

## *Georgina Gentry*

## *Shirl Henke*

## *Anita Mills*

## *Becky Lee Weyrich*

A TOPAZ BOOK

TOPAZ
Published by the Penguin Group
Penguin Books USA Inc., 375 Hudson Street,
New York, New York 10014, U.S.A.
Penguin Books Ltd, 27 Wrights Lane,
London W8 5TZ, England
Penguin Books Australia Ltd, Ringwood,
Victoria, Australia
Penguin Books Canada Ltd, 10 Alcorn Avenue,
Toronto, Ontario, Canada M4V 3B2
Penguin Books (N.Z.) Ltd, 182–190 Wairau Road,
Auckland 10, New Zealand

Penguin Books Ltd, Registered Offices:
Harmondsworth, Middlesex, England

First published by Topaz, an imprint of Dutton Signet,
a division of Penguin Books USA Inc.

First Printing, March, 1994
10  9  8  7  6  5  4  3  2  1

PUBLISHER'S NOTE
These stories are work of fiction. Names, characters, places, and incidents
either are the product of the authors' imagination or are used fictitiously,
and any resemblance to actual persons, living or dead, events, or locales is
entirely coincidental.

# Contents

# Dream Lover

———◆———

*by*

*Jennifer Blake*

# Chapter One

The man in the portrait was her dream lover.

Erina Littlefield stood staring at the old oil painting with her blue-gray gaze wide and fixed with disbelief. It could not be remotely possible; the person captured in that painted image had been real, had lived in another age, another time. Yet, she had never been more certain of anything in her life.

The portrait sat propped against the wall in the main bedroom of the derelict French Quarter mansion, next to the dirty, gray-white marble fireplace mantel. The life-size figure of a man in his thirties, it was set in a heavy frame of carved wood from which the gold leaf had flaked in drifts. Though filmed with dust, yellowed by ancient varnish, and speckled with mold, it was still reasonably clear.

He was dressed in a velvet-collared forest green tailcoat, a cream cravat and waistcoat, and tan trousers strapped under highly polished boots. Standing at ease beside an ornate table, he rested his right hand on the surface near a book which lay as if it had just been put down.

His hair was brushed back in rigorous dark brown waves, though a soft curl had escaped to fall forward over his forehead. His eyes, under straight, black brows, were as dark as bitter chocolate, and held a watchful intentness. The bones of his face were boldly angular, his nose straight. He did not smile,

though the precisely molded contours of his mouth
hovered on the edge of some secret amusement.

It was him. Erina would know him anywhere.

How could she not know the man who had come
to her with warmth and caring in the darkest hours
of a thousand restless nights, summoned in wordless
supplication, or sometimes with a sigh? How could
she not recognize the turn of his square jaw, the line
of his throat and width of his shoulders. And the
mouth. The mouth that she had kissed, gently,
sweetly, in passion?

How could she not identify the body she had clung
to, wrapped herself around, slept against while she
dreamed. She knew the depth of his chest under
those old-fashioned clothes, the hardness of his
thighs. And more.

She had felt his tenderness, tested his patience,
awakened his infinite capacity for inventiveness. She
had shared with him so many small jokes, so many
important and unimportant insights. He had held her
in his arms to keep the pain away while she sat in
the dentist's chair, and lain with her under the green
sheets to hold her safe during minor surgery. She
had laughed silently with him at midnight, and allowed him to make love to her at noon while she sat
demurely at her desk.

Her dream lover. Keeper of her secrets and her
innermost heart.

Erina realized abruptly that she was holding her
breath. She exhaled on a soft, wondering sigh. A moment later, she shook her head as the thought came
to her of how long it had taken her to discover this
painting.

Every time she had passed the old Rouquette mansion since it had come on the market she had felt the
impulse to stop. Something always got in the way:
she was running late for an appointment, it was her
turn to catch the phones at the real estate office, or

she had to get home in time to cook dinner. Of course, she had not had to worry about the last in nearly a year, not since her divorce.

But today, the timing had been right. The woman she had been scheduled to meet at the restored Victorian on Julia Street had failed to show. Erina had waited for half an hour, and that was enough. As she was heading back toward the office, she felt a sudden yen for coffee and beignets as an afternoon pick-me-up, and swung her car in the direction of the Quarter.

She sat for a while at an outside table in the Café du Monde. The café was one of her favorite spots in New Orleans. She loved the view on either side of the graceful old Pontalba apartment buildings dating from before the Civil War and the greenery and wrought iron of Jackson Square before it.

She could feel her nerves unwinding as she lifted the oval of her face to the spring sunshine and felt the breeze from the river stirring her soft auburn hair. The wheeling flight of the pigeons around the spires of St. Louis Cathedral beyond the square had a timeless quality, as if the same birds might have made identical patterns against the sky for countless decades. The rustling leaves of the trees overhead made a sound like the whispers of a thousand secrets. There was a curious peace for Erina in the reflection that the trees and pigeons would remain long after most of the people eating and drinking around her were gone.

It was the rumble of thunder that made her get a move on. She didn't want to be caught in the narrow streets of the Quarter during a rainstorm, especially with rush hour traffic just getting started.

There had been a small fender-bender on the main route out of the Quarter. Erina made a quick detour, turning into the quiet side street where the Rouquette mansion stood. She slowed as she approached it.

It was the lockbox on the double front door that made her turn into the drive. She had the master key, since she had needed it to be able to show the Julia Street house. She would take a look around while both the traffic and the rain that was beginning to fall cleared.

The old house was a raised villa, with a colonnaded upper gallery reached by a double set of steps. There was a mansard roof to give light and air to the second floor, and a great many Italianate details grafted on to what had originally been an elegantly simple French colonial planter's cottage.

Still, the house was in desperate need of repair. A corner of the gallery, or porch, sagged from a missing column; the millwork of the entablature was rotting away and the paint had peeled to expose gray boards.

The interior was in no better shape. Scrap lumber and chunks of wall plaster were piled in every corner, along with bits of filthy carpet and curtains and other unnameable trash. Windowpanes were broken, and grime covered the old wavy glass that was left, combining with the rainstorm outside to make it almost too dark to see. A strong smell of rats and mildew and ancient, nonfunctional drains hung in the air.

Yet, looking more closely, Erina could make out traces of past beauty. The cornices and moldings, though gray-black with dust and old spiderwebs, had been carved with meticulous grace. What looked like a corroded metal lid turned out to be a tarnished silver tray when she picked it up. The knob of the door that led into the hallway where the curving staircase stood was painted with a design of roses and forget-me-nots.

There was a skylight made of heavy glass panes above the staircase. It was leaking with the rain, the warm drops making a wet splotch on the moldy walnut treads. Erina stepped carefully past it, also avoiding the places in the railing where balusters were missing.

The first upstairs room she entered was empty except for an old armoire that had been too big to move. Near the armoire sat a wooden box holding crumbling wax candles. There was also a small barrel filled with shredded wood straw. As she pressed down on the straw with her fingers to see if the barrel was empty, the jeweled jet button of a hat pin poked upward, a sign that someone else, some other time, had also searched the barrel.

An odd chill moved over Erina. She shivered with it, turning quickly, half expecting to see someone behind her.

Nothing.

She was reminded, however, of another reason the house might have remained on the market. Claims had been made for years that it was haunted. There were the usual stories: lights that moved inside empty rooms, voices heard when no one was there, doors found unlocked when they should have been secured.

Erina had heard the tales long before she became a real estate agent. She had grown up only a few streets away. Even back then, when she was ten or twelve, the house had stood empty. It had come on the market just after Erina got her license following her divorce, placed by a legal firm after the elderly owner died in a California nursing home.

In a curious way, visiting the old house was like coming full circle. Erina's love of the old things, particularly the old houses that were now her specialty, dated from the days when she had first seen this place.

Just a couple of weeks ago, she had been talking about the house to her older sister Joanne, telling her how she would love to buy it and fix it up.

"Lord, Erina, that old barn?" Joanne, practical as only a twice-divorced attorney can be, had demanded. "It would take every last penny of your part of Mom and Dad's estate, not to mention what it would cost to heat and cool!"

Erina had to agree. "But just think of waking up in the middle of all those beautiful architectural details and wonderful space. Besides, it would almost be like living in another time."

Joanne shook her head with its stylishly short haircut. "You, my darling sister, are hopelessly out of it, but then, you always were. I remember when you used to moon around that old ruin, having tea parties in the jungle of a garden with playmates who weren't there. But it's time you stopped thinking about houses and antiques and concentrated on men. Buy yourself some new clothes, get your hair cut and curled, find some other perfume besides that old lady's tea rose you wear all the time."

"I like my perfume, and the last thing I want is a man," Erina told her with a shake of defensiveness in her tone.

"I'm not talking about love and marriage, honey lamb. There's also dinner and dancing. Nights on the town. Sex. You remember sex?"

Erina wrinkled her brow in a parody of difficult thought. "I'm not sure I do."

"Yes, well, it's obviously time for a refresher course. I'm worried about you, Erina. You sit around sometimes with a look on your face as if you were somewhere else entirely, or wish you were. You've got to snap out of it, get with it. So your ex wasn't perfect: somewhere out there is somebody who is. But you aren't going to find him hanging around old houses. Unless you go for carpenters?"

She didn't go for carpenters or any other kind of man, Erina thought as she mounted the dirt-crusted stairs, trailing her fingers up the curved walnut rail-

ing. She didn't want one, didn't need one. She had
her own method, mental and blameless, of coping.
She didn't tell Joanne that, of course. Her sister
wouldn't understand, certainly wouldn't consider a
dream lover a worthwhile substitute.

The master bedroom was on the back corner of the
house, well away from the street. Its full-length
French windows opened onto a small balcony that
overlooked the courtyard garden on the side of the
house where Erina had once played. To the left of the
windows was the doorway into an octagonal corner
tower. Within the tower's dimness, the floor could
be seen sagging dangerously to one side.

A magnificent half tester bed in scarred rosewood
sat against one wall. The half tester had collapsed to
dangle precariously like the blade of a guillotine. The
amazing thing was that such a valuable piece had
not been stolen. Unless, of course, it was protected
by its ghostly owners.

Smiling a little at her own whimsy, Erina turned
toward the fireplace on the opposite side of the room.
It was then that she saw the portrait, and stood still
while her smile trembled at the edges.

Her dream lover. Just a dream, nothing more. Until
now.

Erina moved closer. Almost against her will, she
reached out to touch the canvas, with its thick, crackled paint. Following the curve of the man's full bottom lip with her fingertips, she closed her eyes. It
seemed she could almost feel the warm throb of
blood, of life.

How silly. It was just a portrait.

But so close, so very close to the real thing. If a
vision or a daydream could be real.

Sinclair. That was the name she had given him.

He had been with her almost as long as she could
remember, since the time when she played around
the old house. She wondered if it were possible that

she had seen this portrait back then. She could not
remember ever being inside the house as a girl, but
she might have glimpsed it through a window. Perhaps the impression had remained with her, giving
form and color to her imagination.

Sinclair had, at first, been no more than a friend
and companion. He had become something else
again after she married Thomas, her ex-husband. It
was then that she had learned to allow this man in
her dreams the liberties of physical closeness.

Thomas, an ex-marine with a *semper fidelis* tattoo
on his right biceps to prove it, had thought women
should never work outside the home, that taking care
of a husband was a wife's duty and salvation. The
money he earned was his, while the interest income
from what she had received after her parents' deaths
in a plane crash was "theirs" to blow on beer, fish-
ing, bowling, and an occasional night out.

Thomas had never been a man of imagination. The
deep and slow pleasures of erotic exploration were
not only a mystery to him, but offended the puritani-
cal streak he kept hidden inside. Sex for him was an
objective to be reached as quickly as possible.
Though he made noises about Erina's lack of enthusiasm, she sometimes thought he preferred it when she
lay like a beachhead while he took her. Compensa-
tion in some form had become necessary.

Poor Thomas. Her ex-husband had always told her
she lived in a fantasy world. When she tried to discuss some intriguing idea she had read about or to
tell him some wildly impractical thing she wanted to
do in the distant future, he would never listen. "Get
your nose out of the damn books, Erina," he would
say. "All that stuff is moonshine, not worth two
cents. People have to live in the real world."

She hadn't much cared for the real world. She still
didn't.

Two days after Thomas moved out of their apartment for a hot affair with a bar waitress, she hardly missed him. Six months later, she had reverted with relief to her maiden name. Now it sometimes seemed that her marriage was the dream, while reality was in her fantasies.

Once more, she touched the painted face of the portrait, tracing over the broad forehead. She could, she thought, summon Sinclair right now. If she closed her eyes, she could see him with perfect clarity, could compare the image in her mind with that on the dirty canvas.

Her eyelids drifted shut. She breathed deep, once, twice. She whispered his name, calling it in the soft gray corridors of her mind.

*"Sinclair?"*

Yes. Oh, yes. Here he came.

He was smiling and shaking his head as if she was asking a bit much of him, but he would comply out of purest affection and his need to see her. He was in his shirt sleeves, a loose-fitting shirt of blinding white linen tucked into dark trousers that were fastened with straps under his boots. The light in his black eyes was warm with promise, and with something more that appeared there only for her.

He was alive, so alive he made her heart swell in her chest. And he was exactly like the man in the portrait.

Sinclair's pace slowed, and a frown appeared between the dark ridges of his brows. He stretched his hand out toward her.

Behind Erina's closed eyelids, she saw the flash of lightning. It outlined Sinclair in its bright glare.

Just the rainstorm, she thought, as her eyes snapped open and she caught the dying flicker of light, heard the roll of thunder and the splatter of rain. She had almost forgotten it in her enthrallment with the painting.

It was then that she heard the scraping noise of a

footstep. It sounded behind her, in the direction of the door leading into the rest of the house. She swung around so quickly that her hair in its soft pageboy belled out around her face.

The huge shape of a man was outlined in the door frame. His clothes were wrinkled and stained, and a sour smell wafted from them. His hair hung over his eyes so that he stared at her through the lank and greasy strands, blinking as if he had just awakened.

His gaze focused and his mouth twisted in an abrupt leer. He half shuffled, half swayed toward her. "Well, look what we got here."

It was every female real estate agent's worst nightmare. Alone in an empty house with a man, some drunk sleeping it off, a vagrant, maybe a criminal in hiding. No way to call for help. No one to hear if she screamed.

Erina retreated a nervous step as she said, "This is private property; what are you doing here?"

"Just whata you care?" he growled, easing closer.

The urge to run for it pounded through her. He was blocking the main way out. The octagonal tower room leading from the bedroom was a dead end; she couldn't go that way.

"You're trespassing," she said almost at random. "You'll have to leave."

"Who's gonna make me? You?" The man laughed, an unpleasant, grating sound.

There was another narrow door half-hidden behind the fireplace. It might give access to the rest of the house. Angling in that direction, Erina said, "As a real estate agent, I'm obligated to report—"

The man lunged. She stumbled backward, slamming against the wall with the impact. He dug hard fingers into her arms, crushing her against the wall while he hunched his rigid groin against her. She twisted, wrenching away from him, almost breaking his hold. He shoved a leg between hers, hooking behind it to buckle her knee. A scream caught in her throat as she went down.

Pain and sickness exploded inside her as she struck the floor. The man's weight drove the air from her lungs. He was on top of her, pressing her down, holding her legs immobile with the heavy bar of his thigh. He tore at her clothes with vicious, raking fingers.

A blood red haze rose behind her eyes. She couldn't breathe, couldn't move. She felt a hand thrust between her knees to wrench her skirts upward.

From deep in the core of her being there rose fierce rage. Curling her fingers into claws, she dragged her arm free and reached like a striking snake for his eyes.

He jerked his head backward. Gasping for air, she braced her feet and heaved under him. As he rocked to one side, she rolled, surging upward, snatching for the raised edge of the marble hearth to pull herself free.

The man cursed. He swung his fist in a punch with brutal strength behind it. It caught her behind the ear and she was flung against the marble mantel. Her temple struck the molded edge. Blackness rose as in a boiling cloud behind her eyes. She felt the cruel grasp of hands jerking, tearing at her clothes, even as she collapsed to the floor.

Somewhere on the edge of consciousness, she heard herself cry out. The sound was a plea, a prayer, a single name.

*"Sinclair!"*

And a shadow moved, emerging from the ruined tower room. It glided forward in lithe strength and controlled fury.

Above her, the vagrant stiffened. He released her, struggling to stand. A hoarse noise of terror gurgled in his throat.

There was the meaty smack of a solid blow, followed by another and another. Thick curses and sobs of terror. Rasping breaths, scrabbling sounds. Running, staggering footsteps. Silence.

Strong hands, infinitely tender, touched her. She was picked up, cradled in a gentle, familiar clasp against a firm chest. She swung dizzily, then felt herself carried with deliberate, steady steps.

Erina, hesitating on the gray lip of a dark tunnel, sighed and slipped into the comfort of its mouth.

# Chapter Two

The soft, melodious chiming of a clock urged her into wakefulness. Erina's eyelids felt as if they had lead weights attached. She was able to lift them, finally, on the third try.

The clock was sitting on the white marble mantel of the fireplace opposite the bed where she lay. A priceless French antique of gold-painted porcelain, it had an ornate design of vine leaves, flowers, and cupids. Matching candlesticks flanked it on each end, glowing with the light of wax candles. Centered above it was an oval mirror in a gold leaf frame that was tilted slightly forward at the top.

The mirror reflected the bed in exacting detail. Of polished rosewood with a carved pediment topping the half tester, it had a starburst of creamy yellow silk underneath it. Bed curtains of heavy satin lined with cream were draped from under the pediment and tied to the tall, fluted posts. Beneath them, also tied back at present, was the gauzy muslin of mosquito netting. The wallpaper seen in the mirror's silvery surface, and also on the wall behind it, was marked in stripes of green and gold and cream in such pale, soothing shades they were almost nonexistent.

A frown of puzzlement gathered between Erina's eyes. What was she doing in such a finely restored museum of a house? Why in the world had she been put to bed in a perfect antique reproduction, and on

outrageously expensive sheets with the glazed stiffness of starched linen and trailing vine leaves em-
broidered on the hem? And who had put the granny
gown on her, one of fine white lawn with a high-
buttoned neck and long, ruffled sleeves?

A soft rustling came from somewhere near the
head of the bed. The face of a woman appeared from
around the bed curtains. Dressed in a plain cotton
dress with starched collar and cuffs, she wore a cap
edged with crocheted lace over her grizzled hair. She
was dark-skinned and possibly in her late fifties. She
came closer to lean over Erina.

"Mademoiselle? Ah, *mais oui. Voilà, m'sieur!*"

Erina followed the woman's gaze as she turned
toward the French windows on the far side of the
bed. A man stood on the balcony just beyond the
open doorway, outlined against the gray light of evening. He turned at the maid's call.

It was Sinclair.

Every emotion and half-formed idea inside Erina
scattered. She felt lost, disoriented. Her head began
to pound with a sudden, virulent pain.

There was pantherlike grace and force in his tall
form as he stepped inside and came to stand at the
bed's high, ornate footboard. His gaze flickered over
Erina without expression. Resting his hands on the
carved wood in front of him, he said with suppressed
violence, "Who are you? And what are you doing in
my house?"

The lover of her dreams, the man in the portrait,
the flesh and blood man who stood before her: how
could they all be the same? This must be what it
was like to go insane, this sense of everything being
completely solid and real while a small portion of
the brain recognized in panic that it was impossible.

She closed her eyes, fighting for calm, for some
kind of self-control. When she opened them again,

Sinclair was still there, still waiting with barely contained impatience for her answers to his questions.

"My name," she said after a long moment, "is Erina Littlefield."

"You have no French. It is as I suspected; you are of the Irish."

She stared at him as the odd phrases spoken in deep-toned and strangely accented English trickled through her mind. "No," she said finally, "I don't speak French. And I suppose I do have Irish ancestors."

His expression did not waver. "Who brought you here?"

She cast back in her mind for some wisp of memory, but there was nothing except an image that could not possibly be correct. She moistened her dry lips and swallowed with difficulty. Her voice husky, she said, "I have no idea."

The man at the foot of the bed made a brief, sharp gesture toward the dark-skinned woman. She nodded and stepped toward a table near the bed. Glass clinked on glass. A moment later, the woman brought water in a crystal goblet to Erina and lifted her head to help her drink.

Cool, without a trace of chemicals, yet with a faint scent of mud, the liquid slid down Erina's throat. It was not easy to drink with the man watching her so closely, however. She stared at him over the rim of the goblet, just as he was staring at her.

He was wearing rather elegant evening wear, a fact that had not really struck her until that moment because it seemed so natural to him. And yet, there was something odd about the formal clothing. The vest he wore was brocaded, and the tails of his coat much longer than ordinary. His shirt collar was worn turned up with only the slightest roll over the cloth at his neck, which was wrapped and tied in the fashion of an especially fancy ascot. The emerald stickpin at his throat, holding the white satin folds, was fancier than most men would consider acceptable. He looked, in fact, as if he might be wearing a costume.

As Erina signaled that she was finished, the water goblet was removed. The dark-skinned woman stepped to place the glass on the table, and Erina saw that the skirt of her dress reached the floor. She was also wearing a costume. Crazy.

Or perhaps not so crazy, after all. It was possible the clothes were for authenticity in the renovated mansion. Some people who bought and restored old houses were fanatic about such things, at least on special occasions. That was it. It had to be.

The moment she seemed comfortable again the man who looked like Sinclair said, "How can you not know how you came to be here? Did you get into the house by yourself?"

His small gesture of consideration and her arrival at a reasonable explanation for her surroundings gave her the courage to say what was at the back of her mind. "I thought that you— That is—didn't you bring me?"

He stared at her for long seconds, his eyes hard and opaque as blackened steel. Directing his gaze toward the other woman, he said, "Leave us."

"Mais, m'sieur—?" There was the sound of protest in her voice.

His dark eyes were level and unrelenting. Something the older woman saw in them made her lower her lashes. She flung a quick look of doubt at Erina, then turned and moved swiftly from the room.

As the door closed, the man stepped around the bed to Erina's side. Her heartbeat accelerated as she watched him come. He was so familiar, yet unfamiliar, that her response to him seemed all hay-wired. One second she felt a comforting ease with him, the next she was supremely self-conscious and aware of him as a man. His physical presence was so much more vivid and powerful than the man in her dreams. Yet there was something in his eyes, a troubled perplexity behind his anger, that touched a chord of response inside her.

She flinched a little as he reached toward her. His face tightened, but he only picked up her wrist. With a quick movement, he pushed the long sleeve of her nightgown to the elbow.

The purple splotches of bruises made dark patches on her arms. Turning them to the light of the candles, he said, "Did I do this to you?"

Her gaze flicked upward from her exposed arm to where he leaned above her. "You?" she said in puzzled tones. "Of course not!"

"You're certain?"

"Absolutely. It was—just some squatter in the old Rouquette mansion."

"Squatter?" he said, as if the word had no meaning for him.

"A vagrant living in the old house. I disturbed him, and he—"

"He attacked you?"

"You stopped him. Don't you remember?"

There was pleading in her tone. She thought that if the shadowy figure she had glimpsed and this man were the same, then she might not be going insane after all. There could be a simple explanation for everything: the candles, the costumes, the room, the bed, everything.

"No, I don't remember," he said, lowering her sleeve and placing her wrist carefully on the mattress before he turned away from her.

"But you have to; you were there!"

His shoulders tensed. Then he sighed. Without turning his head, he said, "I don't remember because I was—not myself this afternoon."

She frowned at his back. "Not yourself?"

"I am subject, you must understand, to periods

when I lose contact with what is happening around me. Sometimes I fall into an unnatural sleep. At others, so I'm told, I walk and speak and act as I might at any other time, only I have no memory of events that occur. Usually these periods last only a few minutes. At other times, it may be hours, even days."

"Blackout spells," Erina said, almost to herself.

"An apt description. Actually, it's the falling sickness. Or as we French Creoles style it, the *grand mal*, actually *petit mal* in my case, since I am spared the rigors of more serious attacks."

Falling sickness. *Grand mal*. She had seen the names for his illness in autobiographies and historical novels. Napoleon had been subject to such attacks, she thought, and Caesar. Then it came to her.

"Epilepsy."

There was surprise in his face as he turned to stare at her. "So the Greeks called it."

"And you had an episode this afternoon?"

He inclined his head. After a moment, he went on, his tone carefully neutral. "One of the more peculiar manifestations of my illness is delusions. Things I am certain I saw and did while seized with the malady I discover later never took place. Then there are incidents of déjà vu, where things I have never seen, never done before, people I am seeing for the first time, seem familiar. As an instance of the last, when I found you here on the floor and picked you up to put you on the bed, I—"

He paused and looked away while his hands closed into fists. Watching him, Erina felt a squeezing sensation in her chest. Through chill lips, she said, "You thought you knew me?"

"Peculiar, is it not?" Facing her again, he squared his shoulders. "That is why I asked if it was I who— injured you."

"You think you might have done it while you were

out of it? No, it didn't happen. It didn't happen that way at all."

She watched him, wanting so much for him to believe her. At the same time, there was such a confusion of ideas in her mind that she felt dazed with them.

Parapsychology was a growing science. The studies of ESP, mind transference, astral projection, and so-called out-of-body experiences were in their infancy. Was it possible there was something to these mysteries?

What if each time she summoned her fantasy companion she had in some way triggered for this man who looked so much like him an incidence of what he called *petit mal*? What if, in some manner beyond normal comprehension, he was able to walk into her mind while temporarily insensible, was able to do and be all the things she had required of her dream lover?

Dear God.

No. It was impossible.

She was an idiot for thinking such a thing for even a second. The resemblance was a fluke, that was all.

The words as impersonal as she could make them, she said, "Isn't there something that can be done for you, some medicine you can take?"

His gaze hardened. His voice flat, he said, "No. Nothing."

"But I thought I read somewhere that there's a simple drug therapy for epilepsy, one that will allow people with minor cases, like you, to lead perfectly normal lives."

"You are mistaken."

She wasn't and she knew it. She opened her mouth to tell him so.

It was then that she heard the carriage.

She knew what it was because she had heard the sound in dozens of movies and television westerns.

Its approach could be followed from some distance away, the *clip-clop* of horses' hooves, the rattle and jingle of harness, the faint squeal of an axle in need of greasing.

One reason it was so easy to recognize these sounds was the quiet. The unnatural quiet.

She listened hard, but could not hear the ordinary noises of New Orleans, that insistent grumble so familiar it usually went unnoticed. There was no drone of car and truck engines, no hiss of tires on pavement and blast of horns, no dull vibration of distant machinery. These things had ceased as totally as if the city no longer existed.

Onward the carriage came, its pace steady but unhurried. But now, mingling with the noise could be heard a few faint, almost unnoticed sounds after all. Crickets shrilled and tree frogs croaked, and a fly buzzed at the window, which stood open and unscreened to the evening air. Somewhere children shouted as they played and dogs barked. And there was a call from several streets away, faint, persistent, almost indecipherable in its thick French accent.

*"Calas tout chaud! Calas!"*

Rice cakes. Hot rice cakes.

Such things had been sold by street vendors in New Orleans a century and more ago.

Erina levered herself upward on one elbow. Her head swam and she bit back a gasp. After a second, however, the room began to steady.

"What are you doing?" he demanded.

She paid no attention to the question. Sweeping back the sheet and silk coverlet, she swung her legs over the edge of the mattress. The bed was high off the floor. She could see a set of bed steps on the opposite side, but that didn't help her just now. She clung to the bed curtains as she slid down until her feet touched the floor. The hem of her gown rode up, exposing her legs to her thighs.

The man in evening dress averted his gaze.

The gesture, Erina thought, was made not from his own embarrassment, but to preserve her modesty. She hesitated, oddly affected by that sign of awareness and courtesy. She could not think of a single man she knew who would have bothered, or who could have made her so self-conscious by the action.

Then it was forgotten as she heard the clatter of the horse-drawn vehicle coming closer. She took a wavering step toward the window.

The man moved in close to her side at once, placing a supporting hand under her elbow. Disapproval in his voice, he said, "You'll fall if you aren't careful. That's a nasty bruise on your temple; you should rest."

His nearness and the heat and strength of his clasp sent a tremor along her nerves. Her heart began to beat with sickening strokes. Dizziness assailed her and she swayed where she stood. He reached across her back, encircling her shoulders with his arm.

She turned her head to stare up at him with wide eyes, letting her gaze touch the strong planes and angles of his face, the faint stubble of beard under his skin, the way his hair grew in a slight peak on his forehead. He was real, so very real.

"Come, let me help you back into bed." There was a faint note of concern in the roughness of his voice.

She drew breath with an audible gasp. "No, I'm fine. I—I have to see out."

His gaze held hers for long seconds. Finally, he said, "As you wish."

He did not remove his support. She was glad of it as she made her way to the French windows and stepped out onto the balcony.

The carriage was just passing in the street. Its body gleamed a rich maroon in the dusk. The horses that stepped high before it were matched grays. The coachman on the seat wore a burgundy red coat and a top hat, and held his whip at a jaunty angle. Inside the carriage, barely seen in the dimness, rode a woman with a bonnet on her head and a shawl around her shoulders. Opposite her was a child with her nose pressed against the glass; she had ringlets tied in bunches in front of her ears. A pair of lean and rangy dogs, strays perhaps, loped alongside the horses, pretending to nip at their heels while keeping a wary eye on the driver's whip.

Erina closed her eyes tightly then opened them again as if that would change things. It didn't. The carriage rumbled away down the street, its wheels splashing in ruts filled with muddy water from a recent rain. Birds flew down from the tree limbs overhanging the narrow road to peck at grain fallen from feed bags.

Below the balcony was a lovely little paved courtyard garden in which a tiered wrought-iron fountain played. Climbing roses reached upward to scale the wall of an octagonal tower that was attached to the room where Erina stood. The last time she had looked down into that side garden, it had been an overgrown ruin.

Turning slowly, Erina moved back inside. She stood staring at the doorway leading into the tower room, the room from which she had seen Sinclair come.

Her gaze was almost fearful as she looked up once more at the man at her side. With a small catch in her voice, she said, "I don't think I—quite caught your name."

"I beg pardon," he said quietly, "it was an oversight. I am St. Clair Rouquette."

"Sinclair—" she whispered.

"You give me the English form as the Americans do, mademoiselle. It is St. Clair, if you please."

The difference was slight, but she heard it as he emphasized it for her. "Yes, of course."

Rouquette. She was in the Rouquette mansion. The Rouquette mansion as it had been—how long ago? A hundred and fifty years, maybe a little more. On top of that, the New Orleans she had known, with its traffic noise and paved streets, its street lamps and directional signs, had disappeared. Even the air was different. Gone was the smell of car exhaust and decay. On the evening breeze were the fresh scents of flowers and green growing things, and also the faint odor of dust and horses. The air inside the room carried the smells of burning wax from the candles and also linseed oil, perhaps from the hand-rubbed polish on the furniture.

No. She refused to believe it. It wasn't logical. It wasn't possible.

She felt like Alice after she fell down the rabbit hole. Or as if she had fallen into one of her own fantasies.

But there had to be a way to establish normalcy, a way to prove that she was where she should be. There must be something.

In abrupt inspiration, she said, "I would like to go to the bathroom."

St. Clair Rouquette loosened his hold on her. "Bath room? You wish to bathe?"

"I wish to—" she paused as she searched for an unmistakable idiomatic expression—"I wish to use the toilet."

Amusement warred with disapproval in his face. "You are very outspoken, are you not? I'll ring for Theodora to assist you."

"I don't need any help if you'll just point the way."

He lifted a brow, then guided her farther inside the bedroom with a touch on the shoulder. Stepping away, he moved to the door set into the wall beside the fireplace and pushed it open. Without quite looking at her, he said, "You will find what you require in here."

She could feel relief moving through her along with a hectic urge to laugh. How could she have been so silly? Any house that had a modern bathroom had to be a restoration. As for the rest, she must be somewhere in the country. Why she had been brought here, and by whom, she could not imagine, but she would get to the bottom of it or know the reason why.

Brushing past him, she stepped into the bathroom and closed the door behind her. She turned.

It was not a bathroom. There was no toilet, no lavatory, no tub. There was, instead, an armoire, a shaving stand, a bootjack, and a washstand on which sat a pitcher and bowl. There was also a sturdy wooden chair with an enclosed bottom and a seat fitted with a hinged lid which she recognized from her antique books as a closestool, a form of chair used to conceal a chamber pot.

She was in a dressing room.

The clothes in the armoire were hung on hooks instead of wire hangers. The soap in the shaving mug had never been adulterated by any form of detergent. The only razor in sight was a straight-edge blade in an ivory handle. There was no plumbing hidden in the washstand. The closestool was functional.

Erina's face felt stiff and blank when she emerged from the dressing room. She saw St. Clair Rouquette standing at the French windows once more. She stopped with her hands clasped together at her waist. In a tight voice, she said, "The date? What is today's date?"

"The 30th of April. Why?" He watched her intently.

"And the year?"

"It is 1848."

She turned away with stiff movements. Reaching the bed, she picked up the linen sheet that trailed over the side, rubbing the material between her fingers.

Smooth, one hundred per cent linen of a kind not readily available in this century. And who in the modern world had time to embroider vine leaves on such a utilitarian item? Yet, she must be dreaming. She had to be.

"Why has your hair been cut?" The question from the man at the window carried curiosity and a hint of accusation. "Were you ill?"

She lifted a hand to run her fingers through her hair, which just cleared her shoulders. The hair had not been changed; it was still her classic pageboy. Trying to concentrate on his question, she said finally, "No, not ill."

"Head lice, then?"

She swung to look at him. "Good grief, no!"

"My apologies," he said at once. "Conditions are not the best among your people, and I only thought, that is, I know the problem isn't unusual."

Her people. He meant the Irish. The year of 1848 was, if she remembered, the time of the potato famine, when the Irish had poured into New Orleans as they had the rest of the States. Taking the place of the more valuable black slaves, they had been put to work digging ditches and canals to drain the city. Unused to the heat, new to the diseases of warm countries, they had died by the thousands of typhoid and dysentery, malaria and yellow fever. Their despair and poor living conditions had brought the usual brawling, drinking, and low morals, causing them to be pushed into a ghetto of sorts known as the Irish Channel.

"I'm an American," she said sharply.

"Yes, of course. As are we all, fortunately or unfortunately. Perhaps your hair was cut as a punishment?"

Did he mean a public punishment or merely a private one? She had no idea, and, in any case, she could not force her mind to grapple with the possibilities. She said, "It was just more convenient."

"For the sea journey, I see. It's a great pity."

She couldn't cope with the implications of what he was saying, much less form a coherent answer. Her head felt as if it were about to explode and her knees had a tendency to buckle. Climbing into the bed once more, she pushed the down pillows against the headboard and leaned against them. She closed her eyes and a small silence fell.

It was St. Clair who broke it. "You spoke just now of the old Rouquette mansion. I don't know what you meant by that, for there is no other. Did you come—were you sent to see me?"

"If I told you I came out of curiosity and nothing else," she said without looking at him, "would you believe me?"

"I might. There are women who have a taste for the bizarre."

Her eyelids snapped up. "What?"

"Why else would you agree to come to me?"

"I didn't—" she began.

"Oh, come," he interrupted with weary distaste flickering across his features. "I don't object to the demimondaine, but I prefer there to be no subterfuge. If you did not expect me to guess your game, you should have played your part with more skill."

"I have no idea what you're talking about." That wasn't strictly true. She could guess, but she didn't like where her suspicions were leading her.

"Please. You have little womanly reserve and your language is less than modest. You don't object to being alone with a man, indeed, appear quite unconcerned at being visited while in your bed. You were brought into my house and my bedchamber by a paramour, of whatever name you choose to call him, who used rough tactics to see that you remained when your curiosity, and perhaps your courage, failed you. Your hair was cut at some time in the recent past, perhaps in prison before you were transported for petty theft or, more likely, selling your favors. The thing becomes obvious."

"You think—"

"No, I know. And while I appreciate your beauty and have a certain sympathy for your plight, I warn you I resent being taken for a fool."

"You actually believe I'm a prostitute," she said with amazement threading her voice. She reached up to touch the hair that he seemed to find so significant.

He watched her gesture with grim appreciation, but made no answer.

Sitting forward a little, she said, "Because I don't speak and act like some refined version of a simpering French Creole lady, you think I was brought here for your use? Why in heaven's name? Did you send for a woman?"

Anger rose to darken the olive bronze of his skin. "Certainly not!"

"Then why would you consider any of this possible? Who would supply you with a woman if you didn't ask for one yourself?"

"My personal needs and wishes are not something I care to discuss—"

"Too bad! You're the one who brought it up! I am not for sale. And I want to know where you get off suggesting that I might be."

"Come," he said, "are you sure you aren't acquainted with a good friend of mine? Have you never met, and I used the word loosely, a man of some reputation named Brissot?"

"Never in my life," she said through her teeth. For good measure, she added, "I haven't spoken to him, wouldn't know him if he walked into the room, and certainly haven't slept with him, if that's what you're insinuating."

"He must have seen you somewhere. There is no one else who would dare. Or care."

There was pain in his voice. Hearing it, she leaned back slowly against the pillows once more. She stared at him for long moments. Finally she said, "What I don't understand is why you would need to have a woman brought to you in the first place. Why not go out and get your own?"

"I have no need for ladies of the evening, nor even a light o'love."

Light o'love, what a quaint, yet neat, expression. "So what's wrong with a wife?"

"Nothing. Or there wouldn't be if there were a single female of good family in all New Orleans willing to chance the devil's curse."

"The devil's what? You don't mean your epilepsy?" Amazement was strong in her voice.

"The Greeks used to say the sickness was caused by the gods, an affliction sent for some past sin or as a destructive whim. Now we blame the devil. It's all the same."

"There's really no woman who will marry you?"

"Marry? There are none who will look at me, dance with me, or even come near me. Bloodlines are everything, you understand. Even if the girl herself would accept the risk of bearing a child who shares the curse of its father, her family would not permit it."

"So you think your friend fixed you up?"

"What?" His frown was black.

"You think your friend, this Brissot person, sent a female companion, albeit a reluctant one." Albeit. The language he used was getting to her.

"I found you, naked and in a swoon, in my bedchamber. If you can't, or won't, tell me how you came to be here, then what else am I to think?"

*Found. In his bedchamber. In this room, this house.*

His question was, she thought, a very good one.

The only trouble was, he would never believe the answer, not a man who talked about swoons and devil's curses.

How could she expect it, when she wasn't sure she believed it herself?

# Chapter Three

Whoever and whatever this Erina might be, St. Clair thought as he watched the confusion and distress in her face, she was unlike any woman he had ever met.

She was lovely in a fresh, natural fashion; her complexion was wonderfully clear and her hair, without the usual coating of pomade or tortured braiding and curls, shone with vitality even if it was rather short. Her gaze was clear and straightforward, with a marked absence of either coquetry or paralyzed modesty. Her apparent lack of awareness of him as a man invading her boudoir was refreshing, and also oddly affecting.

She made him, against his will and in spite of better intentions, want to come close to her. There was fragrance in her hair and an erotic appeal about the curves of her slender form under the voluminous nightgown that sent his pulse hammering in his head. When he held her so briefly there on the balcony, the reaction had been immediate, intense, and so obvious he had been afraid she might notice. It had been all he could do to stop himself from sweeping her up and putting her back in bed, then joining her there. She was apparently destined for a marvelous career in her chosen profession.

And yet, if she was a *fille de joie*, she could not have been long at the business. There was nothing jaded about her, no hint of scars or disease about her smooth-skinned body that he had seen as he gazed on her nakedness while she was unconscious. She made no effort to attract him, seemed in no hurry to conclude her transaction with him so she could be gone.

She had been injured, of course, perhaps more than her paramour had intended; her manner and comments had been quite dazed at times.

The sudden need he felt to find the man and beat him senseless knotted his fists. How the blackguard had brought himself to bruise her delicate flesh passed understanding. Even less obvious was how he could permit another man to possess her.

Of course, the man need not have been her lover. He might have been a father or a brother, instead. Such things happened when people were hungry enough, and the recent immigrants among the Irish were often desperately hungry.

Excuses. If she would not make them for herself, then he would make them for her. The next thing he knew, he would be trying to save her from her bleak future prospects. It was a sign, if any were needed, of his own desperation.

And his folly. She hadn't seemed frightened or disgusted by his affliction, but rather curious and inclined toward practical remedies. For that, he was grateful. Still, it was unlikely that even a starving harlot would be willing to stay with him for more than a few hours. That being so, it would be as well if he made full use of the time available to him.

His voice carefully even, he said, "I seem to have neglected my duties as host. Perhaps you would care for something to eat, a little broth and bread or a light custard? Or Theodora could make you a tisane."

She stared at him a moment before she said, "A tisane is some kind of herb tea, isn't it? That should be fine." She added. "Thank you."

He moved to tug the bell rope. While he waited for Theodora to appear, he said, "Where do you live?"

She opened her mouth to speak, then apparently changed her mind. "You wouldn't know the area."

"You might be surprised."

She moved one shoulder in a small shrug. "I have an apartment in Kenner."

"An apartment?" He could feel the stiffness of his frown. He was also disturbingly aware of her intent gaze as it rested on his face, his clothes, his hands.

"Three rooms. Rented."

"Ah, you are a boarder." He hesitated, then asked anyway, "You live alone?"

"Except for a cat named Budweiser."

The flippant, almost mocking, quality in her voice flicked him on the raw. It was as if there were hidden meanings in her answers he was not supposed to grasp. That was all too likely, since he was unfamiliar with many English words, such as this Budweiser. "What of the man who brought you? Will he be waiting somewhere for you?"

"I told you, nobody brought me here," she said with a flash of irritation like lightning in her gray eyes. "As for the man you saw, I suppose you scared him so he won't stop running until he crosses the river."

"Unlikely," he answered.

"You think so?" she asked. "Look at your hands."

As he held them up, he noticed their stiff soreness. The knuckles were grazed; one on his right hand was split, as if it had landed against bone.

"I think," she said with soft emphasis, "that you did some serious damage to him."

"Good," he said in clipped satisfaction. He paused. "Unless he is the kind who will take it out on you?"

She closed her eyes and sighed. "Why should you care?"

He could not tell. By good luck, he did not have

to since Theodora came into the room at that moment. He turned to give orders for a light repast to be brought, as well as the tisane he had first suggested. Theodora disapproved; he could tell by the flounce of her skirt as she curtsied and took herself off again. He would try a reprimand if he thought it would do any good. It wouldn't. She had taken care of him and his house for as long as he could remember, and it was her nature to be protective. The trouble was, his housekeeper seemed to think he was responsible for the condition of his guest, and that his future intentions were less than honorable. It was possible she was right about the last.

Then it happened. Behind him, he heard Erina Littlefield speak his name with that small difference that she gave it.

"St. Clair—"

He turned back, and a small breeze through the open window blew the scent of the woman in the bed to him, the mind-stopping fragrance of clean female and China tea roses. He met her watchful gaze and saw there a look of such doubt and longing that he felt his heart turn over inside him.

And suddenly he was lost in shadowy remembrance of the most persistent of his *petit mal* illusions. A woman came toward him with sure steps and clear, smiling eyes. Dressed in some silky, clinging nightgown of a fabric like none he had ever seen, she was everything he had ever dreamed of wanting. She melted into his arms, lifting her lips for his kiss. He picked her up, carrying her to a bed that magically waited, sinking down with her into its softness. Free and open, they gave themselves to each other, removing clothing, touching, holding, gliding together in such perfect harmony that their blood sang with its wonder. Her voice whispered soft requests, and he answered them in perfect rapport, attuned to every nuance of meaning, giving every ounce of strength he possessed.

This was the woman. He would know her anywhere.

He had thought she was a chimera, a dream that came both asleep and waking, one sent to relieve his unbearable need to be accepted, to be held with simple human warmth, and with passion. What if he had been wrong?

Madness. He must be very near the edge. It was always a possibility with his malady. It was not the disease itself that caused it, of course, but the despair of being always set apart, always alone.

He opened his mouth, and words he had not intended, could not recall forming, emerged on his tongue. "Stay," he said. "Don't go back to wherever you came from. You have been injured and I feel in some way at fault. It will be my pleasure and my honor to care for you."

Her gaze was assessing, yet shaded with something near wonder. "You say that, even thinking I'm—no better than I should be? Or are you saying it because of it?"

"My motives may not be pure," he said with irony, "but you have my word that you will be free from attack until after dinner."

She lifted a winged brow. "That was actually a joke," she said in soft amazement. "At least, I think it was?"

Was it? He hardly knew. "You will remain, at least for a few days?"

She looked away from him. "I don't know if I can."

"If you wish it, I will undertake to keep you safe."

A faint smile twitched a corner of her mouth. "I expected nothing less. You always have—" She stopped.

"Yes?"

"Nothing. You kept me from harm before."

She glanced at him, and his gaze locked with hers. He was unable to look away. The need to step to the bed and gather her close against him, fitting every inch of her body against his own, was so strong that his head swam with it and he felt perspiration break out across the back of his neck. Fear of an attack of *petit mal*, there in front of her, made him wrench backward toward the door.

"Don't go!" she cried.

The panic in her voice stilled his own. He could feel it fading, feel his equilibrium returning. He released the breath he had been holding. "You should try to rest."

"Yes, but I would rather—everything is so weird, and I'm not certain I want to close my eyes in case this is just a dream and the nightmare will still be there when—when I wake."

He understood very well what she was trying to say. He sometimes felt himself that he would prefer to live in his delusions.

There was a chair on the near side of the bed where Theodora had been sitting before. He moved to shift it, pulling it closer and seating himself where she could see him. "Rest," he said quietly. "I'll keep the nightmares at bay."

The tension eased from her face. Still, she watched him for long seconds. "You'll share my dinner you ordered?"

He hated broth; he had had enough of it in his days as an invalid to last several lifetimes. Theodora would be amazed. The news would undoubtedly cause considerable speculation later in the servant's quarters. He would hear about it from his man in the morning.

"Yes, certainly," he said.

She hesitated. "Maybe I shouldn't have asked. You look as if you're dressed for a night out."

"You mean for an evening's entertainment? No. Don't, please, let it concern you."

"There's no one waiting for you then?"

"Waiting for me?" he queried, uncertain of her meaning.

"Your wife. A date. Whoever else is going to the party."

He smiled with a decided curl to his mouth. "There is no party, certainly no wife."

"You live alone then?"

"Quite alone, other than during the *saison des visites*. Then my brother and his wife, with their young family and various nursemaids and cooks, arrive from the plantation."

"The plantation," she repeated in blank tones.

He inclined his head in agreement. "My sister-in-law feels the confinement of the country. She lives for the theater and opera, and of course the balls, of the winter."

"No date, either?" she said.

"I'm not sure I understand this word. I thought we had agreed on the day of the month."

Her glance slid away to somewhere beyond his shoulder. "I was—referring to a lady friend, someone you might be escorting for the evening."

"I was not going out," he said shortly. "There is nothing to prevent me from keeping you accompanied."

"That's all right then."

He made no answer. It might not be all right, but he did not intend to let that stop him.

There was baked chicken and fresh bread, asparagus vinaigrette and a bottle of wine, as well as the broth. Theodora was, perhaps, more attuned to his needs than he had imagined. He permitted her to serve Erina and himself, then sent her away. He preferred to be unobserved while he was watching his unexpected guest. The pleasure was too singular to allow distraction.

Erina appeared to have little appetite, though she drank her broth and ate a few morsels of chicken. Sipping her tisane, she made a face.

"I don't suppose you have any aspirin handy?" she said with a droll look in her eyes.

He repeated the unfamiliar word, then shook his head. No doubt it was an Irish herb.

Her breasts, twin mounds with small circular shadows that were her nipples barely showing through the cloth, rose and fell in a sigh. "I thought it might be a problem."

With an effort he removed his gaze from her chest and said, "Perhaps if you could describe it—"

"No," she answered in quick denial as she drank again. "Never mind. This is fine."

There was a long pause. The tisane, St. Clair suspected, had been laced with orange flower water, which in turn contained laudanum, the extract of the opium poppy. He was certain of it as Erina's eyelids drooped and the cup in her hand tilted at a precarious angle. Theodora had her methods of making certain a person rested as he well knew, having been subjected to them himself until he was old enough to circumvent them.

Rising to his feet, he rescued the cup, then lifted the tray from Erina's lap. She murmured something, and her eyelids drifted shut.

St. Clair set the tray aside, then returned to perch on the side of the bed. She was asleep, her lashes making dark, curling shadows on her pale cheeks.

His lips tightened as he reached out to brush the bruise at her temple with his fingertips. The bone underneath was intact, he thought. She might be headachy for a day or two, but she would be all right. The bruising would fade, and the fearful memories.

The silky auburn curls seemed to cling to his fingertips as he threaded through them. Disturbing their soft strands brought that faint hint of rose that tightened his loins. He wanted to bury his face in that scented softness, but that would be tempting fate, and also his command of his baser impulses.

Her lips were beautifully shaped, smooth, delicately moist at the line of their joining. She would taste of tisane and her own sweetness.

Did he dare? No.

Her breasts peaked the white lawn in a compelling fashion. They weren't large, but were perfectly shaped to fit his cupped hand. He could measure without, quite, touching. Would she wake, he wondered, if he closed his hand slowly, took the nipple between his forefinger and thumb and rolled it as delicately as he might a small and incredibly luscious berry?

His eyes felt like hot embers in his head; his brain was simmering in his skull. Never in his life had he wanted a woman so much.

*"I'm not for sale!"*

She had flung those words at him, and he had been astonished to hear them, but not unhappy. Now he regretted them. And wondered how they could be tested.

Tomorrow, if she was better, he would find out.

Discretion and honor were fine things, and he had no wish to be a dupe. But still less did he feel like accepting the martyrdom of useless self-denial.

Her hand lay on the coverlet. Picking it up, he uncurled the lax fingers and brought it to his mouth to place a kiss in the palm. The skin there was smooth and delicate and sweet; he could not resist a single brief touch of his tongue to taste.

Lowering her hand again, positioning it just so beside her, he let it go. He stepped back from the bed and turned, leaving the room. The door closed soundlessly behind him.

Erina entered the parlor, then came to an abrupt halt, overcome by a sense of dislocation. The plaster medallion that she had last seen shattered in pieces on the dirty floor was pristine white and attached to the ceiling above a crystal and bronze d'or chandelier. The draperies that had been faded and ragged now hung in heavy, silken folds at the windows. A parlor set in sea green velvet edged an Aubusson carpet woven in luminous shades of green and rose and gold.

There were two men seated at a table placed near the open window where lace undercurtains wavered in the morning breeze. As she hesitated in the doorway, they rose to their feet. One was St. Clair. The other was a slender dandy with sandy blond hair and a mustache, and a smile that crinkled the corners of his warm blue eyes.

"Oh, excuse me." Erina began a quick retreat.

"No, wait," St. Clair said. Coming toward her, he took her hand and placed it on his arm, holding it there as he led her into the room.

"St. Clair, you devil, who have we here?" The other man moved forward with amusement and interest in his face.

"Permit me, Erina, to present my good friend, Denis Brissot. Denis, Mademoiselle Erina Littlefield."

This was the man St. Clair had suspected of having her brought to his house. Erina felt her face congealing as she reached out automatically to shake hands.

"Delighted, mademoiselle," Brissot said, taking her fingers in a light clasp and turning them as he bowed over them. "St. Clair, I am enchanted, and so I warn you."

There was no amusement in St. Clair's face. He was watching the two of them with measuring eyes.

Erina wondered if he had brought her into the room for the express purpose of seeing how she might react to Brissot, and he to her.

"Please don't let me interrupt your discussion," she said, favoring both men with a small smile as she tugged her hands free. "I was only looking for something to read."

"You read? But I thought—" St. Clair stopped as he saw the look on her face. "Forgive me. There will be no books in English."

She had almost forgotten that she was supposed to be an Irish prostitute, therefore naturally illiterate. She had spent the past three days sleeping, eating the small, delicious meals that were brought to her, and generally regaining her strength and equilibrium.

The afternoon before, she had been visited by a dressmaker and her assistant bearing bolts of material, a set of fashion plates, and one or two fashion dolls. When she had protested at the necessity of having clothing made for her, St. Clair had pointed out with great reasonableness that she could not wear his sister-in-law's nightgown forever, and there was no other way to achieve a gown of any quality. Still, she dithered, unwilling to make a choice. He finally lost patience. Indicating a white India muslin figured in gold, another in aqua and cream stripe, and a rose silk, he instructed the dressmaker to make two day gowns and an evening ensemble to her own design. Swift work, he added, would be well rewarded.

With one thing and another, Erina had almost begun to feel comfortable in the house, and in her role as guest. Suddenly, that comfort was gone. The striped muslin, with the corset, petticoats, and pantaloons that went with it, all chosen and paid for by the man beside her and delivered not an hour ago, felt as if they were made of lead.

"Never mind, then," she said, her voice stiff. "I'll

just go and sit in the garden. There are roses there I have never—that is, the roses are wonderful."

"We'll bring our wine and come with you," Brissot said. "I feel the need of fresh air."

Had the offer been made in a polite attempt to ease the awkwardness that hung in the air? Or was it from curiosity? So bland was the smile that went with it, Erina could not tell.

It made no difference, in any case. St. Clair moved to the door and held it open, ushering Erina and his friend across the central hall to the side door which led into the courtyard garden.

It was a place of warm sunshine, gentle pastel colors, drifting flower scents, and shadows moving softly on the brick walls. The water bubbling up from the fountain and pouring from its bowl made a soothing murmur.

There were wrought iron chairs in a grape leaf pattern placed under the limbs of a tree with fernlike foliage and pink powder puff blooms. The three of them moved in that direction. Realizing as the men paused and stood waiting that they could not be seated until she sat down, Erina chose a chair. St. Clair stepped to hold it while she settled into it with her skirts billowing around her feet.

The tree above them was a mimosa, fast-growing, short-lived, but prodigal with its seedlings. Once Erina had played at tea parties in the shade of the tree's progeny, just here, not far from the fountain. How distant in time that seemed, almost as if the child she had been were someone else entirely.

"So tell me, mademoiselle," Brissot said, "where do you come from, and how long will you be with us here in New Orleans? Are you related to St. Clair that you are visiting with him? And what can I do to make your stay more pleasant? You have only to command me, I swear, and it will be done."

Erina searched her mind for nice, noninformative

answers to the spate of questions. While she hesitated, St. Clair replied for her.

"Erina knows not where she comes from, nor how long she will be staying. For her relationship to me, there is none. I found her, insensible and quite naked, on the floor of my bedchamber. If you are wondering why she has no chaperon while in my house, she seems not to require one so why should I?"

Erina felt the hot color begin somewhere in the region of her navel and rise in a wave to her face. St. Clair's purpose was, no doubt, to shock in the hope that one of them, Denis Brissot or herself, would say something to indicate prior knowledge of each other. The effect, however, was to expose her to his friend. She felt that betrayal like a slap in the face. It hurt, not the least reason being because it was unexpected.

"Fascinating," Brissot said in soft amazement as he rested his gaze on his friend's taut features. "You found her, and so you kept her."

"What else was I supposed to do?" The words were curt.

"Shout hosanna, I should think," Brissot answered in musing tones. "It isn't every day a man is given a gift from the gods. Even you, who scorn my offers of women, seem to recognize that much."

St. Clair gave him a dark look. "Wouldn't you agree the gods owe me a gift or two?"

"They aren't known for paying their debts. And what will you do with her now?"

Erina sprang to her feet. "He will do nothing with me," she said, her voice shaking and her eyes bright with anger as she stared from one man to the other. "I don't belong to him; I belong to me. I decide where I go, and when. And I have no intention of staying here while the two of you talk about me as if I were a—a two-bit whore on a slow Saturday night!"

She whirled and took a quick step away from them. Suddenly there was a spinning sensation inside her head. Darkness crowded near. She gasped, swaying, clamping her hands to her eyes.

St. Clair was beside her in an instant. "What is it? Erina? Tell me!"

His voice was solid, something to hang on to in the whirlwind. His hands on her arms were steadying. The blackness receded. The spinning slowed. Wobbled. Stopped.

"I think," she said indistinctly, "that I had better go and lie down."

"Yes. I'll get Theodora," he began.

"No! No, I think she went to do the marketing. Anyway, I don't need her."

Theodora would fuss and mutter and give her something to make her sleep. She had come to appreciate St. Clair's housekeeper, but she didn't want her now.

"Then I'll come—"

"Stay with your friend," she said. "I'll be perfectly fine."

He let his hands fall away from her, but he did not move. Behind him, Brissot stood watching.

Summoning a smile, Erina inclined her head toward the other man. With a trace of irony in her tone, she said, "A pleasure, Monsieur."

Denis Brissot bowed with a faint snap of his heels. "Until next time, mademoiselle."

"If there is a next time," she returned, and felt a grim smile curve her mouth as she saw St. Clair stiffen.

Turning from them both, she walked away.

But there was no rest in her bedchamber. For one thing, she was too disturbed, and for another, the room was still St. Clair's bedchamber even if she had ousted him; there were reminders of him everywhere.

One of the most potent of these was the scent of

linseed oil. It had nothing to do with furniture, she had discovered that morning, but came from the tower room.

That connecting octagonal chamber was St. Clair's retreat. There he kept the medical books of his father, who had been a physician, also the household records and ledgers pertaining to the family plantation in St. James Parish. In addition, one corner was cluttered with easels and canvases, with oil colors and brushes and all the other paraphernalia of painting. The linseed oil, used for thinning the colors, was among these items.

There were a number of canvases in various stages of completion. One was a river scene, another a somber view of a funeral procession. The largest, set on a low easel in front of a full-length mirror, was a half-finished self-portrait.

Erina wandered into the tower now to stand staring at the painting of St. Clair. There was technical skill in the execution, an exacting color sense, and more than competent brush work. The clothing, the stance and background were the same as in the one she had seen in the derelict mansion. And yet, there was something not quite right about the painted figure. She thought it was in the eyes. They were too blank, the expression passionless and barricaded. It kept everything inside, gave nothing away.

At some point between this moment and the late twentieth century, St. Clair had learned enough to do much better. She knew, because she had seen the final work. But for now, the portrait appeared very like the artist, a man locked inside himself.

It hurt her to look at it.

She turned away, moving back into the bedchamber. There, she stopped. And standing there in the middle of the room, she felt a sudden, terrible need to get out of the house, get away, run, search for something, anything to hold on to that was real and solid. To search, perhaps, for the future.

She had felt the urge hovering inside her from the moment she suspected the truth, even while she rested and regained her strength. As long as St. Clair was nearby, offering stability and comfort, it had not reached the stage of action. Hearing him discuss her as if she meant nothing to him made her realize he was not, could not be, the Sinclair she had created, that she was basing her whole security on no more than a foolish fancy.

She would go. Now.

She donned bonnet and gloves, not because Theodora had told her she should not be seen without them, but because she did not want to be conspicuous. It would be bad enough to be outside the house without chaperon or companion; that much had been impressed upon her in the last hour.

There was no difficulty in leaving the house. Theodora was gone. St. Clair and his friend were still in the courtyard garden; she could hear their voices coming from that direction. The downstairs maid was out in the kitchen wing behind the house, talking to the cook as she prepared the noon meal. A houseboy who was polishing the brass door knocker opened the door for her, then bowed her down the steps.

She moved slowly at first, staring around her, looking for the familiar. But nothing was the same. Streets were more narrow, front entrance areas wider. Curbs and sidewalks were of brick and stone or were missing altogether. There were no street markers against which to check her bearings. Houses appeared stripped of detail, when in reality they had not yet received their late Victorian embellishments.

A farm wagon loaded with vegetables and pulled by a raw-boned mule passed her. She saw a boy bowling a hoop running along in front of a black

woman who puffed after him. A carriage came toward
her. In it was an ancient female in shiny black faded
to purple at the seams, looking desiccated and bored.

By degrees, as she moved deeper into the French
Quarter, her footsteps quickened. Her heart beat high
in her throat. Her head began to throb. She saw a
pair of sailors coming toward her with long, greasy
hair tied back in a queue and striped jerseys. She
crossed the street, holding her skirts above the caked
mud lying in clumps on the brick paving.

Another block, and another. She crossed a street
and rounded a corner.

Jackson Square. There it was before her.

Only it wasn't. Rather, it was the old Place
d'Armes as shown in the faded and yellowed prints.
It was larger, wider; its iron railing was lower. There
were no flowering shrubs and winding paths, no
rearing statue of Andrew Jackson, no Pontalba apartment buildings with black lace iron balconies on either side. It was only a grassy and bedraggled parade
ground with a few trees and a wide, beaten path
across it from Chartres Street to the river.

The river itself had changed, running much closer.
Gone was the Moonwalk, the high wall of the levee,
the wide batture between the city and water. Steam-
boats, like so many floating birthday cakes, were
drawn right up to the low dike of a river wharf,
jostling each other as stevedores heaved sacks on
brawny shoulders to take them up the gangplanks
and rolled barrels down. From that direction, drifting
on the still air, was the sickly smell of raw rum and
molasses, rotted fruit, fish, and mud.

And the St. Louis Cathedral, which faced the river
and naked parade ground, had lost its spires, or
rather, had not yet gained them. With its rounded
bell towers, it had a Spanish aspect that made it seem
completely foreign. The buildings on either side, the
Cabildo and Presbytre, were in bad repair, and with-

out the mansard roofs that would be added in a few years from now in the face-lift provided by the wealthy and scandal-ridden Baroness Pontabla.

Standing there looking around her, Erina felt bereft and suddenly afraid. She had tried to ignore the evidence, not to mention the simple facts as St. Clair gave them to her, tried to pretend it didn't matter. She could do it no longer.

She was standing in New Orleans in the year 1848. She was here, with the paving of ballast stones from arriving ships under her feet, the sun shining on her head, the bodies of people she had always thought of as long dead moving around her. By some means she could not begin to understand, much less duplicate, she had transcended time and space and matter to reach this place, this year, this day.

Now what?

The dizziness, the darkness, was crowding her again. She needed to sit down somewhere out of the sun. Or maybe she needed to lie down, to sleep and possibly dream a dream from which she could awake.

"There you are. I knew I'd find you."

The words were rough-edged, grimly self-satisfied. Hard on them, her arm was taken in a firm grasp and she was dragged around. St. Clair's face swam before her. She reached out to clutch his coat with both hands, holding tight.

"Is something wrong?" he said in totally different tones as he ducked his head, trying to see under the brim of her bonnet. "Are you faint?"

"Yes. No. I don't know. Oh, St. Clair," she cried in despair, "everybody and everything is gone—my sister, my friends, my home and town, my place in them. I don't have a penny to my name, have nowhere to live, nowhere to go. What in heaven's name am I going to do?"

His face changed, softening. "Come home with me," he said.

She loosened her grasp to wipe at the moisture sliding through her lashes with the edge of her gloved hand. "How can I? You don't want the kind of woman you think I am in your house. I have to find work. There must be—"

"The kind of work a lovely woman alone is likely to find, you may as well do for me."

She drew back further. There was a tight pain in her chest as she said, "Are you suggesting—"

"Be my *cherie aine*, my cherished one, my light o'love, and I will take care of you as long as you can find it in your heart to remain. When you go, as you must and surely will, you won't be poorer for it."

It was a bald proposal made on the street under the discreet observance of several curious onlookers. She might have been insulted if she had been of the same time, and was, maybe a little, even so. But, lifting her head to look at him, she saw his set stance, the tension at the corners of his mouth, and the suspended look in his eyes. She saw and was touched by the courage required for him to speak those words.

He expected a refusal, perhaps with horror and loathing. He might even expect the physical retaliation of an open-handed blow, the virginal maiden's traditional slap.

The breath she drew was deep. She said, "You may think you know what and who I am, but you don't. There are things I should tell you that you might not believe or understand."

"There is nothing you can say that will change my mind. I thought I had lost you just now, and I nearly went out of my mind. I also understand more than you may believe. Your independence, for instance. You said you are not mine, and I accept that, as much as I might wish it otherwise. I am asking, most humbly and with all due respect, if you will give yourself to me for whatever time there may be."

This was the man she had known in a thousand dreams, her lover and loving companion. This was her Sinclair. Or at least he was as close as she could find, as near as she could bear.

She could not refuse; she hardly even considered the possibility. It wasn't desperation, nor was it gratitude for the offer of basic necessities. It was, rather, that he wanted her, needed her, and she finally understood something of major importance.

"Yes, of course I will," she answered him quietly but with confidence. "Why else am I here?"

# Chapter Four

"I'm not what you think," Erina said.

They were sitting in the garden with the remains of their lunch spread on a table set back under the mimosa. The air was somnolent with warmth, the scent of the mimosa blossoms overhead, and the hum of bees. Spring was fast turning into summer, in the way it had of doing in New Orleans.

She had debated with herself all through the meal over whether to risk telling St. Clair the truth. He might think she was lying to make herself look better, or else that she was crazy. It couldn't be helped. It would be taking unfair advantage to become a part of his life without letting him know exactly what he was getting.

He looked at her for long moments, his gaze steady upon her. Finally, he said, "Tell me, then, if you must."

She did, and in detail. Nothing was left out, from her childhood visits to the house and her dreams, to her marriage and divorce, her job, and the details of the evening she had been attacked. His face, as he listened, mirrored disbelief, annoyance, and grim implacability. There were also fleeting moments of softness and a species of wonder.

She expected many comments, many questions from him when she finally fell silent. She did not look for the one she got.

"So you really are Madame Erina. And this husband, this Thomas," he continued with a twist of distaste to his lips, "why did you marry him?"

"Hormones," she answered. "Or maybe I should say the confused desires of a young woman who doesn't know anything about love. He asked, which plays more of a part in what women do than most men ever realize, thank goodness. Loneliness was another reason, the need for somebody to help stop the drifting feeling inside and make the future begin."

"Yes," he said softly, "I think I see. Sometimes, dreams are not enough. But you didn't love him."

"I thought he loved me and that would make it all right. I was wrong on both counts."

"But you married him in the church, lived with him as his wife?"

She looked at him curiously as she agreed, wondering what was in his mind.

His gaze was bleak. "Divorce is a difficult matter in these times, a thing involving lawyers, courts, and even the legislature. Even if these obstacles can be overcome, it is strictly forbidden to one of my faith. The nearest thing that can be arranged is an annulment. This is not impossible, even for marriages which produce children, but requires special circumstances, special dispensation from Rome."

Was he saying he could never marry her? She hadn't even considered it, couldn't believe the thought had crossed his mind. She searched for a way to make this plain to him without appearing to assume too much.

Before she could find it, he leaned back in his chair. Crossing his legs, he changed the subject.

"So what is it like living in this future so many years from now? You speak of a car, which I imagine to be some form of transport, and of a phone that seems to be used to communicate. Explain these things."

She did her best, going on to tell of many other

miracles of modern life that she had taken for granted, from airplanes and computers to the garden tractors and harvesting combines that had taken the place of slaves.

"Medicine," she went on, "has made great advances. People in my time seldom die of things like appendicitis and childbirth problems, smallpox, malaria, and yellow fever, or childhood illnesses. And this problem of yours would be a small thing indeed, something easily controlled."

"Don't mock me," he said with a dark look from under his straight brows.

"I wouldn't, I promise. You would be able to do whatever you pleased: run, jog, drive a car, travel, get married, work if that was what you wanted. Anything at all. People do it all the time."

"If only—" he began, then stopped.

He was silent, gazing past her with a faraway look in his eyes while he considered it. Finally, he shook his head, a single gesture of regret and, perhaps, denial.

Turning back to her, he watched her for a moment, then his lips curved in a slow smile. "And in the midst of these many wonders," he said in soft tones, "you dreamed of me."

The heat that moved over her was uncontrollable. She met his gaze, her own seeking, half afraid, for mockery. "You believe me, then? You really do?"

"Why not?"

"It must sound so wild, so impossible." No one she had ever known, least of all her ex-husband, would have listened with half the patience, or have been half so accepting.

"Perhaps I believe it for that reason. Or could be I'm merely credulous."

"Or you prefer it to the alternative?" she asked with thoroughly modern cynicism.

"If you mean by that I would rather consider you

my personal miracle instead of a light woman," he answered quietly, "then you may be right."

She watched him for a long moment. Driven, finally, to speak the thought that was in her mind, she said, "Did you pray for a miracle?"

"On my knees. For years."

The tightness that rose in her chest forced tears to seep into her eyes, pooling among her lashes. "I doubt," she said with difficulty, "that I'm anywhere near so holy."

He smiled, his gaze caressing as it lingered on her face. "Good. I have no use for angels. And I would rather you didn't disappear again in a puff of incense."

"I don't think I know how," she answered in husky tones.

"No?"

"For all I can tell, you brought me here, and may have the power to send me back again."

"If I do, I'll never use it."

She tilted her head, her eyes dark and vulnerable. "Promise me?"

He only smiled. Rising to his feet, he held out his hand. "Come into the house," he said. "It's the siesta hour, and you should rest."

"And you," she answered as she moved beside him.

"Oh, I intend to, at least a little."

The smile he gave her was open and rich with sensual promise.

St. Clair might belong to the Victorian era, but it seemed there was no prudishness in him. It could have been because he was French and of New Orleans, which made him a breed apart. Or possibly it was because he had been born and reared before the arrival of Freudian theory or the sexual revolution to make him self-conscious.

On top of that, he lacked all sense of the press of

time. There was no hurry whatever about the way
he led her into the bedchamber, no desperate haste
or fumbling anxiety as he drew her to him.

He cupped her face in his long artist's fingers, his
fingertips testing the texture of her skin and the fragile bones underneath. His gaze moved over her
brows, her eyelids, the line of her nose, the smooth
point of her chin. His lips followed, delicately brushing. By the time he reached her mouth, her own lips
were tingling, parted for the touch and taste of him.

Warm and sweet, his kiss was everything she had
ever pretended, more tantalizing than dreams. He
traced the sensitive edges of her lips, lapped the corners to collect their moisture, dipped inside. Sinuous,
inciting, his tongue touched hers. Made bold by the
rise of languorous pleasure, she met his incursion,
twining her tongue with his in gentle invitation. With
small strokes, he traced the silken underside, swirled
along the glazed edges of her teeth and, retreating,
encouraged her to venture into his mouth in her turn.

Complying, it was an instant before Erina noticed
his fingers at the row of tiny buttons down her back.
He worked his way along them with patient preci-
sion, laying her back bare. He stroked the smooth
skin there, smoothing the edges of her day gown
away from her shoulders, letting the neckline dip in
front.

Trailing a line of heated kisses from the corner of
her mouth and along her jaw, he descended by
inches to the curves of her breasts, which were
pressed upward by her corset. His soft breath wafting over the blue-veined contours made them prickle
with the tiny rises of gooseflesh. He smoothed away
that delicate roughness, inhaling deeply in wordless
satisfaction as the white curves acquired a faint rose
bloom, like blushed peaches, under his care.

Erina tilted her head back, closing her eyes against
the delicious onslaught of longing. She smoothed her

hands over the muscles of his shoulders and felt them bunch and lengthen under her palms with his movements. There was something so exquisitely right about this moment, something so perfect, that she felt her heart swell in her chest.

He was hers. He always had been, always would be. There were things about him she had never guessed, things she had not expected. Yet in his essential nature, he was as she had formed him in her mind. He was her dream lover, for this moment, and for all time. She knew it, she felt it in the very depths of her being. And if she was wrong, if she was deluding herself, she didn't want to know.

With a small, incoherent murmur, she buried her face in his neck. Blindly, she found the stickpin that held his cravat and opened it and pushed it into the folds before unwinding them. She sought the studs of his shirt, pulling them from their placket layers and dropping them to the floor. Spreading the open edges wider, she pressed her lips to the hollow at the base of his throat and stripped the fullness of linen and the coat he wore over it down his arms.

With a laugh deep in his throat, he stepped away long enough to free himself of the entrapping material. Bending then, he put an arm behind her knees and one at her back and lifted her to the bed. Joining her on the high surface in a swooping leap, he bowled her backward into the softness of the cotton mattress, then rolled above her. Resting his weight on his elbows, but pinning her with his knees, he began with infinite slowness and an infinity of kisses to release her from her confinement of corset and petticoats.

"You are so beautiful," he said as he searched at the edge of her camisole for the coral brown circles of aureoles centered by budded nipples.

"Soft as silk," he said as he found and discarded

the combs Theodora had used to sweep her hair to the top of her head.

"Perfect," he murmured as he shifted from her, dipping to nuzzle the flat, white surface of her abdomen, scraping gently with the faint stubble of his beard. Moving lower still, he opened her thighs with firm pressure to journey into uncharted realms of fine silken curls and tender folds, seeking sweet nectar.

"Oh, Sinclair," she said in aching delight and recognition. Hearing his low chuckle, she realized her mistake, but was too lost in the mounting, spreading sensation inside her to retrieve it. She made, instead, an amends of caresses as she reached out to him.

His flanks were lean, fitted with long, firm muscles, as his trousers were stripped away and kicked aside. "Beautiful," she said as she followed the angular masculine line, feeling the delicious rasping of rough hair against her skin.

Her adventuring touch slid along his hip bone and forward to where he hovered, taut, vibrant, warmly throbbing. Clasping, holding, she murmured, "Like iron under silk." And smiled a little as she heard his soft exhalation.

Then leaning to trace the seam of flesh that decorated the underside with her tongue, she paused to whisper, "Perfect," on a wafting sigh, then continued.

It was a beguilement, one so rich with wonder they were lost in it. It flowed constant around them, inside them. Their hearts beat high with it; their skin took on its glow. Their every breath, every calculated and eager caress, pushed it higher, sharpened its edges. The need it fueled spiraled upward, suffusing them, coalescing in their bodies as a parched and exacting need.

Erina's breath expanded in her chest. Her blood pulsed in hot torrents in her veins. The surface of her skin was so sensitized that the lightest touch sent shivers of sensation along her nerves. Drugged and heavy with desire, she clenched her hands on the muscles of his arms in mute appeal.

He answered it in a swift roll above her once more. She felt the sure touch of his fingers as he eased his way, then he entered her in a warm, fluid slide. A small cry rose to her throat as she felt the stretching fullness. She clenched around him in giving, liquid pulsing. Then as the wrenching spasm eased, he began to move, seeking a rhythm that she could share.

It came, easy and natural. The friction was blessed, bringing soft gasps and cries of gratification. Endless, effortless, it sounded the limits of endurance, of will, of sanity. It found them in a sudden internal upheaval, in the vivid, silent joy that burst inside them.

Time ceased. There was nothing but this, no one except the two of them. Nothing mattered, nothing could or ever would, so long as they could come together, heart to heart, body against body, to create this bliss, this consummate grandeur.

Incapable of thought, unable to move in the grip of inexorable splendor, they held each other. And somewhere in the spinning fringes of her mind Erina knew the truth beyond a doubt.

This was, in the end, the only real miracle.

The early summer was wet. Sometimes it rained all night, at others the showers came every day during the siesta hour, clattering in the courtyard outside the window as they made love. The streets became quagmires. The river crept around the city, flooding the outer edges and driving snakes and frogs into the center of town. Theodora began to mutter about floods and fever seasons going together.

Between the rains, the sun came out hot and bright to raise the humidity to suffocating. Vines and shrubs in the courtyard leaped into rampant lushness. Lin-

ens left unaired developed gray mildew spots and
leather in the back of the armoires sheeted over with
green mold. The citizens of New Orleans steamed
like seafood in a broth.

Erina, used to air conditioning, felt the heat like a
damp, hot blanket wrapped around her. There were
times when she couldn't breathe, felt she wouldn't
be able to stand it an instant longer. Then a breeze
would wander from the direction of Lake Pontchar-
train; it would cloud up and shower, or else the day
would fade into the long, comparatively cool
twilight.

The window in Erina and St. Clair's bedchamber
became a bone of contention. Erina could not bear to
sleep with it closed, while St. Clair seemed convinced
that night air was dangerous. Besides, he said, the
candlelight attracted moths and mosquitoes, and
their fluttering and whining outside the mosquito
*baire*, as he called it, kept him awake. He compro-
mised, finally, by opening the window halfway, and
dressing for bed in the dark. And he spent a good
half hour every evening tucking the mosquito netting
securely under the mattress to seal out insect
intruders.

The netting was so heavy, however, that it blocked
what little movement of air there was in the room.
Erina often waited until St. Clair slept, then lifted the
muslin near her face so she could breathe.

She was in the courtyard one morning, pulling the
weed seedlings that sprang up daily in the cracks
between the paving stones. Denis Brissot found her
there.

"What are you doing? Why not call one of the
houseboys for that task," he said as he strolled toward
her.

She rose from where she knelt on the paving, turning to him with a smile. He was a constant visitor,
St. Clair's only true friend, and she valued him for

that, though she was never sure what he thought of her.

"Were you looking for St. Clair? He went to the market. There was this sudden urgent desire to have squab for lunch, since I've never tasted them."

"I'll wait for him, if you don't mind. But really, must you grub in the dirt?"

"I need some occupation for my time," she said, giving him her hand with a smile as he came nearer.

"Bored already?" he said quietly, searching her face as he made his bow.

"Not at all. But I'm not used to a life of leisure, you know, and Theodora runs everything so well I don't dare interfere. There is just so much shopping I can do. I'm making progress with my French, but even St. Clair can't teach me to read it overnight."

"And there is only so much time you can spend bewitching him?"

She freed her hand. "I don't know what you mean."

"Come, don't be coy. You have changed his life: I've never seen him so outgoing and interested in the world beyond his door as in these last few weeks. He never mentions his illness, hasn't had to shut himself away with it since you came. I am astounded. And terrified."

"Terrified?"

"For what will happen to him when you go."

She moved away toward the chairs under the mimosa. Turning to him with a frown between her eyes as he followed to drop into the chair across from her, she said, "Why should I go? Unless you think he will send me away?"

"There's little danger of that." The Frenchman gave a dry laugh. "You are his life."

The pleasure those words gave her was like an ache. "You think so?"

"Hasn't he told you?"

She shook her head.

"If not, it's because he is also afraid. He knows that if he loses you, it will be worse by far than it was before. He did not then know what was missing from his days, you see."

She gave him a steady look. "Let me set your mind at rest, then. I have no intention of leaving, now or ever."

"What if you cannot prevent it?"

A small frisson ran over her, and she shivered with it in spite of the damp heat. It took every ounce of self-possession she had, still she merely raised an inquiring brow.

"Yes," he said with a nod, "St. Clair told me. I'm not at all sure I understand or accept this story of yours, but I know that a woman capable of making St. Clair believe it is capable of anything."

"You are—very plain spoken."

"This is one of the few chances I've had to talk to you without St. Clair near at hand, and time may be short."

"I appreciate your concern, and even share it, but I think this is something between St. Clair and myself. And I'm not sure he would like being discussed behind his back."

Brissot snorted. "I'm sure he wouldn't. Are you going to tell him what I said?"

"I don't think that will be necessary," she answered, her gaze straight. "I expect you have already done your best to warn him."

He watched her for long seconds. Finally, a smile tugged one corner of his mouth. "I don't really blame St. Clair for being besotted. If I ever find a woman like you, I'm going to marry her, with or without the approval of the Church. Having said which, I expect it might be best if I go away now and return another time, after all."

"Was there some reason you wanted to see St.

Clair, some message I can give him," she said as she watched him rise to his feet.

"As it happens, yes. There was a sailor died last week at the Hotel Dieu with yellow fever. Now it's among the Irish, and they're falling like flies, not unusual with newcomers. People are leaving town early for the country; a half dozen of my good friends and their families will be on the Saturday packet heading upriver."

"You are thinking of going away also?"

"My mother asks for my escort to St. Louis, or possibly White Sulphur Springs. I can hardly refuse; my younger sister and my father died of the fever a few years ago. I'm all she has left, and she lives in horror of seeing me snatched away from her."

"Perhaps you will return to say good-bye to St. Clair, then, before you leave?"

"I was hoping that the two of you might come with us."

But Erina had learned enough of St. Clair to know how unlikely that was. Supersensitive about his moments of inattention, he would never venture into a situation where he must be constantly among people. He might take her driving or to attend the theater behind the comforting privacy of one of the loge grilles usually reserved for pregnant women and those in mourning, but his house was his refuge. He would not leave it for more than an hour or two.

"I hardly think—" she began.

"If anyone can persuade him, it's you," Brissot said with a wry smile.

She shook her head. "It might be too much of a strain or embarrassment. I wouldn't want to be the cause of that."

"You can at least mention it, can't you?"

She smiled and agreed that she could, though she wasn't at all sure that she would. And it wasn't necessary, after all. St. Clair had heard the news at the market.

"Yes, I know about it. Brissot came by," she said when he brought it up.

"Ah, yes, his mother always cries hysterically until he takes her out of the city." St. Clair shook his head with a smile.

"A lot of people are going, it seems," Erina said in tentative tones.

He surveyed her in thoughtful silence. Finally, he said, "If we quarantine ourselves, perhaps there will be no danger."

"That might do it, or might not. Yellow fever is carried by mosquitoes." She went on to explain something of the process.

"This is another of the discoveries of your century? It seems possible; mosquitoes are certainly something we have in plenty. So do you want to join those who are leaving the city?"

"I want to do whatever you usually do, whatever you think is best."

"You want me to take responsibility," he accused with a smile in his eyes.

"I want to be with you where you are happy," she said, each word distinct, "and that's all I want."

The look of love that rose in his eyes was almost like pain. He reached for her, and the subject was discussed no further.

It was two weeks and three days later that Erina noticed the headache. It started as nothing more than pressure behind her eyes and a faint soreness in her skull. By degrees, her eyes began to hurt, and the pressure increased to constant pain. She felt achy and so tired she could hardly move. Deciding to go to bed early, she had a tepid bath brought to the dressing room. As she stepped from the copper tub, she almost fell in her weakness. She caught herself and reached for the towel. Suddenly, she was chilled to the marrow of her bones.

Sometime later, when St. Clair came to bed, she turned toward him on the mattress, huddling against his warmth. A sharp exclamation left him. Rolling from the bed, he kindled a sulphur match and set a whale oil lamp to burning.

*"Mon dieu,"* he whispered as he brought the light to the table near her pillow. His gaze was wide and dark as it rested on her face.

"What is it?" she whispered.

"What have I done?" he said softly, almost to himself. "Ah, my love, what have I done?"

What followed was a confusion of light and dark, of wet, burning heat and shuddering cold. It was distant voices muttering, discussing, hands pulling at her and urgent pleas to drink, to eat, to sit up, lie down. And always, St. Clair's face, haggard and pale, hovering above her.

After what seemed hours, but might have been days, she roused to be desperately sick to her stomach, ridding her body of vile black matter she recognized as the result of internal bleeding. Sleeping again, she dreamed of drowning in a black sea, and woke clinging to St. Clair's hand. Sometimes she could hear herself talking about the other time, babbling about ice and soft drinks, about hospitals and doctors, vaccines and antibiotic cures.

"Yes, yes, I know," St. Clair whispered in despair against her hair as he held her. "If only you were there. If only I had taken you away upriver. If only I could—"

"No, no, no," she whimpered, caught in her nightmare and her fears. And feeling his hold tighten, hearing his sigh, she was safe again, for a little while.

The priest came at dusk on what might have been the second day, but could have been the third. His face was lined and thin, his eyes reflected a thousand consoled miseries, and some beyond consolation. His cassock was simple, his Bible worn. He stood praying beside the bed for long moments, before he turned to St. Clair.

His voice, soft, dry, beautifully modulated, whispered in the quiet. "The lady consents?"

"She would, I am certain, if she could," St. Clair replied in low tones.

"She is of the faith?"

"I don't know. With death so near, does it matter?"

"Death sometimes takes a detour, my son."

"Pray God. Our children will be blessed, then, regardless, to have her for a mother."

"There is no impediment to the sacrament?"

St. Clair's voice, when he spoke, was firm, unequivocal. "None."

The silence, then, was one of rapid yet profound consideration. The priest drew breath. He said, "Let us proceed before it's too late."

Words, flowing words. Erina heard them as from a great distance. They eddied around her, lifting her, carrying her, making little sense. Latin, possibly. Was it? She was so tired. That quiet voice could, if she let it, send her to sleep. Yet it seemed there was something not quite right.

She couldn't think. So weak. Was this the last rites? Could she be that sick? She knew she must be, still there was a part of her that refused to consider it possible. She was going to live forever, or at least a hundred and fifty years. How else was she ever to return from where she had come?

"Will you, Erina Littlefield, take this man to be your wedded husband—"

The words were in French, so that it took a moment for her to decipher them. She opened her eyes, shocked into something near rational thought. St. Clair knelt on the bed step beside her with her hand in his. The priest in his vestments stood waiting for her answer with patience in his face.

"St. Clair?" she said, a zephyr of sound.

"Answer as you will," he replied, his gaze holding hers.

Dark, his eyes were so dark, and held so much passionate grief and determination. This was what he wanted of her, and also what she needed, to be bound by a spiritual tie, something beyond lust, more than a promise. And if a mistake had been made in another place and time, what did it matter? They were here. This was now, the only time they might have.

"Yes," she whispered as her eyes drifted closed. "Yes, I will."

Moments later, she heard the priest's benediction. St. Clair's coat rasped with a noise like sandpaper against the starched sheet. His mouth brushed her heated lips.

She smiled. Sighed. Settled deeper into her pillow, deep into gentle darkness.

It was, after all, a lovely dream.

# Chapter Five

He had accomplished what he wanted, the marriage was done. The answer to the problem of her living husband had come to St. Clair as he sat with Erina three nights ago. It was very simple, really. There was no impediment to her being wed. The man she claimed to have married was not yet born. His own tie to her must precede the other by the century and a half and more she had traveled to come to him. The union with this man, this Thomas person, was nullified since it must occur afterward in time.

He recognized the sophistry of such a conclusion, of course. Still, it satisfied the letter of the requirements of the Church, if not the spirit, and that was close enough for him. It was done and could not be changed.

Now there was one last thing that must be accomplished for Erina. The trouble was, he wasn't sure he had the heart for it, much less the stomach.

He had tried desperately to find a way around it. Doctors, nostrums, nature's sweet time: nothing had helped her. She was dying, the fever was consuming her. He had waited as long as he could before coming to this last possible solution. Pray God he had not left it too late.

He stood on the balcony outside the bedchamber and stared down into the deepening twilight shadows in the garden below. It had become her favorite place. What would it be like without her? Useless.

Barren. Though a thousand blossoms flowered there in the years ahead, they would always lack fragrance or substance.

He had known it couldn't last. Yet somehow he had dared hope, had dared believe for a few short moments that heaven might allow him some degree of normal life, some happiness.

That hope was gone.

What would he do, afterward?

He didn't know; he couldn't see that far. There was only a vast nothingness beyond this night, this coming moment. It was possible, even probable, that his episodes of *petit mal* would return. The idea held no fear. There was comfort in the visions that came to him in his illness, and no reason to fight them.

Self-pity. He thought he had conquered that weakness long ago. He had been wrong. But he would harden himself against it. He must, even if the effort turned him to stone.

Swinging slowly, he stepped back inside the bed-chamber and walked around the bed to stand looking down. Erina's lovely face was so flushed, her lips such a dark, unnatural red. The pain of seeing her that way closed like a fist around his heart.

Rage at fate, at circumstances, at Erina herself rippled through him. How dare she come into his life only to leave it? He had been fine the way he was, not happy or satisfied, no, but resigned. There was no pain in resignation.

The anger was life-giving. He could use it, must have it. If he nurtured it, it might be enough to see him through.

Putting his hand on Erina's shoulder, he shook her. When she did not rouse, he shook her again, more roughly.

"Erina," he said in hard tones. "Wake up. It's time for you to go."

Her eyes, as she raised her lashes, were fever-bright and not quite focused. Her parched lips made a faint dry whispering sound as she tried to speak. "What? Oh, Sinclair, I was dreaming—"

"The dream is over. You can't stay here any longer; you have to go back."

"Back?"

There was no comprehension in her face. Despair brushed him, but he pushed it away. "Back to your own time," he said. "Back to miracle medicines. This is no place for you now."

"But I can't." The words were fretful. She closed her eyes and turned her head away.

"You must," he said, catching her chin in his fingers and forcing her to face him. "There is nothing for you here. If you stay you will die. Do you understand me?"

"I want to be with you," she protested, her eyes closed.

His hands began to tremble. To stop them, he grasped her shoulders and wrenched her toward him. Through his teeth, against the tearing sensation in his chest, he said, "I don't want you. Can't you understand? I have no use for a dying woman."

Her eyes opened, then closed again halfway. Through them he caught the glitter of fear, the beginning shimmer of tears. "But I love you," she said so softly he had to put his ear to her lips to hear.

He thought his heart would burst with the agony; he could hear its thunder in his ears. He swallowed hard, trying to control the harsh rasp of his breath. "You never loved me, never knew me, never cared what I needed. You loved a vision, a man out of a dream. I fit your silly fantasy, and so you used me. But it's over. Do you hear me? It's over!"

"No," she moaned. Her lashes fluttered as if she was trying to stay conscious, trying to reach out to him, but could not quite find the strength.

"Yes!" he insisted. "Did you think I loved you?

Do you really think I could? You are too different with your endless tales of imaginary wonders, your discarded husband and easy favors. You're no better than the loose woman I took you for. What can such a woman mean to me?"

"Oh, Sinclair—" Her eyes were open now, though dull with grief beyond comprehension.

"You cannot even say my name right. Doesn't that tell you anything?" He released her with a hard push. "Listen to me. Listen, because your life may depend on it. I am not the lover of your dreams. I cannot fulfill your childish and ridiculous yearning for the perfect man. No mere mortal can."

Dry, feathery, the words came. "But I'm safe with you."

"Safe? That's only another illusion. There is no such thing as safety. All living, all loving, is dangerous. There is no other way."

"But I want—to stay—here."

There was a slow shimmer of tears rising toward the gray-blue irises of her eyes. He couldn't stand it, refused to look at it.

Breathing slow and deep against the pressure inside him, he spoke in tones made vicious by strain. "You want to hide, to avoid the pain of the world where you were born, of being alive. You are afraid of the risk. But it won't work. Get away. Get out of here. Go and find something real. Go, before it's too late!"

"Don't. Oh, please, don't—"

"Don't what? Don't tear down the walls of your dream world? Don't let in the light so you can see how frail they were? They are built of air and disappointments, lies and longing and fables from books. That's all, pitifully all."

She shook her head in answer, closing her eyes tight. Tears seeped from under her lashes and pooled like silver beads in the dark hollows under her eyes.

Desperation touched him with the sting of a lash. He couldn't stand her tears, couldn't bear the suffering he was causing. He sprang to his feet, facing her with his hands knotted into fists. "You can't stay here. You can't, because I won't let you. Can you comprehend that? You have to go. There is nothing here for you. There never was."

"Oh, Sinclair, please—"

He had to get away. If he stayed, he would throw himself down beside her, fold her in his arms, and hold her close while he begged forgiveness.

"No," he said, the word so harsh it tore at his throat. "Get out of my house. You are not to be here when I come back. You hear me? Go!"

Wrenching around, he groped blindly for the door. He found the knob and managed somehow to blunder out of the room. He thought he heard her cry out behind him, but he could not stop to be sure.

Air, he had to have air. His heart was battering at his breastbone and the agony in his mind was so acute he could not think. He would suffocate if he could not find a place to breathe, some dark spot to be alone and unseen with the sorrow and the terror spinning around him.

Night had fallen, spreading its gray blackness under the trees and shrubbery of the garden. He made his way to the farthermost corner and stopped there. Tilting his head back, he stared up through the tree limbs at the great tin basin of the night sky with starlight shining through its holes.

What had he done?

Would Erina survive it?

Would he?

There was a noise from above and behind him. He turned with panic beating in his brain.

It was as he feared. Erina was standing in the open window of the bedchamber, silhouetted against the yellow lamplight from inside. Did she see him? He could not tell.

She was moving out onto the balcony, her progress slow and uncertain. The wonder was that she could move at all, she had been so weak.

She seemed to be searching the garden below. He should step forward, let her see him. But what good would that do?

Now she was weaving, unbalanced, clinging to the balcony railing with a frail grasp as she leaned out to see. A warning rose in his throat. He opened his mouth to call.

Her braced arm gave way. She staggered, toppled. She was falling, plunging downward in boneless, plummeting grace.

He sprang forward. His muscles bunched in frantic, straining effort. His feet skimmed the flagstones. He had to catch her, to keep her from striking that hard, unyielding surface. He was racing, racing against death and time.

He lost.

Erina struck the paving. She lay still, a pale blur in the darkness ahead of him.

He came closer. He ducked under a tree limb and swung around the base of the mimosa. Ahead of him was the spot underneath the balcony, bathed in starlight, where she had fallen.

She wasn't there.

He jolted to a halt. Somewhere inside his head, he heard a soft cry, his own soul's wailing.

Gone.

Was it all an illusion? Had she really fallen? Or had she never been there at all?

He didn't know, and the disorder of his thoughts combined with his grief was insupportable. There was a roaring in his ears, a shudder and catch in the beating of his heart.

Gone?

He should make his way upstairs, walk into his bedchamber and discover if she still lay in his bed. He wanted to do that, needed to do it. Yet the effort required more strength and courage than he could spare.

And as he stood there, he saw the gray, obscuring fog of his *petit mal* approaching. He felt it enclosing him, immobilizing him, quieting him. He did not fight it, but closed his eyes and took it into his empty heart.

"Erina, talk to me, honey bun. Open your eyes. Please open your eyes. Say something, anything. Oh, Erina, please, wake up. Wake up!"

The voice was familiar. It belonged to a woman, but it was not Theodora.

Listening in passive assessment, Erina heard the concern, the fear, and the doubt in it. There was something about it that tugged at her mind, bringing with it a faint alarm. She wasn't sure what it was, but knew it was important.

She was comfortable, yet there lingered an impression of pain. She thought that if she moved too quickly, or even at all, it might return.

Her body seemed light, as though she had lost weight. She was weak beyond words. More than anything else, she could find no will to move, no worthwhile reason to make the effort to speak.

"I can't get through to her, Doctor. What am I going to do?"

"Give it time. She's been one sick lady."

"It's been ages. She's so still, like she isn't even here. I can't stand it; she has to come out of it."

Loving concern and exasperation. Erina thought about it while long seconds, or perhaps hours, ticked past. Oh, yes. Yes, she had it.

She lifted her lashes by slow degrees to stare at her sister. Her voice breathless, hardly more than a whisper, she said, "Joanne, what—are you—doing here?"

Joanne screamed and grabbed Erina's shoulder. "Oh, God, she said something! Nurse, come here! Did you hear her? She's going to make it. I told you she would! She's going to be all right."

But she wouldn't be, not ever. Because the room in which she lay was tiny, air-conditioned, gray-curtained, sterile. Filled with medical marvels attached to her body with wires and tubes. It was an intensive care hospital unit.

Joanne was beside her, leaning over her, holding her hand. But St. Clair was not there.

Erina closed her eyes, blotting out everything.

It was more than forty-eight hours later that she was placed in a private room, and another twenty-four before anyone was allowed to speak more than a few sentences to her. She was glad. She wasn't ready, might never be ready. She was well aware, however, that a demand for an explanation was inevitable.

Her sister, when she visited her on the fourth morning, was bright and cheerful and came bearing a potted hydrangea with huge blue mopheads of flowers. She chatted about traffic and parking problems, but her eyes were luminous with curiosity as well as compassion.

It was after a short silence that she said, "You don't have to talk about it if you don't want to, Erina, but I have to ask. Where in the world have you been for two whole months?"

Two months. Such a short time, yet forever. Erina moistened her lips. "I'm not sure you would believe me if I told you."

Her sister cocked her head as she watched her closely. "Were you out of the country? You seem to have picked up this funny little accent."

She hadn't realized. It really wasn't surprising, she

supposed, when she thought about it. "No, I never left New Orleans. I was at the Rouquette mansion. Do you remember me telling you about it?"

"Remember! You have got to be kidding; I've haunted the place. And everybody knows you were there. Your car was found in the drive and your clothes scattered all over the upstairs bedroom. They found traces of blood. The story was on TV, in all the newspapers. God, Erina, you have no idea how terrified I've been! When you didn't show up everybody was sure you had been raped and killed, and your body carried off somewhere."

Joanne's face was pale and her eyes wide with remembered horror. Recognizing it, Erina said, "I can see how it must have seemed. I'm so sorry."

"You mean that's not what happened? You weren't attacked?"

"Not exactly. There was a man, and we fought. He meant to—but someone came."

"Who?"

Erina took a deep breath. She closed her eyes a second, then opened them again. "St. Clair Rouquette. He dragged the man who attacked me off, then he—took me home with him."

"Who is this Rouquette guy? And why in hell didn't you call and let us know you were okay? For God's sake, Erina!"

"I couldn't call, there were no phones. And I couldn't let you know because—because there's no way to send a message between 1848 and the present."

Joanne closed her eyes. She shook her head, a slow, gesture of disbelief and despair. Long seconds passed, then in a voice soft with pity, she said, "Oh, Erina."

"You don't believe me." Erina's voice was flat.

"Honey—"

"It's true. It happened."

Joanne raised a hand. "No, listen, Erina. Please. What happened is that you were raped, hurt, taken off somewhere and kept for weeks as some fiend's sexual playmate."

"No, he didn't, he wouldn't—"

"It happened, honey, face it! I don't know who he was or where he took you, but it's the only thing that makes sense."

"You're wrong. I saw—"

"Honey, honey, just listen to me, will you? There's no use hiding behind some sweet self-deception; it isn't good for you. And what happened to you wasn't sweet; it was mean and vicious and criminal. So maybe this guy got to liking you, I don't know. Maybe he got tired of you, or just felt sorry for you after you came down sick. Whatever the reason, he apparently brought you back where he picked you up and put you out. You were found wandering around the old Rouquette place in your nightgown."

"And what do the doctors say was my problem?" Erina spoke with quiet reason, because getting angry would not help.

"Yellow fever. That's why I asked if you had been out of the country. I thought maybe you were taken to South America, Africa, some little Caribbean island where such a thing might still be hanging around."

"It was epidemic in 1848."

"Erina, please!"

"I was there, Joanne. I saw the cathedral the way it was before they changed the bell towers. I saw the clothes, the carriages, the street sellers. I heard the way people talked, saw the way—"

"You've been reading about those things for years; it wouldn't take anything for you to make all that up and see it in your mind. I don't know for sure why you think you went back in time, but I have a good idea. What happened was so awful, you've blanked it out. In its place, you substituted this fairy tale that lets you feel good about yourself."

Was Joanne right? She seemed so sure, and all Erina could muster to prove what she said were memories. And what were memories except visions in the mind?

"Or just maybe," Erina said in slow consideration, "it was all a dream."

"That's right," Joanne said with relief rising in her voice. "That, or a hallucination brought on by your high fever. It was touch and go there for a while. Your doctor said the only thing that kept you alive was sheer will power. You wanted so much to live."

If Joanne wouldn't believe her, then no one would. She could keep trying, keep dredging up details and forcing people to listen, but she saw that it might be dangerous. Like her sister, they would think she was compensating for her traumatic experience. They might even think she was mentally unbalanced, if not completely insane. It would be safer to pretend, and let them think what they would.

It had been easier in St. Clair's time, but then, people had no dependence on psychological explanations. They still believed in miracles.

In the days that followed, Erina was visited by a psychiatrist, a counselor, and a policemen. Each of them, in their own way, wanted to help her deal with her problem. By then, however, she had found her feet and memorized her answers for all the endless questions. There were just two, and she used whichever seemed appropriate at any given time. One was, "I don't know." The other, "I don't remember."

Finally, she was allowed to go home. Joanne had seen after things for her, paying the rent on her apartment, taking Budweiser, her cat, home with her to feed him. The rooms were stale and musty, her possessions strange, as if they belonged to another person. It didn't matter. Anything would do until she was ready to move.

She had made a few decisions while she lay regaining her strength. She put the first of them into operation almost immediately. Two hours after she left the hospital, she made an offer to buy the Rouquette mansion.

"Are you nuts?" Joanne asked when she discovered what Erina had done. "That old place must have terrible memories for you. I'd have thought you'd want to avoid it like the plague."

"I love the house; I always did."

"And hanging around it nearly got you killed! Think, honey, think. You'll be alone there at night. What if that lunatic comes back?"

Erina bit back the retort that hovered on her tongue. Instead, she said, "I appreciate your concern, Joanne, but I'm a grown woman."

"In other words, mind my own business."

"In other words, be glad that I finally have something I want. I haven't exactly been the most outgoing person since Thomas and I split up. Now I have something to work for and even live for. You may not think it's what I need, but it's what I want."

Joanne watched her a long moment. Finally, she said, "All right. I won't say any more."

She did, of course, but it didn't stop Erina.

When the house deal was finalized, she plunged into renovation and restoration. Her apartment was a litter of plans and elevations, of contractor's bids, of plumbing and electrical catalogs, paint chips and drapery samples. She took pleasure in chasing down wallpaper that was the exact replica of what had been there before. It was an adventure to track down the craftsman who could duplicate ceiling medallions and balusters. Every daylight hour she could spare was spent sanding doors and moldings and stripping and refinishing antiques; clearing out and carting off junk and sorting through the good bits that were left.

And now and then, when she stood in the old house or sat in the garden eating her brown bag lunch, she would stare around her, remembering.

But she did not summon Sinclair, did not even try. She was too afraid of what it might indicate if he came, but also of what it could mean if he did not.

It was necessary to borrow money to finish the restoration. The deed to the house was required for collateral. It was while going through the sheaf of papers she had received from the lawyer that she found the provenance for the house. Included was a great deal of historical data, a part of which was a capsule history of the Rouquette family.

There it was, in the spidery copperplate of another era straggling across the heavy sheet of parchment. St. Clair Nicholas Antoine Rouquette, born August 3, 1815. Succeeded to ownership of the house on the death of his father from pneumonia, February, 1839. Chronically ill, wandered from home June 26, 1848. Declared dead, November, 1848. Left no issue. Ownership passed to his brother, Claude Francois Pierre Rouquette, born March 10, 1817.

St. Clair had lived. There it was in black and white. He had lived, and he had, perhaps, under the influence of some *petit mal* delusion, wandered away to be struck down by a carriage, drowned in the river, or perhaps robbed and left dead in some alley. His brother had come to town from the plantation to take up residence, add Victorian touches to the house, and rear the children who would carry the Rouquette name into the twentieth century, if no further.

But he had lived; she had not made him up. St. Clair had once lived. She might have discovered this fact before, if she had not been too afraid to search the records.

Tears crowded her chest, pooling around her heart.

The grief inside her was unending, the salty residue of all the things that might have been.

She had left him, but not of her own will. As she allowed herself to look back now, she saw that neither had it been by his will. He had sent her away to save her life, and for no other reason. The shouting and the hurtful things that had been said were for one purpose, to convince her to release her hold on him and his time and go.

It had been his strength of will and his might that had carried her to his century. Why should he not have had the resolution and power to send her away again?

Then when she was gone, his illness had come back. He had been declared dead in this same month that she had finally found evidence that he had lived. And she missed him, longed for him, grieved for him with every fiber of her being. This man who had been gone from this earth so many long years before she was born.

She saved the courtyard garden until last. She had a fountain cast, using the broken pieces to construct a mold. A pink mimosa seedling, descendent of the long dead original, was found in a corner, and returned to its place. The flagstones were cleaned and replacements found for those that were broken and missing. She discovered, in an antique shop on Magazine Street, chairs and a table of wrought iron in a grape leaf pattern just like those that had once sat in the morning shade.

Finally, it was done. The last drape was hung, the final mirror installed. The carpenter's truck disappeared down the street. The antiques Erina had searched out were delivered and hoisted up the stairs. She hauled her boxes of clothes and dishes from the apartment and put them away in the armoire and the cabinets of the new kitchen that had been built to look like those from the old butler's pantry. She ate her dinner of fast food in the garden, then went inside as night fell. She turned the new deadbolt lock on the front and back doors, and slowly climbed the stairs.

The bedchamber was the same, exactly the same down to the delicate stripe of the wallpaper and the starburst under the half tester. There was a whale oil lamp on the bedside table and candlesticks on the mantel.

She struck a match and made the room glow with the old-fashioned lighting. Passing into the dressing room, she took a bath in the claw foot tub she had installed, then put on a nightgown of white lawn with long, ruffled sleeves and a high neck. She brushed her hair, which had grown to well past shoulder length now, and left it hanging down her back. Then she moved with steady, deliberate steps back into the bedchamber.

It was time. She could not live with fear forever, and would not be controlled by it. If St. Clair was gone, then she would take what consolation she might find in a fantasy of his image. If she could not have what was real and true and fine, then there was no shame in pretending.

She closed her eyes, breathed softly once, twice.

The house smelled of paint and dust, floor finish and, yes, linseed oil. Tomorrow, she would throw wide the windows and air out the newness.

She breathed deep again, trying to relax. Tomorrow, she would order the climbing roses to run up the wall. They should be planted in December.

She couldn't concentrate. Maybe she was still afraid, after all.

She walked to the high post of the bed and leaned her head against it. Her voice soft, broken, she said aloud, "Oh, Sinclair, please. Please come."

Nothing. Silence, except for the ticking of the porcelain mantel clock. Even the dim gray corridors of her mind were empty.

"St. Clair," she whispered with wet, burning tears rimming her eyelids. "I miss you so."

And then there came a quiet footfall from the tower room. She noticed, for the first time, that there was a light glowing there. It cast a man's shadow across the floor. He appeared in the doorway.

St. Clair. Gone from 1848, vanished into another time, but alive, very much alive.

It was St. Clair, and yet he was different. His hair was short, trimmed neatly above his ears. A worn navy T-shirt was stretched over the width of his chest and tucked into faded jeans. There was a smudge of jade green artist's oils on his face, and he stood wiping his hands on a rag that carried the smells of linseed oil and turpentine.

He smiled with gladness and promise in his eyes as he tossed the rag aside and began to walk toward her.

"Where have you been, *ma chere*, my very dearest love," he said. "I've been waiting for you for ages—"

# Love
# For Sail

———⋅✦⋅———

*by*

## Shirl Henke

# Chapter One

"The dirty rotter stole all my rats!" Abel Goode slumped limply against his sister as she half led, half dragged her twin into the big kitchen.

"Forget the measly old rats. You're bleeding like a butchered hog," Sammie chided.

"Measly? Bart Griffin at the Billy Goat Saloon pays half a dollar for every rat over ten pounds."

Sammie helped her injured brother onto a chair, shuddering at the image of those awful fights staged by saloon owners on the Barbary Coast, pitting trained terriers against huge fierce wharf rats. "Well, you lost those rats, but you can always trap more," she said philosophically.

"You're always looking on the bright side," he muttered glumly. "We ain't never going to get out of here if I don't make some money. Then when'll you see your Sandwich Islands?"

"We'll get there someday, Abel," she replied with a weary look on her face. Ever since she was a child and one of her mother's employers had given her a picture book, Sammie had been fascinated by the tropical paradise. Growing up in poverty, living in a city shrouded with fog and blasted by chill winds year round, she had dreamed of sailing to the Sandwiches.

Shaking herself, she looked down at her brother,

who had grown silent. "Oh, Abel, that's a terrible gash on your head! What did he hit you with?"

Abel tried to reply but suddenly two Sammies with long taffy-colored hair and frowning faces danced before his blurry eyes. Everything went black and he started to slide off the chair.

"Gerrard, come quick!" Sammie yelled frantically.

Gerrard emerged from the pantry. "What devilment has that fool boy done now?" His pinched face paled when he saw the blood oozing from Abel's temple.

"He was down at the piers trapping rats when one of those hoodlum gangs attacked him. Help me get him downstairs onto his cot," Sammie pleaded.

Gerrard shook his head in disgust as he reached for one arm. "Fool boy," he grunted, dragging him back onto the sturdy chair. "He's supposed to deliver the feast I've just created to a ship's master in the harbor."

"Gerrard, is the food ready?" a gravelly voice from beyond the heavy swinging door inquired.

"Pearly'll be fit to be tied if he can't make the delivery on time," he muttered, then called out in a fake French accent, "I 'ave just taken ze lamb out of ze oven, Madam Gates."

Sammie chewed her lip. The cook was right. If her brother missed one more delivery, their employer might not only fire him, but her as well. "Let me talk to Pearly. You take him downstairs before she comes in here. I'll handle it."

Gerrard looked at her skeptically, then shrugged an affected Gallic gesture. *"Bon chance."*

Sammie watched as Gerrard leveled Abel across his thin shoulder and carried the youth downstairs. The tall cadaverous cook had gotten them their jobs as menials at one of the most expensive bordellos in the city. Squaring her shoulders, she pushed through the swinging door to confront the madam.

Pearly Gates was a great Amazon of a woman, six feet tall, weighing three hundred pounds. She possessed an annoying voice that grated like knuckles on a washboard. Her favorite line with all new customers was, "Hell, sugar, my name's as close to heaven as I'll ever get!" But beneath the raucous joviality and rolls of fat, Pearly was a cunning and ruthless businesswoman. Five years on the mean streets of San Francisco's Barbary Coast had taught Sammie never to underestimate women like the madam.

"Where's your brother, missy? Gerrard should have that fancy feast ready for delivery." Her carmined lips drooped over her triple chin. Heavy jowls of pasty white skin swayed when she moved. She took a step toward Sammie, her heavily kohled eyes narrowed with suspicion. "Yer covered with blood. What's goin' on?"

"Abel was attacked on the street. He'll be fine, just not up to making that delivery—but I can do it for him," she hastily added before the madam could remonstrate. "I've finished all my chores early. And I'll work late tonight to make up Abel's lost hours."

The shrewd old woman studied the girl speculatively. Sammie Goode and her twin Abel had come to work for her when they were scrawny sixteen-year-old orphans. But in the past year or so, the girl had finally begun to show promise, her petite body at last filling out with curves in the appropriate places. She'd always had that great mop of shiny yellow hair and big gold-coin eyes. The kind of eyes a man would look into and then purely lose his head. She could easily get twenty dollars a customer for a fresh young thing like Sammie ... if she could ever convince the skittish girl to enter the profession ... or ...

"If you got your chores done, don't worry about later tonight," she said reasonably. "You can take the feast to the ship. Never hurts to advertise our place a bit to the ship's officers. I'll have Pigeon-toed Sal and his boys go along for protection."

Sammie nodded in relief, but before she could return to the kitchen, Pearly detained her with one huge fleshy paw that enveloped the girl's shoulder. "You can't go aboard ship dressed in blood-soaked rags. Come with me and I'll find you somethin' decent to wear."

In minutes Sammie was upstairs in one of the house's twenty bedrooms, looking at herself in the mirror. She was dressed in a pale pink taffeta creation with a low neckline, the kind of gown one of the harlots would wear to attend the opera with a high-toned customer. "I—I don't know, Pearly. It's awfully fancy. What if I get saltwater on it or—"

"Tush. My girls have dozens of beautiful dresses. Rita Mae won't even miss this one." She debated fixing Sammie's hair, but decided the girl would become suspicious if she fussed too much. Best to just let nature take its course. With all that long yellow hair and her creamy flesh accented by the dress, Sammie would catch the captain's eye sure enough. He'd ordered a full-course meal from Gerrard and a woman along with it to tide him over until the ship's cargo was unloaded and he could come landside to pursue his pleasures. She smiled slyly. If anyone could charm the prudish little Miss Goode out of being good, it was Kit Warfield, the gorgeous devil.

The covered silver tray weighed a ton, laden with a big crock of steaming bouillabaisse and a whole roasted leg of lamb. The captain must be as huge as Pearly, she thought with amusement as Salvador Giannini, otherwise known as Pigeon-toed Sal, braked the wagon on which they were riding. While he climbed down, she scanned the busy waterfront, taking in all the raucous sights, sounds, and smells of the brawling lusty city. Just as she was about to climb down, a big baldheaded man wearing one gold earring yelled a filthy epithet at Sal and his men, and the whole pier erupted in a fight.

They had been challenged by a gang of crimps, the men who shanghaied sailors for outbound ships. The gangs roamed the waterfront looking for trouble. Now trouble had found them all—and she was caught smack in the middle. Sammie knew what would happen if Sal and his men were defeated by their competitors—she would end up in a foul-smelling crib, tied to a bed! She picked up the heavy crockery pot and hurled scalding bouillabaisse in the face of a squat, greasy man attempting to climb onto the wagon. He fell back with a shriek, clutching his burned face. Hunks of shrimp clung to his filthy beard and mussel shells clattered off his broad shoulders and bounced onto the wharf.

No sooner had she dispatched that attacker when another climbed onto the wagon bed. Sammie, still holding the crock in both hands, swung it around and connected with the skinny crimp's shoulder, toppling him over the side. Sal's men were outnumbered and going down fast. Frantically, she looked for another weapon, having flung the pot overboard at the last invader. There was always cutlery on the trays. Her hands fumbled with a heavy white napkin as she tried to unwrap the knife.

"Hey, yellow hair. I gotta have me a taste of you," the baldheaded leader with the pirate's earring said as he stepped over Sal's unconscious body and grinned up at her. His smirk evaporated like fog when Sammie flashed the knife and jabbed it toward his throat, narrowly missing his jugular.

"You little hellcat, I'll teach you," he snarled, knocking the knife from her hand. As he climbed up into the wagon bed, she scooted away, groping for another weapon until her hand sank into the hot soft mound of mashed potatoes. She reacted instinctively, flinging a big blob of fluffy white. A direct hit. Her attacker snarled as he rubbed the potatoes from his eyes, but they clung stubbornly to his lashes and eyebrows like clown makeup.

Now he was really enraged. Sammie looked down at the ruins of the tray, searching for something, at least a fork. Then he was on her and all she could do was claw across the big platter until her fingers curled around the hot crunchy roasted leg of lamb. She grabbed the narrow end of the bone and swung the leg like a cudgel, smacking the bald man soundly across the side of his head. With a muffled oath he rubbed his ear, holding tight to her left arm as she shrieked and flailed at him with the leg of lamb in her right hand.

Just as the lamb flew apart at the joint, Sammie wrenched free of his grip and jumped from the wagon seat. Her legs tangled in the long folds of her pink taffeta skirt and she lost her footing, tumbling onto the rough wood planks of the wharf. As she rolled, her head struck the edge of the wagon wheel. A sharp pain lanced through her temple and then all went black. She lay unconscious with the lamb bone still clutched tightly in one greasy little fist.

Stub Malone had seen the fight erupt with the sudden violence of a thunderstorm on the plains of his native Texas. The spunky gal in pink was really a sight to see, holding off three big men with a cook pot and a joint of meat for weapons. The wiry little frontiersman-turned-seaman reckoned she was entitled to a bit of help and quickly drew his Colt Peacemaker. His companion, Rollo the boatswain, pulled a wicked-looking knife and nodded to his mate. But before Stub could get off a shot, the girl went down with that polecat Zorko right after her. Stub took aim and fired, grazing the bald man's left shoulder, spinning him around.

"Call off yer boys, Zorko, or I'll match up the other shoulder," Stub yelled.

Zorko's eyes widened in recognition. "So, the *China Lucky*'s back in town. Give my regards to Kit," he snarled. The brawl ended as suddenly as it had begun. Three of Zorko's crimps and two of Sal's men still stood. They stared down the barrel of Stub's cocked Colt backed up by the hulking boatswain's gigantic knife. Within the blink of an eye they vanished like rats in a midnight alley, leaving Stub and his companion with the unconscious girl.

"Right feisty little piece. Looks to be a real lady, all dolled up this way. We cain't jest leave her here." Stub looked up to Rollo.

"Cap'n won't like it," Rollo replied as he knelt and examined the unconscious girl.

Stub spit a stream of tobacco juice that landed against the wagon wheel with a sharp ping. "Cap'n brings ladies of the line aboard ever time we reach port. He cud spend a mite of time keepin' company with a decent gal fer a change."

Rollo's expression was dubious. The boatswain scooped up the unconscious girl and followed Stub down the pier.

Sammie felt a gentle rhythmic rocking and was dimly aware of the creaking of timber. She opened her eyes but shut them quickly against the glare of the lamp. Her head was splitting apart.

"Easy there, missy," admonished a high-pitched, crackling voice. "That fall like to split your skull."

Sammie licked her cracked lips and tried to speak but the only sound she could make was a strangled croak.

"Naw, missy. Save your breath an' I'll get ya some water."

She was aware that the lamp had been moved and she gingerly opened her eyes to watch the man shuf-

fling away from the bed on which she was lying.
He was short, about her height, dressed in buckskin
breeches and a homespun shirt. The lower half of his
left arm was missing and the shirtsleeve had been
folded and pinned, allowing him to move the stub
of upper arm freely. The wiry little man put the lamp
on a mahogany table and filled a glass with water.
As he moved back to the bed, the young woman
watched his face, which was scarred and grooved
with deep wrinkles. She decided that he could be
fifty or eighty. The brown, leathery face twisted into
what she supposed was meant for a smile.

"Here, missy, you down this. Nice and cool."

Sammie clumsily levered herself into a sitting position and reached for the glass.

He handed it over to her, saying, "Ah ... well. I
reckon you're right, missy. I'd hold it fer ya, but
then"—he nodded toward the empty sleeve with a
cackle—"hell, I usually spill half my tangle-leg on
myself. Never kin figger out why losin' one hand
made the other so blame clumsy."

Sammie sat transfixed, nodding in agreement with
the fellow's pronouncement between sips of water.

He studied her pale face with concern, then, as if
remembering his manners, cleared his throat and
said, "Name's Stub."

Sammie could not seem to make her head stop
bobbing in agreement. "Certainly it is ... Oh, I
mean—I'm sorry, Mr. ... er ... Mr. Stub." Her face
reddened.

The man cackled again. "Don't go apologizin',
missy. Stub's not my real name. It's what they call
me 'cause it sorta fits."

Sammie nodded again. "Certainly it does." My
God, she was insulting the man! To cover her embarrassment she took a bigger swallow from the glass—
and choked. The resulting cough made her skull feel

like it was cleft in two. Dropping the empty glass onto her lap, she clutched her head.

"Bloody hell, Stub, are you trying to drown her?" a resonant baritone voice asked in a crisp British accent.

Another man had just entered the cabin. *Of course, this is a ship's cabin.* Fear squeezed her chest tightly. What were they going to do with her? The newcomer had his back to her, reaching for something on the table. She could see that he was much taller than Stub—slim, with broad shoulders and narrow hips. He was dressed in a loose white lawn shirt and close-fitting trousers. When he turned toward her, he was holding the lamp, which illuminated his face.

Sammie forgot her fears as she stared at the most beautiful man she had ever seen. Long shaggy hair, straight and night dark, framed his mesmerizing face. He looked both youthful and ageless, exotic with cleanly chiseled features, a straight blade of a nose, a square jawline, and sensuously molded lips, but it was his eyes that fascinated. One was hidden by a piratical black patch and the other was as ebony as his hair, fringed by thick lashes. What a shame that such a face had to be marred by the loss of an eye. A faint smile, mysterious and fleeting, curved his mouth, but did not reach that fathomless dark eye. She instantly intuited that this was a man who revealed only what he wished others to see.

"So, this is the waif you rescued on the waterfront." Kit studied the girl. Young, rather fetching if one fancied an aura of innocence, even though he knew damn well any female found on the Barbary Coast was no blushing maiden, no matter what Stub thought. The wide gold eyes and all that wheat-colored hair were remarkable. He could see that her body was slim and well formed since the gown she wore had been all but torn off her in the fight that Stub had recounted to him.

"I'm Captain Christopher Warfield, master of the *China Lucky*," he said smoothly, hoping to elicit her name and some explanation of who she was in return.

Sammie tried not to gawk as she replied, "I'm Sammie—Samantha Goode." Then the names sunk in. *China Lucky.* Christopher Warfield. "Are you Kit Warfield?" she gulped out.

He studied her with amused curiosity. "My friends call me Kit, yes. Have we met before, Miss Goode?"

"No," she replied miserably, wishing the sea could swallow her—and Abel. "You see, I work for Pearly Gates and I was sent—"

"Well, that explains what happened," Kit interrupted with a hearty chuckle. "I understand from Stub here that you used the dinner I ordered as effectively as Grant did the cannon."

When he laughed, something inside of her melted. He looked suddenly young and infectiously good-humored. "Then ... you're ... you're not mad ... about the dinner, I mean? I'm awfully sorry I, er, used it, but there was nothing else at hand and those crimps—"

"No harm done. I can always get another leg of lamb." He studied her with measuring intensity, then turned to Stub. "Send Rollo with fresh water so the lady can wash up."

As the little man left the cabin, Sammie looked down at her hands in mortification. They were caked with dried potatoes and meat grease! "I seem to be wearing your dinner," she said, blushing hotly.

"From what Stub described, I'd say Zorko was wearing most of it." He chuckled softly, then asked, "How long have you worked for Pearly?" *Damn! She looked so deceptively innocent.*

"My brother and I lost our ma almost five years ago. We had lots of jobs, but it wasn't easy." She shuddered, recalling the nights of hunger and the desperate theft of food just to survive.

"It must've been hard," he said, recognizing a bit of himself in the plucky girl. The Barbary Coast and Hong Kong had lots more in common than just Chinese inhabitants.

"We were lucky. Gerrard Schwartz—er, I mean Chef Dupree—was an old friend of our father's. He got us work at Miss Gates's place."

*I'll bet he did.* Kit wondered about the kind of family friend who procured, not to mention a brother who'd let his sister whore. He pushed the thought aside when Rollo arrived with the water.

Sammie gratefully plunged her hands into the big basin and used the soap that lay on the cabinet to bathe the sticky mess from her hands and face. The captain dismissed the boatswain and closed the cabin door as she washed. Suddenly he was behind her, unfastening the tiny buttons on the back of her gown.

"It's ruined, I'm afraid, but never mind, I'll buy you a new one." His lips brushed the nape of her neck as one dark, long-fingered hand held her pale hair.

She froze for a moment, struggling to overcome the sizzling messages his warm breath and even warmer flesh were sending up and down her spine. Holding the now loose dress up with her hands clasped around her shoulders, she turned and faced him. "What are you doing?"

His smile turned faintly mocking. "You look quite the innocent, pet, but don't carry the charade too far." He reached up and took the front of her gown in one hand and began to tug it free as his other hand reached for one of hers. "I've been a good sport about the lost dinner, but my other appetite can still be appeased." He drew her to him.

Suddenly Sammie understood. "That sneaky snake

in elephant's hide! Pearly sent me to you, didn't she?"

One thick black brow arched sardonically. "Isn't that what you just told me?"

"No! I mean yes, but—"

"No more games, pet." He reached for her again, this time impatiently.

Sammie twisted like a greased eel, turning to seize the basin filled with soapy water. When his hand reached inside her opened gown and grazed her breast, she reacted instinctively, sloshing the bubbly mess squarely in his face.

He stepped back with an oath, followed by a string of what sounded like very angry Chinese curses as he shook his head, sending droplets of water flying in every direction. Long fingers combed ebony hair off a face gone dark as a hurricane cloud. "What the bloody hell made you pull that little stunt?"

His shirt clung to his skin. The fine lawn cloth was now translucent, revealing every ridge of muscle on his lean sinewy body as well as a liberal thatch of black hair patterned on his chest. Her tongue clove to the roof of her mouth, which had suddenly gone dry. "I had to stop you somehow. I'm not one of Pearly's whores!" At his look of patent disbelief, she persisted, clutching the granite basin across her chest like a breastplate. "I work in the kitchen, helping the chef—and I make up beds and clean. Honest work."

He stroked his chin now, studying the pugnacious little chit. She reminded him of a cornered squirrel, scolding frantically, frightened to death. "And the world's oldest profession isn't honest as far as you're concerned?"

She stiffened even more. "Hell no." Her face crimsoned. "I mean, just no. It's hard to remember my ma raised me to be a lady, what with living in Pearly's place."

"I can see where that might be a problem," he said

sarcastically. "Well now, what are we to do with you, my pet? Now that the obvious is out," he added, gesturing carelessly toward the bed against the wall.

Her shoulders slumped in relief, yet she felt a perverse sense of loss at the same time. "Take me back to Pearly's?"

He studied her face, pale even in the golden light from the lantern. Could she be telling the truth? "You've had a pretty rough day and it's dark now. Why don't I have Stub bring you a bowl of stew, then you sleep here for the night." At her flash of wide-eyed alarm, he amended, "I mean alone, of course. I'll bunk in with one of my officers."

"All right," she replied, again feeling the inexplicable twinge of regret. "Oh, but what about my brother—he'll be ever so worried. And Miss Gates'll fire me for sure if I don't come back to work tonight."

He smiled cynically. "Somehow I doubt Pearly will think it amiss that I keep you, but I'll send a note for your brother."

"Oh," he added as an afterthought, "in the morning, I'll send Stub to you with whatever we can scrape up in the way of clean clothes—probably my cabin boy's." With that promise he left her alone in the cabin.

# Chapter Two

True to his captain's word, the following morning Stub brought her a pair of breeches, along with a voluminous shirt. Stub was accompanied by Rollo, who brought a breakfast tray for her. Red-faced, the one-armed seaman explained that if she used the piece of hemp he handed her as a belt, the captain's shirt would conceal most of her feminine attributes, which were shockingly revealed by the pants. Feeling curiously refreshed in spite of her restive, dream-filled sleep and the bump on her head, Sammie quickly donned the outfit, then ate her breakfast and headed above deck. As she emerged through the hatchway, she saw the captain kneeling, patting a small black dog.

Kit felt someone's eyes on him and knew it was Sammie. Turning, he inspected her. *Damn, she is a fetching little piece.* His big shirt did little to conceal her lithe curves. With her face scrubbed and her hair brushed, she looked incredibly fresh, wholesome ... and desirable.

"Good morning. Did you sleep well?" he asked, standing up as she approached.

The dog began scampering around and barking excitedly as he sniffed at her. Sammie smiled and nodded at Kit, then reached down to pat the mutt. "I love dogs. What's his name?"

"Joss. It means luck."

"Hi, Joss. Oh, you poor thing!" The frisky little

mutt had only three legs, although he seemed not to notice the absence of the right rear one. Looking up at Kit's eye patch and then over to where Stub was issuing orders to several burly seamen, she blurted out, "Is everyone aboard missing some—I mean . . ." Her words faded away in a misery of embarrassment as the captain threw back his head and laughed heartily.

"Not quite everyone, but after meeting me, Stub, and Joss, I can see how you might think so. I'll leave it to the crusty old Texan to explain how heroically he and Joss came by their misfortunes," he said as Stub walked over to them. "I have matters to attend to." As Stub greeted her, Kit departed.

The little sailor strolled along the deck with her, while Joss eagerly tagged along. Stub pointed out the workings of the ship. "We carry mostly wheat outbound, along with some necessaries like iron pots and such. And wine. Lots of demand for wine in the islands."

"Islands?"

"Sandwich Islands the Cap'n calls 'em, him bein' a Hong Kong Brit. The natives call 'em Hawaiian."

Oblivious of her look of goggle-eyed amazement, Stub continued his exposition. "Heck, missy, Cap'n Kit owns a whole blame cane plantation there. Since them sugar refineries was built here in San Francisco, he's been makin' a right handsome profit on both ends."

"You actually live in Hawaii?"

Stub shrugged his shoulders. "'Much as we live anywheres, that's home, but we spend most of our time at sea. Cap'n's a real restless one."

"I wondered about the English accent. So he's from Hong Kong," she said pensively. Another of those fabled exotic places she had read about all her life.

"Yep. His pa was some sort of Brit diplomat. 'N his ma was . . ." His face reddened as he looked at

her out of the corner of his eye. "Well, she was a
real beauty—part Chinese. She passed on when the
cap'n was just a tad."

"And his father?"

Again Stub seemed flustered. "I reckon you'd have
to ask Kit about that. He don't cotton ta talkin' about
Lord Warfield, though."

Realizing the topic was a sensitive one, Sammie
jumped to another subject. "The captain said you'd
tell me about how you and Joss lost your—I mean—"
Flustered, she reached down and patted the dog,
whose tail began to wag furiously at the mention of
his name.

Stub just chuckled. "How we lost our limbs? Well,
now, them are two real tales of harrowin' adventure
half a world apart. Ole Joss, he usta serve aboard a
whaler in the North Pacific. He fought a great white
shark—dragged a sailor from the jaws of sure death,
but that there shark, he was a mean cuss. Caught
ahold of Joss's leg and bit it clean off afore the crew
could harpoon the brute."

Sammie hugged the dog, who closed his eyes and
basked in the adulation, his black tail thumping
loudly on the deck. "And what about you, Stub?"

His weathered face reddened a bit as he spun the
tale of how he'd been a fearful gunfighter in the
Texas Rangers and pursued an outlaw gang to a
bloody shootout in Laredo. "So ya see, they was all
dead, 'n I had this here bullet in my arm. All alone
out in the middle of nowhere. All's I cud do was to
wrap it up to stop the bleedin', but afore I cud get
back to Austin, why it putrefied."

"Oh! Why, that could've killed you!"

"Would've fer sure, but I knowed what I had to
do." He tapped his forehead with his right hand.
"Lucky fer me it was my left arm. See, I took my
Bowie knife and . . ."

As Stub warmed to his tale, Sammie grew decidedly paler until he realized his gristly slice-by-slice account of the amputation was best abridged. "Well, anyways, it healed up real good 'n I went out lookin' fer new adventures. Then I met up with the cap'n and signed on the *China Lucky*."

"What of Captain Warfield's eye?" she asked, unable to stem her curiosity.

Her companion nodded solemnly. "Well now, a pirate's cutlass is a fearsome weapon. You see Kit—"

Before Stub could get further, a cry went up from the crow's nest high atop the ship. "Whitehallers acomin'!"

Stub let out a volley of oaths. "You best get below decks, missy. Them fellers is plumb crazy."

"But surely you aren't going to refuse to let them board? They come on every ship that sails through the Golden Gate."

"Not the *China Lucky*. Cap'n don't want his men endin' up where the whitehallers send 'em— drugged, robbed, 'n shanghaied by crimps."

"But how—"

Her question was cut short as Kit appeared, grim-faced and armed to the teeth. "Get below, Sammie," he commanded, practically shoving her down the steps. "Lock your cabin door."

Her heart beating a mile a minute, Sammie did as she was commanded, rushing to the porthole to watch the fracas. Several dozen of the large skiffs rowed by the whitehallers bobbed on the water, closing with the *China Lucky*. Each was filled with men shouting out the names of the "boarding houses" who employed them and urging the sailors to come with them.

Sammie knew these men were hired by crimps, who treated the seamen abominably, but most captains were eager to get rid of their crews at journey's end and were glad to have them lured off ship. When the ships were ready to sail again, the captain could simply pay for a new crew furnished by the crimps. The system was run by Barbary Coast underworld leaders and few shipmasters dared to defy them, even if they cared about the fate of their crew.

The first skiffs were within thirty feet of the ship when several shots rang out and Kit's voice shouted, "The first man to touch the side of the *Lucky* won't be! I'll blow the bastard straight to hell."

From the other side of the ship the first mate issued a similar declaration, chorused all around by crew members. One skiff dared to approach. Sammie recognized the leader, the vicious Laplander, Nikko, who urged the others to pull their boats closer. But Kit did not bluff. The instant Nikko's skiff touched the hull of the ship, a shot rang out and his boatswain, who had grabbed a ship's line, toppled back into the boat.

"Anyone else want to try?" Kit's voice taunted.

Sammie's porthole was close to the Lap's boat and she saw the look of violent hate etched on Nikko's face as he snarled, "I'll see you in hell, Warfield!" The skiffs turned about quickly after that, rowing back to the wharf.

A hurrah went up across the deck above her and Sammie breathed a sigh of relief. Captain Warfield was either a brave man or a fool. Regardless, he was a man of strong principle. Why couldn't she seem to get the handsome devil off her mind? It must be the mystery surrounding him—son of an English lord and a Eurasian woman, born in Hong Kong. His ancestry explained the exotic caste of his finely sculpted features.

Immediately upon climbing above deck, she sought him out, standing so tall and commanding among his men. Had she been a fool to resist his seduction last night? If he had been pleased with her, might he have taken her and Abel back to the

Sandwiches? Sammie gave herself a stern mental shake. Whatever was happening to her?

*Here I am mooning over a womanizer just because he comes from Hawaii!* Abel was right. She must stop dreaming about paradise. After all, she'd fought too hard to retain her virtue these past years to simply give it away in return for passage to the islands. But was the impulse simply born of her desire to see Hawaii—or did Christopher Warfield's virile beauty stir her to consider such an immoral act? She pushed the disquieting thought aside.

Kit saw her emerge from below, seemingly unshaken by the violence. She was a game little chit, he'd give her that, but what he needed at the moment was a woman to warm his bed, something Miss Samantha Goode had made clear she would not do.

Sighing, he waited as she approached, knowing what he had to tell her would probably make her as frustrated as it did him—albeit for very different reasons.

Deciding it best to get it over with, he nodded to her. "I'm afraid there's a bit of a problem, Miss Goode." *For both of us.* "You'll have to remain on board for another day until I can escort you safely back to Pearly's."

Her jaw dropped. "Why?"

"You saw those scum who work for the crimps. They'll be laying for any single boat I might send ashore. When I finish unloading the cargo, a large complement of my crew will go ashore with me. Then you'll be safe."

"What's to reassure me I'll be safe aboard this ship?" What made her say that? She blushed as her earlier thoughts about becoming his mistress again flashed through her mind.

Kit's black eye glowed with irritated amusement. "I believe, all things considered, I showed admirable restraint last night," he said dryly. "What makes you think I'd force myself on you now? After all, given your charming ensemble, you scarce look the part of a Circe able to tempt me to mad lust."

Her expression grew mutinous at the insult, delivered in that offhandedly clipped British accent. "You're sure full of yourself, Captain, especially for a lecher who tried to strip the clothes off a grease-covered female when she'd barely regained consciousness!" When his face darkened, she felt a surge of self-righteous satisfaction replace her earlier chagrin. She whirled and stomped off to where Stub was coiling a stout hemp rope, an arduous task for a one-handed man. Joss sat next to him, tail wagging.

The little seaman looked up at her with a shrewd gleam in his eyes. "You and the cap'n have words?"

"He's keeping me here until he's ready to escort me ashore. Stub, I'll lose my job—and no telling what my brother will think with me spending another night here."

Dropping the rope, Stub made a dismissive gesture with his right hand. "Nothin' to worry 'bout. Why the cap'n and Miz Pearly, they go back a long ways. She won't fire you ifn he says not to. He's one of her best customers."

"I'll just bet he is," she muttered beneath her breath as she patted the dog.

Kit watched her storm off, knowing he had been bested and deserved it. The wheat-haired wench was a little beauty and he'd have tumbled her in a trice last night, food-covered or no, if she had not insisted so violently that she was an innocent. Fact was, he'd have a damnably hard time sleeping next door to her tonight. Thank the Lord his first mate had left for shore early this morning. He'd put the good Miss Goode in that cabin and at least have his own comfortable bed back. Feeling restless and more than a little frustrated, he went below deck to work off some of his excess energy.

Sammie chatted with Stub for a brief time, but soon the brisk chilling wind off the bay began to make her bruised head ache. Excusing herself, she headed to the cabin to lie down for a short nap. The wind whipped the waves against the hull, causing loud rhythmic groans to echo through the ship. The noise disguised the sound of heavy breathing issuing from the cabin as she opened the door and slipped inside, only to freeze in shock.

The captain was facedown in the center of the cabin floor, his biceps flexed as he raised his body from the last of a set of two hundred push-ups. Sweat beaded his forehead and pooled between the shoulder blades of that broad muscular back. When he heard the cabin door open, his head jerked up angrily. Then he flattened himself instantaneously onto the floor.

"What the bloody hell do you think you're doing?" he roared.

Captain Kit Warfield was buck naked.

Sammie's feet were rooted to the deck as she stared at the sleek contours of his bare body. Her eyes moved from the curves of his hard, small buttocks to his long hairy legs, then back up to the bunched muscles in his shoulders. He raised his head, propping his hands beneath his chin and returned her perusal. When her bemused gaze met his mocking black eye, she finally regained her senses.

"Do you always lay about mother naked?" she squeaked.

"I wasn't laying about, pet. I was exercising, something I do every day."

"In your birthday suit?"

"I find it easier to move without clothes."

"Sounds heathenish to me." Sammie knew her face must be red as sunrise. She gave a groan of misery and fled. His laughter followed her up the companionway.

Sammie spent the rest of the day avoiding the captain, whose amused glances brought heat to her cheeks every time he caught her eye across the wide, crowded deck. Later that afternoon Stub explained to her the new sleeping arrangements and showed her to the absent first mate's cabin, promising to bring her supper.

When a steady tapping roused her from her nap, Sammie sat up in bed, wondering how Stub had knocked with his single hand holding a tray. She called out for him to enter and her question was answered. Joss trotted beside the little one-armed sailor. The dog was fitted with a pegleg of carved ivory.

"So that was the knock I heard," she exclaimed as Joss began to prance around the cabin, clicking out a tattoo on the polished planks.

"Whenever he gets excited, he really beats the drum. 'Course, whenever we're fixin' to go ashore he gets excited. That's the onliest time we put his dress leg on."

"It's a handsome leg, Joss," she said, reaching down to scratch a floppy black ear. "But why does he need it?" she asked Stub. "He can already run fast as the dickens on the three he's got."

He chuckled as he slid the tray onto the table beside the bed. "You seen him run aboard ship. But when he's been at sea so long, shucks, missy, Joss just purely loses his land legs. He can't stand up, much less walk on land without help. A sailor from the whaler he first shipped out on carved this here dress leg outa ivory."

"Are you going ashore tonight then? I thought the captain said—"

"Naw, missy, we'll all go tomorrow, but ole Joss, he's gotta get used to the dress leg. He ain't been on land for nigh onta two months now."

Joss pranced around the table, sniffing at the tray,

his leg thumping sharply. Suddenly he jumped up and caught the napkin in his teeth and dragged it off the tray.

"Watch it, you rascal," Stub scolded, grabbing the other end of the napkin, which the dog promptly dropped. "He's a terrible nuisance when it comes to food. He'll steal anythin'."

As if to prove it, the dog jumped up and seized a ship's biscuit in his teeth, then raced from the cabin, dress leg clicking out a tattoo like a message in crazed Morse Code. A cursing Stub bolted in pursuit.

Sammie spent the night in restless dreams, under the riveting spell of a fathomless ebony eye, seeing her own body entwined with his, feeling his rippling bronzed muscles. She awakened repeatedly, sweating and trembling, and was relieved when morning finally came. Rubbing the sleep from her eyes, she slipped from the bed and knelt to pull out the chamber pot.

After a thorough search that yielded no pot, she let out a few very unladylike oaths acquired on Pacific Street and stood up. She could hear men above deck laughing and talking, Kit's voice among them. Since he had left his cabin, the least embarrassing thing to do was to use his facility and then return here. She quickly pulled on the voluminous shirt and britches, then slipped from the mate's cabin to the captain's far more spacious one.

Sammie had just replaced the chamber pot and was preparing to leave when the creaking of the stairs made her freeze.

"I'll check those manifests as soon as I finish shaving," Kit's voice called out, drawing nearer.

He was returning to his cabin! She looked about the room frantically, searching for a place to hide. The first thing that caught her eye was the massive wardrobe standing with one large door slightly ajar.

Yanking it open, she leaped inside and pulled it closed behind her just as he opened the cabin door and entered, carrying a basin of hot water.

Kit set the water down and began to strop his razor, all the while experiencing the oddest sensation, as if someone were watching him. Having grown up in the alleyways along the Hong Kong waterfront, Warfield's instincts were as well honed as the razor he held in his hand. Then he saw it. The door to his wardrobe was shut tightly and a swatch of white linen stuck out like a flag of truce between the two door panels. He had left it open.

Whistling casually, he stripped off the silk kimono he had thrown on to go for his morning shower on deck and tossed it casually onto the bunk. He did not know what game Miss Samantha Goode was playing, but he did know she could watch through the ornate grillwork on the wardrobe door. He lathered up his beard and slowly set to work.

It was hot inside the closed-in space and Sammie was immobilized by her shirt, caught in the door. Afraid to try and pull it free, she sat very still, praying he would not open the door. When he shrugged out of the robe and tossed it away, she squeezed her eyes shut—for a second or two. Then treasonously, they popped open as if of their own will. She stared goggle-eyed at his splendid profile. Through the small decorative opening she could see his face and upper body where he stood by the porthole, shaving.

Kit knew she was watching. He could see the reflection of those big gold eyes in his mirror when he picked it up and wiped it. *You want a show, my virginal voyeur, I'll give you one you'll never forget.* He flexed his muscles and stretched, then positioned himself strategically behind the table and turned toward her. He started to shave, very, very slowly.

Sammie could feel every stroke of the razor against his cheek, hear the soft sensuous scrape of the bristles as the keen edge cut that black beard, leaving smooth bronzed skin in its wake. The muscles in his shoulders and arms flexed as he performed the simple toilette. Her throat went dry and she felt the most peculiar fluttering feeling in her chest, a very strange tingling that radiated out through the tips of her breasts and pooled lower, deep in her belly.

Lord above, who would've thought just watching a man shave could do this to a girl? Then he moved casually to the other side of the table, rubbing his clean jaw with those long sensuous fingers. He raised his arms and stretched that whole long lean frame until every muscle seemed to flex and quiver. One hand glided down his chest, rubbing the springy hair that grew in such a cunning pattern. Her eyes followed the narrowing trail of black hair to where it disappeared. His lower body was hidden by the high little table on which his shaving mirror sat. She felt a flash of disappointment. Her cheeks burned and she was positive he would hear her heart slamming against her ribs.

Her worst fears were realized after he turned and slid the robe back on, then strode purposefully across the floor to her hiding place. An odd smile quirked those wide mobile lips as he yanked open the door. The latch caught on her shirt with a loud rip, pulling her forward from her kneeling position in the cramped space. She tumbled out of the wardrobe and rolled to the floor, landing at his feet.

Grinning, he quirked one thick black eyebrow and asked, "Did you quite enjoy the show?"

Sammie struggled to her feet, fighting mad. "You knew! You did that on purpose, just to humiliate me!"

Kit shrugged, the silk of the kimono gliding sensuously over his broad shoulders. "You could've closed your eyes."

Her red face grew even redder as she recalled how

long that ploy had worked. "I want off this ship—
right now," she demanded illogically.

He made a sweeping gesture toward the porthole.
"It's a long swim, pet."

She stormed from the cabin.

Kit watched her leave, noting again the perfection
of her small slim woman's body with the sweetly
rounded derriere, sleekly turned calves, and delicate
ankles. He could imagine burying his face in all that
wheat-colored hair, caressing her pale milky skin.
What had begun as an exercise to teach the frustrat-
ing little snoop a lesson had quite backfired on him.

"Bloody hell, I want to get to Pearly's more than
she does!"

He began to dress quickly and angrily.

# Chapter Three

As the boat bobbed across the waves, nearing the wharf, Kit looked at Sammie, who sat huddled forlornly while Rollo and several other burly sailors rowed them ashore. She had not spoken a word to him since their hostile encounter in his cabin nearly an hour ago.

"You're almost home, sweet home. Why aren't you smiling?" he asked.

"It won't be home much longer. Miss Gates'll fire me for being gone so long—especially when she finds out I didn't—" She ducked her head and refused to meet his eyes.

He sighed. "I'll tell Pearly it wasn't your fault. If I vouch for you, she won't fire you," he added with assurance. Damn the crafty old madam, she had set them both up. Kit was ready to exact a real penalty for being used in Pearly's schemes to "break in" a reluctant new girl.

After cooling off and then seeing how frightened she seemed as they neared shore, the captain felt sympathy for the spunky little chit, whose life had no doubt been pretty brutal for one so young and innocent. Even though he had not taken her virginity, some man soon would. Kit knew what life in a waterfront slum was like.

"You mentioned a brother. Don't you have any other kin—I mean somewhere away from San Francisco?" he asked.

His kindly tone caught her off guard. Earlier he had delighted in teasing her, even laughing at her. She looked curiously at that enigmatic face with its piratical eye patch. Odd, but the defect made him appear even more handsome and mysterious. "Abel and I have no one left."

"What would you do if you could start over someplace else, Sammie?" What the devil made him ask that? He bloody well wouldn't take responsibility for two foundlings.

A strange faraway look came into her eyes as she stared out to sea. "I'd go to the Sandwich Islands." Then she realized how it sounded. Knowing that was his home port, she hastened to clarify the blunder. "I've been reading about them ever since I was a little girl. I still have the books Mrs. Hargrove gave my ma—all about what a paradise the islands are. I've read and reread every page." She dared to meet his gaze and could not resist asking, "Do the Kanakas really go without any clothes?" Then remembering how she had twice caught him mother naked, she cringed.

Kit threw back his head and roared with laughter. "The climate is quite balmy, so everyone tends to wear less than is considered conventional here, but it's been several generations since the natives went without anything but flowers in their hair."

"It sounds like paradise," she said wistfully. "Abel and I will get there one day."

Her mercurial mood shifts intrigued him. All too soon her dreams would be destroyed, but he refused to think about that. "Why did you fasten on the Sandwiches? Was that the only reading material your mother had for you?"

"Oh, we had other books, mostly from rich ladies my ma sewed for, but ... well, you see, we lived on Telegraph Hill. It was so bleak nothing grew there but tough old weeds only fit for the Italian settlers' goats. The walls were kind of thin and the wind would blow into our shack. And the fog would make everything damp and cold and gray. I guess I just wanted green grass and bright flowers, warm air and sunshine. I read that orchids grow wild everywhere on the Sandwiches."

"Yes, that part's true. I guess I've never taken time to think about the beauty of the islands. I spend much of my time at sea. When I'm there, it's only to load up a cane shipment."

"Stub said you grew up in Hong Kong. That's another place I've read about."

A guarded look flashed across his face and he changed the subject as the boat approached the wharf. "I'll have a hack take us to Pearly's. It's not safe to walk."

As if to accentuate his words, the heavily armed men accompanying them climbed up onto the wharf and stood, hands resting on pistols and knives, while he helped her from the boat. Three other boatloads of men from the *China Lucky* had come ashore at the same time. Although they had passed several white-hallers, none had bothered them.

In a few minutes they were riding up Pacific Street toward Pearly's, which was situated in a better part of town on Taylor Street. Sammie sat uncomfortably on the edge of the plush upholstered seat, realizing how wretched she looked wearing britches and Kit's baggy shirt, even if she was riding in such a grand conveyance. She looked surreptitiously at Captain Warfield sitting next to her. In profile he was strikingly elegant, dressed in a suit of fine black merino wool with a deep blue vest of silk brocade.

The wind ruffled his long black hair, straight and shiny as a raven's wing. He ran one hand over it, shoving it carelessly back from his face. Since their conversation on the boat ride to the city, he seemed somehow changed, more approachable, even kind.

She had been so angry with him before that she had refused to notice how the formal clothing transformed him from piratical sailor to prosperous gentleman.

*As far above me as the stars.* Lord above, she couldn't allow herself to think about such a ridiculous misalliance. She had rebuffed his advances once and he had made no further attempts to seduce her. Now that Pearly's girls were so near, she would be quickly forgotten, a raggedy waif in boy's britches. She straightened her spine angrily. *As if I'd ever settle for being some man's plaything.*

Her unhappy reverie was interrupted when the hack stopped. Kit paid the driver, then jumped agilely down and offered her his hand. It seemed a ridiculous courtesy considering her appearance, but when their fingers touched, hot, tingly sparks seemed to fly up her arm as he helped her alight.

They went around to the kitchen, since at this time of morning the front door was customarily locked. The alley door stood ajar. Sammie edged inside, nervous now to be back in familiar surroundings. Had she only spent two days aboard the *China Lucky*?

"Abel," she called out as she rounded the corner into the kitchen with Kit at her heels. "I'm here with—"

A loud thunk sounded, followed by a strident curse in clipped British tones. Sammie spun around.

"That's for you, you scurvy bastard! Takin' advantage of my sister," Abel yelled, swinging a whole smoked ham by the hock bone in the general direction of Kit's head. The first blow had blindsided him from his right, but he was prepared for the second swing and ducked, knocking the heavy cudgel from Abel's scrawny hands.

The ham bounced across the floor, leaving a smear of grease. Abel was hapless enough to step onto the slippery trail in his attempt to avoid Kit's fist. Losing his footing, he fell sharply onto his backside. Before he could squirm up, the big devil with the black eye patch planted one booted foot squarely on his chest, pinning him to the ground.

"This, I take it, is Abel?" Kit asked, looking disgustedly at the ruined shoulder of his suit coat. Damn, he was nearly as grease-covered as Sammie had been when Stub brought her aboard. The boy appeared to be no older than his sister, with the same yellow hair and wide gold eyes. The family resemblance was remarkable.

Sammie looked on in mute horror. Before she could defend Kit from Abel's accusations, her brother yelled, "You miserable sonofabitch! You ruined my sister!" He squirmed and wriggled, trying to dislodge the boot, to no avail.

"No, I did not, as a matter of fact," Kit replied evenly, turning to Sammie. "Just as a point of curiosity, pet, have the members of your family always used food for weapons? I suspect that if you possessed an ancestral coat of arms it would be crossed pork chops over a blob of mashed potatoes."

Sammie wanted to crawl beneath the kitchen table and hide in abject mortification. Ignoring Kit's droll comments, she turned to her brother. "Abel, shut up. Captain Warfield didn't touch me. He—"

"I heard Pearly talking. She sent you to him—in a fancy dress. Where is it now, huh? He tear it off you?" Fire blazed from his eyes but his face was pale as the white bandage wrapped around his head.

"No, he didn't. I ruined it when we were attacked by Green Teeth Gruenwald's crimps. You know there's no love lost between Green Teeth and Pigeon-toed Sal. Captain Warfield's crew members rescued me and took me to his ship, else I'd have been at the mercy of Gruenwald's cutthroats."

Abel calmed down as Sammie's words sunk in.

"You ... you mean you're not—you're—" His face turned brick red, another family trait, Kit thought.

Sammie knelt down beside Abel and Warfield deemed it safe to remove his foot from the boy's chest. Seeing the two of them side by side, he said, "Twins. You're bloody twins, aren't you?"

"What the hell's goin' on?" Pearly Gates bellowed from the door at the opposite end of the kitchen. The old madam's face was innocent of her heavy paints and she was almost decently covered in a garish red satin robe. She looked at Abel, sprawled on the floor with Sammie kneeling at his side and her pale little eyes narrowed to fatty slits, but before she could say anything Kit stepped forward, smiling.

"I know it's early for calling hours, Pearly, love, but I wanted to return Miss Goode and thank you for the loan of her." There was an underlying edge of sarcasm in his voice as he thought of Pearly's schemes. The smile on his lips did not communicate itself to that cold black eye, made even more menacing by the patch on his other one.

Pearly looked nervously from Kit's deadly smile to the girl on the floor, dressed in boy's britches. "I sent her to you all fixed up, Kit, darlin'. If she wasn't—"

"Perhaps we'd best leave brother and sister to their reunion. What we have to discuss is best done elsewhere." Kit took Pearly's arm and headed for the hall door after a cursory nod to the twins.

Sammie watched him walk away and felt a sudden inexplicable sense of loss. On the boat ride here he'd been so attentive and sympathetic. . . . Giving herself yet another mental shake, she glared down at Abel. "If you hadn't tried to brain the captain with a ham, he might have saved our jobs for us," she scolded.

"How was I supposed to know he didn't—well, you know." Abel looked at his sister, who was staring after that pirate like he was a juicy steak and she a starving miner. "Say, are you sure—"

"Oh, bother, I told you nothing happened." She jumped up and headed for the door. "I'm going to see if he's keeping his promise to save our jobs here." With a quelling look at Abel, she slipped down the hall after Kit and Pearly.

The house was quiet so early in the day and Sammie quickly located them by following the sound of their voices to Pearly's office just across from the big staircase.

"I'm not in the habit of deflowering virgins."

"I thought I was doin' ya a favor, sugar. Her, too," Pearly replied with a leer in her gravelly voice.

"My tastes run to the more usual sports in a bordello."

"Well, I can sure help you there. You always did fancy Corey, didn't ya? She's probably up there soakin' in her perfumed bubbles about now. Consider her on the house this time. You just go on up while I settle with that worthless little troublemaker. She owes me for that tray and all Gerrard's fancy fixins—not to mention the pink silk dress."

"As I already explained, Sammie used the food to fight for her life. Apparently, a customary family pastime," he added dryly. "I feel responsible for the girl since you were sending her to me. Bloody hell, I'll pay for your damned crockery and I want your word you'll keep the both of them on. No more tricks, foisting Sammie onto your customers."

"Aw, Kit, you always did have too soft a heart. Don't know how you expect a gal like me to run her business," Pearly complained, then hastened to add cajolingly, "All right, all right. They stay on working in the kitchen."

Sammie could imagine the fiercely intimidating look her pirate must have given Pearly. Hearing the floorboards creak in protest as the fat woman crossed the carpet, Sammie darted away from the door and

hid behind a big Chinese urn filled with palms. Kit
and Pearly emerged.

"Corey's in her tub, you say?" Kit asked, a white
grin slashing his sun-bronzed face. "Think I'll just
have a peek."

As Pearly chuckled, Kit climbed the stairs like a
man long familiar with the establishment. Sammie
felt a sudden tight knot of misery twist inside her as
she slid along the wall and vanished into the kitchen
before her employer could catch her eavesdropping.

"What's wrong with you? That fancy lordship not
keep his word? Maybe it's best if we leave here—"

"No, he kept his word, Abel. Pearly isn't going to
fire us. I don't even have to pay for the tray and
all those dishes I broke." At his quizzical look, she
explained the weapons she'd used to defend herself
from Zorko's crimps.

Abel shrugged, adjusting the bandage on his head.
"Well, then, reckon we ought to get to work. If Gerrard sees this fancy ham like this, he'll slice me up
for stew meat." He carried the big ham over to the
sink and began to scrape it clean.

"Abel," Sammie said, then smiled tremulously.
"Thank you for defending my honor."

His face reddened. "Aw, it wasn't nothing. I only
wish you'd never met that one-eyed sailor."

At the mention of Kit, Sammie's face fell. She could
not get the image of him upstairs cavorting with
Corey in her bubble bath out of her mind. "So do I,
Abel," she replied glumly.

Trying to cheer her, he brightened and said, "I
went rattin' again last night. Sold half a dozen big
ones—three dollars, Sammie. When I catch up with
them bounders who stole my big catch the night before you left, we'll have almost twenty dollars in our
nest egg. Before you know it we'll have our fare to
the islands."

"There you are, mooning around like always,"

Pearly said nastily as she shoved the kitchen door open and stood with her hands on her enormous hips. "Get upstairs and start making up beds. I promised Kit I'd keep you on but you're gonna earn your keep. The hard way now. I offered you easier."

"I'd rather make beds than stain them," Sammie said and slipped past the madam.

Abel applied himself assiduously to scrubbing cookpots until his Amazonian employer waddled out of the kitchen.

Sammie entered the big linen closet and began to load up her arms with clean sheets. As she bypassed Corey's room, she heard muffled splashing and the beautiful brunette's silvery laughter, then Kit's low husky voice saying something she could not quite make out.

*As if I wanted to know*, she huffed to herself and headed into the next room. The bed was a rumpled mess. Setting down her load, she went to work with a vengeance, ripping off the soiled sheets and replacing them with fresh linen. She worked feverishly, trying desperately not to think of Kit and Corey next door. Just as she finished the bed and started to leave, Corey's door opened and their laughter filled the hallway.

"The room next door should be cleaned up by now. We can use that bed," Corey said.

"Anywhere you want, love," Kit answered.

"We wouldn't be switching rooms if you hadn't been so impatient and thrown me soaking wet onto my bed," Corey purred seductively.

Sammie's heart skipped a beat. They were coming in here! She simply could not face them, wet from a shared bath, probably half naked! She bolted across the room through the open doors to the balcony, thinking to climb from there across the wide ledge to the next open window. Sammie quickly straddled the balcony's rickety railing, holding on to the outside doorknob for balance, but when she tried to step down, the ledge was not there. A large piece of it had crumbled away during the winter rainy season and Pearly had never gotten around to having it repaired.

Awash in misery, Sammie hung precariously over the balcony, clutching the knob of the door in a death grip. She could hear the sounds of passion far more clearly now—soft moans, silky laughs, and the swish of clothes being discarded. Unable to resist, she peered around the curtained glass panes.

"Forgive me for interrupting your soak, pet?" Kit asked as he nibbled small wet kisses along Corey's throat.

His tall bronzed body was completely naked as he bent over Corey's voluptuous charms, molding her against him as she ran her hands across his wide muscular shoulders. Sammie could still picture him lying on the floor of his cabin doing push-ups, with sweat glowing on those bunched muscles. She closed her eyes and looked away, biting her lip to keep from crying out and making an utter fool of herself.

Corey felt Kit's growing impatience as he moved them toward the bed. When he laid her back onto the clean sheets, she glanced over at the open door and smiled up at him. "I feel a chill blowing in from the bay. After all, darling, it is rather early in the morning to be working. Be a love and close the doors."

"Your slightest wish . . ." Kit murmured as he turned and strode across the carpet.

On the other side of the door, Sammie almost swooned when he turned in her direction and she had her first look at a naked, sexually aroused male body. Before he caught sight of her, she jerked her head back.

Kit pulled the left door closed but for some reason the right one stuck fast. He yanked hard and it gave a bit, then flew back against the balcony railing. "Bloody odd," he muttered.

On the opposite side Sammie hung on for dear life in the tug-of-war, struggling for purchase on the rickety wrought iron railing. Kit murmured a colorful waterfront oath and seized the edge of the door with one hand, pulling it sharply toward him. As she felt the knob being yanked out of her grasp, Sammie did the only thing possible to prevent herself from being thrown over the side of the balcony—she lunged for the door, but unintentionally clutched Kit's arm instead. Just then the railing gave way and her legs slipped. She was left dangling over the edge of the balcony with nothing to save her but a death grip on Kit.

Unfortunately, the sudden weight on his arm took Kit by surprise and he lost his balance, pitching headlong onto the broken railing. His free hand clawed at the door, attempting to keep himself from being catapulted into the alley below. He caught the knob in a white-knuckled hold, sprawling most ungracefully across the hard rusty edge of broken iron. Both his arms felt as if they'd been wrenched from their sockets. He tore his glance from the precarious grip he had on the doorknob and looked down to where his other arm was being pulled by the flailing Sammie, whose screeching drowned out his curses.

"Stop thrashing like a harpooned whale before you send us both plunging to our bloody deaths! I refuse to be smashed naked in the middle of some Barbary Coast back alley!" he bellowed at her, then swore as a certain very sensitive part of his anatomy came in contact with the cold rusty edge of the railing. Very carefully he extricated himself from the most imminent danger, easing his leg back on the rail. Still holding onto the doorknob with his right hand, he struggled to lift the chastened girl up. "There, grab on now, that's it. Easy, easy," he grunted as he hauled her over the edge and stepped back into the room with Sammie plastered tight as a leech to his naked body.

Corey had thrown on her robe and stood glaring furiously at the pair. "I've had all the aggravation I'll take from you, you stupid little chit."

Before the big brunette could say more, Pearly came bursting through the door, wheezing for breath. Right behind her was Stub with Joss, who began barking furiously while his dress leg clicked a frantic tattoo on the floor. At once the old madam's eyes narrowed on Sammie as Kit peeled her from his body and seized one of the dirty sheets from the pile left on the floor.

"Is there anyone else who should be here, perhaps the mayor and city council?" Kit asked, a killing rage roiling beneath the tightly delivered question.

"I heard you yellin' 'n cussin' 'n Miz Sammie screamin', Cap'n," Stub said, red-faced as he re-placed the Colt he had drawn.

"What the hell are you doing spying on my cus-tomers, girlie? You're too good to service the men for me, but not above a little peek, huh?"

Sammie bristled. "I was changing the linens like you told me when they came in." She gestured to Kit and Corey. "All I wanted to do was get away without them seeing me, but the ledge is broken off and . . ." Her anger fled, replaced by yet another wave of burning humiliation. Why could nothing ever seem to go right when she was around Christo-pher Warfield?

"That girl is nothing but trouble, Pearly. Either you get rid of her or I'm leaving," Corey said petulantly.

The madam looked from Corey back to Sammie and shrugged helplessly. "You aren't gonna argue for her now, are ya, Kit? Looks like she near killed you."

"Or worse," he muttered to himself, surreptitiously rubbing his endangered anatomy beneath the makeshift toga in which he was swaddled.

"That settles it. I'll keep the boy on if he don't get in any more scrapes, but I don't want any more trouble from her. I never seen one little bitty gal kick up such a ruckus in all my born days."

Sammie paled but held her chin up. "I'll be gone as soon as I get my things together."

"You can't just turn an innocent girl out onto Pacific Street," Stub protested.

"By the by, what the hell are you doing here?" Kit asked the sailor in a cold voice.

"We got trouble, Cap'n. Gruenwald's men is makin' threats to burn the *Lucky.* I just got word from Cap'n Nelson. He 'n a couple other masters want to talk to you about organizin' to break the crimps."

Kit swore, looking from Stub back to Sammie. "Bloody hell, go downstairs with Stub and wait for me." With that he strode from the room with as much dignity as he could muster clad in a bed sheet.

# Chapter Four

Sammie sat disconsolately at the small table in the elegantly furnished suite that Kit had rented at the Grand Hotel. She poked her fork into the pink slices of beef and took a bite. Juicy and tender, but she had no appetite. Her conversation with Kit earlier that day replayed in her mind.

"You stay put here until I can figure what the bloody hell to do about you," Kit had said with a scowl.

"I don't want your charity, Captain Warfield," she had replied. "I've survived until now without earning my living on my back."

"And that's what you think I have in mind by bringing you here?" His smile was smug as he inspected her person. She wore her only decent dress, a baggy, faded calico atrocity that one of Pearly's whores had cast off.

She blushed. "That isn't what I meant. You're twisting my words. I'll survive without your help."

"You've been doing a capital job of it since we met," he snapped sarcastically. "I don't know who's more dangerous—the crimping gangs or you. Don't leave this room or I'll paddle your backside."

He had stormed off, leaving her alone with Joss, who now pranced around the table, tail thumping and the dress leg clicking as he eyed her food.

"What am I going to do, Joss? He's right. If I leave here alone, I won't last an hour before I end up in some awful crib." She fed the dog a strip of beef, then another, and watched as he snapped them down with sharp white teeth.

"Abel will lose his job if I show my face back at Pearly's. And Kit doesn't want me...." A tear slid down her cheek. There. She had said it aloud, admitted to herself what had made her so miserable all day waiting in his suite. After comparing her to the voluptuous charms of Corey, Kit had found her sadly deficient.

When she had heard them together, laughing and carrying on, she would have done anything rather than face him. "I did do anything, just about the blame craziest thing a body could!" She shivered remembering the brush with broken bones, if not death. The drop from the balcony to the alley below was at least twenty feet. Yep, that had been "anything," sure enough.

"If I'd done what Pearly sent me out to his ship for, it would've been better. Then maybe he'd have kept me—and taken me and Abel to Hawaii with him."

Just thinking about the way it had felt, clinging so tightly to his hard naked body, made her get all hot and fuzzy-feeling inside—like she had the influenza or something. Sammie pondered her peculiar reactions ever since the first moment she had laid eyes on Christopher Warfield's beautiful pirate's face. Then a plan began to take shape in her mind—if she had the nerve to carry it off.

Kit returned to the Grand late that night, tired and dispirited. The whole day had been spent attempting to stop the Barbary Coast crimps from victimizing sailors. He had met with three other ship's captains who were tired of the crimps stealing their crews. They had walked the length of Pacific Street with a complement of armed crewmen, visiting the deadfalls and rescuing drugged and beaten sailors. But they had not been able to locate the man responsible for most of the mayhem, Green Teeth Gruenwald.

As the designated leader of the war on crimps, Kit knew he had made a dangerous enemy. "The bloody hell with it," he sighed, unlocking the door to his suite. Joss stood up and clicked across the floor to greet him. Seeing the dog reminded him of why he had left the mutt here. To guard *her*. He groaned. What was he going to do with that dangerous little chit? Disaster followed her like Joss followed the galley cook.

The dog trotted over to Kit, quizzically watching the captain sink onto the settee and eye the door to the bedroom warily. In a grumbling voice he said, "I expect your new friend has usurped my bed—and fed you handsomely, else you'd be circling me clicking like a crazed flamenco dancer."

Just as he pulled off his boots and started to unfasten his shirt, the bedroom door opened and Sammie stood silhouetted in its frame. The dim light from behind her outlined her small, astonishingly well-rounded curves through the sheer cotton of her night rail. He had thought he'd seen all there was to see of her poured into the cabin boy's breeches. He was mistaken.

Shyly, Sammie watched his taut inspection from beneath her thick gold lashes, unable to decide if he desired her or was appalled by her. His harsh, inscrutable expression did not indicate which. She swallowed as he stood up and strode slowly across the space between them, waiting for him to make the next move.

Kit touched the open collar of her night rail. The white cotton was soft and thin from repeated washings and the long shapeless folds were darned in at least a dozen places. He'd never seen a female in silk or satin look as fetching. Her heavy mass of wheat gold hair fell straight and heavy over her shoulders and down her back. He touched a strand of the glistening stuff and inhaled the clean wholesome scent of soap and woman.

Then her small heart-shaped face tilted up and she returned his gaze. "A man could drown in those gold eyes," he whispered.

One slim little hand lightly touched his chest. "Are you still mad about this morning?"

He sighed. "No, Sammie, I'm not exactly mad . . . just cautious. You should be in bed." *Stupid thing to say, Warfield.*

"I couldn't sleep. . . . The bed's so big." She gulped, knowing she was being too obvious, yet praying it would work. She rested her other hand on his chest and tried to remember what he had done that night aboard ship when he'd tried to seduce her. His heartbeat accelerated—a good sign. At least she hoped it was. She wet her lips nervously with the tip of her tongue and willed him to kiss her.

Kit looked down at those lush pink lips, so much softer and more inviting than Corey's carmined ones. His head lowered and his arms lifted her up against his body, raising her into the kiss. Her hands slid around his neck without hesitation. The first contact was light, brushing, experimental, as if he were afraid she might evaporate. But she did not. She was warm and real and smelled of pine soap. And he had been without a woman for two months, courtesy of her interrupting him with Corey this morning. His mouth grew restive as he ground it down on hers, willing her to open to him.

When she did he invaded, his tongue plunging deep and thrusting with an age-old rhythm. Sammie felt dizzy and tingling, frightened and pleasured all at once. He did want her! She tangled her hands in his shaggy straight black hair and kissed him back, letting her tongue mimic his, dancing into his mouth until he growled and scooped her up in his arms. When he entered the bedroom, he broke the rough hungry kiss and set her down in the center of the big mattress.

Sammie watched him strip off his shirt, then pause. "This is what you want, isn't it?"

She smiled tremulously and swallowed, then answered in a small voice, "Oh, yes. I didn't realize how much I regretted turning you down until you went to Corey. I know I'm not experienced like her but I'll please you. You won't be sorry for taking us."

His hand stilled on the buttons of his fly. "Us?" he echoed ominously.

Sammie swore at herself. She'd let her mouth run away with her again. Kit didn't have much reason to care for Abel. She'd have to work on that later. "I meant taking me."

"Why is it, pet, that I have the feeling you didn't use 'take' in a sexual sense?"

She let out a shaky breath as her face flamed. "Why, I just meant when you took me back to your ship."

He was beginning to catch her drift. And he didn't like it. "My ship. The one that sails to the Sandwiches. You're selling me your bloody virginity in return for a boat ride to paradise—is that it?"

His cold bitten-off words confused and stunned her. Put that way it didn't sound too good. In fact, it sounded downright awful. "I hoped . . . that is, I wanted . . ." Her voice faded away in misery. What had she wanted? To have Kit Warfield love her and vow to keep her? To make her his wife? One look at his implacable, mocking expression made her realize just how absurd the whole scheme was. She stiffened her spine, shielding her crushed pride. "My first instinct was right. All you want is to use me and send me away," she blurted out in pain.

"Me use you? I believe you have it a bit backwards, pet. I'm not in the habit of taking aboard passengers in return for a toss," he added crudely as he turned and slammed the door behind him.

Kit lay on the Aubusson carpet in the parlor. Although it was no more uncomfortable than many a bunk he'd slept in, he pitched and tossed for hours, restless and miserable. "Why in bloody hell do I even desire the scheming little chit?" he muttered savagely to himself.

She was nothing but trouble. Never had he met a female more prone to disaster. He flexed his aching shoulder as if to remind himself of the morning's brush with death. "Bloody hell, I could've dashed my brains out hurtling over that railing." As to the encounter between his manhood and the rusty iron, the less he thought of that, the better. He was mad to want her. But he did.

Abel dived behind the pile of satin pillows in the corner of Pearly's office when he heard her approaching. He knew she would fire him if she caught him sleeping when he had been sent by the housekeeper to dust the bric-a-brac cluttering the big ornate room. He swore to himself, cursing his rotten luck. It was scarcely midmorning. The madam normally never rose before noon and he had been up all night catching rats. Sammie would skin him if he got fired. If they were ever going to save up enough to escape the Barbary Coast, he had to keep working two jobs, especially now that Sammie had lost hers. She was lucky just to have a place to sleep at the mission, where that ship's captain had taken her two days ago.

Pearly lumbered over to her desk and sat down with a loud *whoosh*, bidding her visitor to do likewise. Abel peeked through the garish mounds of satin seraglio pillows and saw Green Teeth Gruenwald. What was the kingpin of the crimps doing here?

"I don't know what I can do," she whined. "Just 'cause Warfield's a regular customer ain't my fault."

"You need my protection for yer place since Zorko finished off Pigeon-toed Sal," Gruenwald said nastily, chewing on a gold toothpick that blended rather well with the stained crooked teeth that had earned him his nickname. "You do like I say—I say yer gonna help me kill Warfield before he stirs up any more trouble for my crimps."

Abel hunched down, his heart thudding in his chest as he listened to the conspiracy. That was when he felt the first tickling way up in his nose, which quickly grew to an intolerable itch. When he had dived behind the filthy mound of pillows he had sent up a dust plume of tornado proportions.

Abel squeezed his nose with both hands and prayed. In vain. A tiny squeak escaped, like a door opening on rusty hinges, rapidly followed by another.

"What was that?" Gruenwald asked, heaving his big body from the chair.

"Shouldn't be no one stirrin' this early, 'cept kitchen help," Pearly replied. Then she remembered. "Ruthie sent that good-fer-nothin' boy to dustin'!" The madam stood up with surprising swiftness for one of her girth. One big fleshy fist grabbed several pillows and tossed them aside.

Abel sneezed again, but this time he did not bother to hold his nose because he was too busy dodging his Amazonian antagonist, who cursed loudly as she denuded the corner of pillows, hurling them at her victim.

"It is that damn kid! Grab 'im." She hit Abel directly in the face with a purple satin cushion that weighed at least ten pounds, five of which was accumulated dust.

A big beefy fist twisted his shirt collar, nearly choking off what breath he had left. "What the hell are you doin' here?" Green Teeth asked, chomping on his toothpick as he drew an evil-looking knife from his belt.

"No, don't kill him—not yet," Pearly said, a cunning smile creasing her pasty face. She had the solution to her problem with the crimp boss. "I got me an idea about how to get Warfield for you."

Sammie sat at Pearly's desk, her hands gripping the carved oak chair in terror. "I won't do it. You can kill me—I won't lure Kit to his death."

Green Teeth chuckled, enjoying the way the yellow-haired wench trembled every time he came near her. It had been a real pleasure snatching her from that mission. He could still feel her sleek little body wriggling and kicking as he threw the blanket over her head.

"You'll write that note to Warfield, all right, dearie—or else we'll kill yer stupid brother." Pearly nodded impatiently to Gruenwald, who seemed more interested in fondling the scrawny girl than attending to business. "Hell, if I'd knowed she had this effect on every man who touches her, I'd have put her to work two years ago," she snapped, opening the closet door. Abel lay inside, bound and gagged.

"You want 'im healthy, you write what Pearly tells ya," Gruenwald said, rolling the toothpick across his slimy tongue as he casually slid his knife along Abel's throat.

"I'll write what you say," she choked out, "but it won't do any good. Kit doesn't care about me."

Pearly snorted. "Yeah. That's why he was dead set on keepin' me from firin' you. Even wanted to protect yer virtue—until he took ya to his hotel the other night fer hisself." She sighed half regretfully, then chuckled loudly and said, "Kit's just too noble fer his own good sometimes." Feeling Gruenwald's gimlet eyes on her, she shoved a sheet of paper at Sammie. "Just you tell him you're back here 'n thinkin' about whorin' fer me. That'll scald his tail. I bet he comes runnin' to save ya from me."

Pearly's harsh, braying laughter filled the room as Sammie tried to think. If she succeeded in luring Kit here unsuspecting, they'd kill him. She had to warn the captain in the letter—but how? Finally, she began to write with a trembling hand. *Please let it work.*

Kit read Sammie's letter, then crumpled it angrily and threw it across the cabin. Had the little fool lost her mind? Why would she ever dream he'd come running after her? Then with a muffled oath, he dived after the missive and reread it. "Stub," he yelled out the door, "get down here on the double."

As darkness fell, a thick fog rolled off the bay, cloaking the city in gray. It perfectly suited Kit's plans as he and two dozen handpicked sailors made their way to Pearly Gates's bordello. Well before nearing the block in which it stood, they split up into six smaller bands, each slipping off to approach the target from a different direction.

Finally just Kit, Stub, and Rollo were left with Joss dancing excitedly around them—minus his dress leg.

"You think he can run on land good enough without it?" Stub asked dubiously.

"He seems to be hopping around all right," Kit replied dryly. "Anyway, we can't have him making that infernal racket with his peg if he's going to do his part in the plan."

The three of them approached the bordello as fog curled around their faces. Turning to the big boatswain, he said, "You know what to do once you get into the parlor."

Rollo, outfitted like a prosperous ship's officer, nodded, grinning. "Bejesus, Cap'n. Me 'n the boys'll start the damnedest fight you ever seen. Just give us five minutes to get in the place." He swaggered toward the front door of Pearly's.

Kit turned to Stub. "All right, let's get to work." The unlikely trio slipped quietly into that back alley of horrendous memory.

The captain took the coil of rope he had been carrying from his shoulder. At one end was a grappling hook, which he swung carefully and then hurled upward toward the balcony. The railing still hung precariously where Sammie had dislodged it from the wall, but the other side seemed secure.

"I wish this weren't the only room I know is empty," he muttered as he watched the hook tangle in the wrought iron. He yanked it tight while Stub stood watch with a big club and his Colt. Once assured the coast was clear, Kit began to climb up hand over hand. When he had scrambled over the groaning rail, he signaled Stub, who attached the other end of the rope to the light-weight harness Joss wore and helped Kit haul the dog up. By the time the captain and his accomplice disappeared inside, Rollo and the rest of the men would be starting a ruckus, if all went according to plan.

Pearly sat near the parlor piano at a table draped with a garishly tasseled cloth, nervously watching the door. She took a frilly lace kerchief from the low-cut bodice of her dress and wiped perspiration from her mustachioed upper lip. Where was Warfield? She had been positive he'd come storming in, expecting to drag that girl out of her den of iniquity. If she had been mistaken, Green Teeth Gruenwald would cause her no end of trouble.

She cast a furtive glance in the direction of the crimp, who was hiding behind a pair of giant potted palms. A dozen of his men were disporting themselves around the downstairs, pretending to be customers. The others were upstairs with the girl.

Pearly had worked hard to get where she was, one of the premier madams in a city famous for its scarlet poppies. Her enormous three-story house with twenty bedrooms, an ornate walnut bar, a receiving parlor, and even a French chef who served elegant midnight buffets, was the talk of the Barbary Coast. She'd be switched with a buggy whip if a damn-blasted war between ship's captains and crimps was going to jeopardize her business.

"Damn Pigeon-toed Sal fer runnin' off like a dog with his tail between his legs, leaving me to Gruenwald."

Just then an enormous brute of a man strode in and headed to the bar at the opposite side of the parlor. He tweaked his waxed handlebar mustache and threw a silver piece on the bar. "What's the best you have in the house?" he asked, eyeing a big redhead whose freckled endowments were almost popping out the top of her black lace corset. She wore scandalously short silk briefs, and her plump legs were encased in black net stockings whose garters bit deeply into the flesh of her soft thighs.

The redhead giggled under his perusal. "I drink the punch," she volunteered, sidling up to the bar.

"A punch for me and one for the lady," Rollo said expansively to the barkeep, who poured two whitish-looking drinks into tall glasses and shoved them across the polished bar. The redhead sipped daintily while Rollo took a big gulp, then wiped his mustache. "By God, what do you call this stuff?"

Red giggled again. "Milk."

"Just plain old milk?" he asked, knowing full well it must be a far more potent libation.

Another giggle and a nod from Red, and her suitor raised his glass for a refill, saying loudly, "Here's to a glorious cow!"

"You a mama's boy, drinkin' milk?" a tall cadaverous stranger next to him asked, snickering.

"Are you callin' me names, bucko?" Rollo was delighted. This cantankerous sucker was not even one of their boys. He grabbed the man by his starched shirt and lifted him high in the air with one arm, then punched him squarely in the face with the other. At once the whole place erupted into violence as men began to curse and shove while the scarlet poppies screamed and ducked for cover. In seconds the sound of beefy fists connecting with flesh mixed with the splintering of furniture.

Upstairs, Kit followed a swiftly trotting Joss, who paused at every door along the hallway, sniffing at each one. Warfield swore to himself. They'd already checked one half of the rooms on the second floor. "Find Sammie, Joss," he urged, thinking their luck might not hold much longer before they were discovered. Lord only knew how many men Pearly had holding her. That the little hellcat had been harmed he refused even to consider.

Just as Joss stopped at the last door, the sounds of bellowing and glass breaking erupted downstairs. Kit smiled grimly. Rollo and the boys were creating a diversion. Now all he had to do was get Sammie the hell out of here. Seeing the dog scratching on a door at the end of the hall, Kit quickly drew his pistol and flattened himself against the wall. The dog let out a sharp bark and scratched some more. The door opened.

"What the hell?" A big stoop-shouldered man reared back aiming a kick at Joss. "Damned mutt. How'd you get in here—with them bums what started the fight downstairs?"

"No, as a matter of fact he came with me," Kit said conversationally in his clipped British accent.

The thug's eyes almost crossed as the barrel of the .45 Colt pressed against the tip of his large hooked nose. He backed into the room, hands raised. Sammie sat tied to a chair, gagged.

"Untie her and be quick about it," Kit commanded.

Hook Nose complied. "You'll never get outta here, Warfield."

"We can but try," Kit said with a shrug, relieved to see the girl alive and little the worse for her ordeal.

"Oh, Kit, you came," Sammie cried as soon as the gag was removed. "I was afraid you wouldn't— you've walked into a trap, you know."

"Your message removed any doubt about the matter—saying you planned to save your ill-gotten earnings and retire to the place of your dreams—on the Massachusetts coast!"

"It was all I could think of," she said, rubbing her wrists. Then it dawned on her as she looked up at him. He no longer wore the eye patch "Your eyes! You have two of them! I mean—"

He grinned raffishly. "It usually works that way."

Just then Joss began to growl low in his throat as the door to the adjoining room opened. "What've we got here?" Zorko said as the dog dashed around him and began to tear at his pants leg. At the same instant Hook Nose lunged at Kit, knocking the gun from his hand. They went down fighting. Zorko quickly pulled a knife from his waistband while trying to kick Joss away.

Sammie's eyes searched frantically for a weapon. Kit's gun lay on the other side of the two thrashing combatants, unreachable. She had to do something at once so she seized the nearest thing at hand, a bowl of Gerrard's spicy curried chicken, which Hook Nose had been feasting on—and hurled it squarely into Zorko's face.

At first he snorted in surprise and inhaled the sticky sauce up his nostrils. A grave mistake. Then he blinked his eyes. A far graver mistake. As the fiery burn of curry ate away at the sensitive lining of his nose and eyes, the cutthroat pawed frantically at his face, trying in vain to wipe it off. The gravest mistake of all.

"Aaargh!" He went down on his knees as fluids gushed from his eyes, nose, and mouth, knife still clutched in his hand but forgotten. So was the dog, who continued to chew at his pants leg. So was the girl, who picked up the heavy serving tray and coshed him soundly over the head. He crumpled to the floor, out of his misery, unconscious. Releasing his pants leg, Joss rushed around to begin devouring the luncheon on Zorko's face. Curry was one of his favorites.

Kit continued to battle Hook Nose, whose brutish strength was fueled by desperation once he saw his companion go down to defeat. The thug had pulled a knife from his boot as they rolled across the floor and clutched it in his right hand, scant inches from Kit's throat. The captain had a death grip on his foe's wrist, keeping the blade from inflicting a mortal wound.

Sammie ran over to them and aimed her tray at the crimp, who was straddling Kit. Unfortunately just as she swung it down Kit rolled up and pinned Hook Nose below him—and received the flat of the tray across his back.

Warfield let out a burst of profanity at the blow, then smashed his foe's hand against the wooden table leg, causing Hook Nose to drop the knife. Kit raised his fist and punched the crimp in his formidable nose, which gushed crimson, but the force of the blow threw the captain off balance and Bloody Nose rolled on top once more.

Tray raised, Sammie swung with all her might— just as Kit came up on top again. He took the hit against his left arm and snarled, "Get the bloody hell away before you cripple me!"

"I was just trying to help," she protested as he landed several sound blows to the crimp's face.

Joss, who had finished chewing every last morsel of curry off Zorko, now jumped into the fray, seizing another pants leg from the tangle of thrashing limbs.

Kit shrieked as sharp little teeth sank into his calf, but continued the punishing blows to his foe until the crimp finally lay unconscious. He felt Sammie trying to pluck Joss from his pants leg and jerked it free himself. Turning to glare at them, he struggled to his feet. "The next time I'm in a fight, do me an enormous courtesy—try everything in your power to assist my opponent."

Sammie looked over to where his Colt lay in the corner. "If I'd only been able to reach your gun—"

"Don't even think it," Kit said in a deadly quiet voice, striding over to pick up the weapon.

"I did keep Zorko from slitting your throat," she replied smugly.

He looked at the ruins of the bald man's face and grinned in spite of himself. "You should stick to using food as a weapon." He shoved her out the door into the hall. "I have to get you out of here before the little diversion downstairs runs its course."

Sammie clutched his arm frantically. "No! Not until we find Abel. Pearly caught him. He's the one who found out about Gruenwald's plans to kill you."

"Gruenwald. Is he here now?"

"I don't know. After they caught Abel, Pearly must've told Green Teeth about you and me. He sent his men to kidnap me from the mission and use me for bait to lure you here. I won't leave without my brother," she said mulishly.

Sighing, Kit muttered, "Do you know where he is?"

"They had him tied up in Pearly's office closet this morning."

"Damn, that means going downstairs. It's too dangerous for you. Stub's waiting with a rope—below the window in that room," he said, shoving her in the direction he pointed. Get out of here. I'll get Abel."

She shook her head. "I'm not leaving without my brother." With that she darted down the hall and headed toward the back stairs with Kit and Joss in pursuit.

# Chapter Five

Pearly Gates looked around her beautiful parlor house with its genuine cut-glass beads edging the red window shades and the black velvet loveseats with real gilt wood frames. One loveseat had its legs broken off, another its cushions ripped with the stuffing spilling out. The beaded shades were slashed and torn across the wide bay window fronting the street. Several of the combatants had crashed through the glass. Shambles. Everything was being reduced to shambles.

Stub Malone had the great misfortune to walk in the front door at that very moment and call out to Rollo, who was in the midst of dispatching one of Green Teeth's crimps. "You seen the cap'n?"

Rollo let his hapless opponent drop limply to the floor and stepped over the body. "Naw, but he'll be around directly to finish off old Green Teeth."

These men were wrecking her place because she had been caught between Warfield and Gruenwald. This was their stupid fight. Warfield was nowhere in sight—but that obnoxious little Texan who shadowed him was directly in her sights! With a loud growl she thundered across the floor, toppling men like bowling pins. When one pair locked in mortal combat slowed her course, she paused long enough to lift each by his shirt collar and crack their heads together.

"Malone, you runty little one-armed sonofabitch—
I'm gonna kill you!"

Stub saw six feet and three hundred pounds of
female cyclone headed straight at him with mayhem
in her eyes. Paling, he tried to run, but he was surrounded by men throwing punches. He ducked a
flying chair and tried to slip behind one of the
crimps, but Pearly seized him, grabbing his thinning
hair until his scalp stretched.

"Eaooo! I ain't got much hair left as it is,
Pearly—Pearly—no!"

The fat Amazon raised the screaming little Texan
high above her head and hurled him through the
broken window. Stub sailed through the air like a
kite in the Bay wind, landing out in the muddy street
amid the other wreckage from the brawl. He started
to sit up, shaking his dazed head, when Pearly
pitched her second victim out the window. The
crimp landed atop Malone, knocking the breath from
him so violently that he saw stars dancing before his
eyes.

Inside, Pearly continued her rage-fed house-
cleaning, disposing of half a dozen more men, sailors
and crimps indiscriminately, in a frenzy to rid the
premises of both sides in the dispute which had
wreaked havoc on her life's work.

Zorko, his face resembling a well-boiled cabbage,
came leaping down the front stairs, searching for his
escaped prisoner. Unfortunately for him the only female in the room was the one who seized him in
two meaty hands and sent him flying through the
front door, which—also unfortunately for him—was
still intact and closed. Pearly's throwing speed
seemed to grow proportionately to the weight of her
victims. Zorko smashed through the door only
slightly under the velocity of a cannonball.

At the opposite end of the house Kit grabbed Sammie, putting a stop to her headlong rush into the

pandemonium up front. "I know where her office is, dammit. Stay behind me."

They quickly made their way to the office and stepped inside. Joss, barking excitedly, dashed past them and ran back and forth in front of the closet. While Kit checked the room to be certain it was empty, Sammie ran to the closet door and threw it open. Sure enough there sat a pale and bedraggled Abel, bound and gagged, propped in the corner.

His sister knelt and began to tug off the gag. "Oh, Abel—are you all right?" Without waiting for an answer, she turned to Kit. "Help me get these ropes off him."

Before he could do more than slip his knife from its sheath, a voice stopped him. "Well, so Pearly was right. Yer little yeller-haired whore did bring ya." Green Teeth Gruenwald stood in the door, his gold toothpick rolling from side to side in his mouth as he leveled his Remington revolver on Kit while grinning nastily. "After yer gone I'll take real good care of her, don't you fret yerself none. See that she's got a real high payin' job." He laughed mirthlessly.

Joss growled low in his throat, braced on three legs. For an instant Gruenwald glanced at the dog and the gun wavered. Sammie let out a shriek as she heaved a satin pillow at him. He turned and fired hastily at the girl, but instead he hit the missile she had thrown. As the pillow exploded, sending feathers and dust flying in all directions, Kit jumped across the space separating them and knocked the gun away from Gruenwald.

Sammie did not interfere but turned her attention to freeing Abel. The two men rolled across the floor, then separated and came up, each with knife in hand. They circled one another warily, like two pit bulls, looking for an opening. Suddenly Gruenwald feinted high, then slid his blade wickedly near Kit's belly.

Kit blocked the attempt, then shoved the heavier man back as the hafts of their knives locked together.

Sammie pulled the last of the heavy hemp rope from Abel's legs and helped him stand.

"We gotta help Warfield." He tried to move but his legs buckled beneath him, numbed from the ropes.

"Don't interfere," she cautioned, holding him back while she watched the two men in their deadly ballet, terrified that any distraction could cost Kit his life. When Gruenwald scored a hit, his blade slicing wickedly across the captain's arm, she bit down on her knuckles to stifle a scream. Warfield quickly recovered.

By now both men were sweating and bleeding from superficial cuts. Kit glared contemptuously at the crimp. "Getting tired, Green Teeth? You seem to have lost your fancy toothpick, but no matter. Where you're going, it would only melt."

Kit tensed as the crimp's knife arced toward him, then feinted low as if to block the thrust with his knife. At the last instant he turned, graceful as a matador, and his knife found its mark. Gruenwald's face took on an oddly quizzical expression as he crumpled slowly to the floor with his life's blood running red onto the garish purple carpet.

"Oh, Kit." Sammie's voice broke in a sob as he turned to where she stood, frozen, with Gruenwald's gun in her hand. Trembling, she smiled crookedly at him. Her mouth wobbled as she said, "You see? I did follow instructions—oh, but what would I have done if he'd killed you—after I shot him, that is!" She dropped the gun and ran to him.

Kit swung her up in his arms. She embraced him, running her hands up his shoulders and framing his face. "You're all right. Thank God, you're all right!" Tears streamed down her face as she rained salty kisses all over his eyes, cheeks, nose, and mouth. Then she stopped abruptly and stared into his eyes.

"What happened to your patch?"

Before he could answer, the shrill of police whistles sounded over the cacophony of the brawl. Stub appeared in the door and Joss quickly trotted over to him, abandoning his inspection of the deceased Gruenwald, upon whose sprawled form there was not even so much as a snack.

"We better get outta here, Cap'n. Them cops er mostly in the crimps' pockets."

"By all means, Stub." He turned to Abel. "Can you walk, boy?" he asked as he scooped Sammie into his arms.

"Yessir," Abel replied.

They left Pearly's by the back door and vanished into the fog before the police ever stumbled across the mortal remains of Green Teeth Gruenwald, who was eventually buried without his gold toothpick. One of the constables had quickly appropriated it as evidence.

Pearly was left sitting on the floor of her parlor amid the wreckage. In her garish purple gown, she looked like a giant blob of grape jelly. Fat tears rolled down her cheeks, washing away the caked powder, leaving a sooty trail of kohl.

"My bordello. My beautiful, beautiful bordello. Gone. All gone," she hiccupped, oblivious to the departure of both combatants and police.

When they reached the *China Lucky*, Stub, somewhat battered and bruised from his encounter with Pearly, took Abel to the galley, where the cook tended the boy's rope burns. Always hoping for a handout, Joss tagged along.

Below deck in his cabin, Kit faced Sammie, with uncertainty written across his face. "You risked your life throwing that pillow at Gruenwald."

"He'd have shot you—or Joss," she replied, equally unsure of herself.

A smile tilted one side of his mouth. "And we certainly couldn't have Joss shot—he might have lost a front leg and had to hop like a kangaroo. Have you ever seen a kangaroo, Sammie?"

"N—no."

"Would you like to? That is, after we spend some time in the Sandwiches?" He watched the play of emotions move across her guileless face—doubt, hope. Perhaps fear? "You not only risked your own life, but your brother's as well, sending me that warning in the note." He reached out and touched a lock of wheat-colored hair, running it through his fingers like spun gold.

"Are you ..." She paused and cleared her throat for courage. "Are you asking me to stay with you— and Abel, too?"

"And Abel, too," he echoed gravely, still seeming to hesitate.

She dared to look up at him and meet his measuring gaze. "I ... I never meant what happened at the hotel to turn out like it did—but when you put it that way ... well, you were right. I would've been selling myself. Only I didn't see it that way when the idea came on me."

Her face reddened again, a trait he was beginning to find endearing. "Why not, Sammie?" His hand caressed her cheek, whisper soft, and his black eyes glowered.

"You don't leave a girl much pride," she said with a touch of pique in her voice. He hadn't declared himself to her, after all, but she told him anyway. "Because when I thought about you and Corey together at Pearly's—and how I reacted and all, well"—she knew her face was flaming—"I realized that I wanted to be with you—just for you, not because of where you lived."

He reeled her into his arms by gently tugging on the lock of hair in his hand, twining it around his fist until she was pressed flush against his chest. She did not resist. "Could it be that you love me, Sammie? I devoutly hope you do because you see, pet, I love you. I never knew how much until I thought of you in danger, a prisoner of Pearly and Gruenwald."

A joyous smile wreathed her face. "You know I do. I loved you from the first moment we met, I think. Maybe that's why I've done all those blame fool things. I'm not usually so accident prone. But Abel is," she felt compelled to add in all honesty.

"I'll take my chances," he replied, lowering his lips to meet hers in a soft, brushing kiss that grew deeper as she clung to him and opened to his invasion.

A sharp rapping on the door interrupted them, followed by Rollo's voice. "We brung the hot bathwater you wanted, Skipper."

Raising his eyebrows expressively, Kit released her and went to open the door, admitting Rollo and several sailors carrying buckets of steaming water, which they dumped into the enormous brass tub the boatswain set down in the center of the cabin. After they had done their work and departed, Kit raised his arm and gestured to the water.

"I feel rather in need of a bath. After all, a man can hardly get married all sweaty and smeared with blood, now can he? And you will marry me," he added offhandedly.

"Married?" she echoed incredulously. That he loved her and was keeping her with him was so much more than she had dared hope. Without thinking, she flung herself into his arms, toppling them both backward into the big tub with a resounding splash.

He lay in the water as her hair floated around his face and said wryly, "I take it that means yes."

She looked into his eyes, which danced with laughter. "Yes, it does." Her lashes fluttered down.

"Have you ever bathed a man before?" he asked, knowing full well she had not.

Her eyes flew open. "No! Will you show me how?" she asked shyly.

"My greatest pleasure," Kit whispered as he began unfastening the buttons of her dress, a plain gray muslin, courtesy of the mission ladies. "Remind me to take you shopping for a trousseau before we leave San Francisco," he murmured as he flicked her scuffed slippers off and pulled her feet into the tub. "Now, turn around and let me finish my task with the buttons while you pull off my boots."

His feet hung over the sides of the tub. She turned and knelt between his legs, then tugged at his foot gear. She could feel him peeling the soaked dress away from her back and then applying his mouth softly to her spine.

"I was a fool to refuse the first time you tried to undress me," she said dreamily, helping as he pulled the sleeves down and worked the whole sodden mess over her hips. Balling it up in his hands, he wrung it out, then tossed it onto the cabin floor where it landed with a loud splat.

Her underwear was old and much mended, what little she had. The worn white cotton turned translucent in the water. "I remember how you looked in that filmy old night rail. This is even better." His hands slid around her waist and cupped two small perfect breasts. When he teased the nipples they puckered into hard little nubs. She sucked in her breath with pleasure. He smiled, then began to pull away the clinging wet cotton.

Sammie turned to him and began to work his ruined shirt from his broad shoulders, lingering to let her fingers play with the crisp black hair on his chest. "The shirt's beyond redemption and, oh, you're hurt, Kit. This gash on your arm should be tended."

He dismissed it. "It's stopped bleeding and I can

scarce feel it. All the blood's rushed to another part of my anatomy."

She could feel the insistent probe of his erection pressing against her thigh and blushed once more as she tossed the shirt onto the growing pile of sopping clothes. When he climbed out of the tub to pull off his trousers, Sammie closed her eyes—but only for a moment. Then she opened them, unable to resist watching as he stripped. His lithe, muscled beauty robbed her of breath, and frightened her a bit when that rampantly male part of him was freed, hard and pulsing.

Kit watched her gold eyes grow enormous and intuited her natural fears. *I must go slow with her.* Giving her a blinding smile, he knelt by the edge of the tub and picked up the soap. "Turn around so I can wash your hair," he said in a low seductive voice. With that he began to work thick bubbling lather through the heavy golden mass, massaging her scalp with the pads of his fingers until he felt her relax and tilt back her head.

"Squeeze your eyes tightly closed so I can rinse," he commanded before dumping a pot of fresh warm water over her head. Then his hands moved lower, sudsing her back, shoulders, and arms. When he turned her and began to lather her breasts, she cried out in such amazed pleasure he all but lost control.

"See how they respond to my touch, pet," he said hoarsely as she arched into his caresses.

Her nipples were pebbly and hard. They ached yet perversely she wanted him to keep touching them, but he turned his attention lower, gliding his hands over her hips, down her thighs. Then he gently lifted one sleek little leg from the water by the slender ankle and began to massage her foot with suds. She felt her toes curl in delight. When he worked his hands up to the juncture of her thighs, Sammie felt an amazing lassitude swamp her senses. Instead of

being shocked by the intimacy, she felt frissons of
intense yearning sweep through her and had to sup-
press a small cry of frustration when he withdrew.

By the time he had rinsed her off and climbed in
beside her, Sammie's fears had been replaced by a
totally different kind of tension. She watched as he
settled himself comfortably in the water, facing her
as she knelt between his legs. Her eyes were dilated
with passion as he handed her the soap, that dazzling
smile melting her bones.

"Now, it's your turn to wash me, pet."

She took the soap and reached up to shampoo his
head of thick black hair. As she worked, he put his
hands about her tiny waist and pulled her closer.
Then his mouth found her breast and opened hotly
over it, letting his tongue tease a pebbly nipple until
she dropped the soap and had to search the water
for it.

"Keep that up and I'll never get you bathed," she
whispered in a choked voice. But when he stopped,
she turned, thrusting her other breast against his
cheek until he continued.

Her hands glided over those splendid bronzed
shoulders and down his arms, then moved to his
chest. With his eyes closed, she had the advantage
of studying him freely. "Your skin is almost golden
where the sun has touched it," she said, letting her
fingertips trace the wonders of biceps and pectoral
muscles. But when she reached the place where his
chest hair narrowed into an arrowlike vee leading
beneath the water, she stopped and blushed. "I've
washed as far as ... that is ..."

He chuckled. "Just let your hands glide below the
water. Aren't you the least bit curious about what a
man feels like, hmm, Sammie?" He knew her blush
would deepen and spread in pink patches over her
breasts.

It did. But when her hands took up his dare, she

was not alone in breathless discovery. One small silky hand slipped across the ridged muscles of his belly and touched his straining sex. He gasped and shuddered.

"Did . . . did I hurt you?"

He chuckled low and wrapped his hand around hers, guiding it back to where it had been—"No, pet. You did exactly what I wanted you to do."

Kit showed her the motion, then released her hand and she warmed to playing with her new toy. Sammie watched his eyes grow unfocused and heavy-lidded with passion as he lay back, completely in her power. She decided she definitely was going to like this man-woman thing.

When he could stand no more, Kit restrained her gently, saying, "Best finish washing me before I muck up the bath water, pet." She looked innocently puzzled, and then when comprehension struck, so flushed with embarrassment that he was enchanted.

Sammie finished washing him and reached for the last remaining pot of rinse water with trembling hands.

"Watch you don't brain me with that," he warned, only half teasing as she raised it over his head and sluiced him clean.

Kit shook the excess droplets of water from his eyes and stood in the tub, then reached down and pulled Sammie up against him. The slick glide of wet flesh on flesh was irresistible. He took her lips in a devouring kiss. Sammie raised herself on tiptoe, stretching her arms around his neck.

His mouth slanted over hers and she opened for the now familiar invasion of his tongue, even daring to let hers dance inside his mouth to brush, taste, tease.

"The water's getting cold," he said against her mouth as he swept her into his arms and stepped dripping from the tub. Letting her slide slowly down the length of his body until her feet touched the floor, he reached over and picked up several towels, then wrapped her in one and began to rub her hair dry with another.

"I'm dry enough," she said breathlessly. "Once more it's my turn." She slid the towel slowly from her body, letting it rasp along her sensitized skin, then held it up and began to rub him with it as he moved them slowly across the floor in the direction of his bed.

When her knees brushed against the edge of the mattress, he took the towel from her and tossed it away, then lowered her onto the covers and lay down beside her. Feeling her tense, he caressed her cheek with his fingertips. "Don't be afraid, Sammie. I'm going to make it good for you."

"But what if I can't—I don't know how . . ." She thought of Corey and all the other voluptuous, experienced women he had lain with and felt woefully inadequate.

"Shh, don't fret. I'll teach you. You've already made marvelous progress in the water," he added with a low seductive chuckle.

Emboldened, Sammie came into his embrace and he rolled onto his back, laying her on top of him. "Kiss me," he commanded and she curtained his face with the gold of her hair and complied. His hands glided up and down her back, over the curve of her buttocks and down her thighs. He lifted her up above him and suckled her breasts until she cried out with the pleasure. Her nails dug into his shoulders, holding fast as he rolled them over again, placing her beneath him. His hand moved around the curve of her breast, past the indentation of her waist and over her silky flat belly until it came to rest on the mound of gold curls at the juncture of her thighs.

Involuntarily her hips arched as he cupped the mound and his fingers moved lower, sliding between

the wet velvety petals. Kit could feel her trembling
and knew she was ready. He slid one knee between
her legs and parted them, then used his hand to tease
and stroke the delicate little bud of her passion until
she cried out.

"Now," he whispered as he guided his aching staff
to the portal of paradise and probed gently.

"Oh, yes, please." Sammie's voice was low and
thick as she raised up, eager, hungry for his caress.
This was what she had been waiting for. Her body
understood even though her mind did not yet comprehend. She only knew she craved more of him.

Gritting his teeth to keep in control, Kit slowly
entered her. God, she was so tight and hot, sweet
and wet. Then he felt the delicate barrier and paused.
"Only be still a moment, pet. I don't want to hurt
you any more than—"

Sammie couldn't obey. Her body craved more. She
wanted to feel him buried deep within her. Her hips
arched and it was done, a small sharp twinge, followed by the sensation of being stretched, filled,
bonded with her love so incredibly that she never
wanted the sweetness to end.

"Have I hurt you?" he asked in a ragged voice.

"No." She shook her head, holding him tightly,
unable to stop her hips from moving.

Kit waited, struggling not to spill his seed before
he had brought her along with him. But he could
little more resist the compulsion to move than could
she. "Oh, Sammie, my love, what you do to me," he
whispered against her ear as he began to stroke, slow
and deep.

Sammie quickly caught the rhythm, following him
on the wild sweet ride. With every breathless caress
she thought nothing could be better, and with each
succeeding caress he proved her wrong. Several
times he stopped and held her hips immobile for a

moment, as if regaining some inner control while she was wantonly needy, restless and hungry to resume.

Kit attuned himself to her body, waiting for the signs that indicated she was nearing the abyss, holding himself back until he felt her stiffen and shudder. The tight contractions radiating from deep within her sent him spiraling over the edge.

She could feel it begin, so low and yet so powerful, like a brilliant ray of sunlight melting wax. The glorious spasms spread out from deep within her until she thought she'd shake to pieces. But Kit held her fast in his arms, his whole big body trembling just as hers did. And at last she understood what she had hungered for, sought, and found.

They lay together for several moments, satiated and silent. Then he rolled away from her and pulled her to his side. She fit perfectly against him and he smiled.

Her hand rested lightly on his chest, tracing the cunning patterns of hair, then glided up to touch the contours of his face. Suddenly she stopped and bounced upright in bed. He turned his head curiously and looked up at her.

"You're not blind in your right eye," she accused.

He caressed her impudently tilted pink-tipped breasts with two good eyes and grinned. "I never said I was."

"But Stub said you'd lost your eye in a battle—with pirates."

He laughed. "Stub is a born yarn-spinner, I'm afraid. Did he also tell you that he was a Texas Ranger who had to amputate his own arm after a gunfight? And that Joss lost his leg saving a sailor from sharks?"

She considered the romantic and improbable tales, a smile tugging at the corners of her mouth. "Yes, although I have to confess the story about you was the most believable."

Kit chuckled. "I had an infection in my eye and the doctor recommended I wear the patch to protect it from wind and sun for a month or so, until it healed."

"And Stub and Joss?"

"Stub, as nearly as I can piece the story together, got drunk in Galveston and passed out in the gutter. A beer wagon rolled over his arm. The surgeon had to have two men hold him down before he could even chloroform him to perform surgery."

"Poor Stub. His version does sound better," she said with a chuckle.

"As to that rascally Joss, it seems he'd been caught stealing a chicken by a Chinese cook who was good with a cleaver." Kit shrugged. "The captain of the ship he had served on was a whaler who carved scrimshaw. He made the dress leg."

"Well, if they weren't heroes before, they certainly are after rescuing Abel and me." She leaned down beside him and whispered, "I haven't thanked you for that—or for letting my brother come with us."

"Oh, I can think of a way for you to thank me," he murmured, pulling her back into his embrace.

# *Epilogue*

They were married in an old Episcopal church on Powell Street late the following afternoon with Abel and Stub as witnesses, along with several dozen hushed sailors who had not seen the inside of a church in decades. Having decided to sail on the morning tide, Kit and Sammie had an intimate wedding dinner aboard the *China Lucky* that evening.

"Aren't you pleased we hired Gerrard?" she asked, looking at the magnificent feast set before them.

"He's certainly an improvement over our old cook. Rico's willing to tolerate him in the galley as long as he debarks in Honolulu with us." Kit eyed the roast capon and mound of fluffy whipped potatoes appreciatively. "After years of eating out of garbage heaps, fine food has really become a passion of mine . . . but not the most important one," he added devilishly.

Sammie studied him in the flickering candlelight. "Stub said you were the son of an English lord and a Chinese lady." How little she really knew about her new husband.

"For once he told the truth, or what he knew of it anyway. My mother was Eurasian but I doubt society would call her a lady." His eyes were sad as he explained. "She was sold to my father by her family in Hong Kong, to be his mistress. He treated her well enough, I suppose. Even paid to have tutors for me."

His expression hardened as he continued. "She died when I was twelve. After that I became an en-

163

cumbrance he no longer wanted. The tutors vanished. So did my beautiful home. I ended up in the streets, on my own. Much as you and Abel did, I imagine," he said softly. "That was one of the first things that struck a kindred spark when Stub brought you aboard."

"You've come a long way—from the slums of Hong Kong to being master of this beautiful ship and owner of a sugar plantation," Sammie said proudly.

"I vowed one day I'd be rich, even when I spent those wretched years starving in back alleys." He shrugged. "It took a lifetime of struggle and hard work, and a bit of luck along the way, but I finally realized my dreams—or at least part of them. They were never complete without you."

"You've made my dreams come true, too, Kit. And the most wonderful thing of all is that I don't care where we live—I'd even follow you to Massachusetts."

He grinned. "Now that is a fulsome compliment indeed, coming from you."

They sat down to the sumptuous feast Gerrard had prepared. Kit carved the roast capon while Sammie dished up the elegant pureed vegetables and crusty sourdough bread. Watching Sammie struggle to be dainty cutting her joint of capon with knife and fork, Kit smiled and picked up his own piece. "Just pull it apart with your hands, like this." He demonstrated.

Sammie blushed. "And here I thought you wanted me to be a lady." She picked up her capon and followed his example. The leg joint immediately popped apart, sending the spicy juice flying across the table—straight into Kit's face.

With an amazed oath his hand flew to his left eye, which began to burn like fire. Blinking his good eye at his wife, he said balefully, "I suppose it's a bloody good thing I didn't throw away the patch."

At her look of red-faced horror, Kit began to

chuckle, then to laugh. "Don't fret, love. If the old cliché is true that in the land of the blind the one-eyed man is king, then marriage to you will doubtless prepare me to become emperor!"

# Old Love
# and
# Lilac Lace

by

Becky Lee Weyrich

# Chapter One

A ragged, faded photograph of a tall man on the hotel veranda, an 1892 menu offering twelve courses from the Jekyl Island Club, and a vintage gown of beaded lilac lace were the only items Lydia Aynsley Winslow had to offer the curator of the newly established millionaires' museum on Georgia's coastal isle.

Her invitation had arrived two months ago. It read:

You are cordially invited
to spend a glorious weekend
March 13-15, 1992
at the
JEKYLL ISLAND CLUB HOTEL
to commemorate with other descendants of the members
the 106th Anniversary of the Club
and to attend ground-breaking ceremonies for the new
MILLIONAIRES' MUSEUM

In discreetly small print at the very bottom, the invited guests were asked for either tax-deductible cash donations toward the museum's upkeep or items that had belonged to their ancestors to be added to the collection.

Unlike her wealthy ancestors, Lydia found ready cash in short supply these days. Gran's final illness and her months'-long hospital stay, had forced Lydia to put the old hilltop house in North Conway, New Hampshire, on the market to pay all the bills. It was the only way. Taxes alone on the place were eating her alive. For several years now, the tourist trade had been off, and her great-grandmother's home hadn't nearly paid its way as a bed and breakfast. She had begged and borrowed to keep the place so that Gran wouldn't have to go to a nursing home. But now Lydia had only herself to consider. Maybe when she went to Jekyll for the reunion she'd stay there for good. Surely, with her years of experience in pleasing customers, she could get a job at the hotel. There was certainly nothing left for her here.

As for the small print on her invitation, Lydia had decided to donate the three things that had been so much a part of her life and had fired her imagination all these years. She hated to give them up—especially the photo of her Prince Charming—but at least the precious antiques would be well cared for and preserved in the permanent collection on Jekyll.

Lydia's midnight blue eyes sparkled with excitement and her heart beat a bit faster when she stared down at the sepia tones of the old photograph. She hadn't seen the picture in years. She'd had no time for dreaming since those long ago afternoons "playing Jekyl" in the attic. Gazing now at the man she and Gran had called Prince Charming, the memory of one particular "dinner party" came back to her as vividly as if she were staring at a reflection of the past in a mirror. She'd been a starry-eyed girl of twelve then, on the very brink of everything, or so it had seemed.

"That was almost fifteen years ago," Lydia said with wonder in her voice. "Seems like only yesterday."

Lydia stared at the old photo thoughtfully. Had she really seen what she thought she saw that long ago afternoon? Or had it simply been a trick of her own imagination?

*       *       *

Buttery sun melted through the stained glass in the dormer window, making the crystal beads on the antique lace gown shimmer like tiny rainbows. Lydia Aynsley Winslow—her honey gold hair pinned atop her head and her deep blue eyes shining—turned this way and that, posing between a pair of cracked mirrors that had long ago been banished to the attic. She marveled as the reflection of her great-grandmother's fancy dress duplicated itself into infinity.

When she held her breath and listened very closely, it seemed she could almost hear the visual echo: "Lilac lace ... lilac lace ... lilac lace ..."

The attic was Lydia's favorite place in the old mansion in North Conway. And playing Jekyl was her favorite game.

Lydia knew that Jekyll Island, Georgia, was a real place; she had even found it on a map. But to her it seemed as much a fantasy location as the Land of Oz. Stories about her fascinating and mysterious ancestor, Lydia Bennington Aynsley—for whom she was named and who had spent one glorious season on Jekyl back before the second *l* was added— seemed every bit as enchanting as tales of the wizard's Emerald City. She loved to dress up in her great-grandmother's things and pretend that she was far away on that remote island with its wild beach, its elegant hotel, and its atmosphere of romance. More than anything, Lydia had always wished she could travel back through time and actually *be* on Jekyl ... truly *be* that other fascinating Lydia.

Carefully holding up the hem of the lilac lace gown, Lydia placed two of her dolls at a small pine table with its miniature china dishes set for four.

"There," she said. "Please make yourselves comfortable, Mrs. Rockefeller, Mrs. Morgan. I'm sure Prince Charming will join us soon. He's always prompt, you know." Then, cupping her small hand to her mouth, she whispered, "Excellent breeding never fails to show."

Lydia left her glass-eyed ladies for a moment and returned to her great-grandmother's steamer trunk. After a brief search she found the other items required for a perfect pretend-dinner party—a Jekyl Island Club menu, dated March 13, 1892, and an old, torn photograph with the initials P.C. written in fading ink on the back. The tall young man in the picture was dressed all in white with a straw boater perched at a rakish angle on his head. Although his face was in shadow, the gleam of his dark eyes was obvious as was his come-hither grin. He seemed to be flirting with someone just out of the picture. There was absolutely no doubt in Lydia's mind that the object of his rapt attention was the lovely Lydia Bee, as her great-grandmother had always been called.

Torn photo in hand, Lydia returned to the table. "Ah, ladies, I hope we haven't kept you waiting overlong." She dramatized each word and spoke in what she assumed might have been the highly cultured tone of the exceedingly rich, exceedingly wellbred Lydia Bennington Aynsley. "My darling prince was detained by Mr. Gould and Mr. Vanderbilt, both of whom desperately needed his advice on certain important financial matters. Besides being handsome and charming, he's ever so clever with money, you see."

Lydia seated herself grandly, with a flourish of beaded lace. She set the old sepia-toned picture on the fourth chair. Once Prince Charming was in place beside her, she gave him an adoring glance. Gran always claimed that Lydia Bee had been in love with this man, so of course Lydia was, too. She wasn't exactly sure what loving a man was all about, but she guessed it had to be something wonderful that could make a girl, by turns, marvelously happy or

terribly sad. According to Gran, it had made Lydia
Bee perfectly miserable.

Gazing at the haunting picture, Lydia couldn't believe that any man with such a winning smile could
ever make a girl unhappy. When Lydia had ques-
tioned Gran on the subject, she'd said she truly didn't
know what had happened. "The way I heard it told,
one minute they were in love, and the next minute
my mama married my papa, and that was that. But
she kept the picture of her Prince Charming, so I
think that in her heart of hearts she must have loved
him secretly all her life. But she was a lady and he,
I'm certain, was a gentleman, so they never saw each
other again after she left Jekyl."

Another odd thing, Lydia mused thoughtfully, was
that no one knew his name or where he'd been from
or what ever happened to him.

Lydia sighed and reached over to touch his image.
"I would so like to know you better, sir. Someday
maybe I'll find out all about you. I'm sure you won't
make *me* 'perfectly miserable.' "

For a few moments, Lydia pretended to be a
waiter, pouring invisible wine into tiny goblets and
handing around imaginary menus while Lydia herself clutched the only real one.

"Why don't I order for all of us?" she suggested.
"Let me see. I believe we'll begin with the Club specialty, cream of lettuce soup, followed by sweet-
breads with spinach."

When Lydia was younger, she had hated spinach.
But that was before she found the old menu. Once
she saw that it had been served at the Jekyl Island
Club, spinach became one of her favorite foods—not
only during these attic make-believe sessions, but
downstairs at the real dinner table as well.

"Have we an *r* in this month?" She glanced about,
pretending that her stay on the island had been such
a whirlwind of excitement that she couldn't keep

track of the day, much less the month. "Ah, yes! It's March now, isn't it? In that case, we'll have oysters on the half shell, followed by ..." She broke off and glanced up at the imaginary waiter. "What game do you have fresh from the hunting party today?" She waited a moment, then responded to the silence. "Wonderful! We'll all have wild boar with sweet potatoes *au sucre*, fresh garden peas, and whole bananas, fried. And for dessert, champagne with our *meringue glacée*." (Lydia had no idea what *meringue glacée* was, but she imagined that it must be as delicious to eat as it was to say, and she felt certain that Lydia Bee had adored it.)

The light in the attic turned from bright butter to old amber as the pretend-meal progressed. Lydia laughed often and gaily at the witty remarks from Mrs. Morgan and Mrs. Rockefeller, but her gaze went time and time again to her Prince Charming. She could tell by the wicked-sweet gleam in his eyes that he wished they were alone, that there were things he wanted to tell her. Important, private things!

She leaned toward him and shielded her words with her hand as she whispered, "I'll meet you later, down by the big oak that hangs over the river."

He smiled back at her and she thought she saw him wink.

The foursome were just finishing their imaginary cherry brandy and their make-believe bonbons when a voice from the real world interrupted their charming dinner.

"Lydia? Are you still up there?" Gran called. "Supper's ready."

Lydia rolled her eyes. *When* would Gran learn that the evening meal was *dinner*? How could Lydia Bennington Aynsley's own daughter make such a dreadful mistake?

"Coming, Gran," Lydia answered.

She left Mrs. Morgan and Mrs. Rockefeller to finish

their dessert wine, but gently lifted Prince Charming from his chair. For safekeeping, he would have to go back into the steamer trunk with the menu and the lilac lace gown.

Holding the photograph against her faintly budding breasts, Lydia paused between the two dressing room mirrors for one last glance at herself. She held up the picture so that it, too, was reflected without end.

"Oh, how I wish you were real," she said with a sigh. "There are so many things I want to ask you— so many things I'd like to tell you."

Just then, she glanced back at the mirror. She caught her breath and goosebumps pimpled her flesh. There staring back at her, from far off in the distance, was a tall man in a straw boater. He seemed to be beckoning to her. He was there and then he was gone. But in that instant, Lydia saw the gleam of his dark eyes. It was as obvious as his come-hither grin.

"Lydia? Don't make me have to climb those stairs to get you down here."

There was no need for Gran's warning. Lydia was out of the gown and out of the attic, flying downstairs in jig-time. She wasn't sure what she felt about seeing the man; she'd have to think it through carefully. But she knew if she had seen him, she'd just seen a ghost.

During supper that night, Lydia made a decision. She had played Jekyl in the attic for the very last time. But somehow she knew that would not be the last time she'd see her Prince Charming. She had wished for it too long and too hard. And as Gran was fond of telling her, "Be careful what you wish for, child. You just might get it."

Still gazing fixedly at the old photo, Lydia realized that her curiosity was as keen now as it had been when she was twelve. Who was that dark-haired man with the brooding eyes? And what had happened between him and her great-grandmother? What had gone wrong that had caused Lydia Bee's father to whisk her away from the island and back to New England before the end of the January through March season of 1892? And if Lydia Bee had truly loved that handsome stranger, why had she married another man less than three months later?

She brushed back a lock of honey-colored hair impatiently. After all these years, she was still wishing she knew more about the two of them. But all the answers to her questions were lost in the dim mists of family history. Maybe, at last—now that she was actually going to Jekyll Island—she'd have her chance to unlock the mystery that had haunted her all her life.

Carefully, she packed the gown, then zipped and locked her bag. It was time to leave for the adventure she'd always dreamed of.

# Chapter Two

As the crow or the jet flies, Jekyl Island, Georgia, is a long way from North Conway, New Hampshire. To Lydia the distance seemed measured in time as well as miles. One hundred years ago, her great-grandmother, Lydia Bennington Aynsley, had traveled a similar route to spend her single shining season on the island, then a millionaires' playground. Now, a century later, Lydia Bee's namesake was returning to the site of her illustrious ancestor's former glory.

Lydia stared through the subtly tinted windows of the limousine, which had been waiting for her at the Jacksonville airport, courtesy of the hotel. Mesmerized, she watched the green-gold marshes wind away in the distance. It seemed, too, that she was feeling the years, decades, and generations roll back. The thought that she would soon arrive at the old Jekyll Island Club to walk the same halls her great-grandmother and Prince Charming had walked, gaze at the same centuries-old oaks, wander the same beach of powdery white sand was a dream Lydia had held dear since she was a little girl, playing dress-up in the attic and listening to Gran tell her about that long ago, golden age. Lydia could almost hear Gran's voice now as her mind wandered down old paths.

"Ah, that season of '92 was a triumph for Lydia Bee. She was the belle of the island that year, with all the fine young lads trying to catch her eye. *One in particular*. That was before the crash, you know. Her father was still rich then—rich as a king. He put your Morgans and your Rockefellers to shame. As for Lydia Bee, her papa made sure her every wish was granted." Then Gran's voice would drop to a whisper as she added, "It's a crying shame he couldn't make her dreams come true as well."

Lydia missed Gran so much. For years the two of them had presided over tea for the guests in the sunny front parlor of Lydia Bee's grand old house. And every afternoon the talk would turn to tales of those old, golden days. Their visitors had loved hearing Gran's stories of how, even after the financial panic of '93 when the great fortune once possessed by the Aynsley clan had been lost, the family had continued to cling to old rituals and their palatial Victorian mansion in North Conway.

When Lydia thought about the sales contract she had signed before leaving New Hampshire, relief mingled with regret. She would miss that house almost as much as she missed Gran.

Lydia's thoughts left the past and returned instantly to Jekyll Island as the last bridge across the causeway from the mainland came into view ahead. A lone brown pelican swooped silently over Jekyll Creek. The water in the river was low, exposing mud flats and oyster beds along the verge of the marsh. To the left of the bridge, a marina and dock jutted out into the river. In the old days Lydia knew that fine yachts had tied up there—J. P. Morgan's *Corsair*, William Kissam Vanderbilt's *Alva*, and, of course, the Aynsleys' *Snowbird*. But now she saw only a tired-looking shrimpboat with its nets up, drying after a long day's haul.

Just beyond the bridge lay the island like a sparkling, green jewel in the late afternoon sun. Lydia felt her excitement soar as her chauffeur turned off the main road onto a curving, moss-draped drive. Azaleas blazed scarlet, coral, and fuschia everywhere she looked. Even through the lush stands of oak, palm, and oleander, Lydia could see the turret atop the old Queen Anne–style hotel. She felt suddenly as if she were returning home after a long exile. But how could that be when she'd never set foot on Jekyll Island before?

Along the narrow road, bordered on the left by the river, they passed several of the millionaires' shingle-style "cottages," some with sparkling facades, others still undergoing the restoration process. She knew from Gran's tales that the wealthy financiers who had built these places considered them no more than rough hunting lodges. But Lydia also knew from Gran's stories that they were truly grand houses, with many bedrooms, indoor plumbing, crystal chandeliers, walk-in safes, yet no kitchen facilities. A century ago, everyone had taken their meals in the posh dining room at the Club.

Lydia Bee and her Prince Charming among them, she mused silently, wondering what it would be like to dress every night for a twelve-course dinner, to have servants at your beck and call, to spend your days in games, conversation, and the pursuit of romance. And to have a handsome suitor who was more than willing to provide that delicious romance.

The limousine rolled to a smooth stop under the hotel's porte-cochere. Lydia stepped from the car in a happy daze. She breathed deeply, drawing in the island's unique perfume of tangy salt air, honey-suckle, and freshly mown grass—a far more exotic blend than the pine green scent of New Hampshire.

An eager young bellman descended upon her to carry her one bag. "Welcome back to Jekyll, ma'am."

Lydia stared at him, puzzled by his greeting. "This is my first visit here," she replied.

He frowned slightly. "You look mighty familiar. I

thought for sure you'd been a guest at the hotel before." Then he grinned. "No matter! You'll love it, I promise, ma'am. My name's Raymond and I'll see you to your room after you check in."

He led the way through the old billiard room to the registration desk. But Lydia lagged behind, craning her neck at the circular turret, peering through the rippled glass of the tall windows that opened from various parlors onto the wide veranda, and glancing curiously at the fanciful architecture of the place—square bays, round porches, nooks and crannies everywhere. And all of it painted in soft pastels to blend with the gentle shades of the marsh and water and sand.

She was so entranced with the hotel itself that she never noticed the man standing in the shadows of the veranda, staring at her with a mixture of pleasure and disbelief on his angular face. He was dressed all in white, with his straw boater cocked at a rakish angle. And the gleam of his dark eyes was as obvious as his come-hither grin.

"Welcome back," he said.

But Lydia heard nothing.

Paxton Carmichael had been waiting a long time for this moment. He'd always wondered what happened to her after she left, although he knew why she went away. Her leaving, of course, had been the cause of his accident, and the reason he'd come back and stayed for so long, waiting.

"What else could I do?" It was a question he had asked himself often through the years. He never bothered to answer it. He knew.

He'd never blamed her for going. How could he? He'd known from the outset that his chances were slim. She had to go back. And her father had been there to make sure that she did.

"That damned, cantankerous old fool!" Pax muttered. But deep down, he knew that fathers were like that back then—were expected to be. It was part of every father's job—support the family, provide a proper home, keep the good name unsullied. And make damn sure the children do the same.

He'd seen her that morning she left. He had tried calling out to her, but, of course, by then it had been too late. He knew her father had forced her to go. He guessed that before boarding the *Snowbird* she must have turned and glanced back at the hotel—directly up at his window, wondering if he might be there. But he wasn't. He'd left long before dawn to keep their secret rendezvous. She didn't know that; she never would.

In his mind's eye, he could see her face as plainly today as he had so long ago on that fateful morning. She was crying as she stood at the railing. Her sapphire eyes glittered with tears. Her gorgeous halo of honey-gold hair looked limp and dull as if her maid hadn't been allowed time to brush it before she was hustled away early to avoid the gossipy breakfast crowd at the Club. She had looked so sad, so young and helpless and lost.

He'd been lost, too, that morning. Lost without her. Lost forevermore, he'd thought.

He should never have allowed things to go so far. If he'd been half the man she thought he was, Pax reminded himself, he'd have demanded her father's permission to marry her. A showdown on the dock at dawn would hardly have been the gentlemanly thing to do, but he would have preferred being branded a cad to enduring the pain of going on without her, of seeing her wed to another man.

"Yes, Carmichael, you should have confronted her father," he muttered. "But you never got around to it, did you?" He tipped his hat down lower over his eyes, as if he felt the need to hide from the world, needless as that gesture was now. "There's no fool like a young fool. You blew it, old chap!"

He wondered suddenly if she'd remember which room was his. He'd kept the same one all these years, hoping against all hope that she might return to the island someday. She had come back once for a brief stay. She came with her husband and child during the season of '99. She'd looked much older, then, and the merry glint had vanished from her once brilliant, night-sky eyes. He'd wanted to talk to her, to let her know that nothing had changed, that there was no need for her to look so desolate. But with all the others there—the Rockefellers, the Morgans, the Cornings, the Pulitzers, the Vanderbilts, the Lorillards—he'd never found his chance for a moment alone with her.

"Did she even realize I was still here?"

He'd watched her from a distance those two weeks she was back at the Club. Just seeing her had provided some solace at the time. But, oh, how empty his days had seemed when she went away again! Even emptier than before because he knew she was unhappy and there wasn't a blasted thing he could do.

He'd watched her husband, too. The man was older than she by three decades and he wore a permanently joyless expression. How could anyone married to her be unhappy? he'd wondered then, and still wondered now. It was not surprising, given the man's surly temperament and dour countenance, that he was never offered full membership by the fun-loving Jekyl group. Instead, they were considered "strangers" by the in-crowd and allowed to remain on the island no longer than a fortnight—Club policy.

It was hard for Paxton to think of her as a stranger. She had been so much a part of everything in the old days. All the fun, all the excitement, all the romance of the place back in '92 had seemed to center around her—around his Lydia Bee.

He left the shadowed alcove of the veranda and sauntered toward the old billiard room. She should be registered by now. He had no intention of letting the others monopolize her this time. He meant to make his presence known as soon as possible. He had things to say to her, things that he'd been storing up for years and years. He had the unsettling feeling that this would be his last chance to set things right between them—his last chance ever to bring their two worlds together and unite their souls with the love that refused to die.

Lydia kept glancing over her shoulder as she walked toward the reception desk. She had the oddest feeling that someone was watching her, sizing her up from all angles. The sensation wasn't unpleasant, however. Far from it. She felt the warmth of approval and affection flowing into her. Yet when she looked around, no one in the throng of hotel guests seemed to be paying the slightest attention to her arrival. She shrugged off the odd feeling and turned a smile on the receptionist.

"Hello. I'm Lydia Winslow, here for the reunion."

"Ms. Winslow?" The perky blond desk clerk scanned her computer screen. "Ah, here you are. You'll be in the room once occupied by Lydia Bennington Aynsley."

"She was my great-grandmother." Lydia sensed a sudden need to authenticate her ancestry to the young woman. Now that she was finally here after so long dreaming about coming, she felt a bit out of place. The other guests were all expensively dressed, the women dripping with diamonds—even those who were wearing shorts—while Lydia had arrived in the one decent suit she owned, a charcoal twill she'd bought for her college graduation several years ago.

The clerk, identified by her brass name badge as Elsie from Atlanta, smiled brightly at Lydia, seeming to sense her apprehension. She leaned closer over the counter and whispered, "I've been hearing stories about Miss Lydia Bee from some of the other reunion guests. It seems she broke quite a few hearts while she was on Jekyl."

"Really?" Lydia answered, smiling back, pleased at the thought. "I hadn't realized that her notoriety would precede her. I can't wait to talk to the others and hear all their tales about her."

"You'll meet them all at dinner tonight, Ms. Winslow. Here's your key and a schedule of events. I hope you enjoy your stay."

"Thank you, Elsie. I'm sure I will."

Lydia gazed down at the heavy brass key in her hand. It sent a little shiver along her spine to realize that she'd be sleeping in the same room that Lydia Bee had once occupied.

Raymond from Jesup, her bellman, showed her out onto a sunny veranda overlooking a fountain and an interior courtyard. Lydia scanned the faces of the dozen or so guests seated at tables, searching for someone familiar. Then she smiled at her own foolishness. How in the world would she recognize any of these people? Her heart gave a little flutter when she spied a man in white, wearing a straw boater. She was certain she'd seen him somewhere before. She blinked, looked again, and he was gone. But that warm, appreciated feeling was back, coursing through her stronger than ever.

*You've got some wild imagination, Lydia Winslow!* she observed silently.

A minute later, her guide led her back into the hotel, to a cool, shadowed room where a mounted boar's head stared glassily down from above the massive terra-cotta fireplace.

"Back in the millionaires' days, this was the main entrance to the Club," Raymond explained. "It was decorated all in olive green and rust red, with black velvet drapes and dark wood paneling. The Club's superintendent, Mr. Ernest Grob, used to meet arriving guests at his desk in front of the fireplace and have them sign in."

Subtle light streamed in through a stained glass window over the entrance. For a moment, Lydia imagined she could almost hear the distant whispers of long ago greetings and feel the movement of the air as guests, arriving from their yachts, opened and closed the huge front door.

"Would you like to take the elevator, ma'am, or use the stairway?"

The young man's voice snapped Lydia back to the present. She glanced toward the wide staircase with its hand-turned railing of dark, polished wood. She could imagine properly-corseted Victorian ladies gliding down those stairs to the dining room. It was the perfect setting.

"I suppose my great-grandmother would have taken the stairs." She smiled at her companion.

"Yes, ma'am, I reckon she wouldn't have had much choice. But those really aren't the stairs she'd have used. You see, when the State of Georgia bought Jekyll back in 1947, they tore out the old staircase to put in the elevators."

Lydia gasped audibly at the thought of such wanton destruction of history.

"And that wasn't the half of what they did," Raymond continued. "You should have seen this place after they got finished with it. I guess they must have had a warehouse up in Atlanta full of white paint they wanted to get rid of. They slapped that stuff on every surface in this hotel." He turned and pointed down a long hallway that ran off the entry. "That's the hall of mirrors down there. All the frames used to be gold. The restoration folks were able to strip the white paint back down to the original dark woodwork you see now, but there was nothing they could do to return those mirror frames to their original look—too much fancy work on them."

"That's terrible!" Lydia exclaimed.

"It's still a mighty pretty sight. The mirrors are set so you just see yourself on and on and on when you stand in that hallway."

Lydia's old mirrors in the attic came to mind. She remembered how she'd loved that illusion of infinity. "I'll be sure to go down and have a look later."

"The staircase?" he asked, getting back to his original question. "This one's an exact copy of the original—next best thing," he assured her.

It still wasn't the same, Lydia told herself, but the hotel was almost the same and the very room where her great-grandmother had slept awaited her on the second floor.

"The stairs!" she answered emphatically.

They were halfway up when Lydia felt a blast of icy air. "My word!" she exclaimed. "The air-conditioning certainly works. I hope there's a blanket in my room."

"The air-conditioning hasn't been turned on yet, ma'am. We've been having a lot of cool days lately and nights that are downright cold."

"But I just felt it," Lydia insisted. "It chilled me to the bone."

The bellman's freckled face crinkled into a grin. "That was probably just our resident ghost. Don't worry, though, ma'am. He's friendly enough. He just gets his kicks from giving folks the shivers now and again. He spooked me a time or two when I first came to work here. He's been pretty quiet the past few months, but I figured this reunion would stir him up."

"Why do you say that?" Lydia asked.

They were outside Lydia's room now. The air in the wide corridor felt close and warm. Not a hint of the chill from moments before lingered.

"Because my guess is that the ghost has been here ever since the days of the millionaires. I think he was one of them."

"Really?" Lydia was intrigued.

"Yes, ma'am, I believe it." He gave his carrot-colored head a firm nod as he opened her door and set her bag on the luggage rack. "I think I may even know who he was—the guy folks say died right here on Jekyll and is buried down the road in the old du Bignon cemetery."

"Oh, tell me about him!"

"He's in a lot of the old photos around the hotel. Good-looking guy. I'm pretty sure it's him because . . ."

"Hey, Raymond!" Another young bellman stuck his head in the door. "Elsie needs you downstairs, soon as you finish up here. There's a busload checking in."

"Right with you!" Raymond answered.

Lydia quickly fished in her purse for a tip so that he could be on his way. "When you have time later, I'd love to hear more about this ghost."

Raymond glanced down at the bill Lydia had pressed into his palm and grinned. "You bet, Ms. Winslow! It'll be my pleasure. Anything you want, now, you just ring the desk and I'll see right to it."

The massive door closed slowly after Raymond. A moment before it clicked shut, Lydia felt another rush of cold air. The room was freezing suddenly. She clutched her arms and shivered.

"I don't care what Raymond said, I'm sure the air-conditioning is on."

She glanced longingly toward the tall double win-

dows that faced the river with its warm breezes.
"They won't open," she said with a sigh. "In hotels
they never do."

But to her delight a moment later, she felt the window glide up easily with only the slightest effort on
her part. There were no screens. The warm, perfumed air of Jekyll Island flowed unfiltered into her
room, banishing the chill.

"That's better!"

She stood at the open window, gazing out over
the sparkling pool and manicured lawn toward the
dock and the river. The whole scene before her shim-
mered in golden light as if she were viewing it
through the old amber-colored glass in the attic back
home. She closed her eyes, trying to grasp the reality
that she was finally on Jekyll Island, and that long
ago Lydia Bee must have stood at this very same
spot, staring out at that oak tree hanging low over
the road near the river's edge.

"Oh, how I wish I could see what she saw and
feel what she felt that season of 1892!"

"Your wish is my command, dear lady," a husky
voice whispered in the room.

All Lydia heard was the sigh of the wind in the
oaks and the rustle of the chintz drapes at the window. But she felt something—she wasn't sure what.

At first she thought Raymond had come back. She
felt a presence very near. It was the same feeling
she'd had downstairs earlier. Then something touched
her shoulder. She turned quickly, but found herself
alone.

"I'm just tired from the trip. And Raymond's talk
about the ghost has me jumpy. I'll be fine once I've
had a shower and changed."

As she unpacked—taking special care with the old
lilac lace gown—Lydia surveyed her room. Surely,
the flower-papered walls were recently redone. She
wondered what they had looked like a century be-

fore. Framed photographs of Club members on the wall drew her immediate attention. Both delight and a sense of déjà vu came over her when she spotted Lydia Bee in a group of young ladies at the beach. Of course, she had seen pictures of her great-grandmother before, but this one could have been Lydia herself. She'd never before noticed such a marked resemblance, especially around the eyes and mouth.

While she stood gazing at the old photos, her lips began to tingle suddenly and the room seemed to swim around her in a blaze of light and color. Gripping the carved bedpost, she closed her eyes and sighed. She felt warm and protected suddenly— wonderfully loved.

The dizziness soon passed, but the feeling of exquisite pleasure remained. She realized she felt almost as if she'd just been kissed. She ran the tip of her tongue over her lips. Moments before, her mouth had been so dry. Now her lips felt moist and soft.

"It's the humidity down here," she reasoned. "I'm wet and sticky all over. Time for a long soak and some lighter clothes."

She headed for the bathroom to turn on the shower, but the phone rang before she could get there.

"Ms. Winslow? This is Elsie at the desk."

"Yes, Elsie?"

"I hate to bother you while you're getting settled in, but I've had a request I thought I'd better check out with you. One of the other guests—a Mr. P. Carmichael—left a message at the desk, asking to be seated at your table this evening for dinner. Is that all right with you, ma'am?"

Lydia thought for a moment, combing her memory, trying to place the name, but she couldn't. "Did he say he knew me?"

"No, ma'am. As I said, I didn't speak with him,

he just left a note. I assume he's one of the reunion guests, but he's not listed as having registered yet. He's probably on one of the tours and will sign in later. It struck me as odd, though. He wrote his message on an old piece of Jekyl Island Club stationery. The paper was all yellowed and brittle and had the Club's crest on it. I can't imagine where he got it. Anyway, he goes on to say that his great-grandfather knew your great-grandmother and he'd like to talk to you about the two of them."

Lydia caught her breath. Her heart raced. What luck! This was better than she'd ever dreamed. She wouldn't have to search out the dark-eyed stranger's kin. One of them had come to her.

"Oh, please do seat us together. I'm eager to hear what he has to say."

"Fine, Ms. Winslow. Dinner's at eight and I'll put you both at table 13."

"I'll be there ..." Lydia hung up the phone, then added, "With bells on!"

The sudden blast of chilly, musty air through the room seemed colder than usual to Lydia, but she was too excited to ponder its source. Shedding her clothes as she went, she hurried into the bathroom to shower, then dress for dinner.

A shadowy form, dressed all in white, perched on her bed, smiling.

"And so it begins ... again!"

# Chapter Three

"Can't be too careful on Friday the 13th, especially when you're dining at table 13," Lydia reminded herself.

She clung to the banister, taking each step cautiously as she headed down to dinner. She had decided to wear Lydia Bee's lilac lace gown one last time before she donated it to the museum, but she didn't want to damage it before it was time to turn it over.

A smile trembled on her lips as she made her way toward the dining room. She was as nervous and as excited about this evening as she had ever been in her whole life. Feeling the antique lace, snug about her bosom and brushing the tops of her feet as she walked, made her believe—*almost*—that by some trick of fate she really had become Lydia Bee. Or at least that she had somehow slipped back into her great-grandmother's time.

"How I wish I could," she murmured to herself. "If only for a day, an hour, an instant."

Just to see Jekyll as it had been back before the turn of the century would fulfill Lydia's fondest dreams. Gazing at the old photographs around the hotel had only heightened her desire to go back to that earlier, more carefree time. And, too, there was a certain gentleman in a straw boater she was dying to meet.

"What a lovely gown!" the hostess exclaimed the

minute Lydia walked through the arched entrance to the pink, white, and gold dining room.

Lydia smiled at the bright-eyed woman. "Thank you. It belonged to my great-grandmother."

The hostess gave a soft cry of recognition. "Well, of course! I knew I'd seen it somewhere before. We have an old photograph of Lydia Bee wearing that very dress." She pointed toward the fireplace at the left of the entrance. "Go see for yourself. The resemblance is amazing. And she was standing there by the hearth when the picture was taken."

Lydia hurried over to have a look. The hostess was right—she did look like Lydia Bee. Why, she'd even done her long hair up in a similar fashion tonight—softly upswept into a pouf atop her head. But her eyes lingered only momentarily on her ancestor. The man beside her in the sepia-toned print captured her attention almost immediately. They were smiling at each other, and it was clear that the look in their eyes held something far deeper than friendship.

"They made a handsome couple, don't you think?"

Lydia jumped when a man spoke from directly over her shoulder. She hadn't heard him walk up behind her. She turned, meaning to say that indeed they looked more than handsome, they looked as if they were in love. But the words froze on her lips when she saw his face. Dark hair and eyes—both almost black. A face not really handsome, but far more than simply appealing. There was something in his looks, in his eyes, that told of laughter and tears, great joy and great sadness beyond his years. Around thirty, she guessed. She also saw wisdom and cunning in his face, but a tenderness that spoke volumes on the stranger's gentle soul.

"But you're not a stranger." Lydia hardly realized she'd spoken the words aloud.

He gripped her hand in the warm strength of his and said, "Allow me to introduce myself, Lydia. I am Paxton Carmichael. My friends call me Pax, the same as my great-grandfather's friends called him." He nodded toward the man beside Lydia Bee in the old photo. "May I show you to our table?"

Lydia's thoughts were in a whirl. P. C.—Prince Charming, Paxton Carmichael. Why hadn't she made the connection when Elsie had called about these dinner arrangements? Could it be that she was truly in the company of a descendant of Lydia Bee's lover? She suddenly wondered how her companion would look in a straw boater.

Not until they were walking through the columned dining room and all heads turned to stare, did Lydia realize that she and Paxton had both dressed as their ancestors. His formal black tails and white tie perfectly complemented her century-old lilac lace gown. Once again, had it not been for the electric wall sconces and chandeliers and the pink, blue, and white packets in the silver sugars on the tables, she could have believed that she had somehow drifted back through time.

To Lydia's delight, table 13 was set only for two. She did want to meet all the others, but tonight she was eager to talk with Paxton Carmichael about their ancestors' shared time on Jekyl. Other conversation would simply have bored and distracted her. Once they were seated, however, Lydia found she hardly knew where to begin. She had so many questions for him.

He took the responsibility from her shoulders, going straight to the heart of things. "I suppose you know that Pax Carmichael was deeply in love with Lydia Bee."

"I knew she fell in love while she was here, but I never knew the man's name. There's a picture of him, though, that she kept with her always. I brought it with me."

He frowned slightly, but still he was wonderful to

look at. "A picture of Paxton? Alone? I can't imagine that. He hated having his photograph made. He consented only when Lydia Bee begged him to pose with her."

Lydia confirmed his suspicions immediately. "I think Lydia Bee was in this picture, too. It's torn, you see. I've always suspected that she ripped it herself, to keep someone—maybe her husband—from knowing she had posed with the man in the straw boater."

He smiled broadly, then threw back his head and chuckled. "Oh, *that* picture! Ah, I should have guessed. She was in it all right. They had been to the beach. Lydia Bee had worn the most scandalous bathing costume. Scandalous for that day, at any rate. A storm came up as they were driving alone in his buggy back to the Club House. They stopped for a time in a thick stand of pines, hoping the rain and wind would pass on. The others at the party had headed back earlier when the skies began to threaten. But Lydia Bee was enjoying the rough surf and didn't want to leave. Only young people were in the group that day, otherwise, she and Pax would never have been left alone. It would have been unseemly for that day and age. At any rate, they used Lydia Bee's cloak to make a rain shelter." He paused and smiled at Lydia, the single candle on their table reflecting in his heavy-lidded, jet eyes. "Quite a cozy arrangement, I'd say, being caught together in a storm, away from all the others."

"Quite!" Lydia murmured, feeling herself blush. For no reason she could think of, she felt suddenly embarrassed by what he was telling her.

"If I had a beautiful woman, whom I was wildly in love with, under those circumstances I'm sure I would take as much advantage as I dared. I imagine my great-grandfather was not above stealing a few kisses from his lady-love."

"If your great-grandfather was half as charming

as you, I doubt my great-grandmother could have resisted."

He laughed softly. "Well put, dear lady. And may I thank you on behalf of the men of Clan Carmichael. At any rate, the photograph on the veranda was taken immediately upon their return. Her bathing cloak, lost or discarded somewhere in the woods, her costume wet, wrinkled, in disarray, and her cheeks still all aflame from whatever happened between them in the woods, I don't imagine Lydia Bee was exactly overjoyed to have the Club photographer snapping away like some modern day paparazzo."

Lydia laughed at the thought of poor Lydia Bee caught in a such a fix. "No wonder she tore the photo." She glanced up at Pax through lowered lashes. "But she kept his picture."

"Why not? I've always thought it a devilish good likeness. And the way he's looking at her. Any fool can see he's just handed her his heart on a silver platter." His smiled faded and a bleak look passed over his face for an instant. "It's a shame he couldn't have offered it on a platter of gold. Then her father might have allowed her to accept it."

The genuine sadness in his voice touched Lydia's heart. She felt almost as if she were sitting here talking to the first Paxton Carmichael, hearing *his* pain, sensing *his* loss.

"How do you know so much about them?" she asked. "My grandmother, Lydia Bee's own daughter, never told me any of this."

"That's not surprising. Lydia Bee married someone else shortly after her father took her away from Jekyl. She would hardly have passed tales down through her family about her last fling before settling down. Husbands don't usually take kindly to that sort of talk, so I'm told."

"You aren't married, then?"

He glanced down at his hands—bare of rings—and shook his head. "No, I'm not."

Lydia thought she heard regret in his voice. "Why not?"

As soon as she'd asked the question, Lydia realized she was being pushy, if not downright rude. Paxton Carmichael was a virtual stranger, and his reasons for remaining single were certainly none of her business. Besides, she wasn't married either. But then she'd had Gran to look after when most women her age were dating, marrying, and starting families.

"You don't have to answer that," she said quickly. "I didn't mean to pry. I'm sorry."

"You have nothing to apologize for, Lydia. Your question shows your interest, nothing more. It's nice to have someone as lovely as you exhibit friendly curiosity. It's been a long time since anyone cared enough to ask." Without explaining what he meant by that, he answered her question. "I would have married once. I would have given my very soul to marry. But she belonged to someone else. There was nothing I could do. Even if I had tried, I'd never have found another woman who could come close to her. I've never given anyone else a second look— until now."

He gazed intensely at Lydia, the meaning of his words so nakedly obvious that she felt herself blush.

Only when she looked away did he continue. "I always felt it would have been unfair of me to make promises to any other woman while my heart still belonged to her."

His eyes took on a hard glitter—the look of a man whose very soul aches to shed tears, but who knows both time and place are inappropriate. His voice turned quiet and husky, as if his thoughts were drifting, allowing him to think aloud. "You see, she was more than my love. She was part of me—the part that mattered. When she went away, she took my heart, my soul, my true identity. I was never the same man without her. Since then, I've simply drifted in my own uncharted seas with no moon or stars to guide me."

He gazed into Lydia's eyes again, his face solemn. "Does that make any sense to you?"

The tears that he couldn't shed, Lydia felt gathering in her own eyes. "Oh, yes. I understand," she whispered.

And she did understand. But how was that possible?

The spell was broken as they ordered dinner. Over cream of lettuce soup, shrimp and avocado salad, and an aged steak so tender it melted like butter at the touch of her knife, Pax held Lydia spellbound with stories of the island—horse races on the beach, shooting expeditions to try to rid the island of the pair of wild boar that had been a gift to one of the members, lawn croquette, garden parties, masquerade balls, and the first transcontinental telephone call, linking Jekyl, San Francisco, Washington, and New York City. He talked so much that he hardly touched his lobster. Not until she had finished her dessert and coffee did he return the conversation to Paxton Carmichael and Lydia Bee.

"You know, you're very like her," he said without preamble, knowing that there was no need to identify the party to Lydia.

Lydia smiled, pleased. "My grandmother always said I was pure Aynsley, even as an infant. That's why Gran insisted that my parents name me after her."

He nodded. "Your name was well chosen. But I don't mean that you simply look like Lydia Bee. You've inherited far more from her. I've always heard that in some families certain strong-willed ancestors are duplicated in equally strong descendants. It's only a theory, but I tend to believe it. I suppose it could be considered a form of reincarnation. Or perhaps it has something to do with memory genes. But, Lydia, take my word for it, you *are* your great-grandmother."

"Why, thank you! That's a wonderful compliment."

"It's not meant as flattery. It's the truth. And I think you knew it before I told you."

"I'm not sure I follow you, Pax."

The man was talking spooky now, and Lydia really didn't want to hear it. She was Lydia Aynsley Winslow, born to Peter and Janice Forrest Winslow in 1967, far removed from Lydia Bennington Aynsley, who had been born in 1867. Whatever traits of Lydia Bee's she possessed were heavily diluted by the intervening generations and other bloodlines.

"If you'll excuse me for a moment, I think I'll go powder my nose."

When Lydia rose, Pax did, too. He gripped her arm, refusing to let her leave. There was something almost frightening in his manner. He seemed so desperate.

"Don't go!"

"I'll be right back."

"You don't understand. I know I've upset you. I'm sorry. I didn't mean to drive you away. God, no! Not that!"

Lydia tried to laugh off his words, but he was really beginning to sound a little unbalanced. All the stuff he'd told her about Lydia Bee—there was no way he could know any of that for sure. No family passed down stories like that. You just don't tell your kids that their grandparents spent time groping around in pine thickets in thunderstorms.

"Please, Pax, you must excuse me. I'll be right back. I won't leave."

When she said those last three words, his face went ashen.

"What's wrong? Are you ill?"

He sank down into his chair as if he couldn't support himself. "That's what *she* said. Her exact words."

"Who? Who are you talking about? Do you mean Lydia Bee?"

When he refused to answer her, Lydia turned and hurried toward the archway that led out of the dining room. At the desk she stopped and whispered to the hostess, "I think you'd better go over and check on Mr. Carmichael. He's not feeling well. I hate to leave him right now, but I *must* dash to the powder room."

"It's that way," the hostess pointed. "I'll send your waiter over to check on Mr. Carmichael."

"Thank you."

Lydia glanced back over her shoulder toward table 13. Pax was staring at her, his face pale and his hand clutching his chest.

"Oh, dear God! He may be really ill."

She started to go back to the table, but then she saw their waiter, John, heading toward Pax. Assured that he would be all right for the short time it took her for a much-needed pit stop, Lydia hurried on toward the ladies' room.

It took her longer than she'd expected. Half the women in the dining room must have gotten the same urge at the same time. Lydia quickly freshened her makeup while she waited her turn. All the while, she kept thinking about Paxton's reaction to her leaving the table. Why, you would think they were lovers and she'd just given him the brush-off.

A buxom blonde dressed all in black and diamonds stood beside Lydia at the marble sinks, reapplying electric pink lipstick. She kept eyeing Lydia in the mirror before she finally spoke.

"Hi! I'm Macy Aspinwall-Carter," she said in a deeply southern drawl. "You're here for the reunion, too, aren't you?"

"Yes. Lydia Winslow." She felt too worried and rushed for polite conversation with a stranger.

"That guy you're with sure is some looker."

"Thanks." Lydia could think of no other reply.

"He's not with the group, is he?"

With her thoughts and emotions in such turmoil, Lydia could barely concentrate on the woman's questions. "Excuse me?"

"I didn't know we could bring dates—you know, strangers."

"He's not a stranger. He's Mr. Paxton Carmichael."

"Really?" the blonde said, pursing her lips. "Where's he from?"

Lydia was surprised and embarrassed that she didn't know.

"Well, it looks like we've got a gate-crasher in our midst. There's no Carmichael on the reunion list, and I should know. I helped organize this shindig."

Lydia frowned. "I'm sure you must be mistaken. I think Elsie at the front desk said he'd registered late."

"Look, honey, I don't know what this guy's trying to pull, but you can take my word for it—he's *not* with our group. You just watch him close until I can get the manager. I think we'd better find out what he's up to. Lord, he could be a cat burglar or who knows what!"

The blonde swished her black satin tush out the ladies' room door, leaving Lydia more unnerved than she'd been before. Quickly, she took care of business, then hurried back to the dining room.

The hostess met her, looking perplexed. "I'm sorry, Ms. Winslow, but Mr. Carmichael left. By the time John got to the table, he was gone. Since you seemed so concerned, I called the desk to have them send someone up to check on him." She paused, chewing at her bottom lip nervously. "Ms. Winslow, he's not registered here."

"Are you sure?" Lydia didn't know what to think.

But this bit of unexpected news, coupled with the accusation from the blonde in black upset her beyond all reason.

Seeing Lydia's distress, the hostess suggested, "You might call around to the motels on the beach. Maybe he just preferred to stay at one of them so he'd have a view of the ocean."

"Thank you," Lydia answered. "I think I'll go to my room now."

She left the dining room, but instead of turning up the stairs, she walked straight ahead to the hall of mirrors. No one else was around. She strolled slowly down the wide passageway, glancing this way and that at her never-ending reflections in glass. Not until she reached the very end, the twin mirrors closest to the veranda doors, did she catch sight of the dark figure far back in the mirror.

The hallway turned cold suddenly. She stared hard at the wavy, silver glass, knowing what she saw, but not believing her eyes.

"Pax?" she said. "Where are you?"

She shivered in the ice-cold corridor, and from somewhere far off she heard a voice whisper. "Don't go. Don't leave me again, Lydia."

She whirled about and flew down the hallway and up the stairs. Once she was safely inside her room, she locked and chained the door. After she'd given herself time to calm down, she reasoned that her mind was playing tricks on her.

"Too much champagne with dinner," she scolded gently.

There had to be a reasonable explanation for all this and she meant to find it. Taking the phone book from the desk drawer, she determined to call every lodging place on the island. There weren't that many. She would locate Paxton Carmichael, all right. And once she did, she meant to find out just exactly what he was up to.

# Chapter Four

His escape was a narrow one. A moment longer and his "glow" would have died right under John the waiter's rather beakish nose and before everyone else's startled gazes. As it was, Pax had managed a hasty retreat to the little round parlor just off the dining room in the nick of time. Used only for after-dinner drinks and coffee, the room had still been deserted, while diners lingered over their multiple-course meals. The hostess, whom Lydia had paused to speak to on her way out, was distracted. So no one saw him rise and make a fast exit—an even faster exit once he was safely out of the dining room. Anyone popping into the tiny parlor moments after Pax would have found only a chilly gust in the unoccupied room.

Now he felt alone and empty—trapped within his own nothingness.

"It was grand being back," he whispered to no one, to nothing. The sound of his voice echoed hollowly in the unearthly grayish mist that followed him onto the veranda. When he looked back inside through the windows, he could see them all, hear them laughing and talking. But he could no longer be a part of the scene, so their gaiety made no impression on him. It was the same with the soft night breeze. He knew it was blowing. He could hear the rattle of the palm fronds and see the Spanish moss swaying gently. But he could neither feel the cool wind on his face nor taste its salt tang. It was simply a colorless, odorless illusion somewhere out there beyond his own realm. Without Lydia by his side, he was disconnected from the real world she inhabited.

Moments before, he had had substance. He had been able to feel Lydia's warmth, share her private space almost as if they were on equal footing. But if he dared venture to her chamber now, she would know only the chill that his presence brought. She would shiver, then open a window or put on a warm robe.

Even in that exquisite moment in her room when he had kissed her and his soul had warmed at the sweet, hot taste of her mouth, she had experienced only the dizziness brought by the nearness of his haunted spirit.

"Oh, God!" he raged silently at the black empty sky. (The beauty of the moon and stars were reserved only for the living as well.) "How can I stand having her here, but untouchable on the other side? I was promised limbo. Have I waited all these years only to find out that it's all some twisted, demonic joke—that I've really abided in hell all this time?"

The last silent words out of Paxton's mouth were wails of grief and pain. "Lydia! Come to me! Let me *be* again, my love!"

Lydia replaced the receiver and closed the slender phone book. She stared off at nothing, her mind blank when she tried to think where to turn next.

"Paxton Carmichael is simply not on Jekyll Island." She said the words aloud, trying to grasp the fact. "What if he's gone for good? What if I never see him again?"

At that moment, Lydia realized the impact the man had made.

"Why, you'd think I was falling in love with him!" The thought brought a smile to her lips. She'd never really been in love, except for a crush in high school, then one brief fling during college. It wasn't that she didn't want to love someone and be loved in return. Oh, no! She'd always dreamed of that; she'd had her Prince Charming, after all. But she'd never had time for real love.

It seemed that most of her life she'd been too much in charge. Her father had died shortly after she was born. She and her mother and grandmother had all been forced to keep their shoulders to the wheel to make ends meet. Her mother had died in a car accident while Lydia was in college, and by then Gran was old and infirm. Still living at home, she'd taught kindergarten one year before she realized that her teacher's salary alone would never pay the bills. Back then, she couldn't bear the thought of selling the old house since it had been Gran's home all her life. So she'd come up with the idea of turning it into a bed and breakfast. Her plan had worked and they'd gotten along until Gran took so ill. Even then, Lydia had managed—managed to keep her grandmother at home and managed to pay most of the medical bills.

Lydia sat back and thought about those hard times. She should be pleased that she'd kept things going for so many years and be proud of herself for doing it. She shook her head sadly.

"I don't want to feel proud. I want to feel loved."

Lydia ran her hand over her tired eyes and uttered a sigh. She looked at herself in the vanity mirror. She had thought she looked so gorgeous in the old gown before she went down to dinner. Now she felt too weary to be impressed. The lilac lace suddenly looked like exactly what it was—an old, outdated frock that was slightly too tight since she didn't have Lydia Bee's eighteen-inch waist. Actually, she thought, she looked like a silly child, playing dress-up in the attic.

"Someone else's attic now," she murmured, remembering the signed sales contract. The thought depressed her. But she refused to allow herself the comfort of tears.

"You did all right, girl," she assured herself. "You managed against some pretty tough odds." Then with another long sigh, she leaned forward and rested her head on her crossed arms. "But why couldn't there have been just a little time for something more—a little time for love? Would that have been too much to ask?"

She glanced up at the old photograph of Lydia Bee—young, laughing, happy, and carefree as a long summer afternoon. "You don't know what I'd give to have a man love me the way Paxton Carmichael loved you. Maybe you couldn't be together all your lives, but at least you had each other that one season. Your memories alone should have kept you happy to your dying day."

Feeling ridiculous that she was sitting alone in her hotel room, scolding a photograph of her long-dead ancestor, Lydia switched off the vanity lamp, plunging the room into darkness.

She meant to go straight to bed. She was beyond exhaustion. But the minute the light faded, she heard a voice. Not a voice from downstairs, but a voice right in the room with her, answering her challenge.

"Well, my girl, I should think that someone longing for love would go about the pursuit with a good deal more verve. Don't slump so! Sit up straight, but never dare let your spine touch the back of your chair. Posture and carriage go a long way in this world. Remember that! Teach it to your daughters."

The voice stopped in midlecture as if gathering force for a second assault.

"I don't have any daughters," Lydia fired back, glancing wildly about the dark room to locate the woman. "Where are you? *Who* are you?"

"Who, indeed? You were talking to me only a moment ago, and now you must ask my identity? Where are your wits, girl?"

Lydia looked into the dark mirror before her. Only it wasn't dark any longer. She saw her own reflection there by eerie light from some unknown source. She brushed a wisp of hair back from her eyes. Her image, however, made no move to copy the gesture. The reflection remained perfectly still, staring back at Lydia with reproof in her midnight blue eyes.

"Well, you've met him at last. What do you think?"

"I think I'm either dreaming or going crazy," Lydia moaned.

"Must you think only of yourself all the time? You are neither crazy nor dreaming. You are here for a purpose, just as I am. So far, you have bungled things royally, dashing off the way you did this evening. But why should I expect anything more of you? I did the same bad job of this myself. It looks as if we Aynsley women would learn with time."

Lydia squinted at the mirror. "Great-grandmother?"

"Well, whom were you expecting? The Queen of England, perhaps?"

"Elizabeth?"

"No, silly goose! Have you no schooling? I mean Victoria. Queen Bess died long ago, but that's neither here nor there. Tell me what you think of *him*."

"If you mean your lover's great-grandson, I find him handsome, charming, mysterious, and a touch on the strange side." When the woman in the mirror opened her mouth to speak, Lydia held up her hand to silence her reflection. "Oh, and one more thing," she added frankly. "I find him sexy as hell!"

"Oh!" the image shrieked. "Naughty child! Go wash your mouth out with lye soap immediately!" Then she seemed to lean closer toward the mirror's inner surface as she whispered, "And after you've removed the filth from your tongue, return at once and tell me what you find sexy about him." She twittered behind her elegant lace fan.

That struck Lydia as rather peculiar since she herself had no fan. So how could her mirror-image have one? However, she wasn't given much time to ponder the question.

"Such a delightfully wicked word, *sexy*," Lydia Bee reflected. "I'd never have dared use it, even if I knew it." She cocked her lovely head. "Dear me, I can't seem to recall if it was ever in my vocabulary. You must tell me how he is sexy."

Lydia felt far less foolish than she should have, carrying on a conversation with her mirror. In fact, she was rather enjoying it, she realized.

"Let's see . . . what do I find sexy about him? He's elegant, old-world, and I like the fit of his trousers and the way the dark hair curls on the backs of his hands. It's hard to explain. He's just . . . well, Pax is just *sexy*!"

"*Pax?*" Lydia Bee interrupted. "You mean you knew who he was all along? My dear, you're far cleverer than I gave you credit for. I assumed you took him for Pax's great-grandson."

"Well, that's who he is, isn't he?" Lydia paused, waiting for a response that was not forthcoming. "I mean, that's who he told me he was. You're simply confused because you live in that mirror. They're both Paxton Carmichael. Aren't they?"

Lydia Bee's laughter trilled in the silence. "Oh, he was always so fond of a good jest. You mean he had you fooled right along? Dear, oh dear, oh dear! This is rich!" She sniggered, she chuckled, then she laughed out loud. "I'm sorry, my child. I really am not laughing at your expense. It's just that I'm so happy to find that he hasn't changed. So often it seems death takes all the fun out of most people."

*"Death?"* Lydia jumped up from the vanity stool and moved quickly away from the mirror.

"You didn't know that Paxton Carmichael is dead? But, my dear, how could he be otherwise? Why, he was even older than I am, and that's rather more candles than I would wish to see burning on a birthday cake."

Lydia closed her eyes, squeezing them so tightly shut that it hurt. She crossed her arms and gripped her shoulders with her hands. She would think this vision away. It wasn't really here anyway. She was only imagining this whole thing. If she had a tape recorder running in the room, the only voice it would record would be her own—a one-way conversation that made no sense at all.

"You're right, of course." The other woman's voice refused to leave her be. "I don't think any of your newfangled contrivances would be able to hear my voice. It's possible, mind you, but not likely."

Lydia eased her eyes open and breathed a sigh of resignation. "You can read minds. Right?"

"Oh, goodness, no! At least, not just anyone's mind. But you see, Lydia, our minds are the same. So much of me remains within you that since your birth I've hardly felt as if I passed over. All those lovely afternoons at tea with Mrs. Morgan and Mrs. Rockefeller and my dear Pax—Prince Charming as you styled him. And my favorite gown. Do you have any idea the pleasure it gives a spirit to don such a creation once clothes are no longer a part of one's ethereal experience? You made my old spirit right jolly at times. Certainly, you were more fun than my husband, dead or alive."

"Then why did you marry him?" Lydia meant to get to the bottom of all this. If she couldn't get one ghost to tell her, she'd ask the other.

"You wouldn't understand."

"Try me!"

"It's simply something beyond your realm. Young women in your day do as they please and make their own lives. They marry or remain old maids—'single women,' I believe you prefer to say—according to their own wishes. Such was not the case in my day. When Pax and I fell in love, we knew it could never be. My father's partner had asked for my hand and received Papa's blessing long before I was old enough to understand about love. I would never have known what love meant, if Pax hadn't come to the Club that season."

"That's outrageous! Why didn't you simply tell your father that you were in love? You could have refused to marry the man he'd picked out. What could he have done—*dragged* you to the altar?"

"Believe me, dear, exactly that happened to more than one of my friends. Take my word for it, Pax and I tried everything—more than we should have. That's why I was forced to marry so soon after we left Jekyl."

"You mean ...?"

Lydia Bee cut her off. "Don't ask! Ladies don't discuss such things."

A brief silence followed her words. Lydia was trying hard to digest everything she'd heard when suddenly Lydia Bee said, "My glow is fading. I must tell you quickly why I've come to you."

"Well, I'd really like to know."

"Please, don't interrupt. I haven't much time left. I want you to do something for me, for Pax, and for yourself. He will come to you again. Watch for him in the hall of mirrors. When he appears, he will ask certain things of you—things he's been wishing for desperately all these years. Please, my dear—for my sake and for the sake of love—do whatever he asks. I promise you, you'll never be sorry."

Her image was wavering now in the glass. Her words were choppy as if they were coming from a great distance, through a poorly adjusted radio receiver. Finally, only a faint wail echoed in the dark room. "It will be a dream come true ... a dream come true ... a dreammmmm ..."

For a long time after the sound faded, Lydia sat motionless, staring into the silent darkness. She felt drugged, zombielike. Slowly, she raised her hand to the lamp switch. There was a loud click, then the room flooded with light. She shielded her eyes for a moment. When she looked into the mirror again, she was staring at her own image.

"Did I only imagine that Lydia Bee was here?"

Just then she moved her hand and something fell from the table to the carpeted floor. Lydia reached down to retrieve the object. Her fingers grasped starched lace and carved ivory.

"Her fan," Lydia whispered. "She *was* here!"

When she spread the fan, it released a faint fragrance. She sniffed the delicate lace.

"Lilac—Lydia Bee's favorite scent, Gran always said."

Outside the open window, the wind rose, tossing the clattering palm fronds. Thunder rumbled in the distance, and flashes of lightning turned the black river eerie silver. Rain began to fall—first in solitary, fat drops, then in slanting sheets—but Lydia never noticed the storm. Her own storm was internal.

Weary to her very soul, she climbed into bed, still clutching the fan, still hearing the echo of Lydia Bee's words.

She could close her eyes, but she could not close out her thoughts. When would Paxton Carmichael come to her again? What would he ask of her? And would she have the courage and the strength to grant his wishes?

It was long after midnight and the storm outside had passed when Lydia came suddenly awake.

"It's time," she murmured, rising from the bed.

Quickly, she dressed again in the old lace gown. Every move she made now was deliberate. She knew where she must go. And she knew that when she got there he would be waiting.

# Chapter Five

Lydia hurried along the dim corridors, trying not to make a sound. The whole world seemed to be sleeping. She should have been nervous, moving about the old, phantom-infested hotel at such a lonely hour. But her purpose drove her steadily onward—toward the hall of mirrors, toward the man she knew would be waiting there. If ever there was a time for ghosts to be about, this was it. And there was one ghost she longed to have haunt her again.

Only the whisper of lace and the beat of her heart intruded in the quiet night. As Lydia made her way to the staircase, she could almost feel Paxton's presence urging her on. The glass eyes of the wild boar glared down at her as she hurried through the hotel lobby. A moment later, she reached the hall of mirrors. The lights were low here, too, casting a soft peach-gold glow over everything. She walked quickly toward the veranda door at the far end, where earlier she had seen his reflection.

She paused when she reached that spot, apprehensive suddenly. What if he wasn't there? What if all of this was only a bizarre trick of her imagination? She closed her eyes tightly, fearing the sight of her solitary image in the mirror.

"Please," she begged quietly. "Let him be there."

When she opened her eyes, she saw only her own reflection—on and on into infinity—lilac lace, the gleam of glass beads, and the disappointment on her face. Then, as she turned to leave, she caught a flicker of movement out of the corner of her eye. She faced back to have another look.

"There he is!" she cried softly. "Just over my left shoulder."

A dark pinpoint far back in the distance became the tiny image of a man. As she watched, smiling now, he came into focus. He was gesturing to her, motioning her back the way she'd come.

Lydia moved swiftly to the next set of mirrors. Pax was there. She could see him plainly now. He was smiling at her, motioning again. She understood. Quickly, she walked back up the length of the hall-way. Each time she looked into a new mirror, Pax was larger, more lifelike. At the very last one, she stopped.

"You've come back," he said, his voice husky and unsteady with emotion. "I'd so hoped you would."

He was life-sized now. He seemed to be standing right beside her. Yet only his reflection was there. She stood all alone in the silent corridor.

"Lydia Bee told me I should come."

"She still loves me, then?"

"Was there ever any doubt of that? You meant everything to her. You always have. Why didn't you tell me at dinner who you really were?"

"Would you have believed me?"

"I don't know." Lydia hesitated, trying to think, but too moved by the sight of him to collect her thoughts clearly. It seemed suddenly that Paxton Carmichael—real or ghost—was all she had ever dreamed of. He was indeed her Prince Charming.

Forgetting that he was only a flat, one-dimensional image in the glass, Lydia reached out as if she meant to take his hand. Her fingers struck the smooth sur-face. She uttered a soft cry of surprise. He seemed that real to her. Then suddenly the mirror melted at her touch. His cool hand gripped hers.

"Will you come to me?" he asked.

Lydia couldn't find her voice to answer. She stared down at her arm. Her hand had disappeared into the mirror, into Paxton's phantom image.

"Is such a thing possible?" she murmured.

"Love makes all dreams possible."

"That's what Lydia Bee told me—that this could be a dream come true."

"Your dream. Yes," he whispered, "and mine as well if you'll grant my wish."

Lydia looked up. She was staring directly into his wonderfully warm eyes. He looked different somehow. He seemed younger, exactly the age he had been in the old torn photograph. The sadness she'd noticed earlier had vanished completely. When he gazed at her now, she saw a man filled with the wonder of love and hope for the future.

"You've changed," she said.

"You loved me this way. And I think you could love me again—almost as much as I love you. If that's so, then all the pain of your leaving is gone. We're both the same again. We've wiped away all the sad times. We've been given a second chance."

"How can that be? Everything has changed. I'm not the woman you loved, Pax."

He smiled at her gently. "You still don't understand, Lydia? You can be the woman I love. All you have to do is wish it so and come to me. I've waited so long for you. This may be the only chance we have left."

Lydia felt so strange. Odd memories—not her own—were stirring in her mind. She recalled the soft urgency of his kisses, but he had never kissed her. Had he? She remembered the wonderful thrill of his hand touching her breast. When had he caressed her in such a loving way? Suddenly, she went weak all over and a tremor coursed through her body. She closed her eyes, recalling the delicious wonder of his sensitive, powerful body. He was indeed a magnificent lover. Yet how could she possibly know that?

"Please, Lydia!" His voice was like a silken thread, drawing her heart to his. "Come to me. I'll show you wondrous sights. Come to me now, my darling."

Lydia was still standing in the hallway, but she could feel him kissing her fingertips, letting the tip of his tongue caress the tender center of her palm. Then his hand was on her arm, tugging gently, drawing her inch-by-inch through the mirror and into his shadowy realm. All the while, his pleading voice tugged with equal force at her heart.

He drew her ever closer to the mirror, until her body was pressed to the cool, smooth glass. Her breasts melted through to the other side. She closed her eyes and pressed her cheek to the silver surface. A moment later, she tensed, surprised when she first felt him caress her. But soon her shock gave way to pure pleasure and she sighed as he stroked the old lace of her bodice.

How gentle he was! How knowing!

"Come kiss me, love," he begged.

Lydia turned her face to the mirror. She felt the cold glass, then a rush of cool air, and finally the warmth of his lips pressing hers. She held her breath, sure that she must be dreaming, not wanting the dream to end. His mouth captured hers with a fierce hunger born of pent-up longing. She parted her lips and he accepted her invitation, setting her heart thundering when he fondled her tongue with his.

She knew his kiss. She knew the taste of him, the feel of him. They were not strangers at all. She had known this man for lifetimes.

"Come, darling," he whispered between kisses. "Come all the way to me."

Lydia took one more step and suddenly she was in his wonderful, strong arms. He held her against his hard, lean body, moaning her name between light kisses that he feathered over her cheeks.

She was barely conscious of anything other than the thrill and the pleasure of his embrace. Yet she knew they were in some dark, chilly place where mists swirled about them and the silence was absolute. It seemed to her that he had miraculously managed to blank out the rest of the world in order to make a hideaway for the two of them that was safe, protected from anyone who might try to come between them.

"I've always loved you, Lydia, and I always shall," he said in a mesmerizing whisper—a passionate litany designed to make her believe and accept him. "You are truly my only reality, my only world. My soul lives within you. My heart beats again through yours. Without you I am merely a silent shade of the man I used to be."

Like waves washing up on the distant beach, Lydia Bee's emotions came rolling over Lydia. She knew her great-grandmother's love for this man. She knew the wonder and ecstasy of their loving as well as the terrible, devastating pain of their parting. She knew something else, too. Lydia Bee had carried Paxton Carmichael's child.

"Forget all the pain," he commanded. "Now that you're here, it will never be. We have the power—through love—to change everything that happened."

At the moment he spoke, the pain was drawn out. Lydia forgot the agony of their parting, the suffering when she had lost his much-longed-for child, the misery of her long, loveless marriage. It was spring once more—the eternal spring of 1892. And she was Lydia Bennington Aynsley. She was rich and beautiful and in love for the first and only time in her life.

"Oh, Pax," Lydia said, "it's going to be the best season ever. The very best!"

He threw back his head and laughed until the joyful sound echoed in the dark halls. The gray, swirling mists vanished in a flood of brilliant light. Pax swept into his arms. "Shall we dance?"

"Forever!" Lydia cried. In that instant, her own tinkling laughter mingled with his, and from far off somewhere she heard music.

Suddenly, they were waltzing under gleaming gas chandeliers in the dining room of the Jekyl Island Club. Bejeweled ladies set the night ablaze with a fireworks display of diamonds, rubies, sapphires, and emeralds. And through the tall windows, Lydia could see a million stars vying for their radiance.

"Yes, *stars*, my love," Pax said. "Just look at them. It's been so long since I could see them. It's a miracle. No, *you* are the miracle. You'll stay with me always, won't you?"

Lydia felt dizzy with joy, dizzy with the whirling waltz, dizzy with love for Paxton Carmichael.

"Just hold me," she whispered. "Never let me go."

"I wish it were that easy," he murmured under his breath.

When the music ended, Pax guided her toward a table where several other young people were seated. Another miracle—Lydia knew all their names. The four Maurice sisters of Hollybourne Cottage were there—Peg, Nina, Emmy, and Mamie—with an assortment of beaming young gentlemen from prominent families.

"You two cut a swell figure on the dance floor, Pax." The speaker was Reginald Fairbank, another of Lydia Bee's suitors that season. But Paxton Carmichael had long since cut him out of the pattern. Now Reggie was mooning over Peg Maurice.

"Any man who danced with Lydia Bee would look good," Pax said, squeezing Lydia's hand under the table.

"And might any man have permission to dance with her?" Reggie asked hopefully.

Pax slipped his arm possessively around the back of Lydia's chair and feigned a leer at his friend. "Not unless he's willing to meet me under the oaks at dawn to pay for such presumptuous behavior."

"Aw, Pax, dueling's against the law nowadays," said another of the young men.

"So is loving a woman as much as I love Lydia Bee." His dark gaze steadied on her face with a look of naked hunger. "Or if it isn't, it very well should be."

The Maurice sisters gasped softly and their cheeks turned a uniform scarlet. There was no doubt in any of their minds that Paxton Carmichael was the most scandalous fellow at the Club. Everyone had heard the tales of his long string of romances back in New York. And they knew as well that Mr. Aynsley had promised his daughter's hand to another. They feared for Lydia Bee's honor. They'd even tried talking to her about it, but she refused to listen. It seemed that the poor girl had fallen terminally in love with the handsome New Yorker, who cared not a whit what he said or to whom.

"You're coming to the beach party tomorrow afternoon, aren't you, Lydia?" Mamie asked. "The water's still cold, but we're all going bathing."

Reggie leaned closer into the group. "Pipe down, Mamie. Someone might hear you." He glanced about to make sure none of the older generation were listening in. "We're supposed to keep this under our hats, but we plan to duck out on our chaperons."

Again the Maurice girls' cheeks colored.

"We can't do that!" Nina gasped. "It would be unseemly."

"Hell's bells! It'll be fun," Reggie insisted. "How about you and Pax, Lydia? Will you come?"

"Certainly!" Lydia answered without giving Pax a chance to reply.

"We'll see," he added, not sure he trusted himself alone with Lydia Bee on the other side of the island.

She smiled at him in a coaxing way. "I brought my new bathing costume. I'd hoped to have a chance to wear it."

The sparkle of her midnight blue eyes and the whisper of her voice made up Paxton's mind for him. "We'll be there," he told Reggie.

Pax motioned to a waiter and ordered a bottle of champagne. They sipped their wine and danced the evening away. When only a few of the older folks remained, Pax touched Lydia's hand under the table.

"Shall we take a breath of air outside before I see you back to your room?"

She knew what he had in mind, and felt her flesh tingle at his suggestion. If he wanted a breath, it was one of hers. He had kissed her that way once before—drawing air from her open mouth into his. The sensation had been strangely thrilling. She smiled at him and nodded. She simply couldn't resist him.

When he'd kissed her for the first time, nearly a month ago, she had sat up all night staring at herself in the vanity mirror, trying to see if their intimacy had changed her in any way. At breakfast the next morning, her father hadn't commented on any visible difference in his daughter. Since she was apparently safe, she longed now day and night for more of his delicious kisses.

The air was cool and fresh with salt on the veranda. But they couldn't stay there. Mr. Grob, the superintendant, might spot them when he made his last round before turning in, or one of the gentlemen might come out here for one final Havana before bedtime.

Pax took her hand. "Let's go down to the oak. It's more private there."

Lydia knew the oak he meant. She could see it from her window on the second floor. It hung over the road and the river's edge. To her, it was *their* oak. Pax had carved their entwined initials in the tree's bark only a week ago.

They clung to the shadows along the carriage drive as they made their way to the river. The air felt soft and moist. Being in the darkness, alone with Pax, was like hiding away in some secret, mysterious place all their own. Lydia's heartbeat quickened as they neared the riverbank. She felt a familiar ache throb to life in the center of her soul.

And then they were there and she was in his arms. She'd been waiting all evening for this moment. His mouth came down over hers—hot and hungry and sweet. He clung to her, drawing her body so close to his that she could feel his need for her. He left her breathless, tingling, aching for more and more and more. Her thoughts went suddenly to the hall of mirrors and their unending reflections. Her love for Pax was like those images. But instead of diminishing, each time she was with him her feelings for him grew and grew until they were almost overpowering.

If ever a man had known how to make a woman happy, surely Paxton Carmichael was that man. And if ever a woman had been totally, insanely in love, surely Lydia Bennington Aynsley was that woman. He wanted her; she wanted him. So why should they wait any longer?

Lydia was about to suggest that they slip into the boathouse for an hour or so when Pax suddenly dashed her passionate dreams.

"We'd better go back now," he said abruptly.

"Go back? Oh, please, Pax," she begged, glancing pointedly toward the boathouse. There was no mistaking her meaning.

"How you tempt me!" Paxton said brusquely. "But, Lydia, we can't."

She had her arms around his neck, her lips on his.

She coaxed him with feathery flicks of her tongue until he moaned into her mouth and gripped her tightly in his arms again. For a time, Lydia was sure she had him totally under her spell. But then he gently forced her arms down and stepped away.

She murmured her disappointment.

"There'll be other nights, Lydia Bee, other kisses," he assured her. "We have our whole lives ahead of us, darling."

"Can we be sure of anything beyond this moment, Pax?" There was strange pathos in her voice.

"You can be sure that I love you, Lydia. That I'll always love you. A hundred years from now, I'll still be loving you." He took her hand and placed it with his over their entwined initials on the oak. "As long as this tree stands and bears witness to our love, we'll never really be apart. The oak is the strongest tree on this island, and our love is stronger yet. But you must be sure before we take such a step. I don't want us to make a mistake you'll regret. When you know in your heart and soul who you really are, Lydia, I'll know, too. Then nothing and no one will stand in our way."

"But I *am* sure, my darling. I've never been more certain of anything in my life. I know exactly who I am and what I want. I, Lydia Aynsley Winslow, want you to love me *now*."

A stricken look passed over his face. "It's as I thought," he said under his breath. Then he shook his head slowly. "I'm afraid the champagne and the starlight are speaking for you. When you can say the same thing in the cold light of day, I'll know our time has come."

A moment of tense silence stretched between them. Then Pax laughed—a sound devoid of humor. "God, Lydia, I've always been such a cad. Why now—when I want to make love to you so that I ache with the pain of it—must the long-dormant gentleman in me awake and assert himself? You did this to me, Lydia. Only you could."

His words brought the sting of unshed tears to her eyes. She dared not trust her voice. Silently, Lydia let him take her hand and lead her back to the hotel. They tiptoed in and up the stairs. At her door, he paused only a moment.

"I'd kiss you good night, but . . ."

She wanted that kiss so desperately, yet she understood the danger in such folly. "I know. One more kiss would be one too many."

He gazed at her with the pain of unfulfilled longing in his dark eyes and nodded. "I'll see you after lunch tomorrow?"

She smiled up into his eyes. "Tomorrow and tomorrow and tomorrow," she whispered.

"Sleep well and dream of me." He touched his fingertips to his lips and then to hers. "I love you."

Lydia was tingling all over, trembling with wanting him so. Would their time ever come?

Quickly, she turned and slipped into her room. The tears she'd managed to hold at bay now filled her eyes, blurring her vision. She leaned her back against the closed door, breathing deeply, trying to get control.

She had thought she was so grown up and sophisticated when she arrived on Jekyl a few weeks ago. But she'd been only a child then. Now, for the first time in her life, she felt like a woman. She knew that Pax had done this to her. Pax and love. And wasn't it wonderful!

Wiping her eyes, she looked about. The gas lamp with its painted satin-glass globe was gone from her vanity. In its place glowed a strange lantern without fire. Everything else had changed, too. The bedcover was dark green, quilted chintz with an exotic flower pattern in pastel colors. The walls were papered in a different print. And her maid, Dora, had not been in to lay out her nightclothes.

She walked quickly to the open windows and looked out. She smiled.

"It doesn't matter," she said. "I can bear any changes as long as our oak still stands and Pax still loves me."

A short time later, Lydia Aynsley Winslow fell into bed and went instantly to sleep. She dreamed of Pax and love.

# Chapter Six

Allowing Lydia to go back into that room tore Pax apart. He knew that when she went inside far more than simply a door closed upon him. A century of longing now stood between them once more.

"But I had to let you go, my darling. You aren't convinced yet that you really are my Lydia Bee."

Pax was standing outside Lydia Bee's room. However, he knew that if the door swung open, he would see, not her, but her great-granddaughter. Lydia Winslow would not see him at all. When he was alone, he lost his substance, his impermanent lease on reality. The moment she left him, he'd heard the click of the key to modern times, locking him out. He had seen the stars in the sky disappear when Lydia returned to her own room in her own time. Without her here beside him, he felt cold, alone, and sad—a solitary vagabond in time.

"In limbo," he reminded himself dismally.

Still, he reasoned, there was no other way.

Actually, there was a way he could have kept her with him forever. He could have made love to her and sealed her fate. Once he claimed her for his own—totally and for all eternity—she could never go back to her time.

"You had your chance, old chap," he grumbled, "there at the oak. You blew it again!"

Oh, how he'd wanted her! And she'd certainly made her willingness plain, with her sweet, lingering kisses and glances toward the boathouse. But that would have been cheating and taking advantage. Lydia didn't fully understand yet. Tonight she had been *almost* Lydia Bee, but not quite. She needed some time back in her own realm to think things through. If she wasn't positively certain this was what she wanted with all her heart, he couldn't force her to stay with him. It had to be her choice, her total commitment to love and to him.

Pax knew that Lydia Winslow possessed the old soul of his Lydia Bee. Now it was up to Lydia to examine her heart and discover the full truth for herself.

He sighed, then turned and sauntered down the deserted hallway, leaving a gust of cold air in his wake.

"She'll come back," he assured himself. "Dear God, she *must* come back!"

The bright sun, shining full in her face, woke Lydia the next morning at seven. Without opening her eyes, she turned her back to the windows. She'd been having such a fantastic dream. Why did it have to end? Maybe she could drift off again and pick up where she'd left off.

"Let's see," she murmured sleepily. "We were by the river and Pax had his arms around me. He was kissing me." She smiled and purred. "Hmmm, yes! Let's pick it up there."

Suddenly, her eyes flew open. "That was no dream! Dreams fade the minute you wake up. I remember every detail of last night. Every kiss, every touch, every word that passed between us."

She sat up in bed, rubbed her eyes, then looked at the vanity mirror. "Lydia Bee, are you there?"

No answer. No image in the glass.

"I need you," Lydia called. "Show yourself! Say something!"

Nothing—only birds singing and muffled voices from the veranda below.

"Hey, come on. You got me into this, now tell me what I'm supposed to do next."

Lydia climbed out of bed and went to the mirror, staring fiercely into it. Only her rumpled, first-thing-in-the-morning image stared back at her. No Lydia Bee. No help at all.

The smell of coffee drifted up from the dining room. Lydia turned away from the mirror and headed for the bathroom. She had things to do today—important things—but the first item on her agenda was breakfast. After she'd eaten, she meant to find Raymond and pump him for information about the ghost. She also wanted to visit the old cemetery he'd mentioned to her. She cocked her head and thought for a moment.

"Isn't there supposed to be a beach party today?" She grabbed her list of events for the reunion. Tours of the old cottages and the hotel, a special luncheon, croquet on the lawn, an afternoon tea dance. "But no beach party," Lydia said, puzzled.

Moments later, it came to her. "I'm supposed to go with Pax and the Maurice sisters and Reggie Fairbank," she mused aloud. "Pax said he'd meet me after lunch. But where?"

Lydia's frown turned suddenly to a bright smile. She knew exactly where. And she meant to be there right on time. She could hardly wait to see him again. More than anything, she wanted to spend all her time with him.

"I love him!" she said suddenly with a touch of wonder in her voice. "I really, truly do love Paxton Carmichael! It's as simple as that, and I'll do *anything* to be with him."

Had Lydia turned back to the vanity mirror at the moment, she would have seen the faint outline of a woman's face. She was smiling.

Lydia ran to the bathroom and turned on the shower. A short time later, she was squeaky-clean and dressed in heather-colored slacks and a matching sweater with a single gold chain draped at the neckline. She pulled her long hair back and fastened it with a black-and-white scarf patterned with picture of M. C. Escher's "Relativity." As she gazed at herself in the mirror she thought how appropriate the dramatic design of the scarf was—all stairways and windows and halls going everywhere and nowhere, defying gravity and perspective.

"Defying even time," she said. "Like this old hotel."

When she arrived at the entrance to the dining room a short while later, she was surprised at the change in the place. She had seen it all pink and gold and white at dinner, of course. But the last time she was here, later in the evening, the woodwork had been dark with heavy tapestries on the walls and gaslights dim in the antique chandeliers. That was the way it should be. This modern version of the place seemed all wrong suddenly.

"Morning, Ms. Winslow," the hostess said. "I hope you had a good night."

When Lydia answered, "Marvelous!" the woman grinned at her exuberance.

"May I have table 13 again?" Lydia reasoned that Pax might show up for breakfast if she was in the spot they'd shared at dinner.

"Right this way, ma'am."

Once she was seated, Lydia glanced about. She hadn't met a soul with the reunion yet, except that blonde—Macy something-or-other—in the ladies' room. She really did want to get acquainted with the others. But finding Pax remained uppermost in her mind.

John brought her menu—a huge selection for breakfast, each entrée named for one of the millionaires. Lydia's gaze went straight to the center of the page. "I'll have 'The Carmichael,'" she told John. She'd never tried eggs scrambled with smoked salmon and scallions, but she could hardly resist its name.

The waiter turned to leave, but Lydia called him back. "John, could you tell me if this breakfast is named for Mr. Paxton Carmichael?"

"Oh, no ma'am," he answered. "This one's in honor of Elijah Carmichael, one of the boat captains who used to bring guests over from the mainland in the early days."

"Thank you. That's very interesting." But Lydia didn't smile as she answered. She was disappointed.

Her breakfast, however, lifted her spirits. This "Carmichael," she decided, was every bit as delicious as the one named Pax. She finished it right down to the last crumb of bagel and smear of cream cheese. She even ate the dainty slices of pineapple, orange, and strawberry that garnished her plate.

She was about to leave when Macy Aspinwall-Carter hurried over to her table. "I'm glad I caught you," the blonde in flaming orange said. "That man you were with last night is not registered anywhere on the whole island. We think he was casing the joint, planning a heist. So, if you haven't already, you'd better make sure your diamonds are locked up in the hotel's safe."

"I'll see to it right after breakfast," Lydia answered with a straight face. She hadn't a diamond to her name—not the first solitaire or tiny chip.

"Well, I knew you'd want to know. The hotel management's brought in some extra security guards for the rest of the weekend and they're all keeping a sharp eye out for him. I gave them a full description. If he comes poking around again, they'll catch him. How did you happen to be having dinner with him?"

"Just luck, I guess," Lydia murmured under her breath.

"Pardon?" Macy said, leaning closer.

"We were simply seated at the same table."

"Oh, so you didn't know him or invite him or anything like that. Good! I guess we don't have to worry about you then. But you really should avoid shady characters like that. We can't be too careful, you know."

The longer Macy stayed and talked, the more certain Lydia became that she preferred Pax's company to that of the reunion guests.

"If you'll excuse me, Mrs. Carter, I have something urgent to attend to." Lydia quickly rose and turned for the door.

"That's Aspinwall-Carter, with a hyphen!" the blonde called after her. "Don't forget the Aspinwall!"

"I should have told her Pax came out of one of the mirrors," Lydia muttered to herself. "Aspinwall-witch, with a hyphen!"

Lydia hurried through the hall of mirrors, barely glancing at her own reflection. Something told her that even if she looked, Pax wouldn't be there this morning. It seemed almost as if he'd sent her back for a purpose. If only she could figure out what it was.

When she reached the reception desk, she found Raymond immediately.

"Morning, Ms. Winslow." His grin was so wide it looked like it must hurt.

"Hi, Raymond. If you've got a minute, I'd like to hear some more about your ghost."

"Sure thing! What did you want to know, ma'am?"

"For starters, what makes you think that this ghost is from the millionaires' days?"

Raymond gave Lydia a sly grin. He glanced around to make sure no one was listening, then motioned for her to come closer.

"I'm not accusing anyone of anything, you understand, ma'am, but when lobster or champagne go missing, I can usually count on finding the goods in a certain room of the hotel—a room in the original section of the old building that hasn't been restored yet."

Lydia found Raymond's words hard to swallow. "Are you trying to tell me that this ghost has an enormous appetite and expensive tastes? I never knew spirits could eat."

"I don't think he can, ma'am. You see, anytime something gets swiped, I check that room and, sure enough, there it is—the lobster spoiled and the champagne opened and gone flat. Now, I ask you, would any normal human being go to the trouble to steal stuff, then let it just sit there and go bad?"

Raymond paused and shook his head. "The only thing I can figure is that this guy was used to the high life back a hundred years ago and he hasn't been able to kick his old habits, even if he can't indulge them any longer."

Lydia looked askance at the young man. "How often has this happened, Raymond?"

"Five times in the past few months, ma'am. You don't lose count of something that odd. Another funny thing, too, is that he always pours two glasses of champagne. But neither one is ever touched. It's almost like he's waiting for someone who never shows up. It's kind of sad really."

"May I see this room, Raymond?" Lydia asked.

He glanced toward the desk. "Well, I guess it would be okay for me to take you up there. That part of the hotel is really off limits to guests, but I can sneak you up there by the back stairs. You'll have to watch your step though, ma'am. If you got hurt along the way, I'd really be in hot water—probably lose my job."

"Don't worry, Raymond. I'll be very careful. Just lead the way."

Lydia's heart pounded with excitement as Raymond led her down corridors, up narrow servants' stairs, then down a shadowed hallway. The wallpaper here was not the same as in the other parts of the hotel, and no carpeting covered the old heartpine floor. This part of the hotel reeked of mildew, smoke, and age.

"There was a fire here a few years back," Raymond explained. "I don't think they'll ever get the smell out of this section."

To Lydia it seemed that the final narrow stairway they climbed carried them not just up, but back in time.

"His room's down at the end of the hall, ma'am. It's not much farther."

It didn't seem the least bit strange to Lydia that Raymond's voice had dropped suddenly to a whisper in this place. A louder tone might have awakened and summoned innumerable shades from the hotel's shadowy past—a veritable gaggle of ghosts. Lydia imagined she could hear the swish of long skirts and petticoats, the creak of whalebone stays, and the hollow echo of men's boots upon the old boards. A chill ran along her spine. She rubbed briskly at the goosebumps on her arms.

"I think he knows we're here." Raymond spoke quietly, glancing about the dim corridor. "Sometimes when I come up here, I get the feeling he welcomes the company. But then other times, it seems like he doesn't want to be bothered and I feel like an intruder. You know what I mean?"

Lydia nodded. "Which does it feel like today?"

Raymond paused, cocked his head, and frowned. "Hard to tell. It feels different this time—maybe because I've never brought anyone else up here before. He's definitely not unhappy to have us here. Feels to me like he's really glad we came—like maybe this was all his idea and he's right with us, leading the way." He turned and grinned sheepishly at Lydia. "Sorry, ma'am. I know that sounds downright crazy. I don't mean to spook you."

"It's all right, Raymond. I know exactly what you mean. I feel him, too." She couldn't bring herself to explain just *how* she felt him. A moment before, an invisible hand had touched Lydia's breast and warm lips had brushed her cheek. "I always thought I'd be scared to death if I ever happened upon a ghost," she continued, "but I don't feel that way at all. Open the door to his room, won't you? Who knows? Maybe he'll be waiting inside for us."

Raymond gave an exaggerated shiver and his face looked suddenly pale beneath his freckles. "Now you're spooking me, ma'am."

With a solid, metallic click, the big brass key tripped the old lock. Raymond turned the heavy knob and the massive door swung slowly inward. A rush of fresh air engulfed them, chasing away the musty, stale odor of the hallway.

"He likes his window open," Raymond explained. "Every time I leave the room, I shut that window and lock it. Next thing I know, I'm outside and glance up and it's wide open again. One day a couple of weeks ago, I looked up and saw the window rising all by itself, seemed like. I hot-footed it up here, hoping I'd catch him in the act. But the room was empty when I got here. I closed the window, of course. By the time I got back downstairs . . ."

"It was open again?"

"You guessed it, ma'am. I'd give up trying to keep it shut if it weren't for the boss yelling about it all the time. He thinks some of the employees are sneaking up here to grab a smoke on the job. He figures we're the ones opening that window to air the room out after we've had a cigarette. I've smelled smoke in here plenty of times. But it's those fancy Cuban cigars of his."

"How do you know it's the ghost smoking? Maybe it is one of the employees."

"No, ma'am." Raymond shook his head. "Cuban cigars are illegal nowadays—have been for years. They can't even be brought into the U.S."

"How can you be so sure they're Cuban? All cigars smell alike to me."

"It's the cigar bands, ma'am. I've found lots of them lying around his room." He pointed toward the open window. "Look, there's one on the floor now."

While Raymond walked over to retrieve his proof, Lydia took in the whole room at a glance—bed, chest, armoire, blanket rack, table. There was no lobster today, but two fragile champagne flutes sat side by side on the table, bubbles still bursting on the surface of the golden liquid. Sudden impulse moved Lydia to lift one of the glasses in a silent toast. Then she took a sip. The wine was cool and fresh, recently poured.

Not until she set the glass back on the table did she notice the torn photograph there. She picked it up carefully. It was old, worn and fragile with age. She stared at the likeness of Lydia Bee, her hair wet and disheveled, her bathing costume wrinkled and sandy. But she had never seen her great-grandmother look so lovely. It was her face. She positively glowed with happiness and a sort of wonder. Her glittering eyes were focused on the man she loved—on Paxton Carmichael, who had been standing nearby the instant the shutter snapped, gazing back at her with his heart in his eyes as well, before the picture was torn in two.

"The other half," she murmured. "He's kept it all these years."

The champagne had made her head feel light. Now another sensation mingled with that giddiness. She felt a warm flood of understanding flow into her. He wanted her. He'd made that perfectly clear. Yet he had allowed her to return, to make the decision for herself.

"Looks like we just missed him," Raymond said, staring at the two glasses. "It's fresh poured, isn't it?"

Lydia nodded, afraid to trust her voice at the moment.

He glanced around the room. "Well, that's about it, ma'am. We'd better not stay up here too long. Any other questions about our resident ghost?"

"No, Raymond," Lydia said softly. "I think I have all the answers I need now. Thank you."

Raymond walked back out into the hall. Lydia lingered a moment, just long enough to whisper, "Pax, if you can hear me, I'll be back."

# Chapter Seven

Lydia left the hotel feeling as if she had stumbled across some great truth while she was in Paxton Carmichael's bedroom, but unsure of the exact nature of her enlightenment. She knew, though, that something was happening to her—something over which she had no control. Yet she had no desire to stop whatever was going on.

She felt on the brink of understanding her relationship with Pax. She could almost, but not quite, explain it to herself.

"But then, who could ever explain love, anyway?" she said with a laugh that sounded more like a cry of pure joy.

She came out of the hotel and into the bright sun. The day was warm and beautiful. Spying a gardener planting day lilies along the hotel drive, she strolled over to ask directions. She knew exactly where Pax wanted her to go next.

"Is the old du Bignon cemetery within walking distance?" she asked.

"If you got all day and nothing better to do with it, ma'am, then you could walk," the gray-haired fellow answered with a smile. "But if I was you, I'd take one of the bikes and just follow the trail along the river. The old burying ground's several miles up the road toward the north end of the island. You can't miss it. It's right across from 'old tabby.'"

To her recollection, Lydia had never heard of "old

tabby," yet somehow she knew that it was the ruin
of a house constructed of burned lime and oyster
shells that had been built in the early eighteenth century by Major William Horton, an aide to Georgia's
founding father, General James Oglethorpe. To Lydia's amazement, her newfound knowledge seemed
encyclopedic. She was aware that Horton had come
to Jekyl after the Indians, who had called the island
Ospo, and after the Spaniards, who had established
the mission of Santiago de Ocone here, but before
the French planters, before the millionaires.

She paused a moment to marvel at all the facts she
knew about Jekyll Island this morning that she
hadn't known only hours before. It seemed almost
as if someone were whispering historic details into
her ear.

"And who might that be, I wonder?" she murmured to herself.

She had a good idea. She'd felt him near her ever
since she entered his room. He was with her now.
She wasn't sure where, but she could feel his presence—not the chill of the ghost, but the warm glow
of his love.

Lost in thought, Lydia never noticed the cushiony
give of the plush green grass beneath her loafers as
she walked across the hotel's lawn to the bike rack.
She chose a canary yellow ten-speed, then headed
for the bike path that followed the gentle curve of
Jekyll Creek. At times, the paved trail paralleled
Plantation Road, where sightseers drove along at a
leisurely pace. Then suddenly she would find herself
in deep woods with moss trailing from low-hanging
limbs to brush her shoulders. At moments when she
was alone, with only the green stillness of the woods
and the soft lap of the water to keep her company,
she could almost imagine that she was back in Pax's
time, when the island was still wild and teaming
with game.

The farther she rode, the more lost in her own thoughts she became. Every moment that she had spent with Pax on the island seemed so real. The present, as she had known it before she came to Jekyll, seemed only some far-off shadow of life.

Had she thought about it, she would have realized by the warmth of her cheeks that the noon sun was shining brightly. But she remained oblivious. Nor did she see the sway of the Spanish moss that accompanied the breeze from the incoming tide. All she could think about was Paxton Carmichael.

"What secret do you want me to discover?" she asked, guessing before she spoke that she would receive no verbal answer. She pedaled on in silent thought.

Up ahead on the right, she could just barely see the two-story tabby shell of the Horton house through the trees behind a split rail fence. The du Bignon cemetery sat on her left, almost at the water's edge and locked in deep, green-black shade by the oaks and cedars growing all around. She realized instantly why the family must have chosen this site to bury their dead. The Horton house had been their marker to locate the plot in the deep and tangled forest.

Suddenly, Lydia received another flash of information out of nowhere. The du Bignon family, French Royalists, had come to America in 1792 to escape the madness of the French Revolution. They owned Jekyl Island for nearly a century before finally selling out to the millionaires. On their plantation, the du Bignons had raised long-staple Sea Island cotton until the War Between the States, when the Emancipation Proclamation freed their many slaves and made the extensive cultivation of their land impossible. The federal invasion of Jekyl and the surrounding islands forced the du Bignons to flee their home. They camped out in the wilds on a far end of Jekyl until the Yankee troops withdrew. After long, troubled years, they returned to their plantation house and tried to eke out a living from the land, farming and raising cattle—a heartbreaking attempt at best. It looked as if all was lost until they hit upon a scheme to stock the island with exotic game and sell it as a hunting preserve. They soon found willing buyers in the financiers from New York and Chicago. Pocketing a princely sum, the du Bignons moved to the mainland, building a fine new home on Union Street in Brunswick, but leaving their ancestors to rest forever on their beloved island.

All these thoughts unfurled in Lydia's mind as she walked toward the old cemetery, enclosed in a tabby wall, dark with age. But how did she know these things? When had she learned so much about the island's history? It was a charming fantasy to imagine that Pax was beside her, acting as her ghostly tour guide. But she guessed otherwise.

"Lydia Bee," she said suddenly, without the least surprise. "She must have known. I know all these things because she knew them. Memory genes, like Pax said."

Lydia realized that she knew other interesting things as well. Things about Pax. He was from a once-prominent New York family, who had made their original fortune trading for furs with the Indians upstate. Later, they had been heavily into real estate in and around New York City. But poor investments and foolish extravagance had cut a wide swath through the Carmichael fortune years before Paxton was born in a brownstone on Fifth Avenue on January 1, 1866.

The blunt reality of Paxton Carmichael's birth date—coming to her suddenly out of nowhere—brought Lydia up short on the path. Holding tightly to the wrought-iron gate in the tabby wall, she glanced about, wondering for an instant if she had encountered a time slip that allowed her to see things she shouldn't be able to see and know things she had no logical way of knowing. But a shiny red convertible whizzing by on the road and a light plane droning overhead told her instantly that she was still in her own time, in the very same place she had been moments before. The only change was in her memory.

"I know Pax," she murmured. "I *really* know him—everything about him. He was an only child, devoted to his mother, who died when he was only eight. After her death, he was always lonely. He missed the love of his mother and craved the love of his father. But his single parent had little time for the motherless lad. Mr. Carmichael traveled constantly, leaving his son behind in one boarding school after another. Pax never felt he belonged until he came to Jekyl. He never felt he was loved until he met Lydia Bee."

A shiver ran through Lydia although the sun was hot. "She loved you, Pax. Truly she did. I can feel it. I *remember* it."

At that moment, Lydia knew for sure that Pax was with her. She felt his touch on her arm, his warm breath on her cheek. He was letting her know he understood all that she was experiencing.

"You brought me here for a reason," she said quietly, staring at the empty space beside her. "Won't you show yourself? Can't you share this with me? Tell me what you want me to know."

Only the breeze sighing through the bearded branches of the ancient oaks answered her. But in that moment she understood.

"You want me to see the cemetery. You want me to know the rest of your story."

A shiver passed through Lydia. There was one thing she didn't know about Paxton Carmichael—

when and how he died. She knew she was about to find out.

Beyond the gate, she could see the du Bignon vaults—three horizontal tombs of bricks covered with marble slabs. Toward the back left corner were two small, upright stones, the names and the date, 1912, clearly legible, along with the fact that the men had drowned accidentally. Far back in the right corner stood a solitary marker, unlike any of the others. Shaped like an hourglass, the stone's surface was covered with pink lichen.

Lydia eased through the rusty gate and tiptoed past the tablet tombs. As she drew nearer the hourglass, tears misted her eyes.

"Pax?" she whispered.

She sank to the ground before the small monument. Rubbing at years' growth of lichen, she felt it crumble away. Her fingertips followed the script incised in the stone.

She whispered the epitaph aloud: "Paxton Carmichael, Born January 1, 1866, Died March 15, 1892. Gone but not forgotten."

Lydia leaned her cheek against the cool stone and let tears water his grave. "Oh, Pax," she murmured. "Why? Why did you have to go? I would have come back to you. I love you now as I loved you then. We've always been together in my heart."

Suddenly, the old cemetery vanished in a swirl of gray mist and flying leaves. Lydia felt wind whipping around her. She clung to the stone, calling Pax's name. A moment later, the storm subsided. She opened her eyes.

She was no longer gripping the tombstone. She was clinging to Pax himself.

Lydia was still crying. It was dark. They were standing beside the river.

"You know I don't want to go, but Papa's forcing me," she said. "I told him last night that you and I

plan to be married." She paused to choke back a sob.
"Oh, Pax, you wouldn't believe his rage. He's always
been so kind to me, so generous."

He kissed the tears from her cheeks and spoke to
her softly. "I'll talk to him, darling. I'll explain things.
Surely he'll listen to reason."

"Oh, no! You mustn't!" she cried. "He said he'd
kill you, Pax."

"Do you think I wouldn't die for you, darling?"

"What good will talk do? It's over for us. My
whole life is over without you."

"Don't say that. Don't even think such a thing.
We'll find a way."

Lydia Bee buried her face against his firm shoulder. "There's more to it than that. He's promised me
to another man—his partner, Mr. . . ."

Pax cut her off. "No! Don't tell me the man's name.
I don't want to know it. You'll never marry him anyway. I'll come for you early in the morning. We'll
take a boat to the mainland and be married in Brunswick before anyone knows we're gone."

"Oh, Pax! Is it possible?" A note of mingled joy
and hysteria crept into her voice. "We could take the
small boat, leave right now. In Brunswick, we could
catch the train and be gone before Papa wakes up."

He drew her more closely into his arms. "How I
wish we could! But we have to wait for the tide. I'll
take you back to your room. Then I'll find a boat,
and meet you at our oak an hour before dawn." He
paused and stared down into her wide eyes. "You
know your father will disown you if we elope. Can
you face that, darling?"

"I can face anything as long as I have you, Pax.
You're my life, my heart, my soul."

Silently, they slipped back across the lawn and into
the hotel. No one was about. Pax led the way up the
stairs to Lydia Bee's room. When they reached her
door, he leaned down for one last kiss.

Lydia sensed his hunger and his urgency. It matched her own. What if something happened and their plan went awry? What if tonight, this minute, was their only chance ever?

"Come in with me," she begged. "I need you to give me courage."

"Are you sure, darling?" His hesitation seemed halfhearted at best.

"Please," she whispered.

A moment later, they were in her room with the door closed against the rest of the world.

Pax held her close. "Oh, God, Lydia Bee! What can we be thinking?"

"I don't want to think, my love. I want . . ." Her words trailed off. She knew exactly what she wanted, but she couldn't talk about it. Finally, she managed to say, "How can a love like ours ever be wrong?"

"Before I met you, I was only half alive," he whispered. "The very first time I saw you, Lydia Bee, I recognized you. I knew that you were the one who owned half of my soul."

"Don't ever let me go, my darling."

"Never!" he murmured against her lips. "I mean to make you mine forever."

A fierce wind wailed off the river and slammed a shutter against Lydia Bee's window, but the lovers never noticed the storm. Touching and kissing all the while, somehow they managed to shed their clothes. In a fever of love and need, they tumbled onto the bed.

Lydia Bee felt his tongue trail hot little flicks down the side of her neck, across her shoulder, and then . . . she held her breath as his mouth touched her breast. She rocked on the bed, moaning softly, while he suckled her nipple. Each stroke of his tongue against the tender flesh sent waves of heat and pleasure coursing through her.

She let her hands roam his body. It was hard with

muscles, but soft to the touch. She could imagine living with such a man and loving him every day for the rest of her life without ever discovering all his wondrous secrets.

Sensing that he could wait no longer, Lydia Bee cupped her hands to his cheeks and brought his mouth back to hers. Teasing his lips with the tip of her tongue, she let him know that she was ready, too.

His first thrust was as bold and sure as a lightning strike. And equally as powerful. Lydia Bee gasped softly, but the sound turned instantly to a purr of pleasure. The sensation of being filled and carried to some far-off exotic realm of new wonders built until she thought she might never return to earth. They were truly one now—soaring high above their natural plane. She felt each slide of hot flesh against hers a thousand times over. Every nerve in her body tingled and chimed. Suddenly, she knew they had gone as far as they dared and yet he took her higher. Into a wild night sky where they rode a comet's tail clear to the moon.

The moon! It was huge and hot and throbbing silver light—blinding Lydia Bee, filling her with its liquid fire.

"Oh, Pax, my darling!" she cried.

He clung to her a moment longer, then sagged to the bed beside her.

"My God!" he moaned. "My God!"

The wind blew off the river, cold and threatening. Suddenly, Lydia was back in the cemetery, clinging to Paxton's tombstone, sobbing her heart out. She looked around, confused.

"Pax?" she called, but there was no answer.

A strange dizziness overcame her. She leaned her head against the stone and closed her eyes. When she opened them a moment later, she was on the deck of a yacht, the *Snowbird.* She stood at the railing, still crying as she watched Jekyl Island grow ever smaller in the distance. Her heart seemed to shrink at the same time as she thought back over the past hours. After they'd made love, Pax had left to secure a boat for their elopement. Shortly before dawn, she'd slipped out of her room and hurried to the oak, expecting to find him there waiting for her. The storm had grown worse. Rain and wind lashed the oak, soaking Lydia Bee and sending down showers of leaves and small branches. In spite of the foul weather, she had waited and paced and prayed until the sun was full up. But Pax had never come.

Her father had, however. He'd hustled her on board the *Snowbird* while she sobbed and begged in protest. Now, the lines were cast off and they were underway. But still, no sign of Pax.

"He won't let Papa do this," she murmured to herself. "He promised he'd come. He promised."

It was an ugly day, all gray and blustery. The promise of spring had vanished in one last, mean gasp of the winter. The water in the river was choppy, bouncing the great yacht as if it were a toy boat. Lydia Bee stood alone at the railing, letting the needlelike salt spray lash her face and sting her eyes, but she hardly noticed. The pain in her heart was too great.

"He's not coming," she murmured in misery.

There was something off in the distance she failed to see, but her great-granddaughter saw it now. A small boat casting off from the north beach.

When he had tried to get a boat Pax had found out that Lydia Bee's father had anticipated this plan of theirs to elope. Mr. Aynsley with his iron will and hard cash had hired every small craft on the island, warning that none were to be lent out until the *Snowbird* had cleared St. Simons Sound. Pax had been forced to steal an ancient punt that was tied up in the creek. So he had missed his appointed rendez-vous with Lydia Bee. But there was still hope.

The Aynsley yacht was sailing against the wind, plodding through the deep waves. Pax's skiff—light enough to dance across the surface—could overtake the *Snowbird*. He pulled at the oars until his hands were raw and his muscles burning. He knew what he must do. He'd draw alongside the larger craft, leap to the Jacob's ladder, and be on deck before old Mr. Aynsley knew he'd been boarded. And once he was there, he would try to reason with the old man. However, he was equally prepared to kidnap his love, if that was the only way.

He stroked his oars to the steady, chanting rhythm. "I'm coming, darling. I'm coming." Pax drew ever nearer until he was only a few yards from the hand-some vessel.

Suddenly, the wind shifted. The *Snowbird*'s sails filled and it took flight. The mighty wake struck the frail skiff broadside.

Lydia Bee's name was the last sound Paxton Car-michael uttered.

It was all over in an instant. When his boat cap-sized, Pax took a mighty blow to the head. He was never conscious of drowning. The wind and rain died suddenly and he was standing on what seemed to be solid ground, staring across a narrow bridge into a brilliant white light. He heard his mother call to him to come.

"I can't," he answered. "I have to find Lydia Bee."

"But she's on the other side," his mother answered gently. "You're here now. Come to me, Paxton, and rest a bit. I've been waiting for you so long."

He felt frantic, torn between the two women he loved most in the world. "You don't understand, Mother. I haven't finished things here. I love her. I can never rest without her."

"Ah, *love*," his mother answered, and he could tell

by the sweetness in her tone that she was smiling. "Love makes all the difference, doesn't it, my son?"

"Love means everything," he answered.

"Then go and wait for her in the limbo world behind the mirrors. She will come in time," his mother promised.

The sweet white light faded. For a moment, he felt totally alone and disoriented. But then he was back in his hotel room on Jekyl Island. Back where he belonged—waiting for the woman he loved. Waiting for Lydia Bee.

The wait was long and often tedious. He saw her in 1899, when she came to the island. But she never knew he was there. Through the years, he felt the sorrow and the emptiness of her life. He knew the moment she breathed her last breath and hoped that she would come to him then. But Lydia Bee had grown old and weary. Instead of coming to him, she went beyond limbo to the far side of heaven to rest. Before she crossed the bridge into the sweet, bright light, however, she passed along her love, her heart, and her soul to the infant Lydia.

From that moment, he knew. He knew that she would come back to him . . . that his long wait was almost at an end.

Lydia rose to her feet, swaying slightly. She stumbled and reached for the top of the hourglass, Pax's tombstone, to keep from falling.

"I'm here," she murmured. "Pax, can you hear me? It's Lydia Bee. I've come back to you. Wait for me! Where are you, my darling?"

# Chapter Eight

"I'm here, Lydia Bee. Right here, my love."

She turned slowly from the grave when she heard his beloved voice. He stood a few feet away from her, but it was wonderfully clear that the only distance now separating them was space. She knew somehow that they would never again find themselves on opposite sides of the mirror of time.

"Pretty flowers for my pretty lady."

Pax swept a bouquet of wildflowers—buttercups, daisies, and forget-me-nots—from behind his back and offered them with a bow and a come-hither smile.

"Am I dreaming, Pax?" she whispered.

"Love, when it's shared, is always a dream come true," he answered. "And now that we've found each other again, the miracle has happened."

He offered his arm and Lydia Bee's gloved hand slipped naturally into place. He led her to a waiting buggy and helped her in. The black horse turned lazily and gazed at them through soft brown eyes.

Lydia seemed to remember a yellow bicycle. Slightly bewildered, she glanced back to the graveyard. The tabby wall looked new, one grave was missing, and a cycle with a high front wheel leaned, unattended, against an oak. She looked down at her lace gown with its bustle and flounces. Whatever could she be thinking? Certainly, she hadn't been out cycling dressed this way. The thought left her mind as quickly as it had entered.

She turned and smiled at the handsome man beside her. She loved the way Pax set his straw boater at such a rakish angle.

"I've good news," he said. "The best! I spoke with your father while you were out for your stroll. He's given us his blessing. All that's left is for you to set a date."

Her first thought was to throw her arms around his neck—she was that filled with joy and relief. But when the Maurice carriage rocked by on the shell road, Lydia Bee remembered suddenly that this was hardly the place for such an exuberant show of affection. Instead, she gripped his hand and smiled into his marvelous eyes.

"A date," she murmured. "A *wedding* date! What day is today? You've had me in such a whirl all season that I can't remember from one day to the next."

He laughed, pleased by her charming accusation. "The date, my darling wife-to-be, is March 13, 1892. And it's a lovely day and you're going to make a lovely bride."

For a time, the horse's clopping hooves along the road was the only sound. Lydia Bee seemed too rapt in her own thoughts to speak. As for Pax, he was always a man of few words, but when he spoke he truly had something to say.

"Actually, I can't believe it," he said now. "I was sure I'd have to kidnap you to have you, darling. After I confessed my love, I'd expected to be booted off the island before nightfall by your doting father." He looked at her and grinned. "And I can't say as I'd blame him. You're a treasure, Lydia Bee. Or as we say in the financial world, an asset of the highest order."

Lydia laughed aloud, not even bothering to cover

her open mouth with her lace fan. "Is that all you see in me? An asset? Dear Lord, you'll be a jolly little comfort on our honeymoon!"

"Which puts me in mind of certain matters too long unattended." Pax tugged at the horse's rein and guided the animal off the shell road onto a woodland path. Instantly, they went from bright sun into deep shade, out of sight of anyone passing along the river. "There's a place I want to show you, darling. A special place. But first . . ."

Pax halted the horse and drew Lydia Bee into his arms. His kiss was long and searching. She felt her heart pound inside her tight bodice, and came away breathless, flushed, wanting him with a need that was like wildfire consuming her.

"I love you, Lydia Bee," he said solemnly. "I always have and I always will. If we should ever be parted, I'll wait for you here on our island. I'll haunt the hotel, live behind the mirrors. I'll toast you with champagne every day and dream of you every night. You'll never be free of me. You'll never be without me. I am yours forever."

Lydia Bee felt tears of happiness stinging her eyes. "Let's make a pact here and now," she whispered. "*Nothing* shall ever come between us. Our love is stronger than the oaks and wider than the sea. And I, Lydia Bennington Aynsley, am yours, Paxton Carmichael, for as long as time exists." She leaned forward and kissed him tenderly, then drew away and stared at her own reflection in his dark eyes. "Our love is like the infinite reflection in the hall of mirrors at the hotel. It goes on and on without end."

Pax reached out and spanned her eighteen-inch waist with strong fingers, drawing her closer, kissing her hair. "Will you marry me soon, darling?"

"Oh, yes!" she said with a sigh. "And I'll marry you for always. If we each live a thousand lives, I'll find you in each one. You'll never be free of me."

"Never?"

"Not ever!"

Pax gave a whoop that startled birds from the trees. Then he touched the whip to his horse and headed for the beach. When they broke out of the deep woods, a wild expanse of sand and waves and dunes lay before them. The sun was going down, turning the water all the shades of a fiery opal. The high breeze made the sea oats wave like flags. Gulls swooped overhead. A sense of calm and perpetual beauty surrounded the two lovers.

"Did you ever see anything so timeless, so perfectly lovely?" Lydia Bee said.

"I did," Pax whispered. "The woman who'll be my wife."

They left the buggy and strolled hand in hand down the wide, white beach. Behind them, wet footprints marked their trail. At times the tracks merged and mingled where they paused to touch and kiss, to whisper words of love.

Long after they had left the beach for dinner and congratulations at the Jekyl Island Club, a hungry seagull sailed high above the sand. He eyed a giant heart, drawn with a piece of driftwood in the sand, suspecting ghost crabs of leaving the odd tracks. The gull circled, keeping watch, until well past dark, when the incoming waves began to lap at the sandy heart and its enclosed message sent to the gods:

Paxton Carmichael will love Lydia Bennington Aynsley
until the sands of time have all washed away.
And Lydia Bee will adore her Pax
for much, much longer than that!

# Journey of
# the Heart

by

*Anita Mills*

*Malbern, Northumbria, December 10, 1860*

The little girl waited eagerly, her face pressed so close to the windowpane that her breath steamed it, until the woman could stand it no longer. "Do sit down, Georgie," she said a trifle sharply. "Watching does not make them arrive any more quickly."

"I know." Sighing, Georgina moved to sit on the edge of a chair across from her aunt. "It is that I have not seen Mama in such a long time, I suppose," she allowed wistfully. "And Papa too, of course," she added hastily for benefit of his sister. "But it is Mama who writes to me."

Jane Durant watched as the child fidgeted, first straightening one dark stocking, then the other, then smoothing the starched white smock over her cherry velvet dress. Her small gloved hands clasped each other for a moment, then she leaned forward to look toward the window again. Jane's gaze went past her to the boys who made a snow fort outside, and she felt an intense pride in her unruly brood. Looking back to Georgie, she frowned, wondering if it had been a mistake to dress the little girl so finely. But it was nearing Christmas, and she had not wanted to make any great difference between Georgina and her own sons.

But Laurence was coming, and her brother tended to regard anything spent on Georgie a waste. Well, she hadn't done it for him, Jane told herself mutinously—she'd done it for Meg, who must surely ache for her daughter.

Georgina jumped from her seat again and hurried to the window once more. "Why are they not here?" she asked anxiously.

"The roads are not the best since the snow," Jane answered mildly. "I expect they have been delayed."

"That's not fair! Oh, if I were out there, I should hit them!"

Aware that the latter had nothing to do with her brother's arrival, Jane shook her head. "Georgie, ladies do not hit anyone."

"But his back was turned—Max's back was turned—and Ned and Charley hit him!"

"As he is the elder, I am sure Max can defend himself, my love."

The little girl sighed again. "Sometimes I wish I were a boy, Aunt Jane," she said sadly. "Robin and Johnny are still at home, you know."

"They are not half so grown-up as you."

But as Jane said them, the words sounded ludicrous to her own ears, for how could anyone expect a child of six to understand the bitterness and misplaced hatred of the adults around her? If only Meg had had more spine, perhaps Laurence would have been different, she mused. No, she was deluding herself to think it. Her brother was too filled with his own pride to think of anyone beyond himself. Even his lovely wife was merely a decorative possession designed to add to his consequence.

"Do you think she will like me?" Georgie asked nervously.

"Do I think—? Of *course* she will! She is your mother, dearest."

"And what am I to do with Papa? I mean, do you think he will like it better if I curtsy—or should I wait for him to kiss me, do you think?"

"I think a curtsy is always in order. It seems to flatter men of consequence."

"Like dukes?"

"Like dukes."

"Max says William the Conqueror was a duke, but that was a long time ago, wasn't it?"

"A very long time ago."

"Max said it was a grand time when men wore armor and lived in castles and fought over damned soles, you know," the child confided.

"The word is damsels, Georgie—*damsels*. Unmarried females were called demoiselles, then damsels back then."

"Well, they sounded rather silly to me, for if Max has the right of it, they merely stood in windows and watched everything."

"We do not need to believe every word of the Arthurian legends to appreciate them," Jane murmured.

"Like when they killed dragons," Georgie said, nodding. "Even I know there are not such things."

"Precisely." Jane's gaze strayed again to the window, where her ten-year-old stepson stood brandishing a wooden sword, his booted feet planted atop the snow fort, and it was her turn to sigh. "I can only hope that one day Max will care half so much for the rest of his studies as he cares for King Arthur."

Georgie nodded solemnly. "He says he was borned in the wrong time."

"Born, dearest—*born*. Really, but I must speak to Laurance about a suitable governess for a girl, I think." She fell silent a moment, staring at the sturdy blond boy outside, then she nodded. "Ah, Max," she mused softly, "I would that your own mama could have lived to see you grow up." Collecting herself, she smiled at the dark-haired child across from her. "Come here, Georgie—the bows are already falling from your hair."

But as the little girl slid from the chair and came to stand before her, Jane gathered her onto her lap, where she held her close, stroking the thick, dark hair that hung in waves down the small back, until Georgina began to squirm. Reluctantly, Jane released her and retied the red velvet bows.

New shouts came from outside, prompting the child to pull away and run again to the window. "They are come, Aunt Jane—they are come!" she squealed excitedly. "Mama is here!"

Jane felt a momentary pang, jealousy perhaps that Georgina could have such hopes of the woman who allowed her exile to happen, then she immediately stifled it. Nothing on earth could make her ever wish to trade places with Meg. Nothing. While Charles Durant could upon occasion be a difficult husband, Laurence Esmond made life hell on earth for Meg.

She rose slowly and walked to join Georgina at the window in time to see the boldly emblazoned traveling coach roll up to the portico. Two liveried coachmen jumped down to place polished brass steps, then opened the carriage doors, while yet another marched smartly to the Durant door to announce importantly, "Their graces, the Duke and Duchess of Wymore!"

Beside her, Georgina's dark eyes were round, her expression one of awe, when the pale, almost ethereal beauty that was Margaret, Duchess of Wymore, stepped down. Even Jane, who put little store in such things, had to stare at the vision of spun-gold hair, blue eyes, perfect pink-tinged skin, all set off by soft blue velvet and tipped ermine. Margaret Halley Esmond, the reigning beauty of the decade, the unwilling bride her brother had bought.

Behind Meg, Laurence emerged, his expression one of utter disdain. As she watched him give his arm to his wife, as she watched Meg hesitate ever so briefly, Jane had to wonder how he could have been born to her parents, how he could have grown up in their house, and still be so contained, so cold, so filled with his own consequence.

Georgina had waited long enough. Ducking past Jane, she ran into the foyer, then outside, crying, "Mama! Mama! 'Tis I—'tis Georgie!" But as she crossed the threshold, her heel caught, sending her sprawling down the steps. She landed on her hands and knees at Wymore's polished boots.

Her mother reached toward her, but her father stayed his wife's arm. Looking to where Jane stood in the door, he inquired rather impersonally, "Is she always so awkward? And so unbecomingly forward?"

"She is excited, Laurence," Meg said.

"Georgina, you will stand up and explain yourself this instant," he said sharply.

"Larry, she is but a child," Jane protested.

"Well, Lady Georgina—what have you to say for yourself?" he persisted.

Georgie struggled to her feet and wiped her stinging hands on her red velvet dress, leaving wet marks. "I fell, Papa." Looking upward to where her mother stood, she fought tears. "I wanted to see you, Mama."

"Young lady, that will not do," the duke said sternly. "I would hear you say it properly."

"Larry, she is but six," Meg protested. "And she has skinned her knee."

"I am waiting."

Acutely self-conscious now, the little girl reached up to discover that her hair ribbons dangled, then looked down at the rent in one of her new black silk stockings. Forcing her chin up, she tried to meet his cold eyes.

"I am sorry, Papa," she managed. "It was improper of me to run."

"No. You will say, 'I am sorry, sir, and I beg your pardon for running,' " he told her.

"Larry, she is a child!" Jane all but shouted at him.

He turned to his sister. "If she is to call herself an Esmond, she will learn to conduct herself properly. And I would not say overmuch were I you, Jane, else I shall feel it incumbent to comment upon this ramshackle household you run. How poor Charles is to stand it, I am sure I do not know."

"I am as much an Esmond as you are, Larry," Jane shot back, unrepentant. "But I believe children must be allowed to be children."

"Do you now?" Returning his attention to the small girl, he snapped, "I am still waiting, Georgina."

"Yes, sir." Swallowing, she looked away. "I am sorry, sir, and I beg your pardon for it."

"Much better. See?" he gibed at Jane. "She can be taught good manners."

Slipping free of her husband's hand, Meg bent to smooth Georgie's dark hair. "My, how pretty you are grown!" she exclaimed, smiling. "Such a lovely dress!"

"I wanted to wear it for you, Mama," Georgie answered, swallowing. "I wanted you to hug me in it."

"And so I shall."

For a moment, the child knew the comfort of her mother's arms, felt the softness of the velvet, the tickle of ermine against her nose, and smelled the soft, warm scent that surrounded her mother's hair.

"Oh, my darling, I have missed you," Meg whispered.

" 'Tis enough, Margaret," the duke snapped. "You will spoil the child beyond bearing." Taking his wife's arm, he drew her away from Georgina, then propelled her toward the door. "Come, my dear— you must rest if we are to travel on to Creighton tomorrow."

"But—" Georgie's lower lip quivered, then she turned away. "But I thought you would stay," she choked out. "Aunt Jane thought you would stay the week at least!"

Laurence Esmond shook his head. "We are committed to the Randalls for the holidays, I'm afraid."

"Please, Papa—" She swallowed hard.

"I knew it would be like this," he muttered. "Tell her you will give her the falderols you have brought her before we leave," he ordered her mother.

"But I don't want—that is, I should rather have you and Mama, sir," Georgie stammered.

"Perhaps at Easter," he answered brusquely.

Jane saw her face fall, and her own anger rose at the brother who could never see what he had done. "Georgie," she said, kneeling on the snow-swept portico, "it is all right, love."

But the child twisted away and ran, not into the house, but rather around toward the back of it. Of the three boys who'd watched silently, it was Max who went after her.

"Don't let her catch cold!" Jane called out to him. Turning to follow Laurence inside, she was determined to have it out with him. He was not going to come into her house and upset the child he did not want. Catching up to him as the footman stood ready to show Meg upstairs, she said crisply, "A word with you in Charles's study, if you please."

He turned around. "And if I do not?"

"I'd still have a word with you," she said evenly.

Max found Georgie in the stable, where she huddled against the hay, crying her eyes out. Instead of trying to talk to her, he dropped down beside her and sat there, waiting for her to get over it. Taking his prized pocket knife out from beneath his coat, he began tossing it aimlessly into the straw, picking it up, trying again and again.

"For what it is worth to hear what I think, Georgie—I think Uncle Laurance is an ass." Seeing that her shoulders shook harder, he dared to touch her dark hair. "If it was me, I'd be glad he was going."

"He—he's taking M-Mama!" she sobbed.

"Her too," he said brutally. "You know why Papa doesn't birch me and Ned and Charlie any more'n he does? Because Mama won't let him, that's why."

"Aunt Jane's different!"

"I'll say she is—she's got spine. Aunt Meg ought to get a little of it."

She looked up through red eyes. "What an awful thing to say, Maximilian Durant! Mama loves me—I know it!"

"Oh? Then why doesn't she make him let you live at Wymore? Why is it that we have you?"

"I don't know!" Turning away, she buried her face in the musty hay and clenched her fists. "I don't know!" she wailed miserably.

The boy felt instantly sorry. Leaning over her, he told her, "I don't know either, but you are safe here, Georgie. You got Mama, Papa, Ned, Charlie—and me. You can stay here forever." Patting her awkwardly, he said, "Please don't cry, Georgie. Come on—get up, and now that they are come, maybe you can change into one of your old dresses and we'll come out and play."

"I don't want to throw snowballs," she retorted.

"All right. It's warmer in here, anyway. We'll say the loft is the castle, and I'll be Sir Gawain, and you can be—"

"I don't want to be some silly lady, Max," she muttered, sniffing back the last of her tears. "All ladies do is wear pretty clothes and get waited on all day."

"They spin and sew also."

"Well, I don't want to be one."

"I'll give you the key to my castle."

"No."

"Look, there wasn't anything else for a female, Georgie—they were ladies or servants or harlots."

"Then I shall be a harlot."

"Georgie—" He frowned. "No, I shouldn't have said it," he muttered. "You cannot be a harlot, and that is all there is to that."

"Why?"

"Because— Look, Georgie, forget you ever heard the word, will you? I don't want you to tell anyone you got it from me."

"Why?"

"Because ladies don't know such creatures exist, or at least that's what I'm told."

"Well, if you know, then what are they?"

"They—" He looked both ways, then leaned closer to whisper, "Squire Tucker told Billy they sell their wares for money."

"So?"

"God, Georgie, but you are green. They sell their bodies to men. And you cannot be one, anyway, for you are a duke's daughter, so you've got to be a lady." To prove his point, he added, "You are Lady Georgina Esmond, aren't you?"

"Yes, but—"

"Every female wants to be a lady, Georgie. Papa says I will have a better time finding a wife than Ned will, because when I marry, my wife will be Lady Durant."

Somehow the notion that her step-cousin might wed one day was disappointing. "Who are you going to marry?" she wanted to know. "Lizzie Tucker?"

"Lud, no. I can do better than a squire's girl, you know, for I shall be a baron. Ned or Charley can have her, since they'll just be plain misters. All they get is money, then they have to make their own ways before the world."

"Are the Durants rich?" she asked curiously.

"No, I don't think so. Not like the Esmonds, anyway—that's why Mama took—" He caught himself and stood up. "Come on—Mrs. Burgess will find you something you cannot ruin."

But as they crept past the kitchen door and into the house, they could hear angry voices coming from Charles Durant's study. But before they were halfway up the back stairs, Georgina heard her father announce, "It is decided—she goes to Broadmoor to school."

"Larry, you would not!" Jane protested angrily. "She is too young to be just plucked away and sent amongst strangers!"

"What a harridan you have become, Jane," he said smugly. "And, no, tears will not move me."

"How can Meg allow you to do this?" she cried. " 'Tis unnatural!"

"I am generous enough to the brat," he retorted.

"Generous! *Generous?*" she demanded, her voice rising. "Is it generous to deny a child her mother?"

"Meg had her choice."

"If she chose you, then she is as odious as you are. Larry, please—let me keep Georgie—let me rear her as my own as I have Max," she coaxed. "At least this way, she will have something."

"What a foolish female you are, my dear—to let a little b—" His voice died, then rose again in anger. "How dare you slap me, Jane! How *dare* you?"

"Oh, but you are richly deserving of it, Laurence—I would that I had done it a dozen times before! And maybe if Mama or Papa had, you'd be a bit more civil!"

Before Max and Georgie could run, the door opened, and the tall duke strode angrily out. Spying her, he grasped her arm and dragged her from her perch upon the stairs.

"How long have you been listening?" he demanded furiously. "I cannot abide a deceitful female, Georgina!"

"N-not long. Please, Papa—"

"I say, Uncle Laurence, but—" Max protested.

"Well, if you heard, then you know you are going away to school, don't you?" the duke asked her, ignoring the boy.

"Y-yes, sir," Georgie answered timidly.

"My sister does not know how to rear a girl properly, particularly not as an Esmond," he said, recovering his coldness. "She forgets what she used to be." His eyes swept the dark, narrow hallway contemptuously. "And all for a love match with a widower with an heir," he sneered. "She gave it all up for a love match where her own sons cannot inherit anything."

He dropped his hand and started back toward the front of the house. Georgina blurted out, "Can I see Mama, sir? I should like to see Mama again before—before she goes."

He stopped, but did not turn around. "She is indisposed," he answered. "But I am sure she will wish to give you your Christmas presents this evening ere you go to bed."

"Papa—sir?"

"What is it now?"

Very deliberately, she walked around to face him, then lifting her full red velvet skirt, she dropped a graceful curtsy before him. "Welcome to Malbern, sir."

He hesitated, then nodded. "At least it has not been a total waste here, has it?"

"No, sir."

She stared up at him, wishing desperately for him to embrace her, or to at least pat her head affectionately as her Uncle Charles often did. But Wymore was so very tall, so very stern, that she was afraid to say anything more to him.

Max caught her hand. "Come on, Georgie," he said

soothingly. "We'll get you bundled up, and when we go out, you can be my squire."

But she stood there, holding it inside her, until her father was out of hearing, then she sank to the steps and wailed, "I don't want to go away, Max! I don't want to go to any school! If I cannot have Mama—if Mama cannot love me, then I want to stay here with Aunt Jane and you and everyone!"

"He didn't say when you had to go, did he? Besides, he'll probably let you come to visit on holidays." Pulling his dirty handkerchief from his pocket, he thrust it at her. "Here—find a corner, will you?" Sitting on the step beside her, he said, "You know, I read somewhere that they used to believe wishes made on green sticks had power. We could find a green stick, and you could wish for whatever you want," he suggested hopefully.

"If I could wish for anything, it would be that Papa cared for me—that he and Mama would want me at Wymore," she answered.

"I don't know—that'd be a hard one, Georgie. Maybe you ought to wish for diamonds and silk dresses and—"

"No. If Papa could like me, everything else would be all right, I know it."

*Wymore, Cumbria, April 20, 1875*

The great stone house was dim and musty within, evoking thoughts of a mausoleum rather than the grand ancestral home of twelve generations of Esmonds. Rather than wait in the dark, cloistered confines of her father's study, Georgina paced in the outer hall, a long, marble-floored gallery, where it seemed as though every esteemed ancestor from "Sir Henry Esmond, Baron Staves: 1621–1649," the unfortunate who lost his head quite literally in King Charles's cause, to "Laurence Edward Thomas Esmond, Fourth Duke of Wymore," the father she scarce knew, looked down upon her. Across the way, segregated by someone's notion of importance, were the wives and mothers of all those Esmonds.

Georgina moved to stand beneath the last one, seeing "Margaret Halley Esmond, Duchess of Wymore," as she'd so often tried to remember her. There were no lines of pain in the lovely face, no gray within the halo of golden hair. But the artist, gifted as he was, had been unable to entirely hide the bitterness in those almost haunting blue eyes.

"You should be glad you were not here at the last," her brother Robin said behind her. "She did not go easily, I'm afraid."

"No one told me," she managed to whisper, despite her aching throat. "No one told me."

"Papa said to leave you be—that you could not do anything for her, anyway."

"I might have eased her, Robin. I might have held her hand and told her I loved her."

"He wouldn't hear of it. He said you were settled and could not get away."

"Robin, I was merely teaching literature at Miss Masterson's Academy! I could have come—I could have read to her! I could have seen that she had enough laudanum!"

"I wanted to tell you, Georgina—truly I did." He looked away briefly. "She asked for you, but then it was too late." His mouth twisted from the memory. "She could not see by then, so Johnny put on one of her dresses and pretended he was you, letting her feel the silk on his arm."

"But I should have been here! Why, Robin? Why does he hate me so?"

"He doesn't hate you," her brother murmured evasively. "He just said there was no need."

"No need?" Her voice rose. "No *need*? Robin, there was every need! She needed me—and I needed her!"

"You did not deal well together," he muttered, unwilling to meet her eyes.

"We never had the chance!"

"Ahem," Mr. Thornwell, the duke's solicitor, cleared his throat behind them. "Really, but given the sad circumstances, I scarce think it a time for rancor, Lady Georgina."

The young woman took a deep breath, then let it out slowly. "No, of course not—you are quite right, sir."

"His grace will be down shortly for the journey to the church, my lady," he added more gently. "You and Master John will occupy one carriage, and Wymore and Lord Bratchford will precede you in the other."

Lord Bratchford. It took a moment to assimilate that he meant Robin, who now held Wymore's lesser title. She was to accompany seventeen-year-old John, a brother she had scarce seen. At least she had crossed Robin's path at Malbern when they'd both visited there over holidays.

"Is aught amiss, my lady?" Thornwell inquired politely.

"No." But at twenty-one, she still felt the acute pain of years of slights and rejections. "No," she repeated more definitely.

"Good. After the service, we shall return here for a cold luncheon, then I shall make known the provisions of your mother's will to everyone."

"Yes, of course."

"And his grace says you may have the rest of the day to choose amongst her grace's clothing and books before he disposes of them."

"Out with the old, in with the new," Robin muttered under his breath.

"What?" she asked curiously.

"Had you not heard? Our esteemed papa already has a replacement in mind."

"Surely not."

"Oh, he will wait until the decent time, but he is expected to wed Lady Conniston later." He leaned closer. "As neither of them can smile, it ought to be the perfect match, don't you think?"

"Really, my lord, but—"

The solicitor's words were lost as the duke came down the wide, sweeping stairs. His gaze rested impersonally on them. "Is everyone quite ready?" he inquired coldly.

"As to that, Your Grace, I have been given to understand that Lord and Lady Durant are expected momentarily," Thornwell murmured apologetically.

"God aid that she does not bring the whole brood," Wymore said irritably. "How many is it that she has now, anyway?"

"I am sure I do not know, Your Grace."

"Aunt Jane and Uncle Charles have seven sons, sir," Georgina answered, speaking up. "Eight, if you would count Max."

"Egad. Yes, well, my sister was never content to do anything halfway, I suppose. Though how Charles is to provide for all of them, I am sure I don't know. Eight," he repeated, shuddering.

"Max is twenty-five now, Ned twenty-three, Charley twenty, and—"

"I pray you will spare me, Robin," he cut in curtly. "Suffice it to say that Jane is a fecund female."

"Yes, sir."

At that moment, the butler answered the front door, and Lady Durant swept in. Behind her, Maximilian Durant crossed the threshold.

"Terribly sorry to be late, Larry," she murmured, leaning to kiss her brother's cheek. "But Thomas and Arthur were taken with measles but hours before I left Malbern, so Charles and everyone but Max stayed at home. I assured him that Max's support was quite sufficient." Her gaze strayed to Georgina, and her expression warmed. "Georgie! My, how positively beautiful you are grown! Why, you look a great deal like your mama, don't you?"

"Margaret was fair," the duke said tersely. "And we are overlate."

"I expect it is her countenance," Jane went on, unabashed. "Yes, and the expression in the eyes. What do you think, Max?"

Embarrassed, Georgina took a deep breath, for her childhood friend had grown into perhaps the handsomest man of her acquaintance. And if half the tales she'd heard of him were true, he'd become quite the ladies' favorite for his clean, chiseled profile, his waving blond hair, and his bright blue eyes.

It was the first time he'd seen her in nearly two years. For a long moment, his eyes appraised her, then he nodded. "I think she still looks like our Georgie," he decided, disappointing her.

"Precisely," Wymore said. "As there are but two of you, I see no need for three carriages. Robin and John will ride with me, and you and Maximilian may take Georgina with you."

"She belongs with you, Larry—on this of all days, she belongs with you," Jane protested.

"No. Leave it be," the duke growled. "It is enough that she is here at all."

Stung, Georgina hastened to say, "Actually, I should prefer your company, Aunt Jane." Aware that Max looked at her oddly, she hastened to add, "And that of Cousin Max, of course."

The service had been brief and relatively private, leaving few to accompany Margaret Esmond's casket to its final resting place. As clouds loomed overhead, the vicar spoke over the open grave with haste, then the casket was covered quickly with spaded earth. When Georgina had looked up, Wymore was beside her, his eyes dry, his face inscrutable, as though he did not mourn his wife of nearly twenty-two years.

Upon their return to Wymore Castle, they dined on cold tongue and aspic, then retreated to the dark, dreary bookroom, where seats had been placed for everyone. And as Mr. Thornwell began reading from her mother's last will and testament, Georgina watched her cold, detached father rise and leave the room.

Oddly, her mother had chosen to make her small bequests to servants first, meting out odd pieces of jewelry and sums of cash to those who'd served her well in her years at Wymore. Then came the rest of it—"To Jane Esmond Durant, to whom I owe so much, I give the silver tea service she has admired. To my daughter, Georgina Esmond, I leave one thousand pounds of my own portion, my Chinese pearls, my emerald ring, whichever of my gowns she shall choose, and the diaries I have kept since my childhood. To my sons, Robert Esmond and John Esmond, I leave the furnishings in my chamber and two thousand pounds to be divided equably between them. And lastly, to my husband, Laurence Esmond, I give only that which must legally be his."

That was it, the sum total of what was left of a life now past. Robin and Johnny rose and approached Georgina.

"Uh, if there is any of Mother's furniture you would wish, you are more than welcome to take what you would like," Robin offered.

"It's not my sort of thing," Johnny added. "I mean, I haven't got a place for any of it."

"Thank you, but as she didn't leave it to me, I don't think I ought to take it either," she murmured.

"Er—His Grace would like a word with you, Lady Georgina," Mr. Thornwell said. "You may wait upon him in your mother's chamber."

An odd foreboding possessed her, tightening a

knot in her stomach. "Did he say why?" she dared
to ask.

"No."

Her Aunt Jane and Max had come up behind her.
"If you wish, I will go up with you," the woman
offered. "Or perhaps Max—"

"No," Georgina said quickly. "No, I don't think
Papa would like it."

"Buck up, Georgie," Max told her. "You are a
woman grown now, so you don't have to do anything you do not wish to."

"No, of course not."

Rising, Georgina made her way from the room,
pausing for one long look down the portrait gallery.
Resolutely, she grasped the polished mahogany ban-
nister and began climbing carpeted stairs. Feeling
very much as though her insides had turned to cold
jelly, she made her way upward.

All of her life, she'd been afraid of her father. All
of her life she'd been torn between hating him and
wishing he could somehow be made to love her.
Now she knew it was too late—she might not quite
hate him, but she was equally certain that he was
never going to care a button for her.

The hallway was dark, made so again by the dark,
carved panels lining it. Beneath her feet, ancient
boards creaked under the floral carpet, announcing
her. At her mother's chamber door, she halted, then
summoned enough courage to rap lightly with her
knuckles. The unlocked door creaked inward, sending another shiver of apprehension down her spine.

"You wished to see me, sir?" she managed.

He swung around from where he'd been standing
at the window, staring into the rain. His lips were
pressed together as he regarded her, then he nodded.

"Sit down."

"I think I should prefer to stand, sir."

"I suppose I ought to have expected that," he said, his voice bitter. "She liked to vex me also."

"Mama?"

"Who else? She was forever prating of you—as though it should change anything, as though I might let her have her bastard here." He looked hard at her. "That's what you are, you know. Her bastard." A small, harsh laugh escaped him. "You are no more mine than one of Saladin's pups is."

"But—"

"All you have of me is my name, and if I knew how, I should take that from you. Georgina Maria Frances Esmond, you are a living lie that I cannot abide."

"There must be some mistake," she said hollowly. "No, there has to be."

"I was deceived—your mother was not a virgin when she came to me."

"But Aunt Jane always—"

"Jane is a sentimental fool," he retorted curtly. "She wanted me to forget, to pretend I did not know, but I could not stand the sight of you, Georgina. Even after she agreed to rear you, she was always writing, always wishing to tell me how you went on, as if I should care. Well, I didn't, and I don't. There. Now there is no need for any pretense between us, is there?"

"No, sir, but—"

"But it is not meet for the presumed daughter of a duke to teach, so I am offering you an allowance—on condition."

"I don't want anything from you," she said with an evenness she did not feel. "I don't want to hang on your sleeve at all, sir."

"You will receive five hundred pounds per year," he went on as though he'd not heard her. "In exchange for that money, you will make no other demands on me, nor will you attempt to foist yourself on Robin or John." When she said nothing now, he continued explaining, "You will, however, conduct yourself according to the name you bear, *Lady* Georgina, which means you will not attempt to support yourself in any manner which must reflect unfavorably on the Esmonds. Should you seek employment anywhere, the allowance will stop." He paused to look at her. "Do you understand me?"

"I don't want your money."

"Nonetheless you shall have it—providing you leave Wymore in the morning and make no attempt to contact me again. If you find you have need of something beyond the five hundred pounds, you are to seek out Mr. Thornwell discreetly. And, if you receive an offer of marriage from a suitable gentleman, you are to contract a private ceremony that will not cause undue comment. You may, however, regard your allowance as your marriage portion."

"No." She dared to meet his eyes. "If you are not my father, sir, then I have no wish to further the acquaintance either."

"Bold words for a penniless female," he scoffed.

Her chin came up. "I have the thousand pounds Mama left me, which is a great deal more than I should ever earn at Miss Masterson's, so I shall no doubt survive without alms from the Esmonds."

"Should you change your mind, you need only apply to Mr. Thornwell," he said coldly. Looking about his late wife's chamber, he added, "You have the rest of the day to decide what you wish to have in here. I have instructed Mrs. Whitsell to mark whatever you cannot take with you that it may be sent later." His piece said, he started walking toward the door. "Goodbye, Georgina."

The intense pain she had expected wasn't there. Nor was the pent-up hurt and anger of nearly twenty-one years. No, she merely felt empty of everything.

She waited until he had his hand on the doorknob before speaking.

"I'm glad I am not your daughter, Your Grace. Now I may perhaps find a father who can love me."

He half-turned back to her. "He was a nobody—a half-pay soldier who thought the Halleys had money. And your mother was a weak-witted fool who believed everything he told her."

But after he left, she sank into a chair. She wasn't really an Esmond, and the Duke of Wymore wasn't her father. It explained so much, relieving so much of the guilt that had haunted her childhood. She wasn't to blame—it wasn't her fault that Laurence Esmond did not love her. If her mother had only told her, she could have been spared so much.

She wasn't an Esmond. She sat there, letting it sink in, wondering how she could not have known. But much of her life, she'd heard well-meaning strangers remark that she resembled the duke. A stretch of fancy, nothing more. She ought to be devastated, but she wasn't. And as the realization of what Wymore had told her took hold, she felt almost happy. She wasn't an Esmond.

"Are you all right, Georgie? Mother would have come herself, but her leg is bothering her dreadfully."

It was Max. She looked up, then brushed an errant strand from her forehead self-consciously. "Yes—yes, I am," she answered, forcing a smile.

"You look like you've had a queer start."

"No—not at all. Max—?" She hesitated, then blurted out, "Did you know?"

"Know what?"

"That we aren't related?"

"We've never precisely been related, Georgie. As much as I claim her, Jane is my stepmother."

"I know that." She bit her lower lip, then looked

up at him again. "But Papa isn't my father—did you
know that?"

"No, but it doesn't surprise me."

"Well, it surprised me."

"He told you that?"

"Yes. He wants me out of his life—as though I
have ever been in it," she said bitterly. Her mouth
twisted into a crooked smile. "That explains so much,
doesn't it? Because I am not his daughter, he could
not abide me."

"I don't know as I'd want to be his, truth to tell,"
he said soberly. Walking closer, he laid a hand on
her shoulder. "It's all right, Georgie—you'll come
about."

"He doesn't want me to teach any more—he
doesn't want me to disgrace the family name, Max—
he's so afraid I shall bring discredit upon the Esmonds that he's offered five hundred pounds a year
if I will do nothing. 'Tis rich, isn't it? I'm not an
Esmond, but I am stuck with the name."

"Until you marry."

"Which is about as likely as pigs flying," she retorted. No, I shall be an Esmond in name for the rest
of my life."

"Making it too grim, aren't you?"

She caught herself. "Yes, I am, aren't I? And in
truth, I ought to be celebrating that I have no ties to
him."

"Yes. Poor Robin and Johnny will be his forever."
His hand clasped her shoulder, then released it. "You
might as well come back to Malbern with Mama."

"I have no claim on her now."

"She's always loved you."

"I'm not a child anymore, Max. Next month, I shall
be one and twenty, in case you have forgotten."

"No, I hadn't. But it seems as though you still
ought to be the grubby little girl who played knights
and castles in the hayloft."

She stared at the water on the window for a moment. "You gave me my love of old stories, Max—did you know that? For the past two years I have taught them to other grubby little schoolgirls, and I love them still."

"As do I, Georgie—as do I."

"Do you remember when you were King Arthur?"

"And you could not pronounce Guinevere?"

"I called her Winnie, I believe."

"I remember. I was a dreamer then," he said softly.

"And I wanted to be just like you."

"Did you?"

"I always thought you knew everything," she admitted simply.

"I thought I did." He pulled up a chair across from her, and sat, leaning forward. "I suppose you read where I offered for Miss Robinson?"

"Yes."

"Unfortunately, she proved as empty-headed as she was rich."

"Max, you didn't jilt her?"

"Lud, no—but it was a near thing. I had to throw her at someone else before she would cry off."

"Max! What an awful thing to say!"

"No, you don't, Georgie. Don't you go getting as censorious as the rest of the females. I have always liked you for being different."

"Well, I'm not—or if I am, I don't want to be."

His manner changed abruptly. "So, what *are* you going to do now?"

"I am going to find my father—and hopefully he will wish to be found. If I am not an Esmond, I want to know who I am, I suppose."

"No." He leaned across to her, looking into her dark eyes, feeling incredibly sorry for her. "No, Georgie," he said, possessing her hands, "you are going to marry me."

"*What?*" For a moment, the room seemed to spin

around her. She stared, trying to make sense of him. "Max, have you lost your mind?" she demanded finally.

"You cannot go off alone, Georgie—it just isn't done."

"But you have not even seen me in years—you cannot—"

"Two years. And I have always liked you," he declared flatly.

"But you don't love me—you cannot say you love me, can you?" she persisted.

"People of our class don't marry for love, Georgie. At least we should be comfortable together, for we have known each other most of our lives."

She opened her mouth, then shut it. "I'm not of your class anymore, Max. If the truth were known, I should be counted naught but a bastard."

"It isn't known, and there is no way Wymore can repudiate you publicly now. Besides, there is a great deal to like in you. You read, and you think, and you care." He smiled boyishly at her. "You remind me a great deal of my stepmother, Georgie. And if you are half the wife she is, you ought to make me the happiest man in England."

As she looked into his bright blue eyes, she felt truly tempted. But she knew why he'd offered, and she didn't want to be taken out of pity.

"No," she said slowly. "You might come to love someone, and then you would be tied to me. And I'm not the sort of person who could give you carte blanche to carry on with other females, I'm afraid."

"Georgie—"

"I'm going to look for my father, Max—I have to. If for no other reason than to see him, to ask him if Mama meant anything to him. And I'd know why he did not marry her."

"No, you are expecting considerably more than that, and you risk being hurt all over again."

"But I have to see him. Max, I want to see if I look like him, if I—"

"You are hoping he won't be like Wymore, but you cannot know that. Even if you are to find him, you might not like him at all."

"I am determined he shall like me."

"You cannot expect a stranger to love you, Georgie. Besides, what if you cannot discover him? What if he's dead?"

"He won't be—I know it," she said with conviction. "You once told me to wish upon a green stick. Well, I shall go further—I shall predict that I find him—and I shall make him love me. There, I have said it." She looked across at him. "Do you wish to make a wager that I cannot do it?"

"No, of course not."

"Go on—I don't mind."

"I don't want to take your money, Coz."

"Tonight I am going to read Mama's diaries, and hopefully she will have mentioned my father somewhere in them."

"And if she does not?"

"Then I shall have to ask the Halleys. Someone must surely know of this, don't you think?"

He rose and walked to stand before the window. "You don't want to know what I think. You haven't listened to anything I have said."

She stood up, then moved behind him. "You have always been my dearest friend," she said softly. "But we should not suit, Max—you have been a man of the world, while I have merely taught young girls to appreciate literature. One day you would look at me and feel cheated—I know it. Please—cry friends with me."

"All right." He turned to face her. "Friends."

"Thank you."

After he left to go back downstairs, she felt an intense loss far greater than that of Wymore. Where she had learned to dislike the duke, she had always cherished a girlish tendre for Max Durant. For a moment, she fought the urge to cry, then she reminded herself that he hadn't really wished to marry her, that he was probably vastly relieved that she'd had the sense to turn him down.

Forcing her thoughts from him, she went to her mother's desk and opened the drawers one by one, hoping to discover the journals. As she poked amongst Margaret Esmond's belongings, she felt as though she were some sort of thief. Until she found her own letters.

Her mother had kept all of them, tying them in neat stacks with pink satin ribbon, telling Georgina she'd meant something, after all. Beneath them were sheets of vellum addressed to "My dearest daughter," letters she'd never posted. As Georgina sorted through them, she felt a terrible anger that her mother had been too weak-spined to send them to the lonely child at Broadmoor. Then, at the very bottom, she came across a single sheet, and the masculine scrawl was chilling.

*Here are all of your letters to your brat. As you can see, I franked none of them.*

Wymore was a beast, that was all there was to it. And if there was truly an Almighty in heaven, then he surely must be punished for his hatred, she hoped fervently. God must surely see him cast down to hell for what he had done to his wife.

"Was you needing anything, my lady?" Mrs. Whitsell asked.

Georgina jumped back as though she'd been caught red-handed. "No—that is, I was looking for Mama's diaries. She left them to me," she explained lamely.

"I got 'em for ye," the woman told her. "I wasn't

wanting him to read 'em after she was dead," she added cryptically. "God knows as she didn't have no secrets when she was here, God rest her soul."

"No, I suppose not."

"She was wanting ye, ye know, and Lord Robin was all for sending to ye, but he wouldn't budge—not at all."

"So I am told. Uh—I don't suppose you could fetch them, could you?"

"They ain't left the room." Crossing to where the late duchess's things still hung in the huge wardrobe, she bent down and lifted a board in the bottom. Straightening up, she held a thick stack of journals in her hands. "Don't know how far back they go, but she said she tried to write something every day."

"Thank you." Taking the musty books, Georgina carried them to the desk. "If you will light the lamp, that will be all I shall require."

"Yes, my lady."

*My lady.* She wasn't even entitled to be called that now, but no one knew it. Resolutely, she opened each diary, noting the first date, then laying it aside until she found the earliest one. At first, she was dismayed to see that her mother had apparently used initials for names in most cases.

It had to be 1853. Her fingers traced the date 8 August, 1853, which was two weeks more than nine months before she was born. She read eagerly, her lips forming the words.

*Wm. sent a posey, but Mama made me reject it, saying Papa would have Wm.'s skin if he discovered it. I am the most miserable of females, for it is determined I shall accept Wymore, tho I cannot abide him. This face is a curse, for it dooms me. I shall hate being a duchess, I know it. Tonight I shall have M. carry a note to Wm., tho it breaks my heart to know I shall never have him.*

Wm. William. There it was. But William who? She read on, turning the next several pages, looking for a last name, finding none. But her mother's distress was more and more evident.

> *Danced with Wymore, then Wm. It was as day after night, and so I told him. Next month, he is being posted to Portsmouth, then off to India. I know not how I shall bear it. Wymore kissed me with far more passion than is allowed, but to me it was as nothing. Soon I shall be but as another possession in his house, but I shall still ache for my Wm.*

Maybe it wasn't William, after all, for he was being sent abroad, probably by Wymore's design, Georgina thought cynically. How very like him to manipulate everything.

> *12 August. I managed to escape the house and spend an agreeable hour in the Park with Wm., but I fear Mrs. Thurstan may have seen us. If Papa says anything I shall die.*
>
> *13 August. We are found out, and Papa is furious with me. I see no course but to go to Wm. and hope he will elope with me. Otherwise, I shall be chained to Wymore forever, and I shall never forgive any of them. Have sent M. with a note to Wm.*

The next date in the book was more than a week later, and the tone changed to one of utter despair. No, it had to be this William. Had her mother eloped, after all? She read further, seeking some clue.

> *22 August. I wish I were dead. Wymore has obtained a license from the archbishop, and on the morrow, I shall be wed. Papa threatens that if I do not moan and cry out in L.'s bed, I shall be utterly ruined, and he will repudiate me. It is enough to make me grit my teeth and bear it, for I hope the duke does send me home in disgrace. Then I shall never have to see him again.*

Georgina did not want to read about the forced marriage, so she marked the place and closed the journal. She had to discover the identity of William. But as her mother and her Halley grandparents were gone now, it was going to be difficult, when all she had was a first name. She even considered asking Wymore, but she doubted he would tell her. It didn't matter, she told herself fiercely. If she had to examine troop lists for September of 1853, she would do it. Even if William was perhaps the commonest of English names. But first she would begin with her Halley relations. Though she scarce knew them either, she did know that her mother had had brothers. Brothers who had not cared enough to attend her funeral.

Having made arrangements to leave early through Mrs. Whitsell, Georgina came down in her travel dress well before nine. In the dining room, Robin and Max were already eating.

"Come join us, Georgie," Robin called out.

"A bit of toast, perhaps," she conceded. "And some tea."

"Papa is not yet down."

"I did not expect it." She took a deep breath, then let it out. "Indeed, I do not expect to come back here at all."

"Now, dash it, Georgie, but you got to let us know how you go on. Mama would wish it."

"He wouldn't."

"He's always been given to queer starts," Robin said consolingly. "I can tell you there have been more times than Johnny and I could count when we envied you for living away from here."

"You wouldn't have liked Broadmoor."

"At least you didn't have to listen to him."

She took her seat and laid a napkin across her lap. Not daring to look at Max, she asked casually, "Tell me, Rob—did Mama and—and Papa quarrel a great deal?"

"Not after she became ill. Before that, she tried to ignore him, and he could not stand that, I suppose."

"Yes."

"He bullocks everyone, as well you know."

"I can imagine it. Uh—I don't suppose Mama spoke much of her life before she married, did she?"

"Only that Grandfather Halley was very like Papa."

"But she never mentioned any friends—no one named William?"

"William? No, not that I can recall, anyway. Was he some sort of relation?"

"He was a soldier who went to India."

"Now *that* I would have remembered," he decided positively.

Max seemed to be intent on the sausages on his plate. Without looking up, he ventured to ask, "Where do you mean to go when you leave here?"

"To see Mama's brothers. I thought perhaps to go to Maple Hill, but beyond that I don't know."

"Do you know them?" Robin asked curiously. "They never seemed to have much to do with Mama. In fact, I don't think any of the Halleys ever came here that I can remember."

"No, but I daresay they will not turn me away."

"Papa said they were all queer ducks—odd, given that he is rather peculiar himself, wouldn't you think? Sort of the pot and kettle thing, eh?"

"I suppose." As a liveried footman approached diffidently, she ordered, "I should like a pot of tea and some buttered toast, I think."

"Yes, my lady," he murmured. "And would your ladyship care for poached eggs and sausage perhaps?"

It was a long journey to Maple Hill. "Yes, that will be fine, thank you."

"How are you getting there?" Max asked abruptly.

"Well, I had thought to take the stage."

"No, you'll be squeezed in with every pickpocket and cutpurse."

"I came by stage," she reminded him.

"And who's to get you from the posting house to Maple Hill?" Robin wanted to know. "You ought to ask Papa for the use of one of the carriages."

"Just now I would not ask him for anything."

"Then I'll ask for you."

"I pray you will not."

He regarded her curiously for a moment. "You know, Georgie, you are as odd as he is. How can you wish to ride the stage above the convenience of a private coach?"

"Actually, the people one meets are rather interesting," she responded evasively. "Pass the sugar, will you?"

When her food arrived, she ate in silence, hoping that Robin did not press her further. And yet as she glanced furtively sidewise, she could see that Max watched her. Discomfited, she polished off her food in short order, then rose.

"Well, I daresay it will be a while before we are met again," she murmured.

"Unless the old man dies," Robin agreed. "You would come home for that surely."

"Home? I'm afraid I have not your attachment for the place." She stood there awkwardly, uncertain as to whether she ought to keep up the pretense with him. But if he knew at all, he gave not the least inkling of it. "Yes, well, goodbye, Robin. Max. And you must tell Johnny that I am sorry I did not get to wish him well at Oxford next year."

"I shall walk you out," Max decided.

"Really, but that will not be necessary." She forced a smile, then held out her hand. "I shall treasure

your friendship always—truly. You and Aunt Jane
made my childhood bearable."

"You make it sound as though you intend to drop
off the earth," Robin chided. "Ten to one, you'll be
either at Malbern or here for Christmas. Now that
the old man has let you come home once, there'll be
no end to it," he predicted.

"I don't think so." Aware that Max still held her
fingers, she retrieved them quickly. "I hate good-
byes," she whispered. "Tell Aunt Jane that I shall
write her."

With that, she made good her escape, knowing that
once she made it to the posting house, there was no
turning back. No matter what name she bore, she
didn't belong to them anymore. She didn't belong to
anyone.

The common room of the Blue Duck was crowded
with those awaiting stages, but she managed to
elbow her way through to buy her ticket as far as
Manchester.

"Coach's going to be full," the agent noted. "Five
inside, four on top."

"Five inside? Then I ought to get a reduction in
fare, I should think."

"One's a boy, so he don't take up much room."

"Oh." She looked around briefly. "How long until
we leave?"

" 'Bout an hour, if it is on time."

"Yes, of course. Er—I do not suppose I could en-
gage a private parlor?" she inquired hopefully. "I
could use a strong cup of tea."

"Oh, aye. Maude! Maude! Give the lady a room
for her tea, eh?"

The woman's gaze swept over Georgina, and her
nose went up, indicating her disdain. "Ye traveling
alone?"

"To Manchester."

"Humph! In my day, females didn't go gadding without someone to look after 'em—not unless they was loose women. Now ye got 'em going off to furrin places and cavorting with heathens."

"I should scarce count Manchester a foreign place." When the woman made no effort to direct her to a private room, Georgina drew herself up to her full height. "I should still like a parlor, madam."

"Oh, ain't ye hoity-toity now?"

"Give her the room, Maude."

"And who's paying for it?"

"I am."

Georgina spun around at the sound of his voice, and her breath caught. "What are you doing here, Max?" she managed weakly.

"I guess I am taking you to Maple Hill."

"I have already bought my ticket."

"I'll cash it in for you."

"Here now—I'm running a respectable place," Maude protested.

"Her ladyship would like to be private," he said smoothly.

"Her ladyship? Oooh, and ye wasn't telling me?" the woman said archly, clearly disbelieving him. "Aye, and I am Queen Victoria herself a-working at the Blue Duck, ain't I? No, me fine buck, ye'll have to think a better one than that."

"She is Lady Georgina Esmond," he said evenly. "Wymore's daughter."

Maude's jaw fell open, then she recovered. "Well, how was I to know it, and her a-riding the common stage, I ask ye?" She bobbed a quick curtsy. "If yer ladyship was to follow me this way, I'll get yer tea right to ye."

"Max, you wretch," Georgina muttered under her breath at him. "What *are* you doing here?"

"I didn't think you had enough money. Besides, I told you—I've a fancy to go to Maple Hill with you."

She waited until the woman withdrew from the tiny room. "Wymore won't thank you for bandying his name about."

"I doubt he will ever hear of it." Sitting down, he removed his hat and smoothed his unruly blond hair. "William, eh?"

"Yes."

"Is that all you have to go on?"

"Yes, but I shall find him."

"What if he died in India?"

"I have to hope he didn't. Look, I know you cannot understand, but I should like to see him." She looked down at her gloved hands. "I should like to hear of Mama from him. All I ever saw was Papa—the duke, that is—was him browbeating her. I'd know if she had spirit before. No, that is not quite true—I *know* she had spirit, for she tried to elope with him."

"You found out that much, did you?"

"Yes. She didn't want to marry Wymore at all. It was rather sad reading, I'm afraid. Apparently, she fled with her William, but did not succeed, for in the end, 'twas Wymore who won."

"Tell me—am I that difficult to take?" he asked suddenly.

"No, but you have offered for the wrong reasons." She dared to meet his eyes momentarily, then she looked down again. " 'Twas pity, wasn't it?"

"Part of it."

"Well, as foolish as it sounds, I should rather wait for a grand passion."

"And if it does not come?"

"Then I shall be a spinster. There are worse things, I think. Certainly Mama would have been better off without the husband she got."

"You know, Georgie, you truly know how to wound a man. I would have treated you a great deal better than he treated her."

"I know, but I should always have worried that

you would discover a grand passion of your own later. Please—I don't wish to discuss it."

"I'm still going with you."

"There is no need."

"Maybe it makes me feel like a knight errant—did you never think of that?" he asked. "Besides, you might need me to beard the Halleys for you. They might not wish to rake up an old scandal."

"All right," she decided finally.

"Cry friends again?"

She nodded. "Friends."

She viewed the ancient stone house with misgiving as she stepped down from Max Durant's carriage. By the looks of it, the Halleys had not prospered despite their daughter's brilliant marriage. As she started toward the house, she could see where stones had come loose and been left lying where they'd fallen. Behind her, Max stopped to survey the place.

"Not precisely inviting, is it?" he murmured.

"No. Not at all. But as my grandparents are both dead, perhaps the present owner does not care quite as much for it."

"Still, he is a Halley, isn't he?"

"I don't know—maybe it has been sold."

Taking a deep breath for courage, she marched up the steps to knock upon the scarred door. When no one answered, Max pounded it, calling out loudly, "Is anyone within?"

Finally, an elderly man opened it to peer outside. "Who is it?" he rasped.

Georgina hesitated, then announced, "Lady Georgina Esmond—Margaret Halley's daughter!"

"Eh?" The old fellow cupped his hand behind his ear. "Cannot hear ye."

"Margaret Halley's daughter!" she shouted.

"She married a duke," he answered, shaking his head. "Miss Margaret married a duke."

"And I am her daughter!"

He peered closely at her, then stepped back, muttering that she might have said so. Max leaned over her shoulder to whisper, "If he is all that is left here, we are out."

"Mrs. Watson will be down in a trice," the old fellow promised.

"Are any of my uncles left at home?" As he looked blankly at her, she raised her voice. "My uncles—where are they?"

"Gone to Lunnon."

"Which one owns Maple Hill?"

"Maple Hill? Why, ye're in it."

"You might wish to wait for Mrs. Watson," Max observed dryly.

"And hope she is not deaf also," she murmured.

The old man threw open a door and directed them inside. As Georgina went in, she could smell the musty odor of damp dust, and as her eyes adjusted to the dimness, she could see Holland covers everywhere. The elderly retainer followed her gaze with rheumy eyes, then nodded.

"Lady Halley don't like it here," he explained. As he walked across the room to pull back the heavy draperies, the floor creaked beneath the faded carpet. "They don't come anymore," he added.

"Lawks a-mercy, but what's going on?" a plump, round-faced woman demanded from the hall.

"Company," the old man muttered, leaving them.

As Max removed his hat, Georgina held out her hand. "I am Margaret Halley's daughter, and—"

"Ye don't look like her—not at all."

"You knew her, then?"

"Aye. Prettiest creature on God's earth, she was."

Georgina's pulse raced, and she had to tell herself to proceed slowly. "You were here when she lived at home?" she asked carefully.

"I was her mama's maid afore I was the housekeeper," Mrs. Watson allowed, nodding. "How is Lady Margaret?"

"She died less than a fortnight ago."

"A pity—a terrible pity," the woman clucked sympathetically. "I ain't seen her for years, ye know—he wasn't one as let her come home."

"The duke?"

"Aye. It fair broke my heart when Lord Halley made the poor little creature wed him, it did. But I ain't supposed to say that, I guess."

"No, I already know she didn't want to be a duchess," Georgina admitted.

"Oh, it was more'n that." Mrs. Watson looked around the room, then shook her head. "The place wasn't always like this, ye know. But I ain't being hospitable, am I?" Moving to a sofa, she pulled the dusty cover from it. "Sit down, and I'll have a bit of tea for ye."

"Oh, but I—" Georgina was talking to air, for the woman had already left. Turning to Max, she confided, "I think she knows."

"Maybe." He dropped his tall frame onto the sofa, then leaned back. "Are you sure you really want to rake up an old scandal, Georgie?"

"Yes. No matter what, I want to know where I belong. I've never had that—never."

"Not even at Malbern?"

"Not even at Malbern. I always knew I did not belong there, that my mother lived elsewhere, and that it wasn't right."

"All right, then," he said, sighing. "We shall follow it to the end." He felt silent for a moment, then he said almost absently, "My mother died while I was yet in leading strings."

"At least you had Uncle Charles, and then Aunt Jane."

"But I always wondered about her," he admitted soberly. "I always wondered what she was like."

"You could have asked, and they would have told you. All I knew was that my mother and father did not want me."

"It isn't the same, Georgie. One still wishes to know one's parents."

"Precisely. Which is why I have to find my father."

"Well, now—I got the tea for ye," Mrs. Watson announced, bustling back into the room. Wiping the dust from a table with her sleeve, the woman set the tea tray down. "Sugar, my lady?"

"Yes—and cream also."

"And fer ye, sir?"

"I'll have the same."

As she poured, the housekeeper observed, "Now ye look more like her, sir—I can see the resemblance there."

"Actually, I am no relation," he admitted apologetically. "I am a Durant—Maximilian Durant."

"Oh, well, ye are blond, so I thought—"

"Not that he wouldn't have wished to be," Georgina said hastily. Taking the filled teacup, she balanced it on her knee. "You said you felt sorry for Mama, Mrs. Watson," she prompted.

"Well, I ain't supposed to tell no tales."

"I have read Mama's diaries."

"Then ye must've known she didn't want him."

"She wanted William, didn't she?"

The old woman looked up sharply, then away. "Ye read that, eh?"

"Yes. She tried to elope with him."

"Aye, but it wasn't no use to try it. Lord Halley and Master Thomas went after 'em."

"But they were gone a week, and the scandal had to be hushed up so she could marry Wymore."

"Aye. They wasn't found for nigh to four days, and when she was brung home, I could see where she was beaten badly, poor thing. Her papa said as if she turned the duke down, he'd see poor Mr. Carrick hanged for a thief." Mrs. Watson looked into the empty fireplace as though she could see it again. "They took his lordship's horses, you see, for they was faster than the nags as Mr. Carrick had."

"His name was William Carrick?"

"Aye. And the Carricks were poorer than the church mice—Mr. William's papa had a hosiery business, and he couldn't afford to feed all his boys. That's why poor Mr. Carrick had to be a soldier, don't ye see?"

"He was a common soldier?"

"As I remember it, he was a leftenant—bought his own commission, he said."

"And he went to India?"

"Oh, he came back from there, and he was still a-wanting to marry Miss Margaret, but he was too late. Lord Halley told him if he was to ever try seeing her, he could still have him hanged. Besides, I guess she'd had two babes by then, if I recall it right."

Hope rose within Georgina's breast. "Mr. Carrick—he must have lived close by, then?"

"He was billeted at Manchester with his regiment."

"Then he wasn't from here?"

"His papa's business was at York, I think. Aye, he had a bit of the sound in his voice. It was York," she decided positively.

It was difficult to hide the elation Georgina felt, and now she was eager to leave, to be on her way, but when she cast a sidewise glance at Max, he was frowning. She gulped her tea down with unladylike haste, then set the cup and saucer on the table. Turning to him, she dared to ask, "Do you think we can reach York by nightfall?"

"Possibly."

"Ye ain't leavin' already?" Mrs. Watson exclaimed. "But I was hoping to serve dinner to ye!"

"We really cannot stay, but I thank you ever so

much for the tea. Max—please, let us try, Max," she coaxed. "We are already nearly there, aren't we?"

"No," he answered baldly. "It's still a dashed long distance, given how far we have come."

"But you have fast horses," she reminded him.

It was difficult to dampen her renewed enthusiasm, but he still had misgivings. If William Carrick's father were a hosier, quite possibly William himself might not be anyone she would wish to know. And the last thing Georgina needed was someone to hang on her sleeve, particularly if she didn't intend to take Wymore's allowance.

He shrugged. "I am but along to chaperone, aren't I?"

"Then you will do it?"

"Yes."

Mrs. Watson regarded him curiously, and it was obvious to her that he was a real buck of fashion. "And who's to chaperone him?" she asked under her breath.

"Max is but my cousin," Georgina said flatly. "Actually, as we were reared together when small, he is more like a brother."

But outside, as he was handing her up into his coach, he grumbled, "You did not have to make her think no one would look twice at me, did you?"

"I didn't say that." Sinking back against the well-padded seat, she cocked her head to study him. "You are quite handsome, you know."

"You are a trifle late for flattery, don't you think?" he countered. "I've a fair notion where I stand in your esteem, anyway."

"Quite high, actually. And if you did not mean to see this to the end, you ought not to have turned in my stage ticket."

"What if there is no trace of Carrick in York?"

"There will be—I know it."

"You are a deuced pig-headed female, Georgie Esmond. If he isn't in York, I suggest we go back to Malbern, and I will make discreet inquiries of the army."

"I knew I forgot something! I forgot to ask her if she remembered whether he was a dragoon or what. Max—"

"We are already on the road, Georgie. Besides, I don't think she was pleased with your haste."

"No, I suppose not." She looked out onto the rolling green hills and sighed. "I only hope that York is not filled with Carricks."

She had dozed much of the way. He sat across from her, watching her, thinking that Wymore and his wife had been utter fools. With that thick, dark hair, and those dark eyes of hers, she could have been a credit to them. As the Duke of Wymore's daughter, she would have been the reigning Toast if she'd had a social season in London. But instead, they'd kept her buried like some awful secret, robbing her not only of a birthright, but also of any chance to be loved. And in his opinion, her mother must have been a total ninny for letting it happen.

The carriage rolled to a halt, and he leaned forward to shake her gently. "Come on—we are arrived, Georgie. I say we eat, then inquire about Carrick."

"I'm not very hungry."

"I am."

"All right." She sat up and rubbed her eyes, then looked out the window. "You think I am looking for a needle in the proverbial haystack, don't you?"

"I don't know. I just hope you are not disappointed when you find him. He could be a sot—or worse."

"My mother would not have loved a sot, Max."

"I'm afraid you have a higher opinion of her than I do," he murmured.

It was already growing dark, and the lights of half

a dozen pubs were lit, beckoning to custom. He jumped down, then turned to lift her out. Looking up and down the street, he considered the offerings.

"Which do you fancy?"

"I don't care."

"Then let us attempt Olde Starre, which claims to be 'the oldest licensed pub in all of York,' " he read from the sign in front of it. "And from the smell, the specialty of the house must surely be fish."

She sniffed the air and nodded. "I'd say you must be right."

"Come on—you always were the game one."

It was crowded, a testimony to the popularity of the place. But somehow Max managed to squeeze through to a small table. "Sit down, and I'll order something. Cod or plaice?"

"Bread and soup, if they have it."

Nearly too tired to hold her head up, she sat there, waiting while he spoke to the man behind the bar. The air around her was smoky, steamy, and laden with the smells of food and ale. Off in one corner, two men disputed over a game of darts played in exceedingly close quarters.

"Bread and Cornish butter," Max announced. "He'll bring your soup out to you."

"Thank you."

He set his own plate down, then regarded her smugly. "At the risk of being whisked from my food, I can tell you that William Carrick lives not far from here."

She'd schooled herself to be disappointed, and now she had to assimilate the reality that she could actually come face to face with her father, with the man who'd eloped with her mother nearly twenty-two years before. Her stomach knotted, making the prospect of food unappealing.

"If you don't eat, I won't take you there," he warned her.

"I'm not hungry."

"You've scarce eaten all day."

"Max, what if he does not like me? What if he should turn me away?" she asked, betraying her anxiety. "I don't think I could bear it."

"Then he is a fool."

She stared at her bread. "All of my life, there has been no place for me," she said wistfully. "And now I have gotten my hopes so high that I don't know if I can bear it should he deny me. I don't want to go through life being nothing to anyone any longer."

"Georgie—"

"Don't pity me—please. I have a surfeit of that for myself."

"Yes, you do," he said bluntly. "And if this proves to be a wash-out, then we shall go home."

"No. If he is my father, and he will not claim me, then I shall just have to go on. I can take Mama's portion she left me and open a school of my own, possibly beneath Wymore's nose." She tried to smile, but her mouth merely twisted. "I shall teach disbelieving girls about Launcelot and Guinevere, Gawain and Gareth and Galahad. I still love them, you know."

"I know." His hand covered hers. "We'll see, Georgie."

His fingers were strong and warm and utterly reassuring. For a long moment, she did not move as she considered the man across from her.

"You always made me think I could do anything, you know," she said softly.

"Anything?"

"Yes. For you, I have jumped out of haylofts, ridden impossible horses, and taken more tumbles than I care to remember. Do you remember when I fell into Squire Tucker's pond?"

"Yes."

"You pulled me out."

"Papa did not appreciate my heroism, as I recall. I seem to remember being soundly birched for letting you fall into it in the first place."

"But you were there." Suddenly fighting the urge to cry, she looked at him through brimming eyes. "You were my best friend, Max. No, you *are* my best friend."

"I'm not nearly the paragon you think me," he said finally.

"I missed you more than anyone when Papa— when Wymore sent me to Broadmoor. I cried so much that Mrs. Stevens put me on bread and water until I stopped." Embarrassed now, she pulled her hand free of his. "I shouldn't have told you that, should I?"

"God, but you know how to pull the heartstrings, don't you?" he managed. Picking up his fork and knife, he began dissecting his fish. "Go on—eat up. I know you do not mean to give me any peace until you find Carrick."

There was a light still on in the hosiery shop, and through the window an elderly man could be seen sorting his wares into narrow bins. She peered nervously inside, then whispered, "But he's rather old, isn't he? He doesn't look at all the sort to have dashed for the border with Mama."

"There's only one way to find out." Reaching out, he knocked loudly.

"We are closed," came the feeble-sounding reply.

"We wish to speak with a William Carrick!" Max called through the door.

"William, you say?" The old man moved slowly, stopping just behind the long pane. "Who are you?"

Georgina steeled herself, then announced baldly, "I am Margaret Halley's daughter. I have come to see my father."

For a moment, she did not think he meant to open

the door at all, but finally he unlatched it from inside. As he stood back, she went in. Reaching for Max's hand, she held it tightly.

"Are you William Carrick, sir?"

"No. But what's this, miss? His daughter, you say? Well, it cannot be, for he never wed."

"Then you know him?"

He nodded. "My boy."

"Please—I have to see him—I have to."

"Er—I expect you have his direction?" Max asked.

"That I do. But he ain't at home—dart night, you know."

"Dart night?" Georgina echoed.

"At the Olde Starre. Wednesday, ain't it?"

"Yes."

"Then that's where he is."

She'd probably already seen him. "What does he look like?" she asked eagerly. "Is he tall?"

" 'Bout my size, but heavier. Got no hair neither."

"He's bald?"

"Aye. If ye see him, tell him I've got all of it sorted, eh? And that I've gone on to bed."

"Yes, of course." She caught his hand and pumped it. "Thank you, sir—thank you."

His faded eyes studied her, then he shook his head. "He don't have no by-blows, I know it."

Outside, she drew in the damp night air. "We saw him, and we did not know it, Max—we saw him!"

"Possibly, but the old man did not sound particularly encouraging."

"But it is not the sort of thing one would tell on oneself, is it?" she countered. "He surely would not have gone home and said 'I tried to elope with Lord Halley's daughter,' I shouldn't think."

"I collect you want to go back to the Olde Starre, don't you?" he said, sighing.

"Yes."

"All right. But if Carrick isn't there, I am for getting rooms and looking again tomorrow. I'm dashed tired, Georgie."

She looked up at him, seeing his face in the street-lamp light. He did look rather drawn, and the crinkle lines at the corners of his eyes seemed deeper. She knew she ought to have offered to wait until morning, but she could not. She'd not sleep until she saw William Carrick.

"I'm sorry—truly I am."

"What a little liar you are, Georgie."

Incredibly, he was smiling, and she felt a tug within as she met his eyes. No man, cousin or not, ought to look quite like that. It wasn't fair to any female. Without thinking, she reached up to brush his tousled blond hair back from where it fell over his forehead.

His hand left hers to slide up her arm, then around her shoulder. For a moment, he stared intently into her dark eyes, then he bent his head to hers. She closed her eyes as she felt the warmth of his breath on her skin, the tentative brush of his lips on hers. His other arm closed around her, holding her, as he teased, then tasted, of her lips. Her hands caught at his waist, steadying herself, as she returned his kiss.

All too soon it was over. He stepped back, disappointing her. "You ought not to have let me do that, Georgie," he whispered.

The blood rushed to her face. "I suppose you think me wanton, don't you?" she choked out.

"No, but for what it's worth to you, I doubt I will sleep much tonight." He reached for her hand. "Come on—let's get it over with."

She fell in beside him, trying to match his stride as they walked the few blocks back to the public house. She was going to face William Carrick, she was going to tell him he was her father, she told herself, but now she was so very aware of Max's hand, of the warm strength of the fingers that held hers. She closed her eyes a moment and tried to pray, squeezing out a quick, "Please, God, let him love me—please, let William Carrick recognize me," under her breath.

But as she came to the curb, she stumbled, catching her heel in the full petticoats beneath her gown. Max caught her elbow with his other hand, breaking her fall.

"Watch where you are going, will you?"

"I was praying."

"What are you going to do if he sends you packing? What if he says he doesn't remember her? We men are fickle fellows, I'm afraid."

"At least I will have seen him for myself," she answered without conviction. What she wanted more than anything was for William Carrick to welcome her with open arms. But she also knew that such drama was merely the pulp of gothic novels. More than likely, he would be just like any other older man. "If he turns me away, then I shall have to go, I suppose," she added finally.

If anything, the crowd was worse when they returned to the Olde Starre. Pushing through the crowd, her wide, full skirts caught on nearly everything.

"Please—your pardon," she managed to one fellow who glared at her.

They were still playing at darts, but to her dismay, both men had caps. Afraid of losing her nerve, she approached them. "Mr. Carrick?" she asked tentatively.

"Him," one of them grunted, indicating the other.

"Mr. Carrick?" she tried again.

"Aye."

It was noisy. She swallowed and stood on tiptoe for a better look at him. "Mr. Carrick, I am Georgina Esmond—Margaret Halley's daughter," she blurted out quickly.

He turned around at that. "Meg's girl?"

She nodded. "Please—I should like to speak with you."

"Did she send you?"

"Can we perhaps sit down somewhere—or could we go outside where we may be heard?"

He looked her up and down. "You don't look much like her."

She gambled. "I think I must look a little like my father."

"Wymore?" His lip curled as he said the word.

"No—my real father. Now, may we be private somewhere, sir?"

"Aye." His gaze shifted from her to the man with her. "And who's the fine young buck with you?"

"My cousin."

Max leaned around her to offer his hand. "Maximilian Durant, sir."

Carrick handed his darts to his partner, then drew out a leather wallet to extricate several banknotes from it. "I'm done for tonight, Jamie. Here—have a pint of stout for me, will you?"

"I cannot hear very well in here," she said.

"What?"

"I said I cannot hear!"

"There's a bench at the corner outside," Max suggested smoothly.

"Aye," William Carrick said.

Her heart pounding beneath her ribs, her stomach tight, her throat nearly too dry for speech, she followed him outside. When she looked back, Max wasn't with her. She turned back wildly.

"Max! Max! Where are you?"

"I didn't think you would want anyone else at the reunion," he said behind her.

"But what if he denies me?"

"Are you saying you want me to come with you?"

"Yes!"

Carrick was waiting outside when they emerged. As she stepped beneath the streetlamp, he cocked his head for a moment. "I suppose there is a resemblance," he decided. "It has been a long time."

"Twenty-two years," she said softly.

"Not quite—twenty-two in August," he corrected her.

"Then you do remember?"

"Aye—like yesterday. How is Meg now?"

"She died not quite two weeks ago."

He seemed taken aback. "Dead," he repeated. "No, it was too soon."

"She had a tumor."

"At least she had you with her. Poor Meg," he said sadly. "She was so full of life when we were young."

"Wymore would not let me be there. Please—sit down, sir." She followed him to the bench, then took a place beside him. "He cannot abide me, you see."

"The bloody swine."

"Yes, he is," she agreed. Twisting her hands in the folds of her skirts, she sought to put it to the touch. "Wymore said I am not his daughter."

He looked at her oddly. "And what did your mother say?"

"He did not tell me until she was dead. But I have read her diaries, sir. You eloped with her, didn't you?"

"Gladly."

"And it was four days before you were caught. You must've gotten to Gretna. Did they get it annulled, I wonder?"

"We didn't reach the border." He stared into the street as though he could look into the years past. "She did not travel well in a coach. We had to stop just this side of Gretna, but if I'd have known Halley was behind me, I'd have carried her across in my arms," he recalled bitterly.

She studied her hands. "There is no delicate way to put this, sir." Glad that he could not see the blood rush to her face, she said baldly, "Wymore said she wasn't—she wasn't—" She was going to choke on the word. "Well, he said that she wasn't pure when she came to him," she finished lamely.

"And he waited to tell you until she couldn't defend herself. Now that was kind of him, wasn't it?" he observed sarcastically.

She dared to touch his sleeve. "Please, I have to know—are you my father, sir? I know Mama loved you. She wrote of you often in her diaries. Is Wymore right? Am I your daughter?"

"What did he say to you?"

"He said my father was a half-pay soldier."

He stared again into the street, and for a time, she feared he did not mean to answer. "I wish I were," he said slowly. "I'd like to believe it, but I can't."

"But you have to be! She eloped with you, didn't she? And you were alone together for four days!" she cried.

"Aye, and Wymore had the right of that, at least," he admitted. "But I cannot claim you."

"But—"

He looked helplessly to Max Durant. "I don't know how to say it, sir," he said, lifting his palms up helplessly. "It isn't what I can tell a lady."

"I would that you told me, anyway," Georgina pleaded. "I have to know! If you are not my father, then why did he say it?"

"Durant—"

"She isn't a dieaway miss, Carrick. You'd best go ahead and say it," Max told him.

The older man drew in a deep breath, then looked at her again. Finally, he nodded. "I guess you've got a right to know something," he decided. "All right. We eloped, and there didn't seem to be any reason to wait to celebrate our promises to each other. We shared rooms as man and wife while we were on our way."

"Then you could be my father," she persisted. "You have just said so."

"No." Again, he looked to Max. "The last day out, she was sick from her bloody flux. When Halley reached us, he took her to a doctor." His gaze shifted to Georgina. "I wish it had been different, so the old man would have made me marry her, but as there could not be a child, he forced her to take Wymore. He said he was going to pass her off as a virgin."

"And she told Wymore, hoping he'd repudiate her," Max said softly.

"The duke was wanting her—like she was a thing—like she was a picture to be collected," Carrick recalled harshly. "He would have given anything for her, and it didn't make any difference that she didn't want him."

But Georgina was sitting very still as every fiber of her body tried to deny what he'd told her. If Carrick was not her father, that left only Wymore. She covered her face and shuddered with the revulsion she felt.

"Is she all right?" the older man wanted to know.

"Yes." Max moved behind her to grip her shoulder. "I'm going to take her home. We both thank you for your candor, sir."

"I'm sorry, Miss Esmond," Carrick said sadly. "I wish I were your father. I wish I had something left of her."

Silent tears began rolling down her cheeks. She closed her eyes and clasped her hands so tightly that her nails dug into the flesh of her palms. She was going to pieces and she knew it.

"Your mother was the love of my life," the older man went on. "She was like light itself." When Georgina did not respond, he added helplessly, "I should have fought for her, but she was afraid they'd hang me. It's been nigh to twenty-two years, and I can still remember the scent she wore."

"Come on, Georgie," Max said gently. Coming around to face her, he lifted her. "We're going to Mama—we're going to Jane." One of his hands smoothed her hair before he put his other arm around her waist. "It will be better tomorrow," he promised. "I don't blame you for being disappointed."

Carrick watched uncertainly. "I'm sorry—truly sorry, sir."

"Georgie, it's Wymore's loss, not yours," Max told her.

"Well, if you are done with me, I'd best go inside," the older man decided.

Too numb for speech, she stood within Max's embrace until Carrick was gone, then she allowed him to take her to the carriage. Stepping up, she caught the strap and took her seat. After giving orders to his disappointed driver, Max swung up beside her and pulled her against his shoulder.

And it was as though the hurt of a lifetime spilled from her. She caught the lapels of his coat, twisting them in her hands as she sobbed uncontrollably.

"Don't, Georgie—don't," Max whispered into her hair. "Wymore's not worth the pain he gives you."

"I-I cannot h-help it! He's my father! Did you not hear Mr. Carrick? Wymore's my father!"

"In name only, sweetheart—in name only."

"In blood, Max—in blood! And I hate him!"

"Shhhh."

"No—I hate him! I hate him for all he has done to me and to Mama! He should have loved me! He should have cared—and he never did, Max—he never did!"

"I know."

Feeling utterly helpless, he let her cry until he thought the well of tears must surely run dry. Finally, he tried to sit her up so he could wipe at her wet cheeks with his handkerchief. She gulped for breath.

"But I am all right," she declared. "I am all right—I have to be."

"Of course you are. It is my coat that is ruined," he said lightly. "You are a big girl now, Georgie."

"I have never been anything else," she muttered, sniffling. She moved away self-consciously. "You must surely be wondering what you ever did to deserve this."

"You were always my favorite nonrelation," he assured her.

"You haven't even slept, and here you are back in your carriage. I have led you on such a chase, haven't I?"

"If you hadn't, I daresay I'd have been gaming in a hell somewhere. As for sleep, I told Jem to stop at the first decent-looking place out of York. I wanted to get you on the road first," he explained. "I didn't want to take you in anywhere while you were distraught."

"I feel as though I am living a nightmare, Max."

"I understand your disappointment—I've had a few of them myself."

"Miss Robinson?"

"At the time, yes." He looked out at the disappearing street lamps, then he sighed. "Even things we recognize for the best can hurt."

"Was she very beautiful?"

"Very."

"I'm sorry."

"Don't be. Underneath that exquisite exterior, there beat the heart of a witch. She wanted more than a fortune, Georgie. She wanted a title."

"But you will have one. You'll be Baron Durant when Uncle Charles dies—surely she must have known that."

"I'm afraid my father was a trifle too healthy to

suit her. And when I realized what she was, God forgive me, Georgie, but I introduced her to an earl I'd gone to Oxford with. Thankfully, the poor, weak-minded fellow tumbled head over heels for her."

"And of course she jilted you for him."

"Faster than a thoroughbred can run the derby."

"Still, it must have been an embarrassment for you," she murmured.

"Oh, it was—but nothing nearly so awful as if she'd wed me, I assure you," he answered, smiling.

"You could have found dozens to replace her, you know."

"Once burned, twice wary—isn't that how the saying goes?"

"I suppose." She looked out into the darkness, seeing the faint outlines of a few trees on the horizon. "I don't want to go to Jane's, Max," she said finally. "I should rather go to Wymore."

"Wouldn't it be better if you just forgot him?" he asked gently. "He isn't worth the trouble of a thought."

Again, she was silent for a time. "No," she said slowly, "I want him to know what he has done to me."

"Georgie—"

"I have to do it—I have to." Turning back to him, she tried to explain. "He robbed me of my mother— he robbed me of my brothers, Max—he cheated all of us."

"And you think you can make him care?" he asked incredulously.

"I have to make him know how wrong he was. Beyond that, I don't care if he loves me or not. But if I say nothing, I am a coward. Can you not see?—if I say nothing, I have let him get by with what he has done."

"Georgie, I don't think you can change anything. If I did, I should be the first to suggest it."

"All I ever wanted was to belong, Max—all I ever dreamed of was to *belong*."

"And then? After you have seen Wymore?"

"And then I do not know."

He could scarce see her in the darkness, but there was no mistaking the passion in her words. "All right," he said heavily. "I'll take you there, but I think you are asking for pain."

Max's carriage had scarce pulled up the drive to the castle before her eighteen-year-old brother was running out to greet her. Waving his arms like flags before the coach, he shouted, "Thank God you are come, Georgina! Robin tried to reach you, but you weren't at Malbern," he said breathlessly. "The doctor does not think he will survive."

"Papa—?" she echoed feebly, turning to Max. "Not Papa surely—"

Johnny wrenched open the door and looked up at them. "The day you left—I suppose the shock of Mama's death finally took its toll on him—he had some sort of seizure, and he fell down the stairs."

"A seizure!" Even as she said it, she felt her stomach sink like lead within her.

"It's bad, Georgina. At first, when he did not move, Robin thought his neck was broken, but his limbs convulsed, and he was still breathing. Dr. Pearce says it was a stroke. In any event, his mind's gone."

"No, it cannot be—it cannot be," she said hollowly. "I came back to see him."

"He's paralyzed—all he does is stare or sleep. Pearce thinks it is the end, that he will have another and be gone."

She had to take a deep breath to control the deep, bitter anger she felt. Wymore could not be dying—he could not—he must not. Not before she had the chance to tell him how wrong he'd been, not before she had the chance to make him see what he'd done to all of them.

"Well, he's not going to die yet," she declared. "He cannot."

"Are you all right, Georgina? Didn't you hear what I just said?" Johnny demanded. "Pearce—"

"Yes, I heard you. Help me down, will you?"

"You are rather calm about it," he muttered, reaching up for her.

"I haven't seen him yet."

"But I just told you—"

"I know what you said, but I want to see him for myself." Twitching her full skirt into place over her petticoats, she started for the house. "Forgive me if I seem rather cranky, but I've been to York and back."

"York? What the devil for?"

"It is too long a tale to tell. I'd see Papa first." She turned back, seeing that Max remained in his coach. "Aren't you coming in?" she asked.

"Do you wish me to? I'd thought under the circumstances to go to Malbern."

"Max, I need you now more than ever."

"Dash it, Georgina, but you cannot have gone all over England alone with him," Robin protested. "It isn't done."

"Well, I have."

"But he isn't even really our relation—what is everyone to think?"

"I don't care," she answered tiredly, her eyes still on her stepcousin. "Please, Max."

He regarded her oddly for a moment, a faint smile on his lips, then without a word, he swung down. Going around to the boot, he lifted out her heavy portmanteau and carried it, falling in beside them.

"Deuced strange business, Georgina," Johnny went on. "I don't know what Papa would think of it."

"I thought you said he couldn't think," she reminded him.

"Well, if he recovers, I wouldn't tell him."

"He won't care."

Robin met them inside the door, lifting the portmanteau from Max. "Where in the world have you been?" he demanded. "I thought you were going to Malbern, but when I sent word over, no one knew anything about it." He stopped, and glancing to Max, he demanded, "Say—this wasn't an elopement, was it?"

"No."

"Then where were you?"

"Robin, I have nearly attained my majority," Georgie snapped.

"They went to York," Johnny explained.

"York! What would you want in York, Georgina?"

"I'll tell you later," she promised. "Just now, I'd see Papa."

"It doesn't look good for him," Robin said, trying to prepare her. "He just lies there, staring at the ceiling. It is as though he has already left us."

"Well, he cannot—I won't let him cheat me again," she muttered. Taking off her gloves, she laid them on the reception table, then smoothed her wrinkled gown with her palms. "I'm going up to see him."

"Pearce is there now."

"Then I shall see him also." Reaching up, she tucked a straggling tendril of hair behind her ear, then she settled her shoulders. "Have a footman put my bag in Mama's bedchamber, will you?" With that, she began the climb upstairs.

Robin looked at Max. "What are you going to do, sir?"

His eyes on Georgina's back, he didn't answer for a moment, then he sighed. "I'm just here for Georgie."

"Deuced odd, if you was to ask me."

"I'm not asking."

Taken aback, Robin recovered quickly. "Well, you
are like a brother to her, I suppose."

"God, I hope not."

"Say, whatever happened to the Robinson chit you
was to marry?" Johnny asked suddenly.

"She jilted me."

"You?" he asked incredulously. "Doing it too
brown, ain't you? From all I ever heard, you are quite
the ladies' man."

"And a gamester," Robin recalled. "Did you truly
wager that you could outrun the train?"

"I outran it," Max admitted. "Diablo is one hell of
a horse, and the distance was short."

"I heard you were hell for anything," Johnny said.

"Rumor, dear boy—*rumor*," Max assured him.

Above them, Georgina walked down the long, carpeted hall, her steps slowing as she approached her
father's bedchamber. Outside the door, she tried to
compose her thoughts. She'd come to have it out
with him, and he'd managed to defeat her yet again.
But she'd meant what she said—she wasn't going to
let him get by with it. Her hand shaking, she rapped
lightly on the door.

"Who is it?" came a testy voice from within.

"Georgina—Georgina Esmond," she said almost
defiantly. "I've come to see my father."

The door opened, creaking inward on ancient
hinges, and a white-haired fellow peered out over
the rims of his spectacles. Seemingly satisfied, he
stood back.

"You can sit with him, but I would you did not
disturb him. He is frightened enough as it is."

"Frightened? I understood—"

He lowered his voice nearly to a whisper. "I see it
all the time, but it is worse for those who've been
strong. He is afraid of dying."

"Then he knows?"

"All of them know, Lady Georgina. If there is any time at all, they know."

"How long?"

"Now that I cannot tell, but usually there is another stroke, perhaps more than one."

"I see. Then you see no hope?"

"Well, there is always hope, of course, but the longer he lies like that, the less hope there is."

"Can he hear—if I were to speak to him, would he know it?"

"I was taught that hearing is the last sense to go, my lady." Nodding toward the huge, canopied bed, he added, "I've tried to keep him comfortable. He is given laudanum whenever he is restless. He may have whatever it takes to ease him, but I have suggested six drops every four hours."

"That ought to keep him in a stupor," she murmured dryly.

"It is for his comfort merely," the doctor assured her. "Well, I've done my best today, so if you do not mind it, I shall go down and take my leave of your brothers. Mrs. Whitsell has my instructions, and I have left a copy by his bed. Good day, my lady."

"Good day, sir."

She waited until Pearce was gone before she approached the bed. All her life she'd been afraid of Wymore, and despite what the doctor and her brothers had said, she still was. Again, she wiped damp palms on her skirt. Walking around the bed, she dared to look down at him, and what she saw stunned her.

Lying there, his body outlined beneath bedcovers, he seemed smaller than she'd remembered him. And the harshness in his face was gone, replaced by nearly blank bewilderment. She had to school herself to anger as she sank into the chair beside him.

" 'Tis I, Papa—'tis Georgina."

He did not blink.

"I came back to tell you you were wrong, Papa."

Nothing. In fact, his stare was definitely abnormal.

"I wanted you to know—" She swallowed the awful lump in her throat. "I wanted you to know I *am* your daughter." She leaned over him, so closely that she could hear his faint, even breathing. "I've been to Maple Hill, Papa—and to York to meet Mama's half-pay soldier, as you called him. You lied to me, you know. He isn't my father." She waited for some sign he'd heard, and got none. "Can you not hear me, Papa?" she cried. "You were wrong— oh, so very wrong! I wanted it to be Mr. Carrick, truly I did. I thought if he were my father, he might be happy to see me, he might wish to know how I have gone on, but he wasn't anything to me. Oh, he'd eloped with Mama, all right, but he could tell me why I wasn't his, Papa. She had her monthly course after—after they'd been together. 'Twas why Lord Halley decided to deceive you, you see. He thought there was no harm to be done, but he was wrong also. He thought if Mama cried and pretended, you would not know the difference."

It was useless to think he heard her, and she knew it. She was speaking to a living dead man, nothing more. The man in the bed was but an empty, mindless husk. Without thinking, she reached to touch his hand. It was cold. Her fingers closed over it, massaging it, trying to force warmth where there was none.

"Papa, you have to hear me!" she cried. "You have to! You have to know! I want you to know! Can you not hear at all?"

Whether it was her imagination, or whether it really happened, she could not tell for certain, but it seemed that his fingers tensed within hers.

"You cannot die now, Papa—you cannot!" Leaning over him again, she pushed back his black hair from his forehead with her other hand. "Do you hear me? I'm not going to let you die! You have to get well—

you have to! I've too much to tell you, Papa—I want you to know what you did to me, to Mama, and to the boys! Can you not see, Papa? You cannot cheat me again—you cannot!''

"Here, my lady, what is this?" Mrs. Whitsell demanded from the open door. "Ye cannot shout at a sick man."

Georgina bit her lip to still its quivering. "I know," she managed. "But I had to tell him, and I know not if he heard me at all."

"I brought his laudanum, like the doctor ordered."

"He isn't restless," Georgina protested.

"It's been four hours."

"Yes—well, leave it here, and I shall give it to him."

The woman hesitated. "Ye cannot be oversetting him."

"Oversetting him?" the young woman asked bitterly. "He is too out to know what I have said to him."

"Still—"

"And if you are afraid I mean to overdose him, I assure you I will not. No, I want him to recover—I want him to get well. I want to be able to look him in the face and call him to book for what he did to Mama."

"I don't know—"

"I'm going to do everything in my power to see he gets better, I swear it."

"Well—"

"He'll recover—he has to. He just has to."

"Aye." Mrs. Whitsell regarded her sympathetically now. "It wasn't right what he did, was it?"

"No. And I mean to tell him so—when he is better, I mean to tell him so."

"Aye. Well, if ye need anything, there is the pull beside his bed. I been running my legs off 'cause he cannot use it."

"I shall not hesitate to call for aid, I promise," Georgina declared. "All I ask is the chance to nurse him."

"I don't suppose as anything can harm him now, anyways," the woman decided. "But ain't ye wanting to change the gown and rest a bit?"

"No."

After the housekeeper left, the room was utterly silent, so much so that Georgina felt she could almost hear her own heart beating. She looked at the man who'd denied her, telling herself it was not the time for any more anger. That could come later.

"Georgie?"

It was Max. He walked into the room and took a chair from the writing desk, moving it beside hers. Sitting down, he stared at the man he'd grown to hate almost as much as she did. But Laurence Edmond wasn't there. He could see that.

"What are you going to do?" he asked finally.

"Everything I can to see he survives," she answered evenly.

"Georgie, hate is destructive," he said gently. "It destroys the vessel rather than the object. But for whatever it is worth to you, I feel it nearly as much as you."

"You cannot."

"Let him go, Georgie. Put it behind you."

"No."

"You are a stubborn, driven woman, Georgina Esmond," he said, sighing. "You cannot make anything easy for yourself, can you?"

"When he knows—no, when he admits he was wrong, I shall heal. I know it, Max—I know it."

"What do you want me to do?"

"Can you stay here? Can you stay until it is over, one way or the other? You are the only person in this house who is not a stranger to me."

"I don't make a very good vulture, Georgie. But I'll give you a week before I go back to London."

"Thank you." Reaching out, she clasped his hand tightly, then let go. "It means a great deal to me."

"What do you really think you can do?"

"I don't know. But for the first thing, I'm taking his laudanum. He does not appear to be in pain, so I see no need for it. He's had so much of it, it is no wonder that he just lies there."

"And then what?"

"I shall read to him. The old stories we loved, Max—the old legends. It may not do very much for him, but perhaps it will preserve what is left of my sanity. I'm going to read to him until he is sick of the sound of my voice. And I am going to see that he is fed."

"Can he swallow?"

"I don't know, but I shall think of something. If you are wishful of helping, would you see if he has a copy of Mallory's *Morte d'Arthur*?"

"Yes."

After he left, she returned her attention to her father. He looked older than he had a scant four days before. But it was the smallness that still stunned her. As a child, even as recently as her mother's funeral, she'd thought him tall, overbearing. Now he was neither.

"Papa?" she said tentatively. "Would you have a drink?"

Nothing.

She rose and found the water pitcher, then the clean cloth that had been laid out for washing him. Carrying them back to the bed, she dipped the cloth, then pried open his mouth to dribble the small amount of water into it. His throat constricted, and for a moment, she feared he would strangle, then he managed to swallow.

"We are going to take it slowly, Papa. But you

have to have nourishment. I shall order a broth for you, and when you are better, you may have some minced meat. You are going to get well, if I have to force you to do it."

She'd been there two days, and sometimes she thought she saw improvement, sometimes not. But she read aloud to Wymore until her throat was sore, her voice hoarse. Then she pressed Robin and Johnny into it above their protests. Finally, when they could no longer be persuaded, she turned to Max.

"Only if you will get some sleep," he told her.

"He's better, don't you think?" she answered evasively.

"Georgie, you are a wreck," he countered. "Go to bed for a few hours. It won't make any difference."

"But you will read to him, won't you?"

"Where are you?"

"I am back to 'Sir Gawain and the Green Knight.' "

"All right."

Neither saw Wymore's eyes follow her as she left the room. Exhaling heavily, Max took her seat by the bed and dutifully opened the book to where she'd marked her place. But he was in no mood to read. He looked over at the duke, feeling an intense resentment.

"You might as well recover, you know," he said irritably. "She's not going to let you die."

Wymore blinked, but having spent little time in the sickroom, Max did not recognize the difference.

"If it were me, I'd have been glad enough to see you go—no, I'd have given you an overdose of the laudanum gladly just to get you out of my life. You don't deserve any of this, not so much as one hour of the time she has spent trying to keep you alive. I hope if you do live, you can be made to appreciate half of what she's done."

Wymore swallowed.

"You cheated her, you know—you cheated her horribly. And you cheated Aunt Margaret and Robin and Johnny. You robbed Georgina of her birthright, Aunt Margaret of her firstborn child, and the boys of their sister. You even cheated yourself, for you denied yourself the pleasure of a daughter, you denied yourself the joy of a family. In some stupid effort to punish your wife, you destroyed everything around you."

Max rose and went to the window, looking down upon the vast expanse of green park land. Turning back to Wymore, he said coldly, "If we'd come back, and if you'd have denied her again, I would have been tempted to kill you myself."

Returning to his seat, he opened the book again and started to read aloud. Two pages later, he closed it.

"You ought to have to live with your conscience," he said. "You ought not to get the easy way out."

"It is time to feed him," Georgina announced, returning with a tray.

"I thought you were going to bed."

"I will—after he has his broth." Taking the vacant chair, she held the tray on her lap. Leaning past Max, she placed a napkin over the bedcovers. "Now, let us see if you can swallow any better this time, Papa," she said to Wymore. Dipping the spoon into the yellow broth, she carried it carefully to his mouth. "Here's one," she announced, as though he were a child. Tipping it into a corner, she waited to see if it went down. He swallowed. She tried not to betray the elation she felt.

"Very good. Now—here's two. And I don't mean to stop until it is all gone."

He swallowed again, and she could not contain herself. "Max, he's better—it's going down better! Papa, you are doing very well."

Max watched her feed Wymore until he could

stand no more. He laid the book aside and went again to the window. Behind him, he could hear her coaxing the old man.

She was about to spoon the tenth swallow in, when Wymore's hand raised about an inch or so above the cover. She dropped it onto the floor. "Max! Max!" she said eagerly. "He's moving! Papa, we are winning!"

"Maybe he doesn't want any more."

"No, but perhaps he wants more than broth," she decided. Perhaps he wants something better." Taking her father's hand, she said, "Squeeze my fingers if you would have some finely chopped meat."

He squeezed.

"And perhaps some beef jelly?"

He squeezed again.

"I might even be able to discover a finger of port for you—if you promise to eat everything else, of course."

This time, she could feel it as his fingers tightened on hers twice. "Max, I think we have done it!"

"Not we—leave me out of it. I didn't even want to read to him." Turning back to her, he said, "I think I might ride over to Malbern later today."

"For a visit?"

"No. I have been thinking of going back to London."

She stared up in dismay. "Oh, but you cannot!"

"You don't need me anymore, Georgie. You can slay your own dragons now."

She followed him out into the hall, then stood there, her back against the wall, her hands bracing her body. "I know you must surely think me foolish for saying it, but I don't even want revenge anymore. I don't even care that he cannot love me."

"I don't think you foolish at all." A slight, enigmatic smile played at the corners of his mouth. "I think you magnificent—truly."

"But—"

"I think you are going to make him get well. As I said, Georgie, you are a stubborn female."

All her life she'd felt the coward, the victim of circumstance. But Max was going to leave her. Taking a deep breath, she gambled.

"I want more than that—I want more than Papa's life even."

He regarded her lazily now. "Do you now?"

"Yes." Never having played the flirt, she was somewhat at a loss. Nevertheless, she managed to look up through a fringe of dark lashes. "Do you remember when you offered to marry me?"

"Very well."

"I didn't want to be taken out of pity."

"Georgie—Georgie—"

His hands touched the wall on either side of her, and his breath caressed her face as he bent his head to kiss her. For answer, she threw her arms around his neck, savoring the very nearness of him. His arms closed around her, holding her almost too close for breath. When at last he raised his head, he smiled crookedly into her eyes.

"Does that feel like pity to you?" he asked huskily.

"No—no, it doesn't—and I would you did it again," she said shamelessly. "Oh, Max—I have loved you for such a long time!"

"Uhhhh—unnnnnhhh—"

"Oh, lord—he's choking!" she cried, running back into her father's chamber.

"Uhhhhh—uhhhhhh—unnnnnhhh—" Wymore lifted his hand again, then let it fall. "Uhhhhh—"

"He's trying to speak," Max decided.

"It's all right, Papa," she said soothingly, clasping his fingers. "You are all right. If you can lift your hand now, you can speak later."

Moving to the other side of the bed, Max leaned over him to speak distinctly. "You have a magnificent daughter, Uncle Laurence. I'm going to marry her."

The old man's eyes turned to look up at her, and there was no mistaking the tear that rolled down his cheek. His hand squeezed hers. "Uhhhhhnnnnnn—"

"Does that mean you approve, sir?" she dared to ask him.

He squeezed her fingers again.

"Do you admit I am your daughter?"

Another squeeze.

Her throat ached and her eyes burned with her own tears. "It is too late for us, Papa, and I know it. But—" She looked across to her betrothed. "But with Max's help, I am going to be the best mother I can be. I don't have to wait to be taken into this family anymore, for I shall have my own. And maybe someday I shall be able to bring my children here, Papa."

Another tear trickled down his cheek. His mouth worked, but only the gutteral grunt came out.

"It's all right, Papa—you don't have to love me." She released his hand and went into the hall again, where she leaned her head against the wall. Max watched as she gave in to her own tears. Finally, she raised her head, and sniffed back her sniffles. "He's going to be all right."

"And so are we, Georgie—and so are we."

*Wymore, December 2, 1879*

She sat in her father's bookroom, holding her small son on her lap. Beside her, Max dandled their infant daughter on his knee, beating out a silent rhythm with his foot to entertain her. Robin stood, while Johnny leaned expectantly against the mahogany mantel.

Mr. Thornwell cleared his throat and began to read, enumerating various bequests to ancient retainers. Looking over his spectacles, he paused to smile, then went ahead with his business.

" 'To my eldest child, my only daughter, Georgina, I hereby bequeath the contents of my library, that she may pass it on to my grandson, William Robert Durant, in the course of time. In addition, she is to have the sum of twenty-five thousand pounds, five thousand of which shall be for her sole and separate use. It is small payment for the largeness of her heart, and I would have her know that although we began late, in the end, I have had the utmost admiration and affection for her.' "

She sat very still, grateful that her black veil hid her red eyes. Max reached over to hold her hand. She nodded that she was all right.

"You did not have him very long, but at least you meant something to him at the last," he whispered. "You belonged to him."

"And he belonged to me," she whispered back.

# Cheyenne
# Dream Catcher

by

Georgina Gentry

# Chapter One

She looked up at him, this virile warrior who had captured her. "I never knew love could be like this."

The Apache brave held her in his strong brown arms and kissed her tenderly. "You were my captive, but I became a prisoner of desire. I love you, beautiful white girl, so I will set you free."

Then he stepped away, tears in his eyes, and Heather Huntington Jeeves turned to go. Back at the fort, two men waited for her. She could have either one she chose: Lord Whitefield, with his vast English lands and castles, or Randley Van Cleef, the handsome, dashing Cavalry officer who was also a Boston millionaire. Both had begged to marry Heather and wanted to give the proud beauty anything her heart desired; anything but the true love she had hungered for all her life.

Heather paused uncertainly, looked behind her. Lobo swung up on his magnificent paint stallion and turned to ride away into the Arizona desert. It was her choice to make and she listened now only to her heart. "Lobo, wait!"

He paused, reining the great horse in. "Goodbye, my dear one. You have only to choose between those two handsome rich men who will

lay the world at your feet. I can offer you
nothing."

"Nothing but love," Heather answered, "and
that means all the world to me. Lord Whitefield
and Randley can keep their mansions and
wealth. I'm following my heart!"

Heather ran to Lobo. The chief reached for her,
swung her up on his stallion, held her close, and
kissed her. Together forever at last! She didn't
look back as she and her virile warrior galloped
away into the desert sunset.

THE END

Sharyl Nuemann sighed, closed the romance novel,
and brushed her long brown hair out of her eyes.
"Oh, don't I wish!"

She glanced at her digital watch: 8/20: 6 P.M. No
wonder the light was fading in her cheap motel
room. With the American Indian Exposition this
week in Anadarko, Oklahoma, and so many tourists
in town, she was lucky to get a room at all. She got
up and began to dress. Maybe her mother was right.
Sharyl had left a good job as a bookstore manager
in Newark, New Jersey, on an impulse because of
the western stories she had read. "So where are all
these handsome Indian males?" she asked herself. Six
months she'd been working at the Cowgirl Clothes
Corral over in the nearby town of Lawton and she
hadn't met even an interesting soldier at Lawton's
Fort Sill.

It was almost dark as Sharyl drove east through
town to the Caddo County Fairgrounds. She parked
and surveyed the crowds and the bright, noisy mid-
way with a sense of disappointment. "Somehow, I
didn't expect a ferris wheel and cotton candy."

What had she expected to find in the town known
as "Indian City, U.S.A."? She didn't know for certain

or even why she had come once her fellow employee, Fran, had canceled out when Fran's boyfriend got unexpected leave. Well, at least Fran had loaned Sharyl her car for the weekend.

Sharyl paused, then threaded her way through the crowds. Dusk lay across the prairie like an Indian blanket; rose and lavender and gray. The summer night felt warm as a lover's breath against her skin. Day after tomorrow, she would be twenty-seven, and it had been a long time since she had had a lover or even a date.

*Get real, Sharyl,* she almost heard her mother's condescending tone, *remember you were never as pretty or popular as your sister, so be sensible and give up your silly romantic dreams. Clifford may be your last chance.*

Mother was right; maybe it was time to get real. But not tonight. Tonight, Sharyl had come to Anadarko's big annual event to watch the Indians dance. Monday was soon enough to give notice and make her airline reservations. It annoyed her how smug her sister Mitzi would be when Sharyl admitted defeat and returned to Newark, even though she had come to love Oklahoma.

She looked again at her souvenir watch from her trip to Enid. Around the face was printed Cherokee Strip Centennial Celebration 1893–1993. Almost time. She'd better hurry or she might not get a good seat, since this was a night for the championship Fancy War Dance competition, yet she lingered to walk through the Arts and Crafts building.

Loud music from the carousel drifted through the open doors, mingled with shouts hawking souvenirs at the many booths outside. The scents of frying hamburgers, sweating horses, and dust mixed with the heat around her. As she pushed through the crowds of tourists and Indians dressed in their native costumes, she noticed a small obscure booth in the shadows. A bent old Indian woman motioned to her, and

Sharyl paused. The elderly woman spoke in a whisper as soft as the wind. "Miss, I have magic things to sell, you buy?"

Sharyl hesitated. "I don't know. . . ."

"Come. See," the ancient crone gestured again. "Dream catchers, just for you."

"Dream catchers?" Sharyl looked down at the small objects on the table.

"Dream catchers." The old woman nodded and held one up. "Use as good luck charm or hang over baby's crib; protect from bad dreams; they get caught on knots, only good dreams get through."

Intrigued, Sharyl studied the small silver circles, most not as large as a quarter. The center of each looked like a silvery spiderweb with knots in it and they had chains so they could be worn as jewelry. Her gaze swept over the shadowy display. They were lovely, all right, but the one that caught her eye was a crude one made of bent willow and old rawhide webbing, with a tiny feather hanging from the frame. It drew her like a magnet. That puzzled her since it certainly wasn't as pretty or maybe as valuable as the silver ones. She picked it up. "How much?"

"The white girl has chosen well," the ancient woman smiled and rubbed the big wart on her chin. "This one very special; big medicine. Heart and spirit soar like dragonfly; like eagle on the wind with this."

She knows a Yankee tourist when she sees one, Sharyl thought. "Why a dragonfly?"

"Magic to the Cheyenne; quick and fast; hard to catch, hard to see."

And a predator, Sharyl remembered her high school science, a warrior among insects. "How much?"

"Twenty-dollar gold piece," the old woman said.

She must have misunderstood her. The government hadn't even produced coins like that for maybe a hundred years or more, Sharyl thought. "I beg your pardon?"

"Twenty-dollar gold piece."

Certainly Sharyl had misunderstood her again. No doubt what the old woman had said was something like: "Twenty dollars good, please."

She didn't have much cash and her birthday money was in traveler's checks. "You'll take a check or plastic?"

The old crone looked puzzled. Perhaps she was having a difficult time understanding Sharyl, too. It was probably a foolish thing to buy anyway. Yet Sharyl wanted to own the crude little thing even though the silver ones were finer. Mother and Mitzi would think her a fool. She wouldn't tell them what it cost. Sharyl opened her purse, gave the old woman a twenty-dollar bill. "Is there tax?"

The bent woman looked at her strangely again as if she had not understood. "Dream catcher," she said again, "saved just for you; enjoy."

Sharyl smiled, nodded, and began tying it around her neck as she turned away and hurried toward the grandstand. Well, even if she didn't get any wonderful dreams out of it, it would certainly be a conversation piece back home in Newark, just like her wristwatch.

Pushing through the crowds in the darkness, Sharyl bumped into someone and stumbled. A strong arm reached out and caught her. In that split second, she was aware he was tall and powerful. When she glanced up, she saw only a silhouette of a rough-hewn profile and olive drab shirt. She couldn't see his face, but she felt the heat of his hand on her skin.

"T-thank you," she stuttered, feeling like a clumsy fool, but the vague form only nodded and was swallowed up in the crowd. She stood staring into the darkness, not even sure he wasn't a product of her imagination. No, he'd been too strong and masculine to be a spirit.

Why hadn't she thought of something clever to say or struck up a conversation? Sharyl just didn't have the knack for flirting like her sister did.

Sharyl bought herself an Indian taco and some hot fry bread and found herself a seat in the old grandstand. The big floodlights drew a cloud of bugs and the loudspeakers crackled as the announcer blared, "Good evening, ladies and gentlemen, welcome to the annual American Indian Exposition here in the state of Oklahoma, home to the largest population of Native Americans in the United States. *Oklahoma* is a Choctaw word translating roughly as 'land of the red man.' If you're a tourist, we hope you'll find time to visit our museums, the Cowboy Hall of Fame in Oklahoma City, and historic old Fort Sill in the nearby town of Lawton, where Quanah Parker, last chief of the Comanche and famed Apache, Geronimo, are buried."

Sharyl sipped a soft drink as the announcer droned on. She didn't regret spending part of her birthday money on this little trip at all, but her mother might not understand about Western Dreams, Inc. Sharyl comforted herself with the thought that she simply wouldn't tell her.

". . . our honored Outstanding Indian for our 1993 event is United States Senator from Colorado, Ben Nighthorse Campbell, who is with us tonight!"

A round of applause from the crowd as the well-known Native American waved to the grandstand.

". . . and now will you please stand as the honor guard brings in the flags preceding our grand entry parade!"

Sharyl stood automatically, watching the two soldiers dressed in green fatigues marching into the arena; the American and the blue state flag with the

Osage war shield emblem whipped smartly in the breeze.

"... two modern warriors from Fort Sill, battle-hardened veterans of Desert Storm and Somalia," the announcer said, "representing two of the sixty-seven tribes that have called Oklahoma home, the Kiowa and the Cheyenne. ..."

Without thinking, Sharyl reached up to touch her dream catcher, watching the pair of soldiers. The one who really caught her attention was the taller, broad-shouldered sergeant with a broken nose. He was a bit too rugged to be handsome, but with a little war paint and riding a pinto stallion, he could have easily ridden right out of history ... or an Indian romance novel. *Why did he look so familiar?*

"Get real, Sharyl," she whispered to herself. "Monday you are giving notice at your job and going back to Newark to say yes to Clifford if he finally asks you. This Oklahoma thing was an impractical dream anyway."

Yet for the next two hours she lost herself in the magic of the exposition as hundreds of Native Americans danced and whirled to the beat of the giant drum. She felt dazzled by bright feathers and scarlet war paint, beaded leather, and a riot of colored fabric, jingles on dresses reflecting the light; bells on costumes echoing as warriors stepped to the beat. Oh, it was almost too much a feast for the senses!

Finally, all too soon, it was over. With a sigh, Sharyl joined the others filing out of the stadium. So many handsome braves and she was returning to her motel to watch an old western movie alone. She remembered the virile sergeant from the honor guard wistfully. She hadn't met anyone like him in the six months she'd been in Lawton.

Sharyl reached up to touch the dream catcher around her neck and had a sudden urge to talk to the old woman again. She searched out that shadowy spot. However, now at that location an Indian boy in a POWWOW POWER T-shirt leaned against the wall eating a grape snow cone. "Excuse me, but what happened to the old lady?"

The teenager was handsome except for bad acne scars. After one bored glance, he returned to his snow cone and stared at the pretty Indian girls walking past. "What old lady?"

Teenagers. In his eyes, Sharyl was probably an old lady herself. "The one who was selling dream catchers here."

Now he yawned and shrugged. "Naw, ain't been nobody like that in this spot." He brushed past her. "Gotta go; it's time for the '49."

"A what?"

"A '49; that's a party we sometimes throw ourselves after the tourists have left."

That's all she was—a tourist. "Funny, I would have sworn the old lady's booth was right here. . . ."

Feeling bewildered and a little foolish, Sharyl wilted under the boy's skeptical stare and turned away and headed toward the car. At least tomorrow afternoon she had Western Dreams, Inc., to look forward to.

Back in her motel room, she reread the ad in the local paper, the *ANADARKO DAILY NEWS*. Sharyl was glad now she had made that call.

HAVE YOU EVER DREAMED OF BEING A GUN-FIGHTER, A SALOON GIRL??? Have you ever had a secret wish to be carried off by a handsome Indian brave?? Let us fulfill your wildest dream!! Western Dreams, Inc., will recreate your fantasy for the exposition week special of only $250, costume included at no extra charge!! Our crew has Hollywood experience!! Give us a chance to turn your dream into reality!! Call for a reservation. . . .

She went to the open window and leaned against the frame and stared out. There was only a tiny sliver of new moon. She stood there a long time, watching the breeze ruffle the buffalo grass in the field across the highway. The slight scent of wildflowers and sagebrush rode on that breeze. She might have been back a hundred years ago; it wasn't hard to imagine she was. Then somewhere, a coyote howled in the stillness, reinforcing Sharyl's sense of desolation.

She sat down on the bed, got out her credit card, and called Mother. It rang and rang. Oh, darn, she had forgotten about the time difference—

"Hello?" The sleepy, familiar annoyed voice answered.

"Mother, I'm sorry, I forgot about the time—"

"Is that you, Sharyl? What's wrong?"

"Nothing." Nothing. She was just lonely, that was all, sitting here in a motel in a small Oklahoma town on a Friday night. "I—I just wanted to tell you your birthday card arrived."

"Couldn't it have waited?"

"I said I was sorry." Sharyl leaned back against the headboard and stared at the cover of the novel on the bed. Why was it she was always apologizing?

"Mitzi was always so thoughtful, she would never do this—"

"I know and she's prettier, too," Sharyl said automatically.

"Don't get smart with me, young lady! After all, your sister has married a doctor, is expecting her third child, and is building a new house."

"Must you start on me, Mother?" She wished now she hadn't called. This was another reason to leave Newark.

"Start on you? May I remind you you're the one who called and got me out of bed? You're too much like your father, and—"

"I said I was sorry." Sharyl realized suddenly she had a splitting headache.

"I saw Clifford yesterday when I played bridge with his folks. He said he can hardly wait for you to get home. He's on the steering committee for the ten-year class reunion next year."

Ten years. Had it really been that long since she'd graduated from high school? Everyone but Sharyl would be bringing a husband to the reunion.

"... Clifford would be a very good catch with those appliance stores he manages for his family; a solid citizen."

Clifford. His hair was thinning and he wore bow ties. He also still lived at home with his parents. Had his mother been on him to be 'sensible,' marry, even if he had to settle for Sharyl?

"You did get the plane ticket I sent? Have you given notice at work?"

"Not yet."

"Honestly, Sharyl, when are you going to stop chasing silly dreams? Real life isn't like a romance novel."

*Why can't it be?* But of course, she didn't say that. "No, Mother." Her head was pounding like that giant powwow drum. Of course Mother was right; she was always right. Hadn't Dad given up his dreams of becoming an artist to do commercial advertising because Mother was always right? He had left his widow good insurance when he drank himself to death. "I've got to go," Sharyl interrupted the tirade. "I'll call you later to tell you when to meet my plane."

"Well, for God's sake, don't call so late!" The receiver clicked loudly.

Sharyl went to the open window. The sultry wind carried the distant echo of drums. Somewhere out there in the summer darkness, people whirled to the rhythm of ancient dances, living the fantasy she had only dreamed of. She closed her eyes and listened to the faint beat and wondered about the '49. She reached to clasp the small object hanging around her neck. Dreams.

In her mind, she saw herself dancing in a fire-lit circle with a rugged warrior who looked as if he had stepped right off one of the covers of her beloved novels. He would be half naked and streaked with scarlet paint. They would sway together, his dark eyes intense with desire and the promise of ecstasy to come. She would feel pretty; prettier than her sister, who had been a cheerleader, prettier than anyone as he swung Sharyl up in his arms and carried her away to his teepee to make passionate love to her.

With a sigh, Sharyl turned out the light. Mother and sister Mitzi need never know about her biggest foolish expenditure. Tomorrow afternoon, Sharyl was going to fulfill her fantasy. With Western Dreams, Inc.'s help, Sharyl Neumann was going to be carried off by an Indian brave!

# Chapter Two

The next morning, after a night of wistful romantic fantasies, Sharyl walked over to Western Dreams, Inc.'s, which office was little more than a block away. It looked as down-at-the-heels as the elderly owner, Sid Rosenthal, who claimed to be a retired Hollywood director. He wore a beret and old-fashioned riding pants.

Sharyl was a bit skeptical, thinking if he ever was involved with movies, it must have been back in the silent days of Charlie Chaplin and Mary Pickford. Yet his interest and apparent need for income gradually overcame her reluctance and she related her dream.

He pushed his beret back and nodded knowingly. "Yes, we can do that. You can ride in the same stagecoach with the college boy who wants to be a gunfighter, a schoolteacher who wants to be a saloon girl, and the business C.E.O. who has a secret yen to be a tin-horn gambler."

"Will the Indians be authentic?" Sharyl asked.

"Naw," he shook his head, "real Indians would probably think it wasn't politically correct; you know how they were always portrayed in westerns." He seemed to see the disappointment on her face. "Hey, we've got a real stagecoach, though; bought it at auction when they cleared out an old barn. According to legend, it was on the Butterfield run and was actually attacked by a war party late one summer day in 1868."

"Umm." She didn't believe him, of course, but what difference did that make? "What happened to the people in that attack?"

Sid shrugged and lit a cigar. "Real mystery about one of the lady passengers, but everyone else survived."

He went on talking about arrangements, the old stuntman who would be driving, but Sharyl's mind was elsewhere. 1868. She had read enough Indian romances to know the following winter of that year was when George Armstrong Custer hit that sleeping Indian village on the Washita River not too many miles from here.

Sharyl said, "What about a dress? I'd really like to look like I came from the time period, and—"

"No problem." Sid stood up. "I managed to buy a lot of costumes and props when a studio went broke. Not much call for "B" westerns anymore and kids don't go to Saturday matinees, even in small towns; they play video games instead. Come back about three and we'll get you dressed. If this venture is a success, we've got an investor interested in opening a Wild West theme park."

Sharyl paid her money, thinking that again she wasn't being sensible, but if she was going back to Newark next week, she had the rest of a rather dull life to be practical.

The day passed all too quickly with a trip to the Indian village and the museums in the area. Then she presented herself back at Sid's office, chose a flowered blue calico dress the color of her eyes, with fluffy white petticoats that brought back memories of all those Saturday western matinees. Sharyl joined the other three participants in the dusty, ragged old stage with four fat mules pulling it and a driver who really did look the part.

The four looked at each other as the stage lurched and pulled away as if they'd all been caught doing something a bit revealing and embarrassing.

The schoolteacher must have been at least fifty, with a lacquered, helmet hairdo, eyeglasses, and an implausible gaudy red dress and cancan petticoats. "I teach history," she said lamely, "and I thought if I had the scope of really living the past—"

"I understand," Sharyl said to put the woman at ease. "I feel a bit foolish myself."

"Well, I don't," the paunchy business exec leaned back. He fiddled with his string tie and adjusted his bright satin vest over his paunch. "I've belonged to a western enactment group for years and finally decided if not now, when?"

Sharyl nodded and the college boy took his pistol out and whirled it. "Careful," she said.

"It's loaded with blanks," the lanky boy said in an Ivy League accent, "just like the enactment cavalry and Indians will have."

Sharyl looked out the window of the stage. Late afternoon on a sultry summer day. How easy it would be to pretend that she was really back in 1868.

The teacher interrupted her thoughts as she peered over the rims of her glasses. "I hear this stage was supposed to have been attacked by Cheyenne Dog Soldiers more than a hundred years ago. Anyone know what those are?"

"I do," Sharyl said, "because I read Indian romances."

The businessman sneered. "Slop! Trashy women's paperbacks."

Sharyl looked him in the eye. "You've paid two hundred fifty bucks to pretend to be a saloon gambler and you're ridiculing women's fantasies?"

He turned brick red. "That's different."

"Is it?" said the college boy. "What's a Dog Soldier?"

Sharyl looked out the window at the rough, brushy country they were approaching. With a little imagination and no power lines in the background, they might have very well been on the old Butterfield trail across the Indian territory. "Dog Soldiers were the elite fighting warriors of the Cheyenne; especially the four carriers of the *hotamtsit*, the Dog Rope. Those were the bravest of the brave, riding at the end of the column when the camp was on the move to cover the retreat in case the tribe was attacked."

"A dog rope?" The teacher-saloon girl asked.

"It's a long leather band draped over the shoulder," Sharyl said. "If need be, the four would stake themselves to the ground with those ropes and fight to the death tied there."

The other three looked impressed.

The stage driver leaned over and yelled in the window. "Okay, we're about to start. Miss Neumann, at a certain point ahead, the extras posing as Indians will ride out, attack, and carry you off. You get an evening of powwow and roast buffalo at a camp fire, courtesy of a local caterer, and you'll be picked up about midnight."

"What about us?" the exec yelled.

"You get to experience the Indian attack, then I take you three to the old western town the local reenactment group uses where we'll have extras at the saloon so you three can experience that all evening."

The stage lurched as it started up again, harness jingling. Sharyl felt her heart beat faster as the four looked at each other in anticipation.

The teacher adjusted her bodice over her flat chest. "Do you suppose that story about this stagecoach is true?"

"Naw," the college boy sneered, "just window dressing for the tourists."

The gambler-exec examined the faded red upholstery. "It looks ragged enough to be that old. "Wouldn't you like to know who was aboard that night; what they thought and felt?"

The gunfighter nodded. "I'm taking a class in physics. There's a weird theory that if one gets right in sync with the exact time and place, you could actually go back and recreate it."

"Don't I wish!" Sharyl said. "Let's pretend that we really are those people and give this happening all we've got."

"Fantastic!" the college kid crowed. "We might as well get our money's worth!"

Abruptly, Sharyl felt the stage lurch into a gallop and the driver began to crack his whip and shout, "Indians! Indians!"

"Here we go. I wish I'd remembered my video camera!" the teacher shrieked.

Sharyl was so excited she found herself holding her breath, leaning out the window to watch for the war party. Dust rose up along the dirt road and seemed to obscure the power lines and the fences in the background. In her blue print calico dress, she really felt like a girl of the last century. How many times had she imagined herself in this very scene?

The college boy gasped "Here they come!"

The exec leaned forward. "By God, they look real enough!"

"Shall I scream?" the teacher asked, her eyes big behind her glasses.

"Must you?" Sharyl kept her attention on the riders emerging from the dusty, distant shadows as the stagecoach picked up speed. Her own heart began to pound as the stagecoach bounced along the rutted road. She clutched the door and hung out the window, not wanting to miss a single moment of this once-in-a-lifetime experience.

"Indians! Indians!" The driver shouted above her

and the sound of his whip cracked through the warm air. The harness jangled and the old stage creaked as it bumped along at a faster speed.

Her three fellow passengers were getting into the spirit of the adventure, the men shooting their pistols with deafening blasts and the would-be saloon girl shrieking. Oh, it was all beginning to seem so real!

Sharyl leaned out the stagecoach window and watched the war party. It looked more authentic than she had first thought when she saw them emerging from the woods. She would have to congratulate Sid Rosenthal on the costumes and makeup. The would-be Indians looked grim and determined as they thundered after the coach. The one in the lead, the one on the big paint stallion, seemed almost familiar. He looked like the culmination of all her dreams, all the heroes of all the novels she had ever sighed over. Sharyl reached up to clasp the little dream catcher around her neck. With just a bit of imagination this could be the real thing!

For a fleeting moment as the war party chased them, shrieking and firing, she thought of that long-ago day when this stage had really been attacked by Indians. What was it the college boy had said? Something about getting in sync with time? If it had been just such a day as this, about this time of evening, on this very land perhaps, and in this very stagecoach, could they possibly be thrown back in time to that precise moment during the summer of 1868? Well, it was fun to pretend!

Around her, dust whirled and the stagecoach bumped as it picked up even more speed. Sharyl was thrown back against the faded crimson horsehair cushions. The saloon girl was screaming, but somehow, she wasn't wearing glasses anymore; no doubt in this wild confusion, the teacher had dropped them. Yet she seemed different in other ways, too.

Puzzled, Sharyl looked around. The two men pas-

sengers weren't the two she had begun this trip with
. . . or were they? It must be the way the late sun
cast shadows inside the coach. Sweat made dusty
trails down the exec's face, which seemed fatter than
before. He really looked scared as he reloaded his
Derringer. Maybe he had had practice with that reenactment group. The young gunfighter's face was set,
his eyes without expression. He fired his Colt out the
window and cursed as if he really expected to be
killed.

"Oh," Sharyl shouted with mounting excitement,
"I wish someone had brought a video camera!"

The other three stared at her as if she were slightly
insane.

"A what?" the gambler asked as if he had never
heard of such a thing.

"Never mind!" Sharyl shouted back. "Just concentrate on the Indians!" She intended to enjoy this expensive happening to the fullest. She leaned out the
window and stared at the war party, which was gaining on them. Any moment one of them would ride
up to the coach and the driver would pull over and
she would be abducted. She hoped the caterer had
provided real buffalo meat and that the Indian camp
looked as realistic as the extras now chasing after the
stage. That one in the lead; now, there was the ulti-
mate Indian hero—big, dark, wide-shouldered. He
was a little too rugged to be handsome, but his broken nose only added to his masculine profile. Oh,
yes, he could carry her off any time! What an adventure this was going to be! If only she'd brought her
camera! But of course, she'd probably be able to have
a souvenir photo taken right in the Indian camp.

Sharyl glanced around. In the confusion and swirling dust and gun smoke, the other three passengers
looked truly terrified. They were really getting into
the spirit of the adventure. Of course she could do
that, too, make the happening even more realistic by

pretending they were back in that actual event. Sharyl hung on to the door and leaned out the window, staring at the war party that was most definitely gaining on the lumbering stage. The scent of burning gunpowder made her gasp and her ears rang with the roar. She hadn't realized blanks could seem so realistic. Above her, the driver cursed and cracked his whip, urging the team onward.

Late afternoon shadows lay across the Oklahoma prairie and the road seemed to be passing through an area where there were no power lines and no fences. It didn't take much imagination now to pretend she really was back in that long ago time. Somewhere up ahead, the stagecoach would halt and she would be carried off by the Indians. She hoped the big one riding out front was the one who was supposed to steal her. Amazing how much he looked like Lobo on his paint stallion, except that she was not beautiful like Heather Huntington Jeeves. Well, Sharyl could pretend.

The Indians were riding alongside the coach now. She could see the scarlet paint on the hard, dark body of the leader. Yes, this was going to be great fun! Sharyl was glad she had decided to do this, even if it wasn't sensible. She intended to live this adventure to the max by actually pretending to be a pioneer girl. Now if the actor would only play his part to the fullest!

The coach didn't seem to be slowing down any. Why wasn't the driver following the plan? The road was getting rougher and the saloon girl screamed again as Indians rode on each side of the coach, their horses blowing and lathered. Out the other window, the gunfighter and the gambler fired at their pursuers. Sharyl clung to her open window to keep from being thrown against the roof of the bouncing stage. The grim, handsome face of the leader appeared right alongside. Any moment now, the coach would stop and she would be abducted. Sharyl clung to the door. The leader seemed to be riding almost out of the swirling dust and pale lavender shadows of late afternoon ... or of time. He looked so real, so authentic.

Abruptly, the coach hit a bad bump in the road. Sharyl felt the door swing open as she clung to it. Helplessly, she looked toward the other passengers, but they were staring out the opposite window at the swarm of Indians galloping along on that side of the coach.

"Help!" Sharyl screamed as the door swung wide and she felt air beneath her feet. The others didn't seem to hear her, no one turned as she hung on to the door for dear life. Oh, dear God, she was going to be killed in a freak accident, just like some movie extra. What would Mother and her sister say when they heard how Sharyl had died? Why hadn't she been sensible?

Any moment now, the driver would halt the coach. If she could just hang on a moment longer, she wouldn't end up under those rolling wheels. Sharyl clung to the door and stared down at the dusty road moving beneath her feet. She wasn't going to be able to do it. With a feeling of horror, she felt her hands giving way, unable to hang on a moment longer. She was going to die here, thrown under this galloping stagecoach while the three who might be able to help her stared out the other window, oblivious to her plight.

Even as the door was torn from her weakening grasp and she began to fall toward the swirling dust, an arm reached for her. Sharyl didn't know where she was. It was almost as if someone had reached through a vast emptiness and grabbed her. She opened her eyes and looked up into the fierce, war-painted face of the leader, who held her tightly against his wide chest.

A trifle dazed, Sharyl stared after the coach as it bounced away down the road, her door still swinging wide, the war party hot in pursuit. She felt the powerful horse under her, the heat of the half-naked man against her as he reined in and glared down into her face. If everyone else could act their parts, she could, too. No doubt he had once been a stunt man to have taken her from the stage that way instead of waiting for it to halt. "You—you saved my life," she gasped.

Dragonfly glared down at the beautiful girl in his arms. Once he had even scouted for the whites, learned their customs and their language. But since they had killed his family at Sand Creek four years ago, he had joined the Dog Soldiers. He himself had barely escaped dying in that massacre. A soldier had struck him in the face with his rifle butt, breaking his nose and leaving him for dead among the bodies of his little brothers and sisters. Dragonfly seethed with hate and hungered for vengeance.

As a carrier of the *hotamtsit*, Dragonfly had become a cold, hard killer; the whites had seen to that. He would show no mercy to this pretty girl he had just saved from the stagecoach and who now looked up at him so bravely. "You are my captive, white girl!" he snarled. "I will take you back to our camp for a victory celebration."

"As I expected," she said.

Dragonfly wheeled his pinto stallion, signaled his men to give up the futile chase of the Butterfield stage, and turned back toward the west. The girl felt warm and soft in his arms. She was pretty as well as brave. Desire rose hot in his loins and he almost regretted that after the victory celebration she would be tortured and killed. Tonight, that mane of light brown hair would be only another scalp hanging from his lodge pole!

# Chapter Three

Sharyl took a deep breath and sighed, relieved at having escaped death under the wheels of the lumbering stage that had disappeared in a cloud of dust down the road. It was gone as abruptly as if it had been swallowed up in time. Already the pursuers were riding back to join her captor.

He held her against his naked chest and shouted orders to his men. Whatever language he spoke, Sharyl couldn't understand. It was probably as fake as he was. However, he looked authentic enough, and certainly the whole adventure was better than Sharyl had expected. She must remember to write a recommendation for Western Dreams, Inc.

Sharyl sneaked an excited glance at her watch. Now she was supposed to go to the Indian village for dancing and a cookout, with the stage returning along the road to pick her up at midnight. She should have taken the watch off. The little dream catcher she still wore around her neck fitted into this historic time and place, but a wristwatch didn't.

She let the big Indian mold her body against his half naked one as he turned his horse toward the west. What a hunk! Sharyl noted the sun dance scars on his broad chest. Someone in the makeup or special effects departments had done a good job making those look realistic. In fact, everything about him looked realistic even to the Dog Rope over his shoulder. If he wasn't a real Native American, he could have fooled Sharyl.

Her captor actor glared down at her, hatred and desire etched on his war-painted features. "How are you called?"

"Sharyl. Who are you?"

She saw his eyes widen in surprise. "You are bold, white girl. Dragonfly does not expect such bravery from a woman."

Oh, how many times had she dreamed of living this role with a primitive man who knew how to make her feel like a woman? "I am your captive and at your mercy, I know, but I would not go to my fate like a whining, scared mouse."

He seemed to smile in spite of himself. "Well said! You will provide an evening's enjoyment for me then; in fact, it will be a shame to end it."

Heroines in historicals were always spunky as she had secretly yearned to be. "You have gotten more than you bargained for," Sharyl shook back her hair and glared up at him. "What explanation do you have for speaking English?"

"You question a Dog Soldier?" He glared at her almost incredulously as his men reined in around him, awaiting his orders. "You have more bravery than sense! I never met a white woman like you when I scouted for the soldiers."

Someone had written him a good script, Sharyl thought with satisfaction. Scouting would be a reasonable explanation. "Do with me what you will"— she threw back her head and flung the words in his face in a fiesty, spirited challenge—"I will show you courage!"

Grudging admiration crossed his handsome dark features. "We will see if you are really so brave by the end of tonight's victory celebration."

He held her tight against his brawny chest and turned his stallion and shouted to his men. The war party galloped into the shadows of the west. It was a strange, eerie feeling, Sharyl thought, almost as if she were really riding back into the past. Maybe it was only because she couldn't see the power lines or any planes against the faded blue Oklahoma sky. Sharyl closed her eyes and let Dragonfly hold her against his hard, dark body. The scent of dust and sun and gun smoke were on his warm skin. She pretended he was really carrying her off forever to be his love and roam wild and free on the endless prairies. At least she'd have tonight and that memory could never be taken away from her, even if she returned to a dull but sensible life with Clifford. Sharyl hoped that her three companions were now enjoying their fantasy as much as she was.

She was more than a little aware of the heat of his bare skin against her face, the way the warmth of his body seemed to burn into hers, all the way through her blue-flowered dress. Sharyl stared at the war party that rode with them. Sid Rosenthal had done a good job, all right, all of the extras looked authentic, although maybe their outfits might have "Made in Taiwan" on the label. Even Dragonfly's shield and weapons looked real. His powerful pinto stallion had its tail tied up for war in the custom of the Plains tribes, and red hand prints painted on its shoulders signified its owner had killed warriors in hand to hand combat.

There was nothing to do now but enjoy the adventure she had paid for. She looked up at his sensual mouth and sighed. The fake warrior was doing what he was paid to do and no doubt wouldn't find her all that alluring anyway.

Dragonfly studied the girl he held in his arms as the war party rode into the Cheyenne camp. With her light hair and creamy skin, she was the most beautiful, desirable woman he had ever seen. He re-

minded himself again how much he hated the whites
for wiping out his friends and family four years ago,
so it was only justice that he take revenge on the
white woman. He would enjoy her ripe body, then
kill her and hang that mane of luxurious hair from
his belt.

He reined in his stallion before his teepee. A
thought occurred to him. This girl with the unusual
name of Sharyl was either the bravest woman he had
ever met or she was loco. If she was loco, he could
not harm her. Most Indians had a reverence for crazy
people; everyone knew the spirits looked out for
them. Now that he had this strange, beautiful girl in
his possession, what was he to do? That decision
would be made later. Right now, he would eat,
dance, and celebrate the victory in capturing his enemy's woman.

That decided, he slid from his horse and reached
up for her. She hesitated, looking around at all the
curious brown faces that pressed toward them.
"Come!" he ordered and grabbed her waist. He
threw her across his shoulder like a small sack of
grain. She didn't weigh much.

"Hey!" she complained. "This is a bit too realistic,
don't you think? The women's rights groups will be
picketing Western Dreams if you aren't careful!"

Yes, she must be loco. Facing rape, then death by
torture, the strange white girl was speaking gibberish
that was English and yet not English. He understood
her words, but they made no sense to him. "You are
mine," he snapped as he strode into his teepee. "I
will do with you what I want."

"You are a male chauvinist pig!" The girl shrieked
and began to pound his back. "Much more of this
and I will report you to the National Organization
for Women!"

Yes, the captive was definitely loco. Dragonfly
didn't know whether to be disappointed or relieved

that he might not be able to add her scalp to his belt. A thought occurred to him as he paused, feeling the warmth of her on his shoulder: whites were not to be trusted. That was why the Cheyenne called them *vehoes*, spiders. Perhaps this spirited *vehoe* was clever enough to pretend to be insane, knowing if she could convince him of that, he dare not harm her. Was she sincerely brave and attempting to fool him into letting her go?

With a sneer, he dumped her unceremoniously on a buffalo robe and looked down at her. Yes, whites were good at deception. Dragonfly thought again of the attack that cold winter dawn in that place called Sand Creek and his hatred returned, bitter in his mouth. Yes, he wanted nothing more than to sacrifice and scalp her to avenge his family, who had died four years ago. His anguish had long ago turned to hatred and obliterated any mercy in his heart.

Sharyl struggled to control her temper as she sat in a heap on the buffalo robe and looked up at the big Dog Soldier who glared at her. She must not scold him for playing his part so enthusiastically; no doubt he was hoping a movie scout might discover him. The more she studied him, the more genuine he seemed. He was probably Italian. "Have you played in spaghetti westerns?"

He looked baffled. "You speak English, yet you make no sense, white girl. You do not fool me; some may think you loco, but not me."

"My mother certainly does," Sharyl sighed, "especially if she ever finds out how I spent my birthday money. Very well, we'll play this to the hilt." She stood up and looked him squarely in the eye, although it was difficult because she had to look up at him. She felt such sexual tension between them, it startled her. "I am ready for anything you've planned, but remember, it has to be finished by midnight.''

He smiled but there was no mirth in his dark face. ''Believe me, Sky Eyes, by that time, you will be glad to have it over. You will be praying to your gods to have it ended.''

His strong hand reached out and caught a trailing lock of her hair. His fingers brushed along her shoulder as he fingered the curl. She felt the electricity, the pent-up power behind that arm as he glared at her. ''You know what we usually do with captives?''

''I know.'' She managed to keep her gaze on his, even though she felt the blood rush to her face and could feel her heart beating harder. In a thousand romance novels she had shared this moment with the heroine; that magnetism of a powerful male, savage and primitive, who had her at his mercy; could do anything he wanted with her and she would be helpless against his strength. Despite herself, Sharyl felt her body rising up on her toes, her heart beating hard. His hands caught her shoulders, and he looked at her a long moment and hesitated. His fingers felt sensual and warm through the delicate cotton dress. His high-cheekboned face appeared confused and troubled.

Sharyl opened her lips to speak, but she couldn't get any words out. She ran her tongue along her lower lip and knew he took a deep, shuddering breath as he watched her. Contract or no contract, she had a sudden feeling that if she changed her expression ever so slightly, or let him pull her one centimeter closer so that her breasts brushed against his bare chest through the thin fabric, he would pull her against him, stifle her protest with his mouth, and kiss her as she had only dreamed of being kissed.

It took several deep breaths for her to get her emotions under control and pull away from him. ''I—I think we should go out to the celebration and feasting."

He started, his eyes widening. "You are either the bravest or the most loco white I have ever met. Even the bravest of the Bluecoats would not demand or sneer in the face of death this way!"

She shrugged and smiled. "It's only what Heather Huntington Jeeves would do." She dared not say that if she stayed this close to him for one more minute, she would find herself closing her eyes, pressing against him, offering her lips to him. What would she do if he kissed her? Worse yet, what would she do if he laughed and reminded her it wasn't in the Western Dreams contract?

"You still make no sense, Sky Eyes." He tangled his big hand in her hair, turned her face up to his and looked into her eyes intently as if attempting to discern her soul. "Yes, we will go join the circle, *vehoe.* Let us see how brave you are when you face my people."

It would soon be dark, Sharyl thought, as the powerful warrior caught her hand and pulled her outside the teepee. They walked toward the camp circle, where a big fire burned brightly. A crowd of curious people followed. Certainly she hadn't expected such a large cast. "This looks like a Cecil B. De Mille production," she said. "I don't know how Sid can afford to pay so many extras."

The Dog Soldier looked over his shoulder at her in puzzlement. "You may yet convince the council you are loco, but I think you are merely brave and very cunning." He sounded both admiring and annoyed.

It was only the way a heroine should react, Sharyl thought as they walked to the camp circle. A haunch of meat roasted on a spit over the roaring fire. "I will eat."

He sat down in the circle and yanked her down

beside him. "No one has offered you any food," he snapped. "The warriors will eat first, then the women and children. We don't usually feed the prisoner."

"I was promised some genuine buffalo," Sharyl said, "and if I don't get it, I'll complain to the city council, the local Chamber of Commerce, and the Better Business Bureau that Western Dreams is not living up to its contract."

Her high voice carried out across the circle, and the venerable old men who were eating paused and stared at her and asked questions of Dragonfly.

He looked embarrassed and annoyed, shrugged and answered.

Sharyl listened and demanded. "What did you tell them?"

He glared at her. "I tell them anyone with nerve enough to complain before the council may be loco after all."

An Indian boy with bad acne scars stared back at her from the shadows across the circle. Why did he look familiar to her? Oh, of course, the snow cone boy had a bit part also. At least he wasn't wearing a T-shirt.

A bent old woman with a big mole on her chin hobbled over to serve Dragonfly and then started to move away.

Sharyl reached up to touch the dream catcher around her own neck. Everyone in town must work part time for Western Dreams, Inc. "Excuse me, but you forgot mine."

The old woman looked at Dragonfly questioningly.

"Serve her," the warrior ordered. "Let's see if she then has the stomach for it."

Was that a challenge? Very slowly and deliberately, Sharyl took a bite. The meat was succulent and delicious. Feeling all eyes upon her, she ate with gusto. "What's this other stuff? It's good, too."

"Pemmican," the warrior said. "Tallow mixed with pounded choke cherries and ripe sand plums."

"Tastes like trail mix," Sharyl smiled. "Good, but I don't know about all that cholesterol."

Next to Dragonfly sat a squat, powerful warrior. She peered at him. "Who is that?"

"You are as curious as a magpie. That is my Comanche friend, Mountain. The Cheyenne, Arapaho, Kiowa, and Comanche have been allies for generations."

"Mountain? Good name for him," she nodded as she ate. "I know much from my reading. I also know about the enemy Pawnee tribe and how they stole your tribe's sacred medicine arrows." She looked around. All had paused and were watching her in awed silence. "What is it?"

Dragonfly said, "They think you are either loco or very brave to be eating with the ordeal that awaits you."

He sounded as if he were giving her grudging praise. Somehow, she liked that. She took another bite of the roast meat. "The caterer is to be congratulated," she said. "He ought to franchise."

Again, Dragonfly stared at her and a murmur ran through the crowd.

"What kind of entertainment is planned?" She asked as she set the empty gourd aside.

"_You_ are the entertainment," Dragonfly snapped. "You should know that."

Of course she had forgotten the dancing around the camp fire Sid had promised her. She would really get to take part in it; that was even better than watching. Sharyl wished she had a cold soda, but no one seemed to be drinking anything but strong coffee boiled in a big iron pot and she didn't have a cup anyway. The food was good, but the service could use improvement. She smiled at the warrior, enjoying herself immensely. The event was everything she had hoped for, even to the handsome brave—if only he wouldn't scowl so much. "You're overacting," she whispered confidentially. "A little bit too melodramatic."

"What?" He gaped at her. "White girl, you risk your life to speak so strangely to a carrier of the Dog Rope."

Okay, if he insisted on overdoing it, she'd play along. She smiled as the drums began to beat rhythmically in the pale shadowy dusk of evening. Women stood up and mingled with the men. It was evident they were inviting partners to dance. The big fire threw distorted shadows across the straggly scrub oak and underbrush as the couples moved to the beat. She almost seemed to feel the throb deep in her body like a mating call. She turned to Dragonfly. "I choose you; show me how."

He looked astounded and blinked. Sharyl reached out, caught his hand and pulled him into the circle. "Sky Eyes," he objected, "you must have a shawl, no woman dances the round dance without a shawl."

"I do; Sid forgot to give me one." Sharyl took her place in the circle. The other dancers seemed almost petrified by her actions as they stepped aside. The two looked into each other's eyes as they moved to the beat, and after a moment she forgot the others, forgot everything but his nearness. She saw the expression on his hard face change gradually and knew he wanted her as a man wants a woman. If he decided to pick her up and carry her out into the darkness and make frenzied love to her, she was not sure she would stop him, safe sex notwithstanding.

When the song ended, a fierce rhythm and chanting began, calling warriors to dance the war dance. Sharyl watched as Dragonfly joined the other men by the giant fire. In the mystic darkness, the flames threw distorted shadows across those in the big circle as the dancers whirled and stomped. Sharyl was mesmerized by her captor's movements. He danced with the skill and grace of some wild cougar, twisting and contorting as he stepped. He was naked except for a skimpy loincloth, and his magnificent bare body shone bronze in the firelight. Sharyl wondered what it would be like to have her captor make love to her.

For a long moment, she imagined that powerful, dark body naked between her thighs, his hot mouth on her bare breast. She would wrap her creamy thighs around his lean, hard hips, pull him deep into her, dig her nails into his back. She had only had two sexual experiences, both very hurried and disappointing. But this one, oh, he looked as if he had the skill and virility to make a woman twist and moan under him, offering her breasts and body to him to do as he wanted.

She must not think of that. Probably this was only a second job to Dragonfly. Probably he had a wife and three kids in Anadarko. No doubt he was doing these fantasy happenings at Western Dreams to pay for a car for her or orthodontic work for his son. Still when he whirled and looked at her, it sent a flush of heat up her belly from her loins to her breasts and made her wonder what it would be like to make love under the stars, uninhibited and unashamed, two wild things mating in the moonlight, thinking of nothing but fulfilling each other's needs and desires. The way he was looking at her made her feel like a movie star, no, like a woman; *all* woman.

Sharyl lost track of time as the hours passed. She danced and whirled with Dragonfly and they exchanged heated glances. Finally the dances began to break up and her captor conferred with the ancient chiefs in muttered tones.

"Now what?" she asked as he returned.

He eyed her keenly. "The old chiefs have decided you are mine and I must make the decision as to your fate."

"So what will you do with your captive?" She looked up at him, wanting to be kissed so very badly by this man.

Dragonfly scowled as if loath to give her up. "I am going to take you out and turn you loose on the prairie."

Sharyl sighed. "Oh, of course, it is about time I suppose for the stagecoach to come back. I wish . . ." She broke off. "Only one other thing I've dreamed of and it's not sensible at all."

"Nothing about you is sensible; you are like no other woman I have ever met." He was still staring at her. "Did you not hear? Instead of being sacrificed, I will free you, when what I really want to do with you is . . ."

She waited. His expression left no doubt what he wanted. She had never felt desirable before. The way this virile man was watching her made up for all the times Mitzi got invited to the prom and she didn't, all those times she didn't get elected or chosen for anything. "I—I'd like to ride with you once more across the prairie, under the stars."

"Yes," he nodded, looking disturbed. "The sooner you are out of my life, the better. I think somehow that you are big medicine that is more than just loco."

If only it were 1868, if only she were a white captive and he were a Dog Soldier who could make a decision to keep her with him always. Get real, Sharyl, she reprimanded herself as she followed him out to the horse herd. He's paid to make you feel this way; it's part of the deal, but the stagecoach will be picking you up along the road in a few minutes.

He caught his magnificent paint stallion and bridled it. "A medicine hat," he said, "you know about them?"

Sharyl nodded. "I know that the color on the head

and ears, the color that looks like a shield on its chest, marks it as good medicine."

"Can you ride, little loco one?"

Sharyl hesitated. In her whole sheltered life, she had never been on anything but a carousel horse, and once when she was small, a mounted policeman in the park had boosted her up on his placid old gelding. "I can ride," she said with emphasis. Suddenly, deep inside her soul, she knew she wasn't a loser. She had been bullied by her mother until she believed it, yet now she knew that if her heart was strong and confident, she could do anything. "Yes, I can ride; I know I can!"

He nodded with amused satisfaction as he swung up on his rearing stallion. "Then come, girl with eyes like a prairie sky, we will ride one time into the night and I will set you free so that you bring no bad medicine to my people."

So he intended to play his part to the last; that was good, Sharyl thought. If he worked at a fast food place or dug ditches in his real life, Sharyl didn't want to know about it. He seemed born to fill this role of warrior.

He reached to lift her up on the bareback stallion before him. His strong arms slipped around her waist and he pulled her against him. She felt the heat of his bare skin through the thin calico dress and his breath was warm against her neck. His strong hand was on her waist, up under her breast and she wished he would move to cover her breast and caress it. Her full skirt had hiked up and now Dragonfly put his big hand on her bare thigh to steady her. She felt the heat of it all through her being.

The stallion danced under them and she was too conscious of the untamed male with his arms around her to be afraid of the powerful beast between her bare thighs.

"All right, little loco one," he whispered and she

caught the challenge in his voice, "let's see you handle this horse!"

She could do it; she knew she could; it was part and parcel of her fantasy. Slapping the spirited mount with the reins, she struggled to keep her balance, but Dragonfly held and protected her, his strong arms wrapped around her. Mother would think this was not a practical thing to do. For a split second, Sharyl wondered if this unexpected and unscheduled ride was covered by liability insurance.

"To hell with always being sensible!" She threw her head back and laughed as the medicine hat stallion took off at a gallop across the horizon, running along in the summer heat of the starlit Oklahoma night.

# Chapter Four

They rode at a gallop across the night-swept prairie. Sharyl had never known emotion like this; the feel of the great horse between her thighs, its strong, ground-eating gallop seemed almost dreamlike; the feel of Dragonfly's body against hers sent waves of longing through her. Yet she knew that in a few minutes the stagecoach would return to whisk her out of her adventure and back to her dull but sensible future life in Newark.

The great pinto stallion was lathered and blowing when she reined in. She leaned against the man with a sigh, reveling in the feel of his body against hers, the heat of his embrace, the touch of his big hand on her bare thigh. They came to a small rise. From here in the moonlight, she could see the rutted road snaking across the horizon. "In a few minutes, the stage will come back along that road." She reined in.

Dragonfly murmured against her hair. "Why do you think the stage will return? After our attack, they won't risk it without an escort of troops."

"Of course they'll be back."

"You are a stubborn and strange girl; different than any white I have ever met." He slid from the horse and held up his arms to her. He sounded puzzled, as if he no longer knew what his emotions should be. "Suppose you don't meet them?"

"Then they'll have everyone out looking for me." She slid off the stallion into Dragonfly's arms. "You can just leave me near the road." She glanced at her watch, its luminous dial glowing in the dark. "It's almost time."

"What is this thing you wear?" He caught her wrist.

So he was going to play it for real right up to the very last moment. Maybe it was better that way so they wouldn't have to deal with the awkwardness of parting. "It's my Cherokee Strip Centennial watch."

He shook his head, still staring at it, puzzlement evident on his dark face in the moonlight. "No, a watch is a big thing a white man wears on a gold chain across his vest and this glows in the dark like magic." He surveyed it even more closely. "The dates are wrong."

"No, they aren't." She pulled away from him. "It's been a hundred years since the government let the settlers have a run for the Cherokee land."

He stared at her in a way that sent chills up and down her back. "You are either loco or bad medicine; I am not sure what you are or where you came from."

"I came from Western Dreams, Inc. I—"

"Dreams." He nodded knowingly. "Yes, you are a medicine dream, perhaps a vision that I have begged the Great Spirit for."

"Now, Dragonfly, you talk nonsense, I—"

"Shh!" He put his finger to his lips suddenly and cocked his head.

"What do you hear? The stage—?"

"Shh!" He signaled her to silence. "I hear a rider; could be anyone." He led her and the horse over into the shadows of some scrub oaks. "My people have many enemies."

Well, it was a good way out of an awkward situation. If they got carried away by this strong electric current between them, exchanged phone numbers, and tried to meet later, they both might be disappointed. Somehow, he seemed at home as a warrior on the prairie; maybe this was the memory of him she should take away.

However, now even her ears caught the faint echo of hoofbeats. It's not loud enough to be the stage horses, she thought. Maybe Sid had sent a rider out to pick her up or to tell her why the stage would be late. At any rate, this would mean good-bye.

Dragonfly slipped his arms around her, still watching the horizon. "I see the rider now, maybe he will pass us by."

Pass us by. Western Dreams, Inc., would be upset if they couldn't find her, and yet, the thought that this man wanted her to stay in his embrace a little longer seemed more important than anything else. Sharyl closed her eyes and snuggled against his big chest, liking the feel of his protective arms around her. The beat of his heart in her ear seemed to say: I love you . . . love you . . . love you. Oh, if only he did.

Something was wrong. She felt sudden tension in his lithe frame and his heart pounded faster. She opened her eyes and saw the rider crossing the prairie only a few hundred yards away. He rode a horse pale as a phantom, but he himself was painted with garish war paint, his hair cut in the pronounced roached style of the Pawnee tribe.

The Pawnee were old enemies of the Cheyenne, she had read. Dragonfly stared at the rider with an angry frown that couldn't be faked. It seemed to her as if they were back more than a century before and watching a bitter enemy approach. "Can't we outrun him?"

Dragonfly shook his head and muttered a curse about his own carelessness in leaving camp without a rifle. "We're riding double and my horse is tired. If you weren't with me, it would be different."

Sharyl wondered what the script called for now. "Perhaps he will pass us by."

"Stay in the shadows," Dragonfly whispered. "He's better armed than I am, and if he wins, he'll carry you off for his own."

She leaned against Dragonfly's chest, feeling loved and protected. What an exciting climax to her adventure! The stage was past due to come rolling up the road. Even as the Pawnee cantered abreast of the pair, his pale horse nickered and the medicine hat stallion returned the challenge. Dragonfly cursed softly under his breath, holding her tightly against him even as the Pawnee reined in.

"Who is there?" His superior rifle glinting in the starlight, the Pawnee wheeled his horse and cantered toward them. "Declare yourself, or will you skulk in the shadows like a cowardly coyote with your female?"

Dragonfly whispered, "He challenges me." He set her safely to one side. "My honor is at stake; I will have to fight him."

Something about his tone frightened Sharyl. These two warriors were making it all seem so very real.

Her Cheyenne captor put his hand on the dagger in his belt and stepped out into the moonlight. He shouted his challenge. "I do not skulk, you cowardly pet of the bluecoats, but I have no gun. A real warrior would fight me hand to hand!"

"Well spoken!" the Pawnee shouted back. "I accept your challenge. Tonight the Pawnee will dance around a Cheyenne scalp and all of us will rape your woman!"

A thrill of excitement and apprehension ran through Sharyl as the Pawnee dismounted and strode toward them. A fight to the death over her would be a fitting climax to this adventure.

Dragonfly turned to her. "I intend to kill him for all the wrongs the Pawnee have done my people, but should something go wrong, mount my stallion and ride away as fast as you can!"

"But what about the stage? It's past due now—"

"Don't argue with me!" He pulled his knife.

The two blades reflected the light as the pair approached each other. The scarlet paint gleaming on the cruel face of the Pawnee made him look like something from a nightmare.

It was all just a show staged for her benefit, Sharyl knew that, yet from the way the men moved she could almost believe that they were really going to fight to the death, with her body as the prize for the victor.

Out on the open prairie, the two enemies confronted each other, circling warily. Dragonfly feinted and the Pawnee jumped back, obviously surprised at his skill and speed. "So the Cheyenne is faster than a rattlesnake. Good, I welcome a worthy foe."

Dragonfly snorted. "I am a Dog Soldier, a carrier of the *hotamsit*. We laugh at the Pawnee as coyotes eating scraps from the white man's table rather than hunt like warriors."

The Pawnee threw back his head and laughed. "Yet you have a white mate. She will bear my sons, Cheyenne! Perhaps I will let you die slowly so you can see me take her the first time before your life's blood runs out to feed the buffalo grass."

There was something very wrong, Sharyl could almost feel it, and why was the stage long overdue? There was tension here, deadly hatred that felt too real to be faked. She reached up to clasp the little charm around her neck. All she had wanted were good dreams; how could this nightmare be slipping through?

The Pawnee dove in, blade slashing, but Dragonfly easily sidestepped the knife with a scornful laugh. "You're soft, cavalry scout, from hanging around the forts too long, eating white man's bread."

"Soon I shall feast on your woman's breast!" the Pawnee crowed as he rushed Dragonfly, knife flashing.

"Look out!" Sharyl screamed even as Dragonfly grabbed the other's wrist. The two men meshed, light gleaming on sweating, straining muscles as each tried to use his strength to gain the advantage. The Pawnee pulled his arm free and slashed downward, but Dragonfly was as quick as the darting insect whose name he bore. The enemy dagger cut a glancing blow along his arm. With any other man, it would have been buried by now in his chest.

Scarlet dripped from the cut and Sharyl held her breath, watching the duel. Yes, she knew it was fake blood, but the two were making the fight look so real! Maybe they had both been stunt doubles at one time in Sid's old movies.

The pair of mighty braves meshed and rolled across the prairie under the hooves of the Pawnee's horse that whinnied and reared in surprise. The two combatants paid no heed as they rolled and cursed and battled.

Dragonfly was tiring, Sharyl could see that now even as the two staggered to their feet. The Pawnee was bigger and weighed more. Her mouth tasted bitter with tension. Surely the script didn't call for the hero to lose this fight?

The Pawnee threw back his head and laughed. "And now, Cheyenne dog, I finish you off and take your woman!" With that shouted challenge, he waded in, slashing as he came, but again with speed and skill like a darting dragonfly, her man sidestepped him and brought his own knife up.

The Pawnee seemed to see the light reflecting off the steel as it came down, but though he threw up one arm, he couldn't stop the blow. He screamed as Dragonfly buried the knife to the hilt in his heart. Dragonfly staggered, breathing heavily as he pulled the scarlet blade out. The enemy fell. Dragonfly reached to take the other's scalp. Holding the hair high, he threw back his head and shouted a victory chant.

Even though she knew it was only special effects, Sharyl let out a great sigh of relief and ran to meet Dragonfly. "Oh, that was so exciting, you two almost made me believe it was real!"

Dragonfly staggered toward her. "Little one, you are indeed loco. Any other woman would take my horse and leave her captor to die out here."

She slipped her arm under his and let him lean against her as they hobbled toward the tree. "Here, let me help you and—"

She paused, puzzled. That red stuff smeared on his flesh certainly looked like blood, it even smelled like blood. "It's amazing the special effects Hollywood has come up with." She turned and yelled back over her shoulder to the other actor. "You can get up now! It was a great climax to the adventure!"

Dragonfly shook his head as she helped him to sit down under the tree. "He won't be getting up."

"What do you mean?" She turned and looked out toward the prone form. He still wasn't moving. Apprehension began to rise in her throat. She'd heard of accidents like this on movie sets. She'd had some CPR training, maybe she could do something until help arrived. She started to walk back out there, but the Cheyenne caught her arm. "Don't, Sky Eyes."

Sharyl felt a growing horror. She looked around the horizon, wondering if there was a ranch nearby. "If I can find a house, I could call 911 and they'll send a chopper, maybe—"

"The Pawnee is dead."

She looked down at him and the truth in his dark eyes washed over her. She gaped at the blood on his shoulder. The two really had accidently hurt each other. "Oh my God! When I bought into this, I didn't mean for anything like this to happen!"

Dragonfly shrugged and leaned back against the tree. "He would have killed me and raped you; don't mourn him."

She ran to get a canteen and held it to Dragonfly's lips. He drank greedily as she tore a strip from her white petticoat and began to bind his wound. It was not as bad as she had first thought. "The stage will be here any minute, and maybe it will have a mobile phone so we can get an ambulance or a chopper—"

"As wounds go, it is nothing." Dragonfly shrugged, looked out toward the body. "We fought; I killed him. The Cheyenne will have a victory dance tomorrow. If he had won, you would be under him right now while he enjoyed your body, then took you back to share with the others."

"You—you meant to kill him?"

"Did you not see the fight? He was trying to kill me."

"But I thought . . . ?" What did she think? There was only one logical explanation; no, that wasn't logical either. Her fantasy had turned into a nightmare. It was all too crazy, like some weird dream. When she got help out here and returned to town, she would sort it all out. She glanced at her watch again.

He caught her arm and stared at her watch. It said 1893–1993. "Magic," he whispered. "But it isn't possible."

His fascination with her watch and the date seemed too real to be faked. She thought again about what the college boy on the stage had said about being in sync with the time, actually going back to that exact moment when the Cheyenne had attacked that very stage at this time of year and almost on this very spot. Nothing made any sense—except that this man had just fought a fight to the death to possess her. She looked around at the horizon. She saw no power

lines, no planes flying against the sky even though
Fort Sill was less than fifty miles away. What had
happened to the stage that was supposed to return
for her? "What—what is the year?"

He shrugged. "Indians don't keep time that way,
we go by winter counts. It has been four since my
people were massacred at Sand Creek."

"Sand Creek?" She remembered what she had
read. "Why, that happened way back in 1864—"

"Yes," he nodded, "four winter counts ago."

"Stop it! Do you hear me?" She heard her own
voice rise to an hysterical shriek. "It can't be 1868!"

He shook her hard. "Of course it is! I knew you
were loco. Where do you get this spirit watch?"

Sharyl trembled and tried to think logically. If only
she had a sensible explanation. There was only one
answer, crazy as it seemed. "Dragonfly, you will
think what I'm about to tell you is loco, but I swear
it's true. Somehow, I—I think I have been caught in
some kind of time warp and swept back into your
life!"

He didn't believe her, she could see it in his dark
eyes. He studied her watch again, staring at the
dates. "Then you have come all this way back to
share this time with me? Why?"

She felt tears come to her eyes. "Because I have
dreamed of you with each romance novel I opened,
every western movie I ever saw. There are thousands
like me, yearning for a *real* man, the virile, primitive
mate I have looked for all my life and never found.
We're all sick of the sensitive wimps of our
civilization."

Somehow, now she didn't want to go back to her
own time. In a few short hours, she had lived a lifetime. She loved this man; she realized that now; he
had fought for her and won her and she wanted to
stay forever in his muscular embrace. She reached
up to touch the little dream catcher around her neck.

If this was a dream the charm had brought her, she never wanted it to end.

He smiled sadly. "I don't question because I sense big spirit medicine at work here. I know now how this must end." He closed his eyes and leaned back against the tree trunk with a sigh. "There is an old Cheyenne legend about White Buffalo Woman, who came to my people. The ancient ones tell the tale late at night when the drums beat and we gather around the fire."

And now she knew the answer, too. Sharyl had read many Indian novels. "The Cheyenne only tell medicine tales at night," she remembered aloud, "it is forbidden to tell them in the daylight because the magic ends at dawn."

"Dawn," he nodded, "yes, somehow this must be a spirit tale that ends with first light."

He spoke the truth, she knew it in her heart. "So we only have tonight," she whispered, looking into his eyes. With the coming of morning, the tale must end and they would be separated forever. "It isn't fair," she said. "I was born in the wrong time and place and have spent my whole life looking for you."

He reached out and caught her hand. "It must be magic that hate turns to love in the length of a medicine tale. I will never feel the same about whites again; there are good and bad ones just as among my people."

"We have tonight," she whispered.

He nodded and in the moonlight his black hair shone like a dragonfly's wings. "Yes, and maybe we are lucky at that. Some never find love, but in this whole universe, with all these millions of people, somehow we have found each other. You came into my life and made me see red and white are the same in their hearts. Sky Eyes, let us not think about tomorrow. If we can have only a few hours in each other's arms, let us make the most of it."

It seemed so right that she was in his arms, sheltered in his chest as he kissed her. This wasn't sensible at all, and yet she was letting a stranger make love to her. No, he wasn't a stranger; she had known him from a thousand novels, knew him better than she had ever known the men of her own day. "I love you."

He kissed her face, looked deep into her eyes, his big hand cupping her chin. "I don't question or understand this magic that has brought you into my life, Sky Eyes, but I have wanted you from the first moment I stole you from the stage."

Sharyl hesitated. She who should know enough to be sensible was in the arms of a stranger out on the prairie at some point in time she wasn't even sure of. And yet it felt as if it were destined to happen. "Take me," she demanded. "Oh, take me now!"

Sharyl reached up for his kiss, her lips half parted. His mouth covered hers; gentle at first, then more passionate. His tongue slipped between her lips, dominating, demanding. She threw her head back and let him explore the velvet interior, making the same thrusting gestures that a man's manhood makes when it puts itself inside a woman's body and she surrenders to his will.

Her hands trembled as she reached to undo the tiny buttons of her bodice, so his hands took over, slowly baring her breasts to the moonlight. His hands were calloused and warm as he cupped her breasts in his palms. "Mine," he murmured, "and so very beautiful!"

No man had ever said that to her and with such ardor and feeling. He kissed along her collarbone, then moved lower so that she felt the heat of his breath on her nipple. "I would like to put my child in your belly," he murmured, "and see your breasts swell with milk for both of us."

He bent his head and his mouth fastened on her

nipple where he sucked like a greedy child. The feeling sent such a heat of desire through her body that she arched her back, pushing her breast deeper into his hot mouth as she groaned aloud and clasped his dark head against her white breast.

Encouraged, he sucked harder, squeezing her other breast with his hand. She felt her turgid nipple swell and felt as if she were on fire all the way down to her knees. Whispering words of passion and endearment, his hands stroked her thighs as he kissed his way down her belly. Surely he wasn't going to kiss her there; no man ever had. Then he did and she couldn't think, she could only writhe and gasp at the sensation. She reached to grasp his manhood and he was as big and throbbing as a stallion with his need. He wore only a skimpy loincloth and moccasins and she was half naked in a tangle of white lace petticoats and a blue calico dress unbuttoned all the way down. She wasn't even wearing bloomers, she realized as he touched and stroked and kissed her with wild abandon.

She had never really wanted a man, wanted to be mounted and mated in the primitive way she hungered for now. "I want your seed in my belly," she said urgently. "You have won me, now mate me as warriors have always taken captured women."

"Say that you want me," he whispered.

"I want you," she said and knew the hunger must shine in her eyes, "oh, how I want you!"

He stood and stripped away the loincloth, standing naked and proud as a wild stallion. In the moonlight, his bronze skin shone darkly copper as he reached for her and swung her up in his arms and kissed her breast.

With a low moan, she held his dark face against her as he sucked her nipples into two points of flaming desire. The fire that was building deep in her belly seemed to spread over them both like glowing coals. She ached with her own passion as Dragonfly laid her on the soft, wind-swept prairie grass. He stood over her naked and dark, looking down at her with the unspoken question in his eyes.

She reached up to him. "Come to me," she whispered. "I want you between my thighs, want you deep inside me."

"I might hurt you, Sky Eyes."

She held out her arms. "Then hurt me; hurt me deep!"

He seemed to need no further urging as he fell to his knees before her. She let her thighs fall apart and he reached to lift her to him. Very slowly, he entered her body. He was built big, and for a moment it felt like an iron bar coming into her, an iron bar from the forge, hot as molten steel. His mouth sought hers.

He seemed to fill her totally; completely. She let him do what he would with his mouth as she held his face against her breast, her thighs locking around his lean, hard-driving dark hips. "More!" she demanded, digging her nails into his back. "Oh, more!"

"I'm afraid I'll hurt you. . . ."

"I can't get enough of you," Sharyl gasped and began to move with him. It felt as if he were ramming hard up under her ribs. She could feel the heated, throbbing power of him swollen with the seed he carried to plant in her womb. She saw herself with her belly swollen big with his son, her breasts full of milk. This was both savage and tender; old as time itself, this ritual of two wild, half-naked beings mating on the grass in the moonlight. Nothing mattered but their love and their passion for each other. Tomorrow might not exist, but they had this one moment in time.

"I love you," he whispered. "I'll always love you. . . ."

"I love you, too." She didn't want to think about always or tomorrow; she would settle for this pre-

cious brief moment in his arms to remember forever.
She felt her body responding greedily to his as he
rode her with long, sure strokes. She dug her nails
into his muscled back, holding him to her with her
legs locked around him and his mouth covering hers,
his tongue deep in her throat. She felt him begin to
give up his seed even as her body trembled under
his, asking, no, demanding that he give her what she
wanted.

She tilted up so that he could thrust his deepest
and then her body convulsed as they surrendered to
their need. She was Woman, demanding to be mated,
wanting his seed deep inside her and running down
her thighs, her breasts tender from his eager mouth.
As she felt his hot seed rush deep inside her womb,
she gave way to her own passion. Blackness swept
over her as night runs before scarlet flames in an all-
consuming prairie fire. She meshed and held him to
her, convulsed beneath him, not willing to stop until
she had drained him.

For a long time, she knew nothing; then gradually
she came back to consciousness and he was kissing
her eyes, her lips, her hair. "My woman," he whispered. "I could never get enough of you!"

She felt her own desire began to build again and
he was a virile lover. His eager mouth found hers
and his manhood grew rigid. She could still want
him with an urgent hunger she would not have
thought possible yesterday. "Make love to me
again."

He obliged and for Sharyl his passionate virility
was more wonderful than anything she had ever experienced. She had not known what sensual could
be until this man had lain between her thighs, held
her close, and made love both fiery and gently
tender.

At last they lay in each other's arms, sated and
weary. Only then did she notice the lavender gray

light in the east. So soon? It seemed they had only been lovers a moment. Now with the light, she must face reality and reality meant losing him forever. Tears blurred her vision. "Dawn is coming."

He caught both her hands in his. "I can't let you go. Perhaps the dawn doesn't matter—"

"You know it does." Sharyl looked up into his dark, rugged features, memorizing everything about his dear face. "We can't question; we both know it's magic, but ending too soon, too soon. . . ."

He kissed her feverishly. "I've only just found you. How can I let you go? All my life I've waited and we only had one night together."

Sharyl clung to him. "I'll cherish every memory. It was a dream come true."

He held her close and they watched the pale blush of daybreak spread along the eastern rim of the horizon. "We have the memories of last night," he said, "and no one can ever take those away from us, but I won't let you go." He sounded angry and determined as he embraced her.

"You have no choice." Inside, she was crying, but she must be strong for both of them. Somehow she knew that if he tried to keep her here, it would upset history and bring him disaster. Only one more thing she must do to keep him safe. "Dragonfly, my dear love! I must protect you, so heed me well. Do you remember that favorite camp of your people along the Washita?"

He nodded.

"This coming winter, in late November, the Cheyenne may hold a woman named Clara Blinn and her little boy, Willie, as prisoners there. Yellowhair Custer will be sent one snowy dawn to attack that camp."

He looked at her as if he did not believe her. "How do you know this?"

"Please trust me; I come from the future. You will

know I speak true when Black Kettle and his wife are among the dead, but you will know in time to escape."

He believed her now, she saw it in his eyes. "I will warn my people."

Sharyl shook her head. "It won't do any good, they won't believe you. Another thing; eight years from now in the summertime, Yellowhair and his men will be wiped out at the Little Big Horn River."

"But the future is not good for the Cheyenne, is it?" He peered down at her. "I see it in your face."

She couldn't look at him. "It is not good," she agreed, "but because you have been warned, perhaps you will live to lead your people." She turned toward the glowing dawn. "I must go now, back to my own time, even though I'm not sure how to get there." Maybe she would wake up on the old stagecoach as it bumped down the road, and they wouldn't even have missed her.

He caught her arm. "I'll go with you."

"Oh, if only you could!" She was weeping now, weeping at losing this one true love of her life when she had only just found him. "You can't cross that barrier."

"I'll find a way." He held her close. "If we both want it bad enough, maybe someday, somehow, in another place and time, we'll meet again."

*Reincarnation.* No, it wasn't possible. "I leave this for you to remember me by, my love." Very slowly, she loosened the little dream catcher from around her neck and tied it around his. It meant so much to her, she wanted him to have it. "Sometime, think of me."

"I'll never take it off." He reached up to touch it. "I will find you again, Sky Eyes, I swear I will. Someday, when you least expect it, you'll look up and see a man and you'll know; there'll be a way that you will know I have loved you enough to find you again."

There was no hope of that, but she hadn't the heart to say, Be sensible. He kissed her deeply, thoroughly, holding her close against his brawny chest. She could feel his heart beating against her breast as they embraced.

Now the first warm ray of dawn fell across her face and she clung to him. "I'll never forget if a thousand years pass! Kiss me, Dragonfly, kiss me one last time."

He kissed her; a kiss to remember forever. "My Sky Eyes, my one true love."

Now with the sunlight chasing away the magic, she felt herself being pulled away from him by a force she could not overcome, although she fought desperately to hang on to him. His beloved image was fading into the receding misty shadows of the night.

"Remember I love you," she called as he became almost a wisp of fog drifting like smoke in the bright sunlight, "I love you ... love you ... love you. ..."

# Chapter Five

Slowly, Sharyl opened her eyes. She whispered an endearment, reached toward her lover; then realized she was alone. Where was she anyway? Her head hurt and she had to concentrate to focus her gaze. A pink blush of light splashed the eastern horizon and directly over her face, a fruit-laden sand plum bush trembled in the cool dawn breeze. A slight movement about the leaves; a darting dragonfly, gauzy wings shining iridescent in the first rays of sun. Crushing realization washed over her; a dream, her great love of one night had only been a dream after all.

She sat up and reached to brush the twigs from her tangled hair and looked down at her rumpled blue calico dress. Immediately, yesterday and Western Dreams, Inc., came back to her. She groaned aloud with the pain of her throbbing head and an indescribable sense of loss. Now she remembered bouncing wildly in the racing stagecoach, hanging on to the door as the fake warriors pursued them. That door must have come open when the stage bounced. Sharyl looked about in confusion. Had she actually fallen out, hit her head, and lain here all night unconscious? Of course that was the only sensible explanation.

Feeling more than a little annoyed, she stood up and brushed the dust from her dress. The white petticoat was torn; probably from her fall. What kind of people managed Western Dreams anyhow? "It looks like they would have at least come back to help me. After all, I was lying right by the trail in plain sight!"

Then she smiled and closed her eyes, remembering the taste of a warrior's lips, his virile embrace. Even if it had been only a dream, it had been wonderful!

Sharyl glanced at her watch. She had to return to town and check out of the motel. Fran would be expecting her car back this afternoon. She walked toward the nearby highway. Around her, the Oklahoma landscape came to life. In a nearby pasture, a horse nickered, quail burst up out of the brush and flew at the cry of a hawk circling in a prairie sky the color of faded denim. She hadn't realized that in six short months she had come to love the wide open spaces of the land of the red man. At that moment, she made her decision.

When she reached the highway, she flagged down an elderly rancher in a battered red pickup. "Looks like you had some weekend, miss."

She started to explain, realizing what he must think and decided she didn't really care. She had changed a lot since yesterday. "Yes, an unforgettable weekend," she murmured.

He looked curious, but he didn't ask anything else as he drove her into Anadarko and dropped her off at the motel.

She went to her room, washed the dust off her face, and changed into a pair of jeans. She folded the dress lovingly and packed it. "An unforgettable weekend," she whispered, "even if it was only a dream."

Her phone rang and she picked it up, puzzled. Only Fran knew she was here. "Hello?"

"Sharyl?" said Mother's scolding voice. "What in the name of goodness are you doing? I called your roommate and she said you'd gone out of town to watch Indians dance."

"It's a tourist thing." Sharyl sat down on the bed

and tied her sneaker with one hand. "I thought it would be fun for my birthday."

"Remember, you're twenty-seven today. I hope you'll be a little more mature from now on. You know, one of the things Clifford's mother said bothered him about you was how impractical you are. Just like your father, I told her."

Sharyl had made her decision and suddenly she wasn't worried about either her mother or her sister Mitzi or even Clifford's opinion anymore. She took a deep breath. "Mother, I've thought it over and I've decided to stay in Oklahoma."

"Sharyl, are you crazy? You can't go chasing silly dreams like a schoolgirl. Why, Mitzi and her husband have just been invited to join the country club, and Clifford would buy you a gorgeous house every bit as big as hers—"

"I'm tired of being compared to Mitzi and treated like a child. I'll write Clifford and tell him I've decided I want to stay out here, period. My mind's made up."

"Are you into drugs? That's the only reason for such strange behavior—"

"No, Mother, I'm not doing drugs, I don't even smoke cigarettes."

"But, Sharyl, be sensible—"

"No, *you* be reasonable and stop trying to live my life for me. We'll talk later when you've calmed down."

"We'll talk now, young lady! If your daddy were alive—"

"He'd cheer me on for following my heart," Sharyl said. "Good-bye, Mother." She hung up the phone, feeling sure of herself and satisfied with her life for the first time she could remember. Maybe she would never meet a handsome Indian warrior to carry her off, but she had finally found herself and maybe that could be enough.

She finished packing and went out and put her bag in the car. Dreams. Absently, her hand went to touch the little dream catcher around her neck and she realized with growing horror that it was gone. "Oh, my God, I've lost it!"

Sharyl ran back into her room and searched frantically around for it. With a sinking feeling, she realized she must have dropped it out on the prairie or in the stagecoach or in that old rancher's truck. She glanced at her watch. Fran would be needing her car and it was about forty or fifty miles back to Lawton. There wasn't much of a chance Sharyl would find the small treasure even if she went and searched all those places and she certainly didn't know how to find that rancher. Maybe if she advertised in the paper. . . . Probably no one would think it had value and look for an ad in Lost and Found. Tears came to her eyes. The crude little object had meant so much to her and it was gone, lost forever. Well, there seemed to be no help for it now.

Tears blurred her vision as she closed the motel door with finality and searched along the sidewalk as she walked to the office to pay her bill. No, of course it wouldn't be lying on the sidewalk, she had only hoped so desperately. . . .

She rang the desk bell twice before the short, muscular manager came out of the back room, hastily wiping breakfast jelly from his dark face. She looked at the Indian in confusion. "Do I know you?"

"I checked you in Friday, remember?"

"Oh, yes." She must seem like a perfect fool. Of course he had been part of her dream. She looked at his nametag: Nat Toya, Manager. "*Toya*. It means 'Mountain'?"

He grinned and nodded. "You read Comanche?"

He'd think she was certifiable if she told him how he'd been part of her dream. "Uh, I don't know how

I know; think I heard someone say the meaning, that's all."

"By, the way, miss, someone from Western Dreams, Inc., has been calling since last night, asking if I'd seen you. I rang your room, but told them you didn't answer."

She wasn't about to explain. "I—I got lost in the dark from the stagecoach ride."

He scratched his head. "Reckon so. Sid said the whole crew searched every inch of that prairie without finding you. They were just fixin' to call the sheriff and file a Missing Persons."

"Searched for me?" Sharyl snorted. "Why, I was lying in plain sight by the trail, and—" She paused in confusion. If she had been right there under that sand plum bush all night, they should have found her easily. Why hadn't they? She'd have to sort this all out in her mind and she didn't want to answer any probing questions from Sid Rosenthal. He'd think she'd been tripped out on drugs—or was in need of a psychiatrist. "Do me a favor and call them, tell them I'm fine and headed back to Lawton." She turned to go.

"Oh, miss, speaking of Lawton, I've got a friend, Jim Hevovetaso, who missed his connection with his buddies and needs a ride back to Fort Sill. Since you're going anyway, I told him you might be willing—"

"I don't know." Sharyl paused, not keen on having some stranger sharing the car.

"He's respectable," the manager said. "Sergeant in the army, not too many years from early retirement, has a nice ranch near here."

She hesitated. What would it hurt after all?

"That's him outside, the big guy sharing his hamburger with the dog."

Sharyl turned to look. He was big all right; she could tell that although he was squatted down with his back to her petting the motel's hound pup. The man's hair was so black it almost seemed to reflect light like iridescent wings. He wore a red powwow ribbon shirt, faded denims, moccasins, and a turquoise belt and bracelets. Hevovetaso. What nationality was that? Italian, maybe?

"Jim said he'd buy your gas and I'll vouch for him; really a nice guy, part of Friday night's honor guard at the dances."

Sharyl shrugged. "Sure, why not?" She picked up her purse and walked out to her car. "Hey, fella, if you're going with me, get in." She didn't even look at him as she got behind the steering wheel and buckled her seat belt.

"I'm much obliged," he said in a deep, somehow familiar voice as he got in and slammed the door.

Startled, she stared at him. Native American; somewhere in his midthirties and a bit too rugged to be handsome.

He rubbed his finger across his nose and smiled sheepishly. "Don't blame you for staring. Broke it boxing in the army. I was division champ."

"It—it wasn't that; it was your voice." Of course it was only a coincidence, she told herself, but she continued to stare into his intense eyes. She felt the sexual tension between them mount and he seemed to feel it, too.

"Ma'am, have we met somewhere before?" His dark brow furrowed in puzzlement. "You look so familiar."

"I think maybe we bumped into each other Friday night at the fairground."

"I swear it seems more than that." The way he was looking at her, she suddenly felt desirable and pretty. He looked puzzled and she felt the magnetism crackle between them. "Did anyone ever tell you you had eyes the color of a prairie sky?"

She felt her eyes mist, remembering. "Someone did once."

"I know this is sudden, but there's a '49 next Saturday night. I'd be honored if you'd consider goin' with me."

She turned the key and the engine roared into life. "I was supposed to make plans this coming week to move back to New Jersey."

She saw the disappointment in his dark eyes.

"But I'm not going."

"Good." He grinned and she watched his muscles ripple as the virile soldier leaned back against the seat.

A feeling began to build in her, an instinct that couldn't be denied. "Hevovetaso. It means *Dragonfly?*"

He nodded, looking puzzled. "It's Cheyenne. How did you know the meaning?"

Only then did she notice his other jewelry. *Reincarnation or a dream?* There was no sensible explanation, and perhaps she would never know, but it didn't matter. Deep in her heart of hearts, she knew. *Hadn't he said somehow, somewhere, in another place and time . . . ?*

"Jim, maybe someday I'll tell you, but I'm not sure you'll believe it." Her heart began to sing as she pulled out on the highway and headed south. Sharyl glanced over at him and returned his smile. In the morning sun, the light reflected on her little dream catcher hanging around the sergeant's brawny neck.

**THE TOPAZ MAN**

PRESENTS: *A Dream Come True*

Win a $1,000 cash to create your own ROMANTIC WEEKEND!

* **Describe in 25 words or less your idea of the most enchanting romantic weekend and you can win $1,000 cash to help create your dream weekend. Please write response on a 3x5 card.**

* **Winner will be selected by the Topaz Man!**

Fill out to win your chance at a Romantic Weekend!

NAME _____

ADDRESS _____

CITY _____ STATE _____ ZIP _____

Include 3x5 card, coupon, and send to:

    "A DREAM COME TRUE" SWEEPSTAKES
    Penguin USA, Mass Market Dept.
    375 Hudson Street
    New York, New York 10014

Offer expires May 31, 1994 • Mail received to June 15, 1994
For complete set of rules, write to above address.